To Dorothy,

Thanks for all your
excellent work as the
<u>AE</u> cover girl!

2.3.10

Roof Over Love & Lust

Robert Leahy

gather
community press

Gather Community Press
99 Summer Street, 7th Floor
Boston, MA 02110
(877) 775-7558

This book is a work of fiction. People, places, events, and situations are the product of the author's imagination. Any resemblance to actual persons, living or dead, or historical events, is purely coincidental.

First published by Gather Community Press   5/7/2009

ISBN: 978-1-4389-5862-0 (sc)
ISBN: 978-1-4389-5921-4 (hc)

Printed in the United States of America
Boston, Massachusetts

This book is printed on acid-free paper.

Roof Over Love & Lust

"A roof over lust must be built with love."
Danny Roarke

Chapter 1: Syracuse Spartan

Danny Roarke could not stop. He crossed Main Street in his white Volkswagen and approached the Hollywood Tavern, where Suzi and Antonio wanted to celebrate his first Spartans victory. To his left, Danny saw the full moon above campus, as if the luminous disc portended change. When he looked at Suzi, singing happily to the Beatles with Antonio, he worried that she was pregnant and wondered what their lives would be like at the next full moon.

To his right, before the turn up the hill past the Hollywood, Danny saw St. Mary's Catholic Church. He pictured sitting in the empty stone cathedral on a cold January afternoon – four months prior – as an essay poured out into his journal. As he aimed the car toward the hill, fragments flashed in his head:

Jan. 3, 1969
Meditation in St. Mary's on a Misdirected Life

I realize my mistake.

I've tried to live life as a lifeless experiment attuned to the dictates of reason.

I must create through teaching and hopefully writing.

I am emotional but conditioned not to be.

I'm running towards a light clouded by unanswerable questions requiring a leap.

I want to teach wonder; anything else is worthless.

We must teach the individual to express himself to the limits of his talents and hope each will be satisfied.

An hour before in Syracuse, sweating joyfully, Danny felt each tumbler click to open his locker. He grinned as he lifted his orange Spartans jersey with both hands and wiped his sweaty face. Neither fatigue nor pain throbbing from a red and blue bruise swelling on his thigh drained exhilaration from winning their first professional soccer game.

The departing crowd's excitement flowing from the stadium, matched by bursts of rhythmic fists on metal lockers, continued as Danny tossed his left spike into his open locker. Several Syracuse Spartans programs – in Halloween black and orange team colors – lay on the bench next to him. As he untied his right spike, he sensed someone near him. Leaning forward, he snapped his head left and saw a curly blond haired boy hold a Spartans program toward him.

"May I have your autograph?" the boy asked shyly.

"My autograph? But there are better players..." Danny said, sweeping his hand around the locker room toward his teammates, feeling flushed by embarrassment.

The boy stopped, looked up at the thin man with him. He pressed his program and pen to his chest then stared at Danny.

The man said, "You're great, Danny. That pass you headed to Frankie Odono won the game. You won the Spartans' first game. You're a hero! My son Rickie would really appreciate it, Danny."

"Frankie scored the goal. I got the assist," Danny said, shrugging.

The man patted Danny's shoulder then took several programs from the stack on the bench.

In the boisterous Spartans' locker room, Danny studied the boy's excited blue eyes. Behind Rickie, he saw perfectly built Frankie Odono – their star from Ghana, who scored the winning goal – his white teeth bright against firmly muscled wet black skin. His shirt off, Frankie chattered and laughed in a group of players and fans. He loved their attention.

Danny loved soccer. But no one ever asked for his autograph. Until today, he was an amateur.

But sitting on the bench, his embarrassment faded when he saw Rickie's father wrap his arm around his son's shoulder. As Danny stood to face them, his heart focused the moment.

The boy opened his program to the center, to the sixteen players' photos and bios. He unfolded a newspaper clipping with the headline, "'Local boy' gets kicks for Spartans". He handed it to Danny.

Reading it, Danny realized that he was the "local boy." He wondered why the sports writer saw him as a story. The article summarized his life in four paragraphs: born in New York City, grew up in Litteltown, Long Island, to graduate from State Teachers College in a few weeks as the class of 1969. The article ended with "…a prime example of the development possible in this 'new' sport of soccer, Danny Roarke captained every team he has played for."

Danny stared at Rickie, wondering what was happening to him, and this boy, that suddenly his signature on a program meant something.

"Danny Roarke – Forward, Number 16 – 6'0" 175 pounds. A twenty-one year old local boy," the father read from the program. "Great picture. You look tough, but you're more handsome in person. I bet the women love you. Now that you're a star, you'll have to beat them off with a stick."

"I have a girlfriend," Danny said, picturing Suzi.

Pointing to the program photos, Rickie said, "See, you're the only player from America, Mr. Roarke."

Being called "Mr. Roarke" startled him into thinking his dad had suddenly appeared, but this was the first time he saw the program. The Spartans players were from Europe, Africa, and South America. He noticed his black-and-white photo among the others: a young man with a few days beard growth, close-cropped hair, and a determined look in a photo he forgot their publicity agent took. He realized, at twenty-one, he was the youngest player on the team. But Rickie was right, he was the only player born in the U.S. Rickie and his dad may have thought he was a hero, but what struck Danny was the irony. In the sport he loved, maybe he was a token player, included on the team for ticket sales.

The locker room was wild. Players and fans kept chanting and cheering. Fans pushed through the aisles congratulating players. Players yelled congratulations to each other as they undressed to shower. Men excited about their first victory, in a city that embraced them, wanted them to win, eager to share victory.

Rickie asked shyly, "Mr. Roarke, would you sign my program?"

Suddenly, his signature felt like a gift he had to offer.

"Rickie, call me Danny. I'd be happy to sign. Do you play soccer?"

"I play forward too, on my junior high team. I want to play for the Spartans some day."

Danny wiped his hands on a towel then took the pen and program. He wrote:

Rickie,

Welcome to our team!

Danny Roarke

He was amazed how Rickie's face glowed when he returned the program. It was a thrill for him too, but an odd thrill, as if his signature meant something beyond the game itself, as if using his talent to the fullest was his signature.

As an amateur, he never waved to the crowd, never acknowledged them. He called it "hot-dogging" or "sand-dancing" to acknowledge the crowd. Today, Coach DeSalvo insisted, "Wave when you're introduced. Let the fans know you're here for them, Danny."

Coach DeSalvo said that if soccer was ever to appeal to Americans, it was up to him. But, realizing he was the only American-born player, he questioned whether he was on the team for his talent or his birthplace. As Rickie and his dad headed toward the exit, Danny looked at his teammates. He felt his talent matched theirs. But, then he wondered if soccer was his only talent.

His teammates came to America to play soccer. He was born here, but he struggled to decide what he should do with his life. Since he immersed himself in sports in junior high school, and now, playing the sport he loved in front of thousands of people, he felt he sacrificed other aspects of life to prove himself athletically. Leaving the locker room in his street clothes, he knew he had to prove himself, but he wondered if he had other talent that would become his true signature.

After the game, in his parents' white Volkswagen, Danny drove his girlfriend Suzi and Antonio, his closest friend, the thirty miles south on Route 81 from Syracuse back to State. Along the way, his feelings vacillated from high to low as he caught glimpses of Suzi's vibrant blue eyes and blond hair bouncing in her ponytail. As they approached town, she moved her head animatedly, chatting happily between him and Antonio in the back seat. But when he clicked the turn signal and slowed toward the highway exit, aspects of his life that he had to resolve returned to torment him.

The newspaper article reminded him that graduation was only a few weeks away, but because of the Vietnam War, graduation would end his draft deferment and probably his soccer career. The irony of the popular phrase,

"Free, White and Twenty-one," popped into his head. He thought about his brother Charlie in Vietnam, and their high school goalie Bob Anzione, already killed in the war. As they exited Route 81, east of town, the game's excitement faded into the reality of life in this small town he'd grown to hate.

"Suzi, when we get back, I have to go to the lab," Danny said, turning onto the road into town.

"Not tonight, Danny. Let's celebrate. How about going to the Hollywood?" Suzi asked, kissing Danny on the cheek.

"Yeah, Danny, we have to celebrate your first *professional* victory," Antonio said, reaching over the seat to squeeze Danny's shoulder.

"I really can't. I've got lab tests to run for Dr. McClelland. He wants them tomorrow morning. It was great you two made it to the game. But, if I don't Ace senior research, I can't graduate."

And, if Suzi is pregnant, he thought, as he looked at her, I have to graduate.

"How could you not graduate?" Antonio asked, removing his hand from Danny's shoulder.

"Simple math, Tony. And amusing irony... I'm a chemistry major who hates chemistry. If I don't Ace senior research, I won't have a 2.0 in my major. So, I can't graduate. If I don't graduate, I'm screwed. I'll lose the teaching job on Long Island. I'll be 1A. And Uncle Sam will want me... All I want to know is what country claiming to be free drafts men for war who can't even vote?"

Danny looked at Suzi, whose smile turned to worry.

And it was simple math about Suzi too, he thought. A week ago, she was the first girl he ever slept with, now he was counting days, and hoping for her period.

As Danny drove, he felt campus invade from the hill above town through the windshield. He anguished over four years of indecision and rebellion. He rejected athletic scholarships to better universities, partly, because his high school coach graduated from State, and thought it was the right place for him. He came to State on a Regents scholarship to become a chemistry teacher. But since he arrived, he came to hate chemistry. He hated to go to class to listen to it fill the chalkboard and lecture hall, hated the endless hours of lab, hated textbooks that he forced himself to study, hated any thoughts about chemistry.

"But Danny, your grades in everything else are good. You should have majored in English with me," Suzi said.

"Or in philosophy. You love it," Antonio added.

"A soccer playing philosopher poet, sure! All I know is I have to graduate. I'm an athlete. I can't quit when I'm losing."

"Danny, you're not a loser," Suzi insisted.

"When I left home four years ago, I promised my parents I'd become a chemistry teacher. English and philosophy are nonsense. Not something a jock from Litteltown imagines as a profession. Nor could my parents – who never finished high school – understand as a career."

"You'll make it, Danny," Antonio said.

"Of course he will, Tony. He's just a tormented artist," she said, and kissed him again.

As the white Volkswagen reached Main Street, the Beatles' "Norwegian Wood" started on the radio. When Suzi and Antonio sang about whether he had the girl or she had him, his stomach knotted.

As they passed Saint Mary's, journal phrases repeated in Danny's head: *I realize my mistake. ...a lifeless experiment attuned to the dictates of reason. I am emotional... I want to teach wonder...to express...talents.*

He looked at Suzi and felt a rush of love, followed by a surge of torment that she was pregnant. He looked at Antonio in the rearview mirror, a friend for three years to whom he'd become closer than any other man. As they reached the top of the hill on campus, he knew he had to drop them off and go to the lab to complete the work Dr. McClelland wanted in the morning. Suddenly, the jubilant crowd celebrating the Syracuse Spartans' defeat of the New York Titans felt like a dream image. Instead, he felt his life would be guided by what he wrote in his journal that day in St. Mary's, through his relationship with Suzi and Antonio.

Chapter 2: Trojan Attack

The following Sunday, Danny watched Frankie Odono's corner kick rise toward midfield. Danny withdrew from a knot of players near where the goalie protected the far goalpost. As the ball descended, he ran forward, dove to hit the ball, snapped his head down and left to drive it between several players. First he heard moans from the Boston Revolution fans when the ball bounced into the net, then boos. As he lay on the ground, he saw the goalie retrieve the ball from the twisted net. Danny jumped up, raised both arms above his head. Frankie embraced him and teammates crowded around. The Spartans kept the one goal lead to win the game.

In the locker room after the game, an overweight and balding Boston sports writer found Danny at his locker. The writer said, "That diving header was incredible. How'd it feel to score your first professional goal?"

"The goal felt great, but the boos surprised me."

"It's life or death out there. This is America, sports are religious wars. Our fans hate you," the writer replied, arrogantly.

"It's life or death to me, but it's a sport, not a war," Danny said, puzzled by the writer's attitude.

"Kid, you don't know shit about sports or America," he said, and left abruptly to talk with Frankie Odono, surrounded by happy players and fans.

Danny looked around the locker room as he smacked his spikes together to clean turf from them. The goal was a great feeling, a tangible sign for years of work. But as he thought about what the writer said, feelings that bothered him the past few weeks tightened his chest. He loved soccer. But listening to the writer, he felt he was perpetuating youth, instead of moving toward maturity.

Watching Frankie's enthusiasm while being interviewed, Danny agreed the writer was right that people took it as ritualized war. As Spartans – named after the ancient Greek city of Sparta – our fans want victory. Today we conquered Boston. Next week we attack Washington. Spectators lived through the team. Listening to booing fans and the sports writer's questions, he wondered why he wanted to keep playing. He felt there had to be more important things to do with his life.

After Danny pulled off his sweaty jersey, he looked at the black and orange colors. The Halloween colors felt like a macabre religion. The Syracuse Spartans against the Boston Revolution in an epic battle to honor their home cities. Danny wondered if Americans would ever grow up, or if he would. He loved soccer, but, now, with the pressure about Suzi and graduation, soccer felt like a retreat into adolescence.

After talking with Frankie, the writer returned to Danny.

"Kid, you interest me. You think you'd be on the field if you didn't score?"

"I know it's about goals...about winning."

"Right. When their team wins, it gives meaning to people's lives. Like I said, it's a frickin' religious war."

"What's with you and the war stuff?" Danny asked, becoming irritated.

"Kid, you're part jock but all hippie! You're anti-religion and anti-war. Whoever invented the phrase, 'America, love it or leave it' must have had you in mind."

"What?" Danny asked, angrily.

"Danny boy, you're a spoiled college kid. Frankie came all the way from Africa to play for the Spartans. You're the only guy on the team born here. But you're down on America. You're a prima donna."

"Give me a break. Go bust somebody else's balls," Danny said sarcastically, then leaned over to grab a towel from Randy, the team trainer walking by.

The writer narrowed his eyes and scribbled notes in his spiral pad. "Prima Donna Danny. The Spartans' Anti-American Hero! No one more important than D-a-n-n-y," the writer chanted defiantly and looked at Danny, who stared back.

Danny maintained the stare, but suddenly thought about Suzi. He leaned toward the writer but strained to control his voice. "Soccer's a game, Stud. Hopefully religion isn't. But if you want my feeling about the Vietnam War, I'm against it. And America? I'd prefer not to leave it, but we can do better. We can transform it."

He wiped his face with his jersey, folded it and tossed it in his traveling bag. He wrapped the towel around his waist and walked toward the shower.

The following week the Spartans traveled to Washington to play the Washington Diplomats. Danny was surprised that what he said in Boston made it into the Washington paper on game day. That Washington fans would care about his comments seemed absurd. But a Washington sports writer used the Boston sports writer's comments. The article had the headline, "Spartans' Anti-American Hero a Spoiled Sport."

During warm-ups, Danny stretched along the sidelines with several teammates. But when he started to pass the ball with Frankie Odono, a knot of spectators harassed him from beyond the wall around the field. Several spectators held signs that read, "Fork Roarke!" and "America, Love it or Leave it!"

"Roarke, we're gonna stick a fork in you. You're done in this league," a middle aged man yelled from the crowd. Danny wondered why they were so angry. But each time he touched the ball, he heard the chant "Fork Roarke!"

Early in the game, he was thrilled when he lobbed a pass to Frankie, who timed the ball perfectly and slashed it past the diving goalie for the Spartans' first goal and the crowd's moans. Late in the game, he was jubilant after scoring on a diving head from a corner kick by Sergio, their right-winger from Brazil, to a crescendo of chants, "Fork Roarke!"

In the locker after the game, a Washington sports writer pushed his way into where Danny and several other players were undressing.

The sports writer leaned toward Danny and asked, "Why are you the most hated guy on the field?"

But Frankie put his hand on the writer's chest and said, "Leave Danny alone."

The writer tried to move past, saying, "Frankie, how do you feel about a teammate, the only American on the field, and the fans hate him?"

"Danny will be great. That's why they hate him. If he was no good, no one would hate him," Frankie said, and put his arm around Danny's shoulder.

Danny nodded to his African teammate, as he sat on the bench untying his spikes.

The writer asked, "Danny, why are you so Anti-America?"

Frankie pushed the writer with his bare chest, as if on the field defending against a free kick. But Danny held his hand toward Frankie signaling to let the writer alone.

"Well, Danny boy, what about America, you gonna love it or leave it?" the writer insisted.

Danny leaned toward him and said, "What's with America, love it or leave it? All I said was that we can do better…we can transform it. If fans don't like my suggestion, let them boo."

He walked toward the shower, through the buzzing and banging of a jubilant locker room. Trying to drown out the interview, he stood under a showerhead and turned on the water.

Absorbed into the warm spray, he worried about Suzi. Then he was struck by the dream that haunted him. It occurred during his senior year in high school, the weekend that he was offered a scholarship to the Ivy League's championship soccer team. He dreamed that someone next to a huge budding tree called to him through an open window.

He thought about the dream as he shampooed his hair. He pictured his high school teammate Gunter Schmidt, who the Ivy coach recruited the previous year. That morning, when the coach said, "Danny your talent can improve the team," Danny felt he couldn't play on the same team with self-centered Gunter again. He said, "Thanks, coach, but I don't want to be hired as an athlete at the expense of being a student." He remembered the coach's startled face and handshake that wished him luck.

As water splashed over him, he rinsed his hair then started to soap his arms and chest. The budding tree still meant that his calling was to go his own direction in life. But it tormented him that he rejected a scholarship to a prestigious university and a chance to play with an excellent team.

At State, he was tormented, without courage to change his major while playing on a mediocre team. As he washed his arms and chest, he knew playing soccer professionally proved something, because Gunter was named All-American and he only made All-State. But he was desperate to graduate and obsessed by Suzi's pregnancy. Remembering the dream emphasized the struggle not the solution. Recalling his comment to the sports writer about transforming America, he wondered if he could even transform himself.

As he started to soap his crotch, the dream swirled in his mind. He rejected the Ivy League because the dream dominated his decision. He ached to know how his life would be different had he accepted the offer. He couldn't imagine he would be so pained. But equally important, he wondered if he would have found a woman there to love. The scholarship to Ivy seemed like an enchanted life compared to what he endured at State. But he could not know how his life would be had he chosen differently. That was the harder lesson.

Standing in the steamy shower, he looked at limp flesh surrounded by a sac full of curly hair. He remembered that Gunter married his high school girlfriend when she got pregnant, then divorced her after a series of affairs. Danny felt his testicles through the sac and looked at his limp penis through the foam. He worried that he was heading toward a similar fate. Since sleeping with Suzi, he was obsessed that she was pregnant, but worried how much he loved her. As the soapy water disappeared down the drain, his genitals reappeared. He wondered what this thing between his legs meant to him. Until recently he used it to urinate, the thing as a kid his mom called his "pee pee". Now he had no idea where it was leading him. He couldn't tell if he felt love or lust.

He shook his limp penis, anguished about Suzi. Strangely, he thought back to his first girlfriend Erin. As Catholics, from junior high to high school they only kissed. He remembered the lyrics from "Ebb Tide" and that night at her seventeenth birthday party, as they slow-danced in her living room. As lyrics drifted through his mind, he pictured the gold ankle bracelet with overlapping hearts that he gave her. But entwined as they danced, he got such an erection that he worried his passion for her would lead to mortal sin. For several days afterward, he was afraid to call her. She took his retreat as disinterest and started dating another boy. That still tormented him.

Suzi was the only girl since. Although he moved away from his Catholic upbringing, he wanted to love a girl before he would sleep with her. Standing naked in the shower, rinsing his genitals, he knew his ideas were outdated in these days of "free love". He remembered how Suzi finally teased him into having sex saying, "Danny, I'd hate to see you die a virgin. Sex is no big deal."

"Danny, don't let that writer bother you," Frankie said.

Danny snapped out of his imagination to see Frankie with several teammates approach the showers. Everyone naked.

"Great game, Danny. If you leave America they'd love you in Europe."

"Thanks, Gordie. You think I'm ready for Manchester United?" he teased.

"They'd love you there, Danny Boy!" Gordie shot back.

"Pay no attention to boos. They hate your talent," Frankie said, as the group of White, Black and Hispanic guys each found a shower head.

"If I keep passing and you score the goals, maybe they'll just boo you, Frankie. And Sergio, just aim the corner kicks to Frankie, not me," Danny said, enjoying the team spirit.

"You're taller than Frankie, a bigger target, Danny," Sergio replied, patting Danny's shoulder.

"Forget the boos. Go celebrate with Suzi when you get home," Frankie insisted.

"Thanks for the encouragement, Frankie," Danny said. But looking down at his penis, as he wrapped the towel around himself to walk back to his locker, he wondered what he and Suzi would celebrate.

The night after the Spartans got back from Washington, Danny went to the lab. He walked down the hall, but cringed as he passed the "Better Living Through Chemistry" poster advertising birth control pills – thinking about Suzi and his lost condom.

When he got into the lab, he analyzed the six colored liquids he'd taken four hours to make before the trip. He injected each of the liquids into the Gas Chromatograph and waited for each print out. Afterwards, he inserted samples into the Magnetic Resonance Imager, the MRI. It took three hours to assess six colored compounds containing iron, nickel and chromium. Knowing the results were due in the morning, he kept telling himself it was just like the two-minute warning in a soccer game he was losing; he had to play his best to win. He hated to lose in soccer, but to lose here meant no graduation.

The distillation apparatus condensed time to test tubes filled with pretty colored liquids. He placed sample liquids into the Gas Chromatograph to assess molecules into long complex graphs. To measure various angles and wobbles of their atomic structures, he placed them in the MRI that printed pages of complicated graffiti. After hours in the lab making colored water, his whole life felt meaningless.

Suddenly Antonio appeared at the door. "I was on my way back from the library and saw the light on. So this is the life of the great chemist?" Antonio asked, as he walked toward Danny.

"This is it. Yep! Madam Curie is off tonight," Danny said and held several test tubes to the light, looking at a range of red, blue and green. "Kinda ironic, unwilling to leave chemistry, it controls my life."

"You could major in anything you want. I can't see you doing something you hate."

"No doubt, a great future in philosophy. For years I was a Catholic boy searching for a woman to love and remain celibate until after marriage. While rooming with you, I started my journal defying everything. And then I let Suzi convince me to try sex."

"I told you to use a Trojan and twist the end. You were supposed to stay *in* the Trojan horse, Ulysses."

"I certainly didn't intend to fall out, Tony," he said, forcing a laugh. "There was a lot going on. But she's not worried. I've been obsessed by it for weeks. I can't let her see my journal...all about sex as lust and love. She's slept with another guy before me, so she ridiculed my celibacy saying, 'You should try sex before you worry your life away over losing your virginity.'"

"She's right, Danny, you have to get over it. Chances are slim that she's pregnant."

"Did you see that birth control poster in the hall? Better living if you use the pill. She wasn't on the pill. I got a feeling this fallen Catholic boy ain't got rhythm. I can't forget that the condom came off. I've never worried more about anything in my life. Impossible not to feel she's pregnant."

"Let's just hope she isn't," Tony said calmingly, as he looked at the colored liquids.

"You remember when we were roommates last year and I had to go to my high school friends' wedding? I remember comments my mom made the night I got home. She asked, 'Is the bride wearing white?' I said I didn't know. She added, 'I hope you have more restraint.'"

"She does get to the point," Antonio replied, wincing.

Danny nodded and continued – his feelings like storm surf. "You know her. A strong German woman who doesn't take bullshit. I knew Sally and Tom since seventh grade. The night before the wedding, in his basement where we partied throughout high school, all Tom said was that they would have gotten married eventually. Sally showed Irish resignation. I put my arm around her shoulders, which were tense, and asked how she was. She said, 'My folks are cool with it. I guess Irish-Catholic parents should teach less guilt and more birth control,' and forced a laugh. But the next morning when the priest asked if anyone had reasons against Holy Matrimony, it was tough to keep quiet. All I could think was America and the Catholic Church were forcing them into marriage for the wrong reason." Danny felt awkward rambling on about the past, but more worried about similar pressures for him and Suzi.

"I sure hope you didn't say anything in church?" Antonio said, looking from the colored liquids toward Danny.

"Luckily, no. But as I watched them get married I thought about Hawthorne Circle. You know, near Valhalla where the Bronx River and the Saw Mill Parkways merge to the Taconic Parkway. It was Brother Charlie's favorite spot. He loved the Viking connection with Valhalla, where slain heroes went. But I thought about Hawthorne's *Scarlet Letter*. That's what American Catholics were perpetuating. Sally inherited Hester's Scarlet A. Not for adultery, but abortion. Tom and Sally were forced into adulthood because of their sin of sex. Religion gave no alternatives to pregnancy, forced them to have a family, forced them onto Litteltown's treadmill of resignation, the way Hester Prynne was marked for the sin of sex with the minister Dimmesdale."

13

"Man, you take all this so seriously. Tom was right, they would have gotten married anyway."

"I want to agree, but what about the kid?" he asked, and grimaced. "I thought Hester was heroic. But her daughter Pearl always bothered me in *The Scarlet Letter.* She was a wild child, like she knew that she was ill-conceived. How is their child gonna feel about being born? Seems abortion might be more heroic than what Hester or Sally chose."

"Not legal in the U.S. And certainly nothing Catholics would approve."

"I know. Just feels like Tom and Sally are paying a horrible price. And the kid? Who knows how he'll feel about it all? I don't want to have to go through it with Suzi," he finished, agitated, his hands unsteady as he handled several test tubes.

"Take it easy, Danny. It'll work out," Antonio said, encouragingly.

"I hope so, Tony. Here I am standing in the lab, making colored water. In a country that advocates God and war. I'm trying to figure out the meaning of life and love without God or war. I'm sick of the Vietnam War. Bob Anzione, my high school goalie, was the first from Litteltown to be killed there. Now Brother Charlie volunteered and is in deadly firefights protecting the Air Force base in Saigon. The irony is, if Suzi has a baby, I could get a deferment from the draft. The whole world seems fucking crazy."

As Danny stood at the sink, cleaning glassware from the experiments, he looked up at the lab clock. "Antonio, I don't want to be here again past midnight. I have to finish my philosophy paper about Camus, the French Algerian writer."

"Can I help you clean up?"

"Thanks. But it's quicker if I do it."

As he hurried to clean up, he stopped to grab a piece of paper from his jeans, unfolded it and smoothed it on the counter next to the sink.

"Tony, what do you think of this quote from Camus' journal? I want to finish my paper with it. *I know this, with sure and certain knowledge: a man's work is nothing but his slow trek to rediscover, through the detours of art, those two or three great and simple images in whose presence his heart first opens.*"

"Wow! Yes. That sounds like you," Tony said, enthusiastically.

"I don't know. When I look at that clock, all I feel is I'm wasting time. All I do is make colored water and clean glassware. My folks gave me a chemistry set for Christmas when I was in fifth grade. As a kid, science and sports opened my heart. These days I hate science and I think I have to get beyond sports."

He put the glassware into his locker then looked at the quote again.

Antonio sat on a lab stool holding a test tube filled with green liquid. "Danny, remember the senior award ceremony a few weeks ago? I think

Coach Galsworthy got it right about you when he said, 'Danny has the heart of an artist. He's obsessed by the margin between performance and perfection!' I think that is you Danny. I don't know where either of us will end up, but there is no doubt you're an artist. I see it on the soccer field. If only you could find something else to be passionate about. Whether it's Suzi, or English or philosophy. You're just impatient with the 'slow trek'."

"You got that right, my friend. So far my life just feels like a series of detours. I hope my heart opens soon."

The week after the Washington game, the Spartans played the Troy Trojans. It was their first night game. Suzi and Antonio were there, and Danny's friend Frank, with whom he played soccer in high school, brought his girlfriend Dawn. On a cool spring night, the moon was full over the stadium. Suzi, Tony, Frank and Dawn sat near the home team, surrounded by players' wives and families.

Early in the game, Frankie placed an arching ball from mid-field to Danny near the penalty area. The ball fell so precisely into Danny's stride that defenders couldn't catch him. For the first time in his life, he had the ball alone in the penalty area with only the goalie to beat. The beauty of the pass and the open field in front of him was a dream image.

Looking up, Danny saw the goalie hesitate on the goal line. As Danny went to his right, the goalie rushed him. As the goalie dove, Danny flicked the ball over him with his left shoe tip. He was amazed as it looped into the net. At first he fell to his knees, his head bowed. Then lifting his head and spreading his arms wide, he jumped up and turned to the cheering fans. Frankie ran toward him with open arms and yelled, "Magnificent, Danny!"

As they embraced, Danny yelled, "Gorgeous pass, Frankie!"

Teammates leaped on them to celebrate.

But late in the first half, the Trojans tied the score.

In the second half, Sergio placed a corner kick a few yards in front of the goal, near the far goalpost. Amidst a knot of Trojan defenders, Danny dove to head it into the net.

When he got up from the ground smiling, the Trojan fullback, a rough German player named Helmut Schmidt said, "*Das ist alles*, Roarke! No more, Roarke!"

"We'll see, *Meister* Schmidt. Under the lights and a full moon, I feel lucky," he said, surrounded by jubilant teammates.

Sergio embraced him, saying, "No one has ever scored two goals for us Danny. *Estas muy grande.* Maybe three tonight!"

Toward the middle of the second half, on another corner kick from Sergio, Danny dove to head it, but the fullback Schmidt slammed him with an elbow as he hit the ball. The ball went wide above the goal to the crowd's groans.

Dizzy when he got up, Danny felt near his left eyebrow. When he looked, his fingers were bloody. He ran toward Schmidt, who retreated.

"Ah, the anti-war hero gets mad," Schmidt said, laughing, then stopped and crossed his arms.

"What the hell was that?" Danny demanded, wanting to kick the guy's legs out from under him.

Waving a yellow card, the referee ran toward Danny.

"Calm down, Roarke!" he said, moving between players.

"Ref, that asshole elbowed me in the penalty area, look at the blood!" he yelled, shoving his bloody fingers over the yellow card.

"Watch your language, Roarke."

"My language? He elbowed me, Ref! See? Blood!"

"Watch your language, Roarke," the referee insisted. "I didn't see a foul. The yellow card's a warning. If you don't calm down, I'll make it red. Control yourself, or I'll eject you for foul language. You want to see a red card?"

"You didn't see the elbow? Where the *fuck* were you?" he yelled, the word focusing his anger. "It should be a penalty kick!"

"I warned you, Roarke!" he yelled back, then waved the red card in Danny's face, then toward the crowd announcing the ejection.

The crowd moaned.

"You're done, Roarke. You're out of the game."

"And what's he get Ref?"

"I saw nothing flagrant."

"Nothing flagrant? Look! Blood!" Danny yelled, amazed that he was getting ejected.

"No matter what he did, you can't use language like that. Your team has to play a man short. You're out of the game, Roarke!"

Danny stepped toward the referee, with his arms outstretched. "A guy draws blood, and I get ejected for foul language? What kind of bullshit is that, Ref?" Danny demanded.

Frankie and Sergio grabbed Danny's arms and pulled him toward the sideline.

"*Gutten nacht*, Danny boy!" Schmidt yelled then laughed demonically, as he flicked his finger tips rapidly. "*Auf Wiedersehen*, Danny Boy!"

Strangely, instead of the Trojan player, Danny's high school teammate Gunter's face flashed into his eyes as Schmidt's malicious delight signaled he let himself be manipulated. Looking at the Trojan player, but seeing Gunter, suddenly Danny realized the "slow trek" was more difficult than he imagined

As teammates escorted him to the bench, he looked to Suzi, whose face was filled with disappointment. After he sat alone with his head down, dejected and amazed, eventually he looked up at the stadium lights. Above the lights, he saw the moon, full and silver. Trying to make sense of what happened, he felt it was an ominous omen. He looked at Suzi, and then up to the full moon. Suddenly, coincidences that convinced him she was pregnant flashed in his head.

The night after Suzi and he made love, he met one of his soccer teammates. His teammate was returning from a wedding of a friend who was pregnant at the altar and couldn't wait until graduation because she was afraid she'd have the baby. In the past two weeks, two of Suzi's friends told her they were getting married after graduation because they were pregnant. Now Suzi's period was a week past due.

Looking toward the field, Danny felt it was ironic to be watching Spartans battle Trojans, as if enacting the mythical tale. But looking back to Suzi, Antonio, Frank and Dawn in the stands, he felt he and his friends may be a generation of rebels, but America's rules kept them in place.

Being ejected from a war between Spartans and Trojans for foul language suddenly amused him. But as he watched his teammates defend then attack as the game ebbed and flowed, his thoughts bounced from Suzi to his high school girlfriend Erin.

He pictured Erin as the famous Helen, "the face that launched a thousand ships" into Homer's Trojan War for reasons he never understood. Helen never appealed to him. Ever patient and resourceful Penelope, Odysseus' faithful wife impressed him.

He remembered the day school started their senior year. The first day he was shocked to see Erin holding hands with Randy Guardino, the quarterback on the football team. Erin and Randy were standing outside the library. He realized that by not calling her after the party, she must have thought he was no longer interested. But he never understood why she didn't talk to him before dating Randy. He never got over it. But now, looking for Suzi, who had suddenly disappeared from the stands, he wondered if she were another Helen or faithful Penelope.

As he sat thinking about Erin and Suzi, he stared at the moon thinking life was just love and lust confused as religion and war.

Suddenly, Suzi appeared at the wall behind the bench and yelled, "Great goal, Danny! The referee should've ejected the other guy, not you."

"Thanks, Suzi," he said, happy to see her face. He got up from the bench and walked to the wall. "We're still a goal up. Maybe I'm in the Trojan horse tonight."

"You're always my Ulysses," she said, and smiled broadly. "Your goals are winning the game. Don't feel bad."

Out of the game, he wasn't sure what he felt. The field was where he felt most free. On the field he could express his talent; all else dropped away. With Suzi standing near him, and the playing field forfeited, he was compressed between his past and their future. But in the crowded stadium, the moon overhead seemed somehow benevolent.

"Danny, are you OK?"

"I'm pissed for getting ejected. But remember you gave me James Joyce's *Portrait of the Artist* a couple months ago?" he asked, looking into her blue eyes, noticing her smile.

"Yes, the perfect book for a Catholic boy. But why?"

"Getting ejected because I confronted the Ref reminds me of that quote I read to you where Joyce said he wouldn't serve what he no longer believed in. He figured he would have to leave Ireland and the Church because he had to express himself freely through art. Well, I just got exiled for not keeping my mouth shut in the face of authority protecting himself against his mistakes. I got a feeling, after tonight my life is gonna be a lot of silence and exile."

"I remember that quote about silence and exile, yes. But didn't Joyce also say he would defend himself with cunning?"

"He did. But nights like tonight, I feel too dumb to live. Cunning just doesn't seem like my style. I let that German asshole get to me."

"Oh, Danny, don't take it so hard. You'll be great in the next game."

"I hope so. Well. I'll see you after the game," he said, and leaning over the wall, kissed her cheek.

He sat through the remainder of the game feeling defiant as he thought about the Joyce quote. As he watched his Spartan teammates fight their Trojan enemies, he thought about Helen and Penelope. He wanted Penelope in his life. Looking into the stands to see his friends, he wondered about the meaning of the full moon above them all.

In the locker room, after the game, Rickie, the young boy who asked Danny for his autograph after the first game, brought another newspaper article. Rickie listened quietly as the Syracuse sports writer interviewed Danny.

"Looks like the home town fans love you, Danny. Guess they put up with your anti-American bullshit as long as you score," the writer said.

"I'm not anti-American," Danny replied.

"Sure as hell you're not going to volunteer your pretty face to get killed in Vietnam."

"To get killed in a soccer game would be fine, but not this war. My high school goalie got killed there. So my brother volunteered. He's there now.

He told our mom that it was to keep the Russians out of her flower beds. That's his choice. I want to do something else with my life."

"I heard you got a deferment to teach. Kind of a cop-out for a guy who wants to be an anti-war hero."

"I don't think teaching is a cop-out. But what's happened to free, white and twenty-one in America? The draft makes no one free. Families watch their sons go to war, jail or Canada. What kind of freedom is that?"

The sports writer shrugged and walked toward Frankie Odono surrounded by players and fans.

Holding up the newspaper clipping, Ricky asked shyly, "Danny, are you against the war?"

"Thousands of guys are dying, Rickie. I don't think it's worth it."

"The newspaper says you may quit the team," he added, sounding hurt.

Glancing through the article, Danny read that he was taking a teaching job to avoid the draft.

Danny said, "If I don't teach, I'll get drafted. I won't be able to play soccer anyway."

"But you're a great player. Everybody loves you."

"My draft board doesn't care, Ricky. Anyway, there are more important things than soccer."

"Not to me. I want to play for the Spartans some day."

"Nothing else is as important?"

"No. To play in front of so many people must be great."

"I think it's more important to be a teacher," Danny said, and felt as if a tumbler clicked in his head, opening feelings that he had locked away.

Later, when he and Suzi were in his room in the residence hall where Danny was an advisor, his father called to ask about the game and to talk about plans to attend graduation. Danny didn't want to talk about being ejected from the game, but he was more distressed to discuss it was likely that he would not graduate.

"Everybody is looking forward to you coming home, Danny."

"Thanks, Dad. Hard to believe four years have passed since you dropped me off back in 1965."

"Time goes by quickly. But next week you'll have your degree and be ready to teach."

"I hope so. But the Spartans' coach is asking if I'll stay with the team," Danny said, tentatively, sensing his father would disagree.

"You can't. You've already signed a contract with the school district. A man's only as good as his word. Remember, you put your signature on a contract, Danny! You'll have to tell the coach," his father insisted.

They talked for a short while longer, but by the time they ended the conversation, Danny felt drained. He felt worse as he explained to Suzi what his father said.

"Danny, you can't quit the Spartans," she said, sounding like a stern teacher.

Danny felt trapped, "My Dad's right. I promised to teach on Long Island. I can't break the contract. I have to quit."

"You can't quit. You're one of their best players."

"I signed a contract to teach," he repeated, feeling he wanted to teach.

"Danny, your teammates traveled from all over the world to play here. You're the only American. You have to play!"

"Be serious, Suzi. It's just soccer."

"But you love it."

"I know. But I have to graduate. And with the draft I have to teach. Soccer is a kid's sport. I gotta grow up."

"I don't see you ever growing up. I'm a Capricorn. A practical woman. You're a flighty Gemini, who believes in some illusionary world of fair play and honoring your parents. When my parents got divorced, I learned all that family crap is illusion. We're on our own in this world, Danny."

"I understand that. But, I'm more worried about you being pregnant," he said, startled as he said it.

"You've obsessed about the condom ever since we made love. Danny, you're still sooo Catholic. Still have to keep promises. Still have to obey your father."

"I believe in keeping promises, yes."

"If I'm pregnant, would you marry me?"

"We'd have to get married."

"Why?"

"Abortion is illegal, Suzi."

"Not in Sweden."

"I'm not sure I believe in it anyway."

"You're not sure what you believe. Do you even love me?"

"I love you. But marrying you because you're pregnant would really strain our love."

"Sweet! My friends told me about you. You are screwed up. Some philosopher. If I'm pregnant you'd marry me. Not because you love me, but because you believe abortion is wrong. That's crap."

"I just hope you aren't pregnant," he said, nauseous at the thought.

"I guess you missed the look on my face after you got ejected tonight. My period started during the game. Lucky I had a Tampax with me. I'm not pregnant. So you're *free!*" she said, sarcastically

"Why didn't you tell me on the ride home?" he asked, incredibly relieved as the month of torment dissolved suddenly.

"I was hoping you were going to ask to live together in Syracuse after we graduate next week. But your old man killed that."

"He just reminded me that I promised to teach on the Island."

"That's crap. Everybody breaks contracts. You're afraid to piss off your old man. And you're afraid to live with me because that will piss off your old man and your mom too. Basically, you're a coward, Danny," she said, shaking her head. She pointed to the poster she made for him before the first game. It had his photo on it surrounded by soccer balls; she signed it, "Your biggest fan!" "If you quit the Spartans, you'll be a ball-less wonder," she said, and smirked.

"Suzi, I signed a contract. I made a promise. Now I have to graduate. Anyway, if I don't take the teaching job I'll lose my deferment. I won't be able to play for the Spartans anyway."

"Do what you want, Danny," she said, with an angry flip of her wrist.

"OK. You're right. I don't want to disappoint my parents. But the world is so fucked up these days, that if you had a baby, I could play for the Spartans and still get a deferment. The Vietnam War controls everybody's life in this country. Anyway, if I don't ace McClelland's class this week, I won't graduate and I'll lose my deferment and the teaching job."

"McClelland loves the way you kiss his butt. He'll make sure you graduate. Danny, your biggest problem is that you have more talent than you know what to do with. If only you'd believe in yourself. But now, be a good little boy and go back to your parents on the Island. I'm going to take the teaching job in Boston. You just killed any chance we had. I'm glad I'm not having your kid. Let me know if you ever grow up," she said, then grabbed her sweater from the bed.

"I made a promise. I have to stick with it. You see our relationship like a real estate deal. In the right neighborhood I'm worth a lot to you. As a soccer player I'm hot property. You love the excitement and attention. As a teacher I'm worthless."

"Anybody can teach, Danny. Yeah, I like the excitement."

"But you really don't love me. You don't really believe in me. At least Erin cared about my soul when I believed I had one."

"Oh, that angelic Leo you whine about. Do you remember that she started dating the quarterback of the football team because you didn't call her after her birthday party? She's no Penelope. Yeah, and if you stayed with her, you'd still be Catholic and celibate. Admit it, you like sex, even if we aren't married."

"No doubt. But I need a woman who loves me for who I am."

"I hope you find her, Danny. I tried. You're in another world. Go teach," she said, and swung the sweater over her shoulder and walked out.

Devastated, he stood in the open door and watched her hurry down the hall. She was so confident and he felt so insecure. As the door closed behind her at the end of the corridor, he repeated her words about believing in himself, but he wondered if he ever would.

Chapter 3: The Wandering Begins

June 16, 1969
Suzi was right. I aced Dr. McClelland's research course. I'm a State graduate in chemistry. But she's in Boston to teach English. And so, tonight my twenty-first year ends alone. Love lost seems the cruelest pain.

First Erin, now Suzi. I wonder what it is about me that makes love so hard. I need a woman to believe in me as I try to believe in myself. I loved Erin completely but innocently. I made love with Suzi, but never loved her completely. But now love seems meaningless without passion. I loved Erin purely as a sexless Catholic boy. I loved Suzi and explored lust. But she didn't love me for the man I want to become. Can love and lust blend into a passionate lasting relationship? Is there such a woman?

Suzi was being clever the day I quit the Spartans when she called me "a ball-less wonder." She didn't understand how hard it was to quit, but she may be right. I'm in the bed I inherited from Charlie that he inherited from Rich.

Rich is married for a year this month and working on the Lunar Excursion Module. Brother Rich plans to put a man on the moon next month to fulfill Kennedy's promise. Charlie's in Vietnam keeping the Communists out of mom's flower beds. I feel like a boy in this family and this country. I wonder if I have the balls to ever do anything worthwhile. A man without a great love is nothing...

Danny lay on the bed, writing in his journal. He looked up occasionally at his soccer, basketball and track trophies on the bedroom shelves. Back in his parents' house again, Suzi and the Syracuse Spartans felt like a different life.

Charlie in Vietnam. Always the fighter. When Coach D kicked him off our high school team for fighting, all he said was "I've never learned to turn the other cheek, Coach. But this gives me more time for chicks." Before the game ended, Charlie paraded past the field with his arm around his girlfriend. Charlie's ballsy style played great on the high school patrol between classes. He and his Bandy's Boys had smooth take-no-shit attitudes like Marlon Brando, James Dean, and Frank Sinatra. But when Bob Anzione was the first Bandy's Boy killed in Vietnam, Charlie took it hard. After he left college, he joined the Air Force. My ballsy brother.

Seeing him off after I drove down from State last fall seems so long ago. The folks were working hard to be optimistic, and Spot the dog hid in pain under the kitchen table after getting hit by a car the previous day. But Charlie looked like chiseled rock sporting his black belt in judo.

Charlie insisted we have a beer together in The Flame for the first time. Then we went to Gilgo Beach, where we used to surf. Then he headed his old Plymouth west to Jones Beach. I loved it when we passed the phallic water tower at the main beach and Charlie said, "How'd you like to be hung like that?" He laughed and kept driving.

When we ended in a bar in Greenwich Village, Charlie ordered a pitcher of beer and made a toast. "Here's to you, Danny-boy, and your college friends. Remember, college brother, we owe our lives to this country. We gotta stop the Russians and Red Chinese, otherwise, they'll be in Mom's flower beds soon. I'm going so you won't have to. You think I'm dumb, but I took Anzione's death personally. He was my closest friend. I want revenge on those Commies, so smart wimps with crooked teeth can live the way they want. Now drink your beer and wish me luck," Charlie said, and flashed that don't-fuck-with-me grin.

He knew the crooked teeth comments got to me, but he never seemed to understand how much I admired his courage and commitment to his friends. But when he said, "I want you to see Vicki," being in the city made sense.

When he brought her home his first year in college, she dressed in black, wore no makeup, had marble white skin and blond hair. She didn't laugh. She probably felt guilty about Dad's comment that Charlie spent more time with her than books. Dad alluded to Charlie's mixed college honors that he was the college's best swimmer and diver but had a grade point average near zero.

When Vicki opened the door to her studio apartment, she brushed back her blond hair and said, "Sorry for the mess, I've been working."

She was not in black. She had on jeans, a white poor-boy blouse with red sparkles and red lipstick. The room was filled with brightly colored drawings and paintings of Charlie or her in the nude. She had hand-made candles on the floor against the wall and hot plates and metal pots.

"You remember my little brother, Danny?"

"Little? He's bigger than you," she said, and hugged me.

"Not in ways that count," Charlie said, pulling off his shirt and posing like Mr. America to expose bulging biceps. "There's a body, Danny-boy," he said, pointing to a painting of him. He was Michelangelo's David with an attitude.

"Vicki looks good," I said, pointing to one of her.

"She's too much for you. She's a college graduate and artist," he said, hugging her.

"Starving artist and waitress who sells candles to buy paint," she said, discouraged.

"You'll be Picasso someday, Honey. Make yourself at home, Danny. There's beer in the fridge. Vicki and I have some catching up to do," he said, and walked with her toward a folding screen with a peace symbol hanging on it.

I was surprised, but felt rebellious as they wandered off. I heard them whisper and kiss behind the panel, but was relieved that someone turned on a record. Janis Joplin started singing "Piece of My Heart" and they did sound like they were truly sharing.

Vicki's bookcase was filled with art and astrology books; and I drank some beer and smiled, apparently destined to experience the Sexual Revolution through my brother as Janis added "Summertime" in an intensely sensual voice that seemed to perk up the activity behind the screen.

On the cover of Walt Whitman's poems, Vicki had written about celebrating herself and believing each atom of herself belonged to Charlie too. I remember it sounded like she and Charlie were demonstrating that. Behind the screen they thumped and sighed and groaned while Joplin sang about freedom in "Bobby McGee".

And in their passionate gymnastics the screen rocked. I remember thinking freedom's one thing, but privacy's another. But when the peace symbol leaped to the floor and the screen toppled, I saw love in action for the first time. Still wrapped around Vicki in a position I'd never seen, Charlie said, "Welcome to the show, Danny!" and laughed. My ballsy brother.

I wonder what's in store for Charlie in Vietnam. I worry about Charlie's choice to revenge Anzione. But my heart is with him.

The day Charlie left for Vietnam, I took Spotty in my arms and drove to the Wantagh Animal Shelter, where we got her fourteen years before as a puppy. The vet said the most humane thing to do would be to put her to sleep. When I called, the folks agreed. Even Spotty acknowledged with sad brown eyes that the end of suffering would be preferable. But I felt miserable as the messenger of mercy. As I waited for the vet to put her to sleep, I remembered when we went as a family to the high school football field and took turns to throw a tennis ball and watch her run, and then she'd make us grab to get it back from her mouth, wet with saliva.

And so, tonight Charlie's fighting in Vietnam. Conservative Rich is happily married and planning to land a man on the moon next month. Without Suzi, I'm no longer free, white and twenty-one. Broken-hearted, I start my twenty-second year... I wonder if it will be the year I find love.

He puzzled over his life that night and the next day and the next few weeks as he drove from Litteltown to his job as a lifeguard at Jones Beach. Without Suzie, he felt he'd lost love, and without soccer he'd lost passion. He felt adrift. He avoided the beach parties and bar parties of his fellow lifeguards and read when he wasn't on the lifeguard stand. He wanted a new direction in his life. He read obsessively, mostly literature and philosophy. During the difficult transition, he took a week off from his lifeguard job to plan science curriculum with other teachers from the district where he would teach that fall. He hoped teaching would replace Suzi and soccer.

He read things that he thought beyond the fringe a few years ago. His mother found a book on the living room coffee table as she cleaned for their Fourth of July party.

"Isn't he an atheist?" she asked, holding Nietzsche's *Beyond Good and Evil*.

"He's the guy who said 'God is dead'" Danny jabbed. He remembered Nietzsche's statement about seeing the universal in the particulars, but he figured that pomposity would piss her off.

"I've raised my own Doubting Thomas. Daniel, I know it takes all kinds to make a world, but I don't want you reading that garbage."

"I'll keep it in my room," he said and shrugged.

"That's not the point," she insisted.

"I'll read what I want or I'll leave," he said defensively.

"Then maybe it's time," she said, handing him the book.

Her response startled him, but he felt his heart harden against her. He took Nietzsche's *Beyond Good and Evil* from her, and grabbed Joyce's *Portrait of the Artist* and Camus' *The Stranger* from the shelf under the glass topped table. As he stood, he looked at the textured cardboard brush strokes on the framed copy of "Storm Surf" by Robert Woods above the couch. Feeling superior, he walked into his room and tossed the books on the bed.

She followed him and stood silently in the doorway for a moment. "Daniel, I've been worried about you. Are you an atheist now?"

"I don't know," he said, impatiently, but feeling invaded.

"Danny, you're a smart man. Are you saying there is no God?"

"Mom, I think virtue is its own reward. Why look for a payoff in heaven?"

"You think this life is all there is?" she asked, looking at his journal on the shelf along the headboard

"I don't know, Mom. But this world is all I know. You've always told me I have to be good. I believe you."

"Daniel, Daniel, Daniel," she repeated, slowly. "My youngest child. Why make life so complicated?"

"Mom, I don't know if God made everything or the world just showed up with a Big Bang," he said, impatiently, looking at the journal, as fragments flashed in his mind.

"So, you don't believe in God? How about confession?"

"Remember, I wanted to be a priest. But I just don't think Catholicism works for me anymore. It's all the rules. I don't know Mom," he said, feeling strange talking with her about things that so confused and pained him, things that he'd talked about for hours in philosophy classes and with friends, but still were unresolved.

"So you don't believe in God? Or the Catholic Church? Daniel, this is blasphemy, you know that," she said sternly.

"I know. But how do you explain Buddha? Or Gandhi? Or Moses? They weren't Catholic," he said, astonished by the conversation and the turbulence he felt about sharing his uncertainty with her.

"God works in mysterious ways, Daniel. That's what faith is. That's why I believe in him, why we raised you to believe in him," she said, her voice straining.

"Maybe I've lost my faith…" he said, feeling guilty for hurting her. He looked at the wall next to the door where the plaque of Jesus with a crown of thorns and his exposed red heart dripped blood. He focused on the pale yellow palm frond cross his mother made and affixed to it.

"Maybe you have lost your faith," she said sadly. "You're a smart man, Danny. When Dr. Milani delivered you with the caul, he predicted great things for you. And even in elementary school, they said you had the highest I.Q. they ever saw."

"Mom, that was Litteltown Elementary School, not Harvard."

"Regardless. It hurts me to see you suffering. I want to understand you better. Do you write about these things in that notebook?" she asked, pointing toward it.

"My journal?" he said defensively, suddenly worried she may have read about Suzi. "You didn't read it?" he asked, anger rising.

"Danny, I'm your mother. I love you. I worry about you. But you know I would never invade your privacy and read your *journal*. But, Danny, God is love. Better to believe in him than not."

"That's what the philosopher William James said," Danny replied, his anger subsiding as he changed the subject.

"Smart man. But if you don't believe, that's OK. We named you for the Daniel in the lion's den, who had the courage to love against all odds. And the Irish song, 'Danny Boy.' All the highfalutin words in all those books you read don't mean anything, Daniel. You'll find that life is about love," she said, and he noticed tears filling her eyes.

"I'm trying, Mom. But I've gotta live my way. I had to quit soccer because of the draft and the teaching contract. And Suzi left me. I'm trying to make sense of my life, but I can't do it here. I've gotta get out on my own. I'm sorry. Maybe it is time for me to leave."

He watched her tears flow as she looked at him sweetly.

"Daniel, you have a genius I.Q. But life isn't about being smart, it's about loving."

Tormented, he watched her wipe her tears as she looked from him to the journal and then to the plaque of Jesus' sacred heart. He put his hand on her shoulder and kissed her gently on her cheek, "I'm sorry, Mom."

She watched quietly as he grabbed his soccer traveling bag from the closet and put it on the bed. He took a few pairs of jeans, T-shirts and socks and stuffed them into the bag. He felt terrible as she walked back toward the living room.

He went into the bathroom and took the leather shaving kit that Suzi gave him last Christmas. He caught a glimpse of his face in the mirror. He looked serious, almost handsome, but then he smiled, and saw those crooked teeth that Charlie ridiculed for years. The way the two front ones twisted together seemed symbolic of how he felt his personality was twisted, unable to align.

He zipped the shaving kit closed and noticed the figurine on the toilet tank of a little man flushing himself down the toilet. The phrase etched into the base said, "Goodbye cruel world." It appealed to his Irish sense of humor. Then he read the wooden sign above it that said, "Too soon oldt, too late schmart." His mom reminded him about it often when she said, "Don't let your will get in your way, Daniel. Remember, you're half German." He walked back into the bedroom and tossed the kit into the bag.

He looked at the shelves with high school soccer, basketball and track trophies and his college soccer trophies. He took the wood carving of a seated fertility figure he'd copied from an art book about primitive sculpture that he made when he was rooming with Antonio a year ago. He stopped to consider the plaque next to his bed of the sacred heart of Jesus, a dark eyed, dark haired, dark bearded man wearing a crown of thorns, and the dry pale palm that his mom had shaped into a cross, affixed to it. The red heart was exposed in his chest with thorns piercing it to release drops of blood. In gold on a scroll at the bottom he read, "The pure of heart will see God." As it drew his attention, he thought that keeping pure of heart seemed crucial, regardless if God existed or not.

He grabbed his journal and flipped through it. He noticed the entry that poured out of him that past January. He read through it quickly.

Jan. 3, 1969

Meditation in St. Mary's on a Misdirected Life

I realize my mistake. I've tried to live life as a lifeless experiment attuned to the dictates of reason. How simply unworkable and empty. Life isn't separable from the individual. I can't work at living, I must live as an integrated whole.

I now understand religion. It has nothing to do with God but solely the generation of communion between not to people. God's only gift can be love and churches remain to help people realize it.

My trouble has been with rules. Rules can at best be general guidelines, which describe an ideal. However, the ideal is subject to individual interpretation. Most importantly, it is the obligation of the individual to realize this and act accordingly.

Now I can be an atheistic Christian.

I need no reward for good performed, since virtue is its own reward. Each man must choose his method for living the ideal. If we deny ourselves by denying God, we have created our own hell and need no supernatural punishment. Because of this, we don't need a Christian God, since we have the ideal manifested in the works of Christ and other sacred figures, i.e. Buddha, Gandhi, Confucius, Mohammed, Moses, etc. We realize almost implicitly what the good is. I'm wandering into a labyrinth if I deny the absolute, but I must extricate myself to proceed to essences.

Life then is love. Meaningful life is awareness of this by promulgation of love through the individual's mode of expression. The doctrine of love entails sacrifice and pain, but since it is a worthy ideal and necessary for perpetuation of the human race, I must work at it.

My mode is to create through teaching and hopefully, through writing. My method must be literature, since philosophy is too rational and avoids the feeling needed. Science is out. Since creation in that realm merely adds lacquer to a decorative shell. My task is to return the shell to its true meaning, eliminating the need for lacquer.

Teach feeling then handle the problems. No other way is possible. We must realize beauty. Offer insight then cultivate it.

Confession is to someone who will listen: a close friend or empty page! Not to a black screen with a disinterested but captive listener.

Deny vanity. Pride is less expensive but much more valuable. Vanity is the technician's excuse for pride.

Know thyself first. I am emotional, but am conditioned not to be, conditioned to believe reason dictates. Beauty is my goal, truth my path. Rational is below me since it doesn't impart beauty. My limitations are real. Time will tell if I can overcome them.

I'm running towards a light clouded by unanswerable questions requiring a leap. But life can only be lived not explained! Explanations will stall you in the clouds and lose you forever.

I want to teach wonder; anything else is worthless. If the answer can't come from the individual, no searching is going to help. Striving for self-worth through appropriation is a race towards oblivion. We must teach the individual to express himself to the limits of his talents and hope each will be satisfied.

Suddenly, he heard his father pull into the driveway. He zipped the bag and walked into the living room. As he passed the corner cabinet, he noticed the small bronze Buddha incense burner that bank customers from Chinatown gave his father and the St. Christopher statue at the top, for which his mother made seasonal robes. He continued past the front door toward the small kitchen where his mother was making Irish soda bread.

"What's going on?" Mr. Roarke asked amiably, as they met in the kitchen.

"Danny thinks he can do better someplace else," his mom said, wiping tears with her fingers. She kissed her husband quickly on the lips then looked back at Danny.

He returned her look but quivered inside.

"You going somewhere?" his dad asked, pointing to the carrying bag.

"Out of here," he said, defensively, trying to gather courage.

"Why?"

"Mom doesn't like what I read," he said, shrugging, uncertain what to do.

"Doesn't like what you read?" he asked, looking at his wife.

If Daniel wants to leave, let him," she said, returning his look, knowing he would side with her.

"All you people want is your comfortable home and mon
with either of you anymore," Danny said, feeling a surge of
night he got thrown out of his last soccer game.

"There's no free lunch in this world, Daniel. It's strictly p
his father said, a rare edge to his voice.

"Can't talk to me?" his mother said painfully, as tears rolled down her
cheeks. "Where will you go?"

"Right now I have to go work the Fourth of July at the beach. There will
be so many people the police will probably have to close off access through
the toll booths. After that, I'll see," he said, defensively, but he hated what he
was doing.

"At least come back for the party," his dad insisted.

Not sure what to do, he looked from his dad to his mom. He loved
them, but living at home no longer worked. He was moving in a direction
neither he nor they understood. His Irish dad and German mom felt deeply,
but let little emotion out. Knowing he brought his mother to tears horrified
him, but he felt himself withdraw from both of them as he stood near the
kitchen door and looked at his motorcycle on the driveway.

He could no longer believe what they wanted him to believe, nor be
who they wanted him to be, but leaving frightened him. He was unable to
understand his turmoil or believe they could understand him. The sudden
mercurial surge of anger confused him. He pushed open the screen door
and let it bang behind him. He secured the bag to the back of the Yamaha
motorcycle that Charlie gave him when he left for Vietnam. He cranked the
kick-start hard and the engine jumped to life. He revved the engine. When
he popped the clutch, the motorcycle snapped out of the driveway. He forced
himself to not look back.

He drove around the corner past Tom's parents' house, but Tom and Sally
were living in Connecticut awaiting the baby. He drove past The Flame
Lounge, but that was Charlie's life. He headed to the high school and drove
across the soccer field, but it reminded him too much of their dead goalie
Bob Anzione and his brother Charlie in Vietnam. Finally, he headed to Jones
Beach to work.

The Main Mall was crowded with bus passengers from the city and people
carrying blankets, umbrellas and coolers from the mass of cars in the main
lot. A sunny Fourth of July meant the crowd would go over the half-million
mark and fill the beach so the state police would close it to more vehicles. As
he walked toward the boardwalk then onto the sandy beach, he figured with
all the drinking and celebrating, it would be a tough day.

When he reported to the main lifeguard tower, the lieutenant said, "Some asshole's getting his rocks off slashing women with a razor. Rumor has it he's here today."

"Just what we need," Danny said sarcastically.

"Even crazier, some jilted lover sacrificed himself to King Neptune last night in front of the West Bath House. With today's current, he's probably coming this way. He should pop up blue and bloated by this afternoon."

"Should I set my guard tower further west today?"

"Good idea, Danny. Keep your eyes open. If you see him, run it like a regular rescue. It'll keep people from panic."

Danny nodded his head but closed his eyes trying to take in what he just heard. He dragged his wooden lifeguard tower further west than usual. Then with another lifeguard, he set up two boats and several buoys for rescues. Afterwards, he walked out to the guard tower and climbed up to watch the crowd in the water as he thought about the slasher and the suicide.

Each time a wave broke over the crowd, he looked for anyone in trouble. As the sun moved beyond noon and heat pushed more and more people into the water, Danny tried to forget that there could be a guy out there with a razor cutting women for the thrill of it. It seemed too bizarre. But after a wave break, and the return of a line of noisy bathers resurfacing, he noticed something bob to the surface, floating inanimately beyond the breaking waves.

Hesitant, he watched it for a few seconds, but he knew the lieutenant wanted him to run it like a rescue. He jumped off the tower, grabbed a red buoy and ran through the crowd to the wave break and dove into deeper water. When he reached it, the bloated blue body was floating face down.

As Danny placed the red buoy under the man's lifeless arms, the head flopped back. The expressionless face with blue lips and wide-open lifeless eyes shocked him. When another guard reached him with the towrope, to pull the three of them in, Danny kept thinking that this guy killed himself because of a woman.

As they were pulled through rolling surf into shallow water, Danny pretended it was a rescue. Other guards kept the crowd away and assured people that the guy would be all right. But guiding the floating body in the wave break then lifting it, Danny struggled with nausea.

As he and the other guard carried the body to shore, Danny remembered what he heard. The guy killed himself last night after his girlfriend dumped him. As they maneuvered the body through the rolling surf toward the stretcher from the ambulance, Danny looked at the dead man's face. Blue and bloated, there was nothing to read on the face but wide-eyed death. The decision the guy made in agony last night was final in the afternoon sun.

Danny had never seen a suicide. As he looked into the g,
eyes, it seemed strange that he would kill himself on a public beach.
night, he walked into the surf a half-mile up the beach because he c
live without a woman. Looking from the bloated blue body, beyonc
swimmers bobbing in the waves, out to the horizon, Danny thought abc
Suzi. He wondered if he would kill himself over Suzi or whether he woula
ever find another woman to replace her.

Afterwards, alone on his guard tower, it was hard to focus on the swimmers
as they bobbed along the breaker line. As he watched the swimmers, he
thought this July Fourth Independence Day was incredibly odd. One guy
killed himself because his woman no longer wanted him and another guy
slashed women because he couldn't have them. Always the conflict between
love and lust, he thought.

Within an hour of bringing in the suicide, he missed a Hispanic woman
going down, as a rip current opened and sucked her out. Two sharp whistle
blasts from the main tower caught his attention. He leaped off the tower to
grab a buoy and run through the breakers toward her. The water felt cold on
his hot skin as he swam toward where she splashed frantically. He saw terror
in her chubby brown face, but he felt detached as he swam, and he got too
close. She threw her arms around his head and they both went under, which
felt for a moment like a solution to his life.

Reflexively, he dove deeper. When he went under, she let go. He surfaced
quickly and wrapped her arms across the buoy and then his arm around her.
He started to swim toward his partner Ted swimming out a towrope. But
when the three finally connected and were being pulled in, Ted shook his
head and said, "Textbook rescue, Danny." But neither of them laughed.

Danny knew the suicide had gotten to him. It stirred his unresolved
feelings for Suzi. It was nothing he could explain to Ted, so, as they got back
to the stand, he said simply, "We got her in alive, thanks Ted. Sorry for being
a fuck-up..."

After work, Danny stopped by Frank's house. In shorts, Frank was in the
driveway washing his car as he argued with his father. Angry to be denied
a deferment for a fellowship to Cornell and denied conscientious objector
status by the Draft Board, he defended himself against his World War II
veteran father. Danny hated to hear them argue.

"Frank, how about going to my parents' party? I'm on my way over."

"Anything to get away from this madhouse," he said, turning off the
hose.

Frank was still angry on Danny's motorcycle. When they got to the
party he was ready to fight. At first Danny's folks were glad to see him, but

his mom had become increasingly antagonistic toward Frank over the years, especially his belligerence.

Danny's parents offered them burgers and salads from the picnic table near the grill. The open umbrella covered brother Rich and his wife and a group of partying neighbors. But Ray Murphy, a World War II veteran who lived across the street, commented about Frank's beard as Danny handed him a hamburger.

"You could use a shave son," Ray said.

Frank wouldn't leave the painful silence alone. Antagonistically, he responded, "Since when is wearing a beard a crime?"

That set off Ray Murphy, who had been drinking all day; he yelled, "A shave might teach you some manners!"

Frank replied caustically, "What would an *education* do for you?"

Danny's father interrupted, "Book smart is one thing. You've got a lot to learn about people, Frank."

"Danny, I think you better get your friend out of here," Rich said.

Danny was embarrassed by Frank's arrogance. But at that moment, Rich and his wife with their exclusive house on the affluent North Shore and his folks immersed in the day to day life of Litteltown and Independence Day celebrations with neighbors felt like the enemy. Danny remembered the argument with his folks that morning about what he should or shouldn't read. He said to Rich, "If he goes, I go."

Rich frowned and brushed him off with a wave of his hand, then said, "Don't be silly."

Rich's condescension made him explode. He said, "Frank, I guess we ought to take the hint and leave!"

His mom sensed that he was serious and she reached for his hand. "Get Frank to apologize. I want you to stay."

He knew he was hurting them, but suddenly that appealed to him. It was an opportunity to declare his own independence. He was actually enjoying the drama, which was unlike anything he'd ever done.

"If he goes I go, that's it."

"Then go. I won't have friends insulted in my house," Mr. Roarke said.

"Keep your precious house and friends. I'll take mine."

Starting to cry, Mrs. Roarke said, "Don't be stubborn, Danny, we love you."

"You have what you love. I'm out of here," he said, and went in the kitchen door toward his room. He took a quick look around, and saw nothing left of importance in the room. When he went back on the patio, his mom was crying. His dad stood stiffly near the grill. Rich followed him out the gate to his motorcycle on the driveway.

"You're upsetting Mom and Dad, Danny. Let Frank go and you stay!"

"Run your wife's life, Rich. Leave me alone."

"You're acting crazy, Danny. Maybe you should see a psychiatrist. We could arrange that."

"Rich, you're so straight and so money obsessed, you ought to see a psychiatrist. If my friends aren't welcome here, I'm not welcome here. It doesn't take a psychiatrist to figure that out. Frank, let's go."

"Danny, no big deal if your parents kick me out. You don't need to go."

"Frank, if not today, someday soon. It's better to get it over with," Danny said angrily. Firmly entrenched in his own rebellion, he felt alive for the first time since Suzi dumped him. He jumped on the kick-start. The engine popped to life. He headed to Frank's house.

When they went in, Frank's dad had the baseball game on and was sitting with his wife in the back room. Mr. Rinaldo was wearing a sleeveless T-shirt, smoking a cigar and drinking a bottle of Rheingold, watching the Mets. Mrs. Rinaldo was making a quilt, but got up when Frank and Danny walked in.

"Danny, good to see you. You're more handsome than ever. I like the way the sun is bleaching your hair blond. And your tan, like a movie star, like Robert Redford," Mrs. Rinaldo said, hugging him, something his family never did. "I was so sorry to hear that you and Suzi broke up. How are you? And your family?"

"I'm OK," he said, and he knew he couldn't tell her what just happened as they ended the hug.

"Get you a beer?" Mr. Rinaldo asked, taking the cigar out of his mouth. "Liza get this college graduate a beer," he added. He handed Danny a White Owl Corona and pack of matches.

She left the quilt on the arm of the chair and went into the kitchen. Mr. Rinaldo signaled Danny to the couch next to his reclining chair. Frank sat across from him.

"Workin' these days, Danny-boy?"

"Still lifeguarding at Jones Beach."

"Then what? White-collar job? Your Dad get you in at the bank?"

"I won't sell-out to become Dashing Dan the commuter in a suit," he said, feeling a rush of anger remind him of his argument with Rich.

"College boys! You got a lot to learn, Danny-boy."

Mrs. Rinaldo returned with beer and a ham and cheese sandwich on a hard roll. Danny put the cigar and matches down as she handed him everything, then she sat down and picked up the quilt.

"Danny, I'm making this for Dawn and Frank."

"It's beautiful," he said, reaching to feel it.

"Cold winters in Toronto for draft dodgers, Danny-boy," Mr. Rinaldo said, glaring at Frank.

"*John!*" Mrs. Rinaldo said angrily.

"That's what he is Liza, a draft dodger."

"The Draft Board denied my deferment for the Cornell fellowship and my CO appeal. It's a matter of conscience, Dad."

"I'd say *no* conscience, Frank."

Danny felt that Frank and Dawn moving to Toronto to avoid the draft was courageous, but he had his argument for the night. He kept quiet, drank the beer, and ate the sandwich.

"When your country calls, you go. If we chickened out in World War Two you'd be speakin' Kraut, Frank."

"The Vietnamese are not trying to invade America. It's a civil war that we're butting into."

"Frank thinks *this* war's wrong," Mrs. Rinaldo said, defensively, stitching a paisley quilt patch.

"Ain't his decision. How'd you get out, Danny-boy?"

"Teaching deferment," he said, and looked apologetically toward Frank.

"Lucky," Mr. Rinaldo said.

"Luck of the Irish," Frank said, without bitterness, which impressed Danny.

Mrs. Rinaldo looked up with an enigmatic smile. Danny turned his attention to the Mets, feeling the argument futile, wondering where he was going to sleep. Yogi Berra was on the mound talking to his pitcher Tom Seaver.

"You shoulda played baseball, Danny-boy," Mr. Rinaldo said. "That's where the money is."

"I don't like knickers and knee-socks, reminds me of Catholic school," he said, joking. But he pictured the Hall of Fame in Cooperstown where his mom and dad took them as boys, and being awed by memorabilia of the Yankees: Lou Gehrig, Babe Ruth and Joe DiMaggio. But baseball bored him. Except for occasional heroic moments, it lacked the passion of soccer. "I guess Frank told you I had to quit the Spartans to take the teaching job."

"No money in soccer, Danny. Maybe you should go to Europe."

"Soccer's over for me, Mr. Rinaldo. And I'm too much of an American to go to Europe."

"Too much to visit me in Toronto?" Frank asked.

"No way," he said, Frank's exile incomprehensible.

"Mom?" Frank asked.

"If your father will go," she said, through tears.

Danny leaned over to put his arm on her shoulder. She patted his hand and wiped her tears away with her other hand. Mr. Rinaldo watched the game silently, puffing his cigar. He sat like that for a long time. Mrs. Rinaldo went back to her quilt and motioned Danny back to the couch. No one spoke. Danny remembered his mom's maxim about "When hearing other people's troubles, be thankful for your own, and grab them and run." When he finished the sandwich, he placed the plate on the TV tray next to Mr. Rinaldo.

"Good sandwich, hey, Danny?" Mr. Rinaldo asked.

"Yes, thanks."

He stayed for several more awkward minutes and then excused himself. Mr. Rinaldo shook his hand. Mrs. Rinaldo hugged him and he leaned down to kiss her cheek. He walked out to his motorcycle with Frank; he hugged him awkwardly. "I guess we're both exiles... I'll see you in Toronto."

He started his motorcycle and waved goodbye. He drove a few blocks back to his parents' house. Their lights were on in the living room behind the Venetian blinds. He stared at the house for a long time. He'd lived there since they moved from the Bronx when he was in first grade. Now, sixteen years later, he doubted he would ever return. Finally, he decided to drive to the beach.

Standing on the sand, he listened to the ocean and looked at the stars and moon flashing on the curling waves at the start of a new life.

Chapter 4: Lotus Eaters

The next day, Danny bought a tent to live on the beach. Continuing to work as a lifeguard, he watched the sun rise and set and the stars and moon appear as waves carried the ocean's ebb and flow. He watched the new moon move toward a crescent as Apollo 11 launched from Canaveral on July 16, 1969. Four nights later he stood on the beach and looked at the moon where the Lunar Excursion Module, that Rich helped design, named the Eagle landed. The nights following the astronauts' successful return to Earth, Danny walked the beach, looking up at the moon. He repeated Neil Armstrong's phrase, as the first man to walk on the moon, "One small step for man, one giant leap for mankind."

At summer's end, Danny sold his motorcycle and bought a used white Toyota Corona. He packed his tent and sleeping bag and drove up to Walden Pond in Massachusetts. Leaning against a white birch near the small sandy beach outside Thoreau's cabin, he read from *Walden* about the real meaning of success. Looking from the cabin to the calm water, he felt he was on a journey similar to Thoreau, the humble search to find and express himself. He repeated the word "confidently" several times. Then he read several other lines from the same page about why Thoreau went there and why he left.

Surrounded by white birch trees, Danny felt this pond was Thoreau's answer. He needed to discover his answer, and so, he set out from Concord to the coast. He drove Cape Cod to Provincetown, then Bar Harbor, and around the Bay of Fundy through tiny fishing villages in Nova Scotia and on to Quebec. After a few days fascinated by the French ambience in the old walled city of Quebec, he aimed south to Montreal, then through Vermont and New Hampshire. But the camping and traveling only reminded him that he was wandering not finding home.

Back on Long Island, he rented a small cottage in Rocky Point, near the Sound. The remaining days before school started, he took long walks on the beach and wrote poetry along the dunes as the sun set and the moon rose, hoping to move his life in a new direction, beyond soccer and Suzi. Having let his hair and beard grow when he started to travel, he was pleased with his shaggy rebellious look when he started to teach school.

He loved teaching. He loved working with seventh graders. He loved their enthusiasm. Teaching was as exciting as soccer, but it lasted all day. Teaching was a team sport, and as teacher, like on all his soccer teams, he was the captain.

A couple weeks after he started teaching, he enrolled in graduate school to study education. He wanted to know what was important to teach. But what he was learning he was not allowed to apply to the strictly controlled curriculum of the school district.

But other things happened. Charlie came back from Vietnam that Thanksgiving after losing his leg in a fire fight. It was the first time Danny would see his family since he left on July 4th. Feeling independent in his cottage overlooking the Sound, he wondered how he'd feel seeing his folks and his brothers. As he parked along the curb, he felt awkward for having stormed out. At the front door his dad said, "The prodigal son returns," and shook his hand. His mom kissed him gently on the cheek as he entered. In the living room, neighbors surrounded Charlie.

But Rich was on stage. He gave their parents a model of the Lunar Excursion Module, like some four footed mythological creature, that he placed on the glass topped coffee table and talked about the moon landing.

"We fulfilled Kennedy's promise to land a man on the moon before the end of the decade. We were five months ahead of the December deadline," Rich said, as the family and neighbors sat listening, while Charlie watched quietly and drank gin.

"Is Mars next, Rich?" Ray Murphy asked.

"Someday. But, next for me, Dad got me an interview at the bank. I've finished my MBA."

"From engineer to banker?" Charlie asked, drinking a martini that filled a water glass.

"Rockefeller thinks engineers can steer banks in a new direction. The LEM has changed the world."

"What's it doing for Vietnam? You heard about the draft lottery in a few days, on December 1st. Uncle Sam's gonna draft guys based on their birthday. Happy Birthday!" Danny said, sarcastically.

"The draft won't affect us. You have a teaching deferment," Rich responded, cheerily.

"And that war ain't worth dyin' for, Danny. Keep teachin'," Charlie said, his words slurred.

Danny looked at Charlie, sensing a profound change. Charlie and Rich were right the draft wouldn't affect him as long as he remained a teacher. But the draft ended his soccer career and his relationship with Suzi. The draft had his friends' lives and the fate of a million men determined by a dice roll in a country that advertised freedom, but it cost Charlie his leg.

Danny looked from his mom snuggled close to his dad on the couch, to her hand on Charlie's wrist in the chair next to them. During the evening, Charlie talked little about the war, but it was clear he'd changed his mind about it; having experienced the hell first hand, he was bitter about all that he saw.

Toward the end of the evening, Charlie walked Danny out to his car.

"Charlie, I'm so sorry about your leg."

"I'm fine, Danny. Shit, little brother, I survived Nam. I can handle life from here."

"You are an incredible guy. It's good seeing you again. I wish you luck," Danny said, and hugged his brother like they did when they were soccer teammates.

But Charlie was Charlie, and he survived. The following spring he married his high school sweetheart, with whom he reconnected after he returned. As a nurse, she loved him before the tragedy and was incredibly supportive throughout the long ordeal of rehabilitation. After the wedding that spring, Danny and Charlie got closer than they had for years.

By the start of his second year, Danny's contempt for restraints on what and how he taught overwhelmed his enthusiasm for teaching. He had arguments with his department chairman and the science curriculum specialist and the principal. He wanted to teach philosophy in the school, based on what he was learning in graduate school, but no one would let him.

He loved to work with the kids, but by the third year, he could no longer endure the formalized curriculum. He wanted education more concerned about the meaning of life. But in the schools, the curriculum was prescribed.

By his third year, he had a reputation as combative. That spring, at a faculty meeting, he questioned the principal in a way that angered his chairman.

"Curriculum is prescribed in every course. Do you ever wonder why teachers leave teaching?" Danny asked.

"Our county specialists develop curriculum for teachers to implement, Mr. Roarke," the principal responded, angrily

"Then we ought to get new specialists. I've submitted curriculum that gets lost in the county approval system."

"We don't teach philosophy in the science curriculum."

"Seems I should have some say in what I teach."

"Maybe in a few years."

"Like when I'm your age? I doubt you'll see me in a few years. You've ignored my suggestions for three years. And I've been sitting on a lucky lottery number for three years, so I don't even need the deferment. I want to teach, but you treat me like a seventh grader."

Danny heard murmurs among many teachers, but returned his chairman's stare as tension increased. He made his point. He had been doing graduate work for three years. He felt he had ideas he wanted to try, but if the school district wouldn't listen, he should leave. Within a couple weeks of the argument, he handed in his resignation.

Through his closest friend Antonio, he got an assistantship to take care of other people's children as a dorm director at Green Mountain University, where Antonio had started a doctoral program the previous year. After three years as a teacher, first thrilled then frustrated by it, and barely dating, unable to find a woman who truly excited him, he looked forward to leaving Long Island and his little cottage by the Sound.

In his first class at the university, Danny met Elaine Hansen. She was a slim brunette finishing her master's degree. Her voice and clothes and style exuded sensuality. She intrigued him throughout the semester during a group-counseling course. At the end of the semester, during a weekend group marathon in a large country house, he found her irresistible as they walked through the secluded woods and talked about their attraction to each other.

They dated several times before Danny and Antonio went on the trip they planned to Europe during Christmas vacation. While in Europe, Danny and Antonio planned a beach party in Antonio's apartment; when they got back to the snow covered ground and freezing temperatures, they bought bags of sand from the university's grounds crew. They laid the sand on a tarp in Antonio's living room and placed a small plastic swimming pool on the sand. That night, after the beach party, Danny and Elaine slept together for the first time.

The following morning he woke up and looked at her, her hair resting on her pillow as she faced him. It was an incredible change from the years by himself on the lonely beaches of Long Island. "You are the most sensual woman I've ever met," he said, reaching to kiss her.

"And you are the most charming man I've ever met," she responded after the kiss.

"I guess we really like each other," he added, and kissed her again.

In May, Elaine's parents, Mr. and Mrs. Farrell, visited from Waverly, Oklahoma to see her graduate from the master's program. That morning, Danny trimmed his hair and beard and put on a jacket and tie, which made him late for the ceremony, but in time for the gathering outside the chapel afterward.

Elaine's father wore a dark gray suit. He was sturdily built, almost as tall as Danny, and his silver gray hair was combed back. When Elaine introduced them, the strength of his handshake gave Danny evidence why he was a successful land developer.

Danny wore his only sport jacket, a blue and white seersucker, which matched the blue velvet master's hood over Elaine's black robe. His dark blue shirt contrasted with his bright floral tie. The last time he wore the outfit was as best man at Frank's wedding, a few months before Frank and Dawn expatriated to Toronto because his lottery number was low and appeal for conscientious objector status failed again.

Mrs. Farrell's conversation fluttered like her silk dress. She had a high-pitched voice as she dashed from chatter about her Europe trip, to the house they were building in Arizona, back to social life in Waverly.

"Elaine dear, to think only a few years ago you dropped out of college to get married and have Kirsten. Now you have a master's degree. I'm so proud," she said and hugged Elaine. "Danny stand next to her. Kirsten stand in front of them," she motioned, with an erratic wrist.

"Mother, relax," Elaine said impatiently, but moved close to Danny.

Danny put his arm around her and she looked up at him. Suddenly he felt he was being lured into some plan of her mother. Elaine put her hand on Kirsten's shoulder, still looking at Danny.

"Smile everyone!" Mrs. Farrell chirped.

Elaine smiled up broadly at Danny. He looked back with a tight lipped smile, covering his crooked teeth. Kirsten wriggled in Elaine's hand and clutched her yellow Pooh Bear. Mr. Farrell watched from several yards away, his arms folded. After the picture, Kirsten ran to him and said, "I want a picture with Grampa."

Mrs. Farrell accommodated several times. Eventually, Mr. Farrell escorted Kirsten back into Elaine's hand.

"You like kids, Daniel?" he asked.

Danny nodded uncomfortably. The question caught him off guard. He wondered if Elaine described his difficulty accepting that she got married because she was pregnant then divorced the following year, or if she told him how they argued at times about how to raise Kirsten. He couldn't help but notice that Mr. Farrell seemed fond of Kirsten as long as she minded. Mr. Farrell seemed a man needing adoration and control, a man so different from his father, who genuinely enjoyed children and family.

"We insist that you, Elaine and Kirsten visit us in Waverly," Mrs. Farrell said, as she continued to snap pictures.

"That would be great," Elaine said, "I'd love Danny to meet my friends. And he'd love the ranch."

Danny looked at Mr. Farrell, who seemed to be counting the bricks in Dewey Hall, the building next to the Green Mountain Chapel.

"Elaine, I have a really pretty house picked out for you in Waverly," Mr. Farrell said. "Daniel, you'll like Waverly," he added. "I'm from New York too, but I wouldn't go back."

"Sounds like fun," Danny said, working to be polite, but wondering what Elaine had said about their relationship, and why they saw Waverly, Oklahoma as the only place to live.

"We could visit Garret and Melanie in Aspen then," Elaine said, wrapping her hands around Danny's arm.

Danny liked Elaine's quiet elegance, comfortable style and powerful sensuality. But he was still uncomfortable about her marriage and divorce. She had an impressive brick house on Pearl Street and her independent wealth made him uncomfortable also. He didn't like the thought that any trips to Waverly would have to be at her expense.

The next day Elaine left Kirsten with her parents so she and Danny could go camping in New Hampshire.

They got to Lake Chocurua by early afternoon. Danny pitched the tent and then went to gather firewood. When he came back, Elaine and he went for a hike. On a side trail from the lake toward the mountain, they found a wide pool under a waterfall, where a couple was skinny-dipping.

"Cold but great," the guy said. "I'm Greg. This gorgeous blond is June. Get naked and join us," he added, pointing to his tall blond friend as she stood ready to jump in.

Danny was surprised by the invitation, but it sounded like fun. "C'mon, Elaine," Danny said. "How about it?" he asked, as he started to undress.

Elaine looked at him for a few moments then suddenly pulled off her boots. She stood motionless for a moment, her foot in the cold water, as June surfaced next to Greg. June pushed her long blond hair back then threw her arms around him and they both went under and popped up a few moments later.

Elaine removed her blouse slowly and stood with large hands on long arms across small breasts. Eventually, she removed her clothes and stood with slightly bowed legs. Surfacing after jumping into the cold mountain water, Danny was fascinated by her nakedness. As he watched, she turned suddenly and shimmied her most exquisite feature, her perfect pear-shaped ass. And they smiled at each other.

"Jump, it's the only way," he yelled, exhilarated by the scene, deep in the white birches and pines of New Hampshire's woods.

"Jump! Jump! Jump!" the naked couple chanted.

Finally she did, surfaced quickly and swam tentatively toward Danny. The four of them swam and treaded water. Danny and Elaine hugged and kissed and the happy couple did the same, as the four of them laughed and splashed and played. June climbed the ledge to the waterfall and dove back into the water. Each of them took turns and dove back into the pool. The water splashing from the falls into the pool was numbingly cold, but Danny was exhilarated by their nakedness, the location so idyllic, as the four exposed themselves to each other in playful innocence. Eventually, Elaine got out and wrapped herself in a large towel. Shortly after, unable to endure the cold longer, they all got out and walked back to the camp. Danny and Greg set off along the trail to gather more firewood.

"Well Danny, I'm glad you enjoyed our skinny-dip."

"Was fun, Greg. I guess this makes Elaine's and my life complete. And such an incredible setting. Great place. I've never done that before."

"You gotta lighten up, Danny. It's the Seventies. Be free. What do you do?"

"I'm in grad school in Vermont. Doing a master's in education. I'm thinking about a PhD."

"Wow. That's cool. June and I are doing MFA's at Dartmouth. She's a poet and I'm a painter. Eventually, we'll teach. And you?"

"I have this weird feeling that I want to change American education... even if I'm just a footnote somewhere. But, anyway, skinny-dipping was great fun. June has a classic body. You two married?"

"Yep. This is our first anniversary. She's great making love and I greatly love her. A wonderful combination."

"She is so much the all American girl, beautiful, sweet, geez... Congratulations."

"Thanks. She's wonderful. How about you and Elaine?"

Danny was hesitant to say anything, but felt somehow free in the woods after the surprise encounter with Greg and June. "I'm having trouble getting over her divorce.... But trying to accept her daughter Kirsten and agreeing with Elaine how to raise her. It's tough raising somebody else's child."

"She was married before? I'm sure that's tough for you. But, yeah, if you don't agree how to raise her daughter, that will be tough. But Elaine seems so lovable. Keep that in mind."

"Thanks. I've never wanted kids. But I love Elaine and I like Kirsten, it does test me," he said, and thought about a sexual concern he didn't want to mention.

They carried the firewood back to the camp. With some newspaper and matches, they started a fire that cracked and popped in the covering darkness as aromatic smoke drifted lazily into the tall trees surrounding them. As they piled the wood near the fire, June held out several marijuana joints.

"Anyone like a toke?" June asked, after lighting one and inhaling then holding the joint toward Danny.

"That marijuana?" he asked.

"Yes. Great after skinny-dipping in the mountains," Greg said. "Try it, Danny. You really gotta lighten up. It's the Seventies. The Vietnam War is over and we are free to be whoever we want to be!"

"You two really are artists. Wow. Ah, research is my life," he said, as June handed it to him.

Then he passed the joint to Elaine. The hazy blue smoke blended with the fire's aroma as they sat closer to each other.

"Nice stuff," Greg said, staring at the fire, circling June's waist with his arm.

They passed the joint as the fire burned and sizzled and popped. Smoke from the joint with its rich earthiness blended with the scent of burning pine from the fire as it spiraled up through the birches.

"Hand me your plates," Elaine said, stirring the stew with a ladle.

"Good timing...the pot's making me hungry," Danny said, handing her several metal bowls.

"What do you think of it, Danny?" Greg asked.

Danny smiled quietly to himself, feeling his head begin to percolate. The logic of the question amused him as he drifted into the glow of the experience.

"I guess this kind of research you just *feel*, huh Greg?"

"Danny? Doing feeling research?" Elaine asked quizzically.

"Yes...*feel* it... I know. You're always on me about me calling research *thinking*. But you're right. I gotta do more *feeling* research."

Elaine dropped the ladle into the stew. At first she applauded, then hugged him. Greg and June, with their arms around each other, watched and smiled.

They chatted for a long time around the fire and adjourned to separate tents. It was only a short time before Danny heard June's erotic moans above the rustle of the forest, which made Elaine increasingly tense as they made love.

"You come, Danny. I don't think I can."

"Don't give up," he said, frustrated by what he still couldn't understand nor fix as they made love on top of the sleeping bag.

"Not tonight. But it's getting better, Honey."

"Let's keep trying," he said softly, leaning down to kiss her full lips.

"You come. I'm OK."

He hated her saying that, frustrated again that she would not try. But he pulled out of her as he kissed her softly. He sucked each nipple on her small breasts then slid down to push his head between her legs. He loved her and was aroused however they made love. She held his head tightly in her hands as he teased her clitoris with his tongue. But no matter what position they tried, she was unable to reach orgasm. He believed it was her Baptist upbringing and her grandmother's admonitions about hell fire for sin that were more frightening than the guilt he'd learned as a Catholic boy, but she disagreed, she insisted it was anatomy.

Intent on her, wanting to overcome her frustration, her sexuality remained a mystery in the primeval forest. An image of his first night with Suzi and his fear and guilt flashed through his mind, but now he savored sex. He wanted to please her, to have her open to his love and her own joy. As he varied his pace, the image of her stern Baptist grandmother lingered.

As he teased her clitoris, an image of his parents kissing startled him, but their intimacy never seemed sexual, and here he was with his tongue on Elaine. It was bizarre that in the woods, having heard June savor her climax from the tent in the neighboring campsite, Elaine struggled. Then he had a weird image of Hester Prynne with Minister Dimmesdale in Puritan outfits making love in the woods, although, in the *Scarlet Letter*, Hawthorne gave no lovemaking details, only ominous results.

Teasing and licking her, Danny thought about Elaine's pregnancy in college. She married about the time Sally and Tom got married. Kirsten was a few months younger than their son Joseph. Like Sally and Tom, Elaine married because she was pregnant, whereas Hester Prynne's ill-fated union produced the wild child Pearl without marriage.

Danny thought of Kirsten as the wild child Pearl, because he felt knowing that she was ill-conceived made her difficult. Elaine's sexuality worried him. She was as much an enigma to him as Hester who withdrew from her controlling husband to have an affair with a minister who should have known better. Danny felt that Hawthorne was perplexed by lust, but never portrayed love.

C'mon Sweetie, you're almost there," he said, softly. "I can feel you. I love you. Please let yourself go."

His tongue tiring but his mind no longer wandering, he supported her exquisite butt with his hands as he buried his face between her legs. Finally, intent to please her, he felt her moving to orgasm slowly, almost grudgingly, fighting an internal battle as he caressed her with his tongue. Her musky wetness covered his face and beard as she moaned to climax and clutched his head as she came, releasing tension in her thighs; his relief blended with feelings of love that he brought her there on a night scented by campfires and friendship in the forest.

After the camping trip, grudgingly, Danny agreed to let Elaine pay for his flight to Waverly to visit her family. When Elaine had the limo driver park in the Farrell's circular drive, he couldn't believe the size of the estate. Their house and landscape were like a Spanish hacienda. He thought about Charlie's landscape business on estates in Garden City back on Long Island, places neither of them were ever in. Rich's aspirations on the North Shore approached this, but had not amounted to this opulence. Inside were oriental rugs and rooms full of antiques. But what amazed him were oil paintings by artists he'd seen in museums. It was the first time he'd ever seen an original Picasso hanging on someone's wall.

Later, when the limo driver took them into the matriarch's stucco hacienda, Buddy, Elaine's charmingly gay cousin, met them at the door.

"Danny, so nice to meet you," Buddy said, sounding genuine as he extended his hand, his tan in contrast to his light linen suit. "Elaine, would you and this handsome man like champagne?" he asked. He signaled the black servant wearing white gloves.

"I'd prefer pot," she said, smiling mischievously. "But thanks, Buddy," she added, and hugged him.

Danny shook Buddy's hand while the black servant with white gloves returned with drinks on a silver tray. Elaine and he walked with Buddy into the room to be introduced to the aging matriarch. The conversation in the circle of chairs around her was about a local businessman's ten million dollar swindle of a bank "back East," not Rich's bank, Danny realized, with some disappointment.

The matriarch stood shakily, which seemed to be noted by all eyes, and extended her hand to him.

"Elaine has said so much about you. You're more handsome than she described."

"I'm glad you like her taste," he said. She laughed and he smiled without exposing his teeth, more self-conscious in a group whose wealth was obvious.

"You take care of her. She is my favorite granddaughter," she added sternly, and peered into his eyes. He thought he heard someone sigh at the grandmother's declaration. Elaine blushed, and he realized the assembled group was a family vote, not a coincidental afternoon cocktail party.

His sense about the staunch Baptist matriarch coincided with Elaine's description that there was no compassion in her, especially about sex, which she considered an evil duty. She was the grandmother who tended Elaine, when her father tired of it during her mother's absences in the sanitarium with wild visions of Jesus and heaven. His anxiety convinced him that he was working hard to be among these people, but apart from that apprehension, he realized their money impressed him.

The following morning, Mrs. Farrell insisted he drive her Mercedes 450SL the several hour ride to the ranch, through flat dry brown dust under a cloudless blue hot sky beyond the irrigated manicured gardens of Waverly. The ranch road was rough and dusty and lined with shale and sandstone outcroppings. Finally Elaine and he reached a long low, tiled roof and salmon colored stucco building where bowlegged cowboys ambled through a maze of corrals.

Beyond it was the original wood framed ranch house now used by guests. Inside, oval braided rugs covered wooden floors and bright quilts secured beds. Old rocking chairs in the living room were worn smooth and pictures of several generations lined the walls.

"Let's go for a ride. The foreman left two horses in the corral out back," Elaine said, shortly after they put her suitcase on the bed.

Danny followed her out the back door. She grabbed halters and bits from the wall and gave one to him. She hopped the fence into the corral and cornered a sleek young horse that reared several times until she grabbed his mane and slipped the bit into his mouth. She saddled him quickly and secured the reins to the fence.

"Nice work, Tex," Danny said, impressed.

She took the second halter and bit and secured it to a compliant horse she called Sunny.

"Sunny, Danny-boy's a virgin," she said, and handed him the reins.

"Why'd you tell him that?"

"I'd hate to see your gorgeous butt bruised," she said, and kissed him hard on the lips.

With a quick step into the stirrup, she hopped onto her horse. Danny struggled onto Sunny. He followed her out the gate and bounced along on the hard saddle as she threaded slowly through a knot of cattle grazing just outside a fence that they went through on the way toward prairie that rolled endlessly like sea grass filled sand dunes. He saw willows in the distance on a rise. She broke into a gallop. He tried to follow but couldn't match Sunny's rhythm and bludgeoned by the saddle, slowed to a walk.

He watched Elaine make a fluid sweeping arc through chest high grass as land expanded in every direction and meadow birds fluttered up in front of her as she rode. She reached the crest of the rise almost to the willows and continued around and back to where he remained to chat with Sunny.

"How's it goin' *Tex?*" she said, her voice deep, sensual, emphasizing a drawl she didn't use in Vermont.

"Sunny's back and my butt aren't *simpatico*."

"Hope he didn't damage your privates."

"No, I'm saving that for you," he said teasing, but there was an irony there he didn't like.

They continued slowly through the deep grass along a stream that led past a pond in the hot dry afternoon sun. Over another rise they came onto a ring of oil wells like pink grasshoppers that bobbed their heads compulsively to suck deep into the earth. Danny understood more clearly about the family, and why the group of heirs attuned so closely to any unevenness in the matriarch's movements.

The next day he experienced an improved but still painful relationship with Sunny and admired Elaine's skill more. That afternoon they drove back to Waverly, flew to Denver, and stayed overnight in Boulder. Her brother Garret and his girlfriend Melanie met them and drove to their place in Aspen, where they stayed a few days to hike and make love in the Rockies. They flew back to Waverly to pick up Kirsten for the flight back to Vermont. There were more than a few moments where he began to like the lifestyle and understood Rich's obsession with money. And there were many requests that he and Elaine return soon.

A week after getting back from the overwhelming introduction to wealth in Waverly, Danny and Antonio dropped a rented aluminum canoe into the cold current of the Lamoille River near the dam in Jeffersonville, about thirty miles northeast of the university. Danny lit Tony's cigar, then his own, and helped pile their gear into the canoe's center. They both wore leather hiking boots and jeans. Danny had on a red turtleneck cut to short sleeves. Tony had a denim shirt and a dark blue bandanna.

The river meandered west through green mountains and disappeared around a bend of maple and birch. A few hours later their shirts were off as they paddled hard and perspired in afternoon sun. Casually, Tony motioned to the clouds behind them.

"Rain?"

"Maybe, Antonio. The ponchos are in the plastic garbage bag near the lantern."

They paddled past a meadow filled with cows. In the distance was a man on a tractor. Near them the ground was broken into moist brown chunks along jagged furrows.

"I want a farm someday," Tony said, pointing toward the tractor.

"Back to your Italian roots?"

"In a warmer climate, Virginia or the Carolinas. But it looks like it won't be with Jody," Tony said, his voice strained.

"Why so stressed?"

"I told her that when I finish my PhD, I want to complete a law degree also. But she's tired of the academic life. And I'm getting tired of the beautiful cheerleader type. I met a wonderful woman in one of my law classes. But I feel terrible hurting Jody."

"Wow. Breaking up is tough. You sure?"

"It's been fun with Jody. But it's not love for the long term. With Allison it's really a meeting of mind and heart. I gotta move on. But I also have to be good to Jody."

"You do. She's a sweetheart, but not an intellectual. You really need a bright woman not just a beautiful one."

"I agree. I've been thinking about turning my dissertation into a book, and Jody has no interest. I'm writing about John Rawls' *Theory of Justice*. He talks about justice as the 'veil of ignorance', but I think justice cannot be blind to be fair. I want to work the ideas out in a book called *Justice Unveiled* and then finish the law degree."

"Taking on Rawls will be work. He's a star at Harvard. But sounds like a great challenge for you. How does Allison feel?"

"She agrees I should try."

"I have to meet her."

They paddled in silence past the farm and under a dilapidated covered bridge, then through steep banks thick with foliage. The river eased along quietly. Occasional boulders broke the surface, and they needed to coordinate their strokes to avoid them. Paddling reminded Danny of the excitement of competition. The four years since he'd played for the Spartans were difficult; playing on an amateur team the past fall reminded him that he loved competition, but to play at his highest level counted. He missed the Spartans terribly, an ache like a great love lost that had yet to heal.

As they paddled, Danny admired Tony's fluid arm and shoulder movements in the bow. Since they met back in college, at times he wondered if it was a homosexual attraction. That thought disturbed him. Danny's transition from science and sports toward philosophy and art seemed like an amalgam of male and female that he had difficulty understanding and which had no simple map.

A few weeks earlier, Elaine mentioned that their Europe trip over Christmas, back to Antonio's hometown in Italy seemed unnatural. Danny insisted they were close friends. "Peculiarly close," she said, as they lay in bed together. He thought she might be jealous, but puzzled over her comment. "I'm closer to Antonio than any man, but it doesn't feel sexual." "You're repressing, Danny," she said. "Couldn't intimacy be nonsexual?" he asked. "Sounds like rationalization," she responded.

He puzzled over Elaine's comments, especially times when he felt resistance toward her. He never felt sexually attracted to Tony, just a closeness he never felt with anyone else. Tony understood him, that simple he thought. Their friendship never got difficult. They each cared for the other and never let things get in the way of their friendship. But then, it wasn't a sexual relationship. With Elaine, sexuality always intervened, and the exclusiveness seemed jealously guarded. They had to be true to each other, with Tony the simple fact was that they loved each other like he loved no other man.

As they paddled comfortably, in the distance Danny saw mist and heard rumbling. Behind them, the sky blackened. Down river, on the north bank was a power house.

"Must be Cambridge Falls. We need to pull out."

"Let's run it," Tony said.

"Sure," he mocked, "the rental guy said it's a hundred foot drop! I remember he said something about wanting his canoe back, remember?"

"Where's the whitewater, Mountain Man?"

"Beyond the falls. Remember, he said 'Not *Deliverance*, but tough.'"

They beached on the south bank. They carried the canoe past the falls that plunged to a rock ledge that dropped a second falls to pummel huge boulders below and would have easily crushed their canoe. They labored the canoe down the steep slope to the river. With the canoe back in the water, they hopped into it and paddled toward the boulders, but were driven back by the turbulent whitewater. Tony dismissed the cascading water with a snap of his hand. Danny feigned a scowl back. The water swung them around as they continued downstream.

Within minutes black thunderstorm clouds surrounded them with jagged lightning that cracked into the trees and echoed malevolently toward them to deny the optimistic morning weather report. Wind blew hard cold rain that pelted them and clattered against the aluminum canoe. They hurried into their shirts and ponchos, then paddled hard toward a shoal and beached the canoe over their gear and ran back into the trees to wait as thunder and lightning crashed all around.

When the storm passed, it was almost dark. They were cold and wet. They got into the canoe to look for a dry place. Eventually they saw a house under construction. They beached the canoe and carried their gear into its loft. They stripped down, put on dry clothes from the plastic bag, unrolled their sleeping bags, got into them, and ate their sandwiches.

"Mother Nature must be pissed at us. Close call that time," Danny said, as his body thawed slowly.

"We were born lucky, Danny boy. But next time, no metal canoe," Tony said, and they laughed.

The next morning steam rose from the river beneath an early sun in blue sky as they piled gear into the canoe and pushed off. Danny felt stiff, but worked into the pace Tony set from the bow. Within a few hours the sun warmed the air, and they had their shirts off sweating.

Suddenly, Danny heard sounds like rumbling of a giant gravel truck. In the distance, boulders shimmered in the river. Water percolated and splashed as far ahead as he could see. He slid off the seat and spread his knees and feet wide against the sides for balance, and tightened his grip on the paddle. His heart came alive in his chest.

"Grand Concourse of Whitewater! Stay low, Butch."

"Whooee!" Tony yelled. "Cover me, Sundance!"

Tony settled into the bow. Boulders appeared below the surface. Water rushed by white, gray, green, and blue along the dark rocks. Depth blurred as the canoe bounced and scraped. They rattled across a wide ledge and water sprayed over them. Tony maneuvered through a pair of shoulder high boulders and they dropped hard and took on water as the canoe crunched against something hard that slid them sideways.

Danny struggled to straighten them. His paddle smashed against a rock that almost snapped it from him. They squirted through a funnel of white foam and took on more water. The gear started to float. Danny was soaked to his crotch.

Tony pushed off a boulder with his paddle. They dropped through another chute of white foam, cracked hard against a rock. Danny bounced up and almost out. The canoe veered to the right, slammed against a rock, straightened momentarily, then dropped with a loud crunch and slammed into another boulder. Tony was ejected forward. Danny caromed off to the left.

He managed to hold onto the canoe, but all their gear was sucked out. Tony disappeared for what seemed like too long.

Suddenly Tony surfaced then went under. He tumbled over rocks, popped up again then disappeared. The canoe banged and scraped over rocks as it dragged Danny along.

Danny held the canoe like a rescue buoy to keep a victim afloat in the ocean. But he hadn't made the save.

Suddenly, Tony bounced to the surface and Danny yelled, "Grab the canoe!"

Tony grabbed for it but missed. Danny lunged and caught Tony's forearm as he went under. Stretched between the canoe and Antonio, Danny tried to pull him close but couldn't overcome the current, nor hold both. Tony's free arm flailed the water like a terrified ocean swimmer. He was Danny's most important save. The canoe strained Danny's arm as they bounced through turbulent whitewater. He sucked a deep breath like a dive into the surf on a rescue and let go of the canoe.

Tony pulled him under immediately.

Danny wrapped his arm around Tony's chest, and with his free arm struggled to surface and took a quick breath. Downstream he saw the canoe bang over some rocks and disappear, while they were washed endlessly over rocks and under water.

Finally, Danny stroked violently to get them out of the current. Luckily they were dumped into a whirlpool like eddy. Danny paddled frantically to extract them from the current. In the rush of water, he paddled and kicked and scrambled over several submerged rocks to a patch of beach where they collapsed.

His heart pounded and his lungs ached. It took a long time to catch his breath, but finally he turned toward Tony and said, "You call that stayin' low, Butch?"

Tony coughed several times then said, "You call that givin' cover, Sundance?"

"Mountain Men, my ass. Dumpin' a canoe in whitewater so you don't have to face dumpin' your girlfriend ain't a way out," he said, teasing, but concerned about blood streaming from Tony's head.

Chapter 5: Calypso's Domain

The following summer, after he graduated, Danny moved in with Elaine near Landsome, Vermont, where she worked as a counselor during his second year in the master's program. He walked from the house he and Elaine shared to the mailbox on the gravel road. He pushed the red flag down and extracted the single letter. The return address made his insides quiver. He ripped it open, shocked to read, "You have been accepted into the doctoral program." He looked at the return address: Cornell University and the post mark, Ithaca, August 9, 1974. He carried the letter around to the back of the house, past where he had his potter's wheel under the deck, and walked into the house.

"Elaine, we're going to Ithaca!" he yelled.

She came running down the stairs.

"You've heard?"

He showed her the letter. "A Cornell PhD. Unbelievable! But there it is. They accepted me. Sweetie, I finally get my chance at the Ivy League. Suddenly, the academic big time."

"Oh, Danny, I'm so proud of you. I told you you'd make it," she said, and hugged him.

Feeling jubilant, he held her tightly. Memories and feelings tumbled through him. He rejected the Ivy League in high school. He was tormented as a mediocre student at State. While teaching he became intrigued with education and went to Green Mountain University, where he took academics seriously. The letter signaled life beginning again. He re-read the letter. He felt that this would finally be a chance to prove whether he had any academic talent.

A few days later he drove from Elaine's house nestled in the woods across from Killington Mountain to the university to consult with Kemo – the master potter originally from Hawaii with whom he studied during his master's, taking pottery courses in addition to those for his degree.

"I still can't get the glazes to work, Kemo."

"Daniel, you must design glazes that fit your ideas. My glazes, I develop for thirty years."

"More test tiles?"

"Yes. Make a series of them and place them in different parts of the kiln. Make notes," Kemo said slowly, his angular Asian face pensive.

Kemo held a round leather-hard clay jar in his right hand and shaped it with a wooden paddle that he held in his left. Slowly it went from round to angled planes like an enlarged chestnut. He put it down then tested the lid to see if it still fit. It did. He lifted the jar again and paddled it carefully.

Danny wanted to develop glazes to simulate Lake Champlain at sunset. He wanted color bands from deep purple to orange and yellow, to emulate the Adirondack Mountains across the lake and the sun and sky above to look authentic. But his glazes sat on the jars and bowls and wouldn't fuse to the clay like the ash glazes Kemo made from burnt fireplace logs and applied by brush with maple syrup.

It was the first time since elementary school that he felt a need for chemistry, but trial after trial ended in frustration. Elaine suggested that he make more commercial pieces. She wanted him to make wind chimes and bird feeders. But he wanted the layered sunset over the mountains.

She worked as a counselor in a local agency, but was tired of the internal politics. She wanted to return to Waverly to convince him that her family wealth meant neither of them had to work. It bothered her that he maintained his poor friends, especially Tony, who had continued on for his law degree after finishing his doctorate.

"We could go back to Waverly and live how we want. Danny, you don't need your doctorate," Elaine said, standing on the deck, where Danny worked at the potter's wheel.

He looked up, increasingly familiar with her desire to return to Waverly; but he was angry that she didn't understand how important it was for him to go to Cornell.

"Set up a gallery in Waverly, I'll pay for it. I want to go back. Vermont winters are depressing. If you like snow, there's Aspen or Switzerland, you've skied there. My family likes you Danny. We can travel anywhere."

He thought about it, but continued working on a vase. Her attitude about money irritated him. Her plans involved him in ways he didn't like.

Suddenly, Kirsten ran past the wheel. She kicked a vase he just finished as she ran toward the car pulling into the driveway around front, to meet a friend whose parents were there to pick her up to stay for the night.

"Kirsten," he said sternly, standing.

"It's just a pot, Danny," Elaine said. "She didn't see it."

Controlling his anger, he said, "She's gotta be careful."

"I'm not going to let her get uptight, Danny."

"She just kicked it and ran by. She didn't even listen."

"You have to get her trust before you discipline her. I'm not going with the Baptist hell fire and brimstone approach my parents and grandmother used. Look what all that Catholic repression did to you."

"I think I've survived OK."

"You still have a hard time with my divorce."

"Catholicism dies hard," he responded, "but it's mostly about our differences raising Kirsten."

"Let's not fight. We both need to show we love her."

Elaine walked toward him and put both hands softly on his chest. He put his arms around her. She looked up at him and they were quiet; then he kissed her. They walked slowly toward the car. They said goodbye to Kirsten, as she got into the car; and they watched until it disappeared between the pines along the gravel road. They walked back to the cattle trough that Danny bought to mix clay. Occasionally Elaine, Kirsten, and Danny rolled up their pants or wore shorts on warm days as he threw clay powders and soaked them with a hose while they stomped bare feet to mix the clay.

"Would you help me make clay?" he asked.

"OK, you get it started."

That evening, as the forest cooled near sunset, Danny tossed several bags of dry clay into the trough and soaked it with the hose; then he added buckets of hot water from the kitchen. As twilight faded to darkness, he and Elaine climbed bare foot into the trough. They started slowly to mix the powdery clay. An occasional loud pop accompanied an exultant foot freed from primeval ooze as bubbles burst in a molten mass of ripening clay. It was slow hard work, but eventually the clay became the consistency of ocean edge sand that sucked feet into a frothy wavelike rhythm.

Danny took off his shorts and tossed them on the ground. He helped Elaine off with her shorts. Then he removed his shirt and she took off her blouse.

"Add more hot water, Danny."

He went to the kitchen and carried out two buckets of hot water. In the warm, knee-deep clay they started to make love as fireflies blinked silently in the darkness.

"I'm so glad you bought this trough," she said, and adjusted her hips under him. "This way," she said, and adjusted his hips to hers. "Oh, Danny, I can really feel you inside me."

He felt her solid against the clay. As he quickened his pace, she pushed back and forth hard against him, her arms around his hips. She moaned and moved rhythmically. With warm water and wet clay around them, and fireflies in the distance blinking randomly, Danny immersed in sensuality, kissing Elaine softly, luxuriating in her full firm lips and the magnetic feel of their entwined bodies. They went on and on as fireflies illuminated the night. As they made love under the star filled night sky, Danny felt Elaine transform, as if freed from her past, wanting to connect with passion. What she thought previously was misplaced suddenly appeared in the precise spot for her to climax exquisitely for the first time. Her soft and sensual moans convinced him that they had finally connected.

"Should be a great batch of clay," he said, and kissed her gently as she looked exhausted but happy.

"Oh, Danny, I love you!" she said, and tugged his beard.

"I love you too. I knew we'd get here."

A few weeks later, as Danny sat in bed reading, wearing his environmentalist protest T-shirt *Don't Do It In The Lake,* Elaine was lying next to him. She mentioned again that she thought they should get married before he started at Cornell the following month. It was becoming a humorous ritual. She said they were getting along so well that everyone assumed they were married.

"It would make my family happy. Daddy would stop asking if you were only after my money."

"He asks that?" Danny said, irritated.

"People have money because they think about money. I told him you don't think about it."

"That's not completely true."

He knew that without Elaine's money Kirsten would have been a major problem and their lifestyle would be very different. He thought about his dad's comment that there isn't any free lunch in this world, it's strictly pay as you go; but he was riding a wave of luck with Elaine, for now it kept building, and they were riding it toward the beach together.

"Anyway, since you connected that short circuit between my legs, you've gotten the best part of my virginity."

"Artfully put," he teased.

But he understood what she meant. He liked that idea; it made her unexpected pregnancy, forced marriage, and quick divorce more palatable.

And since she was the first woman he'd been in love with since Suzi, he felt their bond was strong.

"You could even get your teeth capped before the wedding, so you would smile for the pictures."

Her comment reminded him of Charlie's insults. He figured that he should ignore the embarrassment, but it never dissipated. He knew he had to have them fixed. But capping them sounded pretentious.

"I don't think so," he said, then got up. "I have to go take a leak."

In the bathroom mirror, he looked at his snaggle-toothed smile. He could fix them, that's what bothered him. It would have to be the hard way, with braces. He needed the nerve to discuss it with a dentist. It was an embarrassment he lacked courage to admit. But Elaine, like Charlie, reminded him that he couldn't ignore it. Charlie knew the insults got to him, that his Achilles heel was his sensitivity about his teeth. That's why Charlie called him a wimp; he didn't have the courage to fix what he could, and he let it torment him.

While looking in the mirror, he reached inside the medicine cabinet to get some aspirin for the beginning of a headache. He noticed the disc of Elaine's birth control pills, which he hadn't paid attention to in months. But, when he looked at it more closely, he realized it wasn't opened. Alarmed, he took it with him.

"Look what I found," he said, and tossed them on the bed.

"My pills?"

"Lots of extras."

She stared at him as she picked up the disc, "So what?"

"Check the dates."

She looked at the pills quietly then put them on the night table next to her. She looked at him. They were silent for a long time.

"What about the dates?" he asked, angrily.

"They're usable," she said, and she watched him.

"Usable...but *not* used."

"I...I stopped taking them."

"You what? You've lied about taking them?"

"I lied because I love you."

"If you loved me you wouldn't lie!"

"Remember when we made love in the clay, remember? I said you got the best part of my virginity. Then, that day, I knew I wanted to marry you."

"Really?" he said, anger constricting his throat.

"Well. I thought, if I got pregnant you would marry me."

His chest felt like a parachute whose rip cord had been pulled, his breath sucked out. He stood motionless and waited, then suddenly inhaled dizzily, and yelled, "And we'd live happily fucking after!"

"Danny, please. You'll wake Kirsten."

"And...you...didn't...ask...me?" he said, separating each word like an island. He wanted to choke her.

"We've talked about getting married."

"About getting married, yes. Not about you having another kid. Is that how you got your first husband to marry you?"

"No," she protested.

"Then why did you have Kirsten?"

"Mother suggested I go to Sweden for an abortion, but I wanted someone to take care of."

"Someone to take care of? What'd he want? Did you ask? What kind of start is that for a baby?"

"You intellectualize it all. I just did it."

"So now we're supposed to get married. Where's your head at?"

"Why do you think I share my money? So we wouldn't get married?" she said, going on the offensive.

"Let me promise you there's at least one thing in this world you can't buy... That what money does to rich people's heads?"

Suddenly Kirsten came in rubbing her eyes carrying her Pooh Bear. "You guys are too loud, I can't sleep," she protested.

"Come here, honey," Elaine said, and wrapped her arms around her little girl.

"I don't want you two fighting," Kirsten said emphatically.

Danny looked at them slowly as he put on his jeans and slipped into his hiking boots. He slammed the bedroom door against the wall and bolted into the hall.

"Stop it!" Kirsten screamed then she started to cry.

As he banged down the stairs he could hear Elaine soothing her. He went through the kitchen and out the back door. At first he started to jog slowly in the rain. The rain soaked his jeans, matted his hair, and rolled down his face. The water stung in the cold mountain air. He increased his pace. He splashed hard in puddles on the path along the stream, the mud an anointment. He ran faster, sucked cold wet air into hot lungs, inhaled the wet ground and thought about training on the hills around campus at State, the strain natural then.

He ran faster. His lungs ached. He assumed Elaine was pregnant. He breathed wildly, spasmodically, sucked all the air he could. Pain blanked his mind then opened it to the thought of abortion.

His legs burned as muscles strained but moved rhythmically, forcefully. His mouth was dry, his lungs stretched. His heart beat violently, naturally. He pounded the mud. Rain and mud soaked through his clothes, clung wet and cold, and mixed with warm sweat. Running reminded him of soccer, when pain accompanied improvement naturally, but Elaine treated him unnaturally.

He strained to sprint as pain throbbed in his head. Then suddenly, effortlessly, magically, like a second wind in soccer, he was unaware of his feet against the ground, felt an order appear, something elegant, a way to consider an unborn child. A flow of thought ran smoothly in his brain, a principle with three parts: natural, moral, legal.

Because Elaine lied, he realized what seemed unnatural could become natural. What Catholicism called immoral, he called moral. What the country had called illegal was now legal. It felt like an artistic principle about life.

He ran fluidly and understood that a choice was not right or wrong for *all*, but right or wrong for *whom*. Abortion was natural, since not all eggs or sperm were fertile. Abortion was moral, since he did not want a child, wasn't even asked. Abortion was legal, because the Supreme Court recently changed the law, a change with which he firmly agreed. The principle was about mutual consent, and he had not consented to Elaine's plan. She had not even asked.

As he sprinted, he felt the warm flow of blood through muscle. The new principle seemed clear, but he knew he was only part of the equation. Elaine had to agree, or she could have their child without his consent. He wondered if Hester had Pearl without Dimmesdale's consent. Hawthorne had no alternative but to let Hester have the child. Even now, as he ran thinking about the scarlet letter, he knew abortion was much more serious than adultery. But he realized he had given his consent by trusting that Elaine was taking the pills. Until tonight, he thought that chemistry had solved the problem, although really it was chemistry, or more accurately biochemistry that was creating the problem. But in his own mind he saw a solution with his principle of mutual consent.

After a few days of Elaine's morning sickness, Danny went with her to consult her gynecologist about what her body had already announced. When Elaine and Danny got back to the house, his concern spilled in all directions.

"Elaine, it's not fair to anyone for us to get married."

"You want me to have the baby on my own?"

"It's not a toy for a spoiled rich girl. You're asking me to consent to a violation."

"Maybe you should have had a vasectomy."

"Maybe I'll want kids someday," he responded angrily.

"Pregnancy's the chance you take making love."

"Don't you assume the person with whom you're making love is honest? In physics there's something called the Heisenberg Uncertainty Principle. It says you can never know completely the direction and spin of an atom. You can measure one or the other. If physicists can't figure out one atom, who the hell's gonna figure out a whole person? At some point when someone says they love you, you gotta trust them."

"You're intellectualizing. Why not get married? We'd make a cute baby. We can afford it."

"What *you* can afford isn't the point. I don't want a child. I just want my part back, that's all. I want my sperm back. You got it immorally and illegally."

"You're being crazy now. You get crazy ideas like mother used to."

"It's not crazy. I learned one thing in chemistry, that theoretically all reactions are reversible. So theoretically we could reverse this reaction. Unfortunately, medicine is not that sophisticated, occasionally eggs get scrambled. I only want back what you took immorally. You lied."

"Spare me the theatrics. What if I agree to the abortion, would you marry me then?"

The conversation was bizarre. He felt trapped. As much as it tortured the remnants of his Catholic beliefs, he wanted her to consent to go to the local clinic for a safe legal procedure early in her pregnancy. He couldn't predict what she would or wouldn't do, so he wanted to focus on the most important problem. As exciting as their relationship had been, it seemed clear he shouldn't marry her, because he couldn't trust her.

What bothered him about Kirsten's birth seemed to be playing itself out again. Who knew how or why Elaine got pregnant before, but she saw it as leverage, and she was using it because she wanted to be married, and he'd become a good investment. She had been delighted to announce his acceptance to Cornell to her parents, which appeared to make him worth parading to relatives. A second marriage would reestablish her position in the family. As transparent as the scenario seemed, it appeared to be true. To her, his resistance was immaturity.

They argued and agonized for days. And although he'd never been violent, he had intensely angry moments that shocked him, when he realized how people could do violence to each other.

Eventually Elaine agreed that this would be the wrong way to move into marriage. She consented to the abortion at the local clinic. Elaine's choice to get married, have Kirsten, then divorce and raise her alone, like Hester Prynne, seemed less courageous. He did not want to create a child this way. But as sick as he was about it, he honestly felt abortion was the best choice for them, and maybe for Hester Prynne – although Hawthorne would have had no story, or maybe a more tragic and courageous one: the Scarlet A for abortion. All he knew was that within the guilt and shame, he felt a spark of integrity about his principle of mutual consent that required reciprocity in relationships.

It was difficult for them afterward. Elaine accepted the abortion without religious implications that tormented Danny, but she acknowledged that why she married before didn't work now. She resented him, but she still tried to use her money as a tool.

"I'll buy a house in Ithaca, so we can live together to see if we should get married."

"Do you still want to get married?"

"Don't you think we should?"

"I don't know," he said, feeling incredibly distant from her after so many nights sleeping together without physical or emotional intimacy.

They talked about it and talked about it, but a few days before he had to leave to start school, he decided to go on his own.

Elaine made arrangements for movers to take all her belongings to Waverly. She followed Danny in her car to help him get settled in a rooming house in Ithaca before she drove on to Waverly. His decision felt correct, but unbearable.

As they stood on the little porch outside his room, he hugged her.

"I'll miss you…" he said, detached, as if in a world of will not feeling.

"I'm sorry it didn't work out, Danny."

"Me too. I hate for you to leave…"

As she pulled out of the rooming house parking lot, he followed her to the road. He watched her turn and disappear down the hill. He stood looking down the hill feeling abandoned. Not knowing what to do next, he went back to his little room. He put Joan Baez's *Any Day Now* on his stereo. He walked out to the small balcony attached to his room that faced west. He stared at the corner where Elaine turned and went out of sight. He listened to Joan Baez sing the first song, "Love Minus Zero/No Limit" and he felt his life dissolve.

With Elaine gone, all he had left were the tears pouring out of him and rolling down his face. As Baez sang, he felt empty and lost. He thought about Suzi and how it took years for him to recover from her rejection. This time, because he couldn't trust Elaine, he ended the relationship himself, and that felt worse. Looking at the turn where she disappeared, he knew he loved her, although he couldn't trust her and the torment was twisting him with a pain he'd never felt before.

He stood on the balcony, as Baez sang each song written by Bob Dylan that seemed to mirror his life, and he cried for both women.

Dylan was a prophet to his psyche and Baez's gorgeous voice a blade. He listened to each word from Dylan – heir to Walt Whitman's poetic voice of a century before – in Baez's flawless passionate intensity. An exhausting hour later, he tried to agree with her final word to "endure."

He knew from pole vaulting that the energy and effort it takes for a moment of ecstasy over the bar as one pushes higher means simply that there is further to fall. Elaine now gone, starting a doctoral program at Cornell, which sounded glorious in Vermont, became a struggle with loneliness. Amidst his tears, he realized that integrity is a spark that must be tended carefully if wood collected for a campfire stands a chance of keeping one warm.

Chapter 6: Sighting Ithaca

Danny could not forget Elaine. He called her parents the day after she left. The third day, she reached her parents' house and returned his call. Mid-semester she came to visit and they went to a university counselor to talk about getting back together.

"When we're not together, I feel empty," Danny said, looking at Elaine.

"I feel the same way, Danny."

"But is it love, Danny?" the female counselor asked.

"I think so. It's not just lust. I really do love Elaine. But maybe her Taurus stubbornness and my dual Gemini personality affect our relationship."

"I don't do astrological counseling, Danny," the counselor replied.

"My stubborness?" Elaine asked.

"Think about our disagreements raising Kirsten."

"You can't discipline her unless she feels you love her."

"But you indulge her because your parents were so strict. And your grandmother was even stricter with you."

"Is that the major difficulty, Danny?" the counselor asked.

"Yes. I love Elaine, and I'm accepting Kirsten more these days. But growing up, my parents agreed how to raise my brothers and me. I wish Elaine and I could agree about Kirsten."

"Your family is so different than most," Elaine insisted. "Your parents lived for their kids."

Danny nodded. "That's how I see family."

During Christmas break at Cornell, Danny flew out to see Elaine. She met him at the airport. He drove her green Mercedes to her house on a warm clear night, the snow-covered ground of Ithaca replaced by manicured lawns around a small lake. The house was large and comfortable, the wooden floors polished and covered with oriental rugs. Her antique metal cat collection filled the fireplace mantel under the Alphonse Mucha poster of a wistful woman holding a beer mug. Danny put his bag in Elaine's bedroom and met her again in the kitchen. He put his arms around her and leaned back against the counter, pulling her close.

"I've missed you," he said and kissed her warmly.

"I'm glad you came. Let's go to the party."

He kissed her again, softly. She walked into the living room and straightened magazines on the coffee table and picked dead leaves from several plants. Danny sat in the yellow wicker rocker, enjoying her long skirt like a breeze moving her. His feelings for her filled him with expectation.

The party was in an even more affluent part of town. Unfolding along the circular drive, the house was filled with heavy red velvet furniture and large gold-framed paintings. Guests were draped along the fireplace mantel like elegant Christmas stockings, heirs to cattle and oil fortunes.

Elaine drifted away to chat with the hostess, in a bold floral print dress, returned to Waverly from her divorce in San Francisco. Danny drifted through several rooms filed with circles of her friends chatting about business and marriage. One frenetic fellow, a local movie producer, insisted Danny join them. He did for a while, hearing about the producer's vision for a movie called *Oil Barons* about sex and power among Waverly's wealthy. It all seemed possible and well planned, and the crowd of young heirs and heiresses seemed confident in business but intimidated by love. Danny chatted through several more circles of friends, and reconnected with Elaine, suggesting he was ready to leave.

On the ride home they talked in flutters, like birds in a bath, followed by strained silences. Elaine fidgeted, smoked several cigarettes, a habit she re-acquired. Back in the house, Danny put on a Crosby, Stills and Nash album, a favorite from Vermont. He watched Elaine as she sorted mail into pottery bowls he made the past summer. As the song "Our House" started on the stereo, Danny felt he was going to learn something he didn't want to know.

"OK, who are you sleeping with these days?" he asked, surprised that it made sense of the confusion he'd been feeling since she met him at the airport.

Elaine stood several moments staring at him, absentmindedly holding several envelopes in her hand.

"I've been seeing someone since Thanksgiving. I didn't think it would affect my feelings for you. I guess it does," she said, sounding confused.

Amazed, he asked "You've been sleeping with some guy and you didn't think it would affect your feelings for me?"

Suddenly alone in Waverly, with Elaine behind an emotional wall, Danny realized their relationship ended when they split in Landsome, before he went to Ithaca. But then, as now, he couldn't overcome his love for her.

"Why didn't you tell me?" he asked, still stunned.

"I didn't think my feelings for him would affect my feelings for you."

"How could they not?"

"I thought my feelings for you would come back when I saw you. But they haven't. I guess I'm in love with him."

Danny stood looking at her, conversations with Tony running through his mind, as his feelings crashed into each other like angry surf tumbling him before smashing him on the beach. He remembered when Tony said, "She needs a man."

"You couldn't have told me before I came?" he asked, like a driver viewing a car wreck, unable to believe it.

"I thought my feelings would come back," she repeated, sounding detached.

He looked at her, shaking his head. His chest knotted; feelings repeated that he had to let her go, move on, no sense arguing. But his head kept repeating that he loved her, and he wanted her to love him. As he looked at her, he stepped back, tuning for a moment to the irony of the song about how fine a house they shared.

During his long silence, Elaine asked, "How did you know I was seeing someone else?"

"I felt it," he said. "I know my vacillation contributed to it, but if you don't love me, that's all that counts," he said, leaning forward, wanting to hug her, but he controlled himself.

Elaine excused herself and went to bed. Danny sat listening to the album in the dark. Eventually, he went into the bedroom. Elaine was on the phone. By the look on her face he knew with whom.

"You couldn't wait?"

She put her hand over the speaker and looked at him.

Danny kicked the door and felt it splinter around his shoe before it smashed against the wall.

"Danny, please!"

"Tell him I'm out of your life!" he said angrily.

He grabbed his traveling bag and left. He walked around the lake several times and looked back at the house. Elaine's light was on in her bedroom. Danny imagined she was talking to her other boyfriend. He walked beyond the lake, towards a cluster of lights he hoped would be a group of stores. He found a phone booth, called a cab, and went to the airport. He flew standby, anxious to leave Waverly. As the plane rumbled down the runway and light anticipated sunrise, Danny wrote in his journal.

Jan. 5, 1975

Through the window, the Waverly skyline under a clear black sky, pinpoints of light fading above. The plane rumbles toward Chicago and my life pours into my journal... Suddenly, we are off and even that may be a symbol. My first full-blown relationship – the only one I've worked at. The only one that has brought me the fullness of caring for a woman. As a chance to grow it has offered me everything. I've dealt with feelings, fears, prejudices, all sorts of complications and insights. It's been pervasive. I've viewed my life differently while I've been in it. It is hard to say goodbye to three years of work, but I believe we cannot endure. But it's painful to be on my own. Even when leaving is correct, it is difficult.

Chapter 7: Ithaca Reconsidered

Substitute teaching for the day, Danny watched the boys file out of the wood shop at the bell. He put his clipboard on the desk, with the first draft of a philosophy paper he was writing. When the bell rang again, it signaled his twenty-minute lunch break. He stood in the doorway and ate the bagel he brought. He decided to walk the halls and ended in the school library. As the school librarian placed books on the shelves, he approached her slowly.

"Nice quiet job," he said.

"Yes. Until the kids arrive after lunch," she said and smiled.

"Safe haven for me. I've been substituting in wood shop today."

"Substituting? I thought you looked new. How's it going?"

"It's fun. And, it pays the rent," he added with a shrug.

He handed her a book from the cart, so she would not have to step down from the ladder.

"Are you looking for a teaching job?" she asked.

"Eventually. But now I gotta keep a roof over my head and food on the table. I'm a grad student at Cornell, working on my doctorate."

"Impressive. In what?" she asked, descending the ladder slowly.

"Philosophy of education. A bit weird, huh?"

"No. As a librarian, I think teachers need a philosophy of education. Most teachers haven't a clue about anything other than their subject."

"I taught science and chemistry for a few years, but got bored. I love working with kids and I love teaching. Philosophy of education makes me think about what we should be doing in schools and why."

"You sound excited," she said, smiling as she climbed carefully up the ladder.

"I am. Schools can do much more. When I figure out what, I'll write my dissertation," he added, with a short laugh.

"Writing that must be hard. Any ideas yet?"

"Unfortunately, just ideas. But substitute teaching helps me understand kids and see what happens in schools day to day. It's all so interesting…but I think we should spend more time focused on emotional development. Who kids are and who they become…so far just ideas," he said, frustrated.

Danny handed her another book, noticing her left hand had no ring, and then her shiny dark hair in a French braid, but the bell rang, and he had to hurry back to shop class. Walking down the busy hall, he pictured her warm smile and brown eyes and the ease with which she moved up and down the ladder. Her memory lingered as he chatted with shop students about their projects until the final bell.

After he closed the shop, he helped teachers outside the school get students on the buses home. As the final bus left the driveway, Danny walked toward the library, but he didn't see the librarian. Disappointed, he started toward his car, but noticed athletic fields behind the school.

The soccer team was scrimmaging. There was kicking and running and clusters of players around the ball. Little finesse showed as players banged against each other for a ball that bounced haphazardly from offense to defensive players.

Danny watched, looking for talent, but saw little. He thought about the librarian and their conversation about his dissertation. He would have felt foolish saying he wanted to develop a general theory of educating that would work from elementary school through graduate school. Watching the soccer players, he realized he was more passionate about education than he had been about soccer.

He thought about his interest in both. Soccer was as poetic as it was fluid. Each player contributed passion and team spirit and desire for victory governed by rules controlled by the referee. It could be so elegant. And so could educating, he thought, with the teacher as coach and referee to help people understand life as a team sport. He watched for a while longer, musing, enjoying his rambling thoughts, then continued on past the field to his aging car in the parking lot.

As he approached it, he saw the librarian walking toward her car. "Get all the books back on the shelves?"

"Yes, thanks for your help."

"Happy to help. I liked your comment about teachers needing a philosophy of education."

"I wish you luck developing one."

"Thanks. Sounds pretentious to try... I used to be one of those," he said, pointing toward the soccer field."

"You played soccer?"

"Since elementary school. And then after college, for the Syracuse Spartans."

"Wow. Are you still playing for them?"

"No... I'm retired," he said, with a short laugh. But although it had been five years since he quit the team, he ached over it as he stood trying to be nonchalant.

"I like soccer. It's not violent like football," she said, unlocking her car door.

Danny looked at her ringless finger again. He'd enjoyed their conversation, but was hesitant to intrude. "Looks like we have similar views on education *and* sports. It's been nice talking with you. I hope to see you again when I'm subbing here," he said, turning toward his car.

"I look forward to it," she said, leaning against her unlocked door then turning to open it as he started to walk away. "Thanks again for helping," she added. "Oh, my name is Alice Donovan. My number is in the phone book."

Danny nodded, thought about walking back, but didn't feel the courage to risk it. He waved and continued toward his car. His loneliness made him uncertain. But she intrigued him.

He drove to the Teagle Hall locker room on campus to meet his friend Chris for handball. Parking his car, he noticed a tall dark-haired woman walking quickly. She looked familiar, but he couldn't remember from where. As he got out of his car, instead of heading toward the locker room, he walked toward her, trying not to be obvious.

"Lenore Hamlin?" he blurted, startled to see her at Cornell.

"Yes," she said, stopping as he approached her.

"Remember Miss Langstrom's freshman English at State? I'm Danny Roarke."

"What a memory! That was ten years ago. Hard to believe," she said, flashing a wide smile. Her green eyes sparkled as she turned toward the setting sun. "Great to see you, Danny. I didn't recognize you with the red beard and long hair. What are you doing here?"

"How about you first?" he asked impulsively, as he admired her broad smile that was covered by braces then. She was taller than he remembered. He had a crush on her freshman year; now her elegance impressed him.

"I'm doing my master's in the Hotel School. And I'm late for class!"

"Small world... I'm doing my PhD in education."

"That's great. I gotta run Danny. But let's get together. My name's in the phone book," she said then hurried off toward Statler Hotel.

He watched her silhouette against the sun. She moved fluidly in her heeled boots and long coat, her dark hair waving in the cold breeze buffeting her red knit hat. He watched her until she was lost in a crowd of people near the hotel school. Turning toward Teagle Hall, he started to swing his traveling bag back and forth as he hurried toward the locker room. Strangely, he remembered the day Langstrom took them outside on the lawn to discuss Holden Caulfield's rebellious red hat in *Catcher in the Rye*. He remembered the red hat he wore the year he quit teaching on Long Island.

After changing, he hurried out of Teagle Hall across the road to the handball courts. He banged on the small door and pushed it open slowly to enter the court.

"The prince finally arrives. Can't philosophers tell time? We only have the court for an hour, Plato," Chris said.

"What is time? Oh, you mean what time is it? Sorry I'm late. Weird day!"

"Danny-boy, every day is weird for you," Chris responded, throwing the black rubber ball against the wall and catching it.

"I just met a woman I went to State with ten years ago."

"Is she available?"

"She told me to call her."

"Danny-boy, you may finally get lucky. I'm so sick of your whining since you broke up with Elaine. You need to get laid."

"Do I really whine?"

"Danny-boy, if whining were an Olympic sport you'd be guaranteed gold."

"I guess I'd rather just kick your butt in handball."

"Not today friend. Ready?"

Danny stretched his legs and arms, feeling the stiffness go as he did. He threw the ball against the front wall several times with each hand. He tightened his leather gloves then slapped several shots against the front wall and off the side walls.

"We only have the court for an hour, Plato. Are you ready?"

"For you yes. Maybe this is my night. I also met the librarian at Ryden High School today when I was subbing."

"Geez, it would be about time for you to find a woman. But right now, let's play some handball."

Chris served and Danny returned it. They played several quick points that they split. Then Danny kept serving and winning points. Chris played hard but could not match Danny.

"Maybe it is my lucky day," he said, as he approached the final point with a five point lead.

"Maybe so, friend. But let's hope you're as lucky in love as in handball."

"Talent friend."

"Having heard about Elaine, I don't think you've got talent for love, my philosopher friend. Let's hope for luck."

Danny said nothing, just shot a glance at Chris, and focused quickly on serving the final point. Chris took the serve as it bounced from the back wall and caromed it off the side wall low into the front wall. Danny hit it low and hard off the front wall, beyond Chris' reach, ending the game.

"Nice game Danny. As much as I hate to admit it, you are an athlete. I know Jenny and I wish you success with love."

"Thanks, Chris. Maybe something will happen soon. It's been almost a year since I ended my relationship with Elaine," Danny said, feeling optimistic for the first time in months.

"I hope so. You get that paper done for Callahan's seminar?"

"Not yet. But I've got some ideas."

"You *are* a frickin' philosopher! You take all the stuff Callahan talks about seriously."

Danny shrugged, feeling apologetic for being a philosopher, even at Cornell. "I guess I do."

That night, Danny went back to the rooming house and thought about Lenore and the librarian Alice. He found both numbers in the phone book, but was hesitant to call either. Chris reminded him that he had to get beyond Elaine, but moving on was still a difficult and painful transition. Complicating his life with another woman felt like a risk he wasn't ready to take. Instead, as he sat in his rocking chair, he wrote about ideas he was trying to sort out for a paper in Callahan's seminar, where he and Chris met that semester.

November 3, 1975

The person comes to learn those things that are important.

The existentialists talk of experience but focus on anguish and despair – feeling unattached to the world: de trop. The grounding of the person is self-awareness and handling experience. It is from this point that the individual develops his sense of what is important. These problems must become the focus of education. We have tremendous libraries of literature dealing with the human condition. Each person develops a solution by himself. What suffering one experiences is locked within each person. That can't be measured.

We each have a sense of what is important, what we are willing to sacrifice for, what we enjoy. This is a result of experience and reflecting on that experience.

But we need an external observer, a teacher to help us process this information and lead us to new areas – this is what education is about. The need is for dialogue.

The teacher must lead, introduce, share, point, encourage, persuade, etc. The person must process and absorb and process again. The interaction must be maintained and extended – new materials, new experiences, new thoughts. The self is fulfilled when absorbed in processes outside the self – the carpenter and his wood, the writer and his book, the doctor and his patients, the mother and her child, the artist and his art, the lover and loved.

He closed the journal and sat. He enjoyed the warm fatigue from handball. The little room did not feel as empty tonight. Thoughts about Lenore and Alice eased the constraint. He rocked back and forth feeling what he'd just written made sense.

Chapter 8: Ithaca Abandoned

August 1, 1977

A thunderstorm has cleansed the air, but the sky hangs heavy and gray as a crow, feathery fingers spread, strokes the air to maintain himself on wind currents above the balcony. The streets are drying in mottled dark and light patches and everything is quiet. A small breeze bubbles from the back door to the front and the delivery truck outside sputters and coughs, grunts and moves on after leaving its wares. The tea is hot, steaming. After lighting my cigar, the smoky taste of tobacco feels good in my mouth.

Preparing to leave is at times tedious: all nuts and bolts and timing. I'll miss this town. I'll miss the men and women I've met. I never imagined the women I'd meet, but I leave with no thoughts of return.

Agnes, the sweet tall dark-haired Libra teacher who thought I was gay that night my housemate startled me when he came in with his ear pierced boyfriend. Lenore, the luscious Leo intent on managing a hotel in Hawaii. Meg, the Virgo economics major who kept her dissertation in the refrigerator to protect it from fire. Alice, the good-hearted Aquarius librarian who believed that someday I will become a philosopher. Tracy, the Jewish Taurus bookstore clerk with such sweet lips and gracious sensuality of Elaine. Christie the blond Pisces who believes that only art can liberate the planet. But always the memory of Elaine, Suzi, and Erin.

He looked at the list. Most had become friends. Many were lovers but not love. He looked down at the old white Toyota and the trailer. He looked up the hill toward the university. The McGraw Tower clock, visible in the distance, began to chime.

As Danny carried the box of sheets and towels down the stairs to his car, his affair with Lenore flashed through his mind. He pictured the first night he saw her naked in bed – as if seeing beauty for the first time. Elegant in anticipation, her lips soft and warm, her green eyes bright with excitement and her high cheekbones and angular jaw line alluring – an exquisite Leo. Her nipples perched on round firm breasts as she lay on the bed. He savored each nipple to hardness, loving her athletic body and movement. Her long curly black hair sprawled around her as they made love. With her at five foot nine, they were the perfect height for each other. He felt immersed in a *Playboy* fantasy as he delighted in the reality. But the first time and every subsequent time, he never felt connected emotionally. He loved her beauty and the gymnastics of love making, but he didn't love her. He lusted for her. She was smart, beautiful and fun, but he did not love her. And so, several months after their relationship began, he ended it

As he put the box in the trunk, he pictured Alice. He remembered how bright and sweet she was. He enjoyed their conversations about books. He liked how she took an interest in his ideas about education. She encouraged him when at times he felt silly in his transition from athlete to scholar, and had a hard time taking himself seriously as a philosopher. She insisted that he keep at his writing – a gracious warm-hearted Aquarius. But the relationship never ignited. He neither lusted for her nor loved her. They were good friends he thought, as he carried a box of books down the stairs from his second-floor apartment to the U-Haul trailer attached to his aging white Toyota Corona.

Now almost three years since he arrived, he knew it was time to leave. Lenore and Alice helped him get beyond Elaine, but he had not met a woman since Elaine whom he loved. For the past year, unable to focus on writing his dissertation to complete the doctorate, he wrote a novel about Elaine.

He packed several dishes and pots from the kitchen into one of the cardboard boxes he'd gotten from the liquor store, and he thought about the novel. It was hard work, but the first handwritten draft lay on the small dining room table where he'd written it, finishing just before his birthday in June. He put the box of kitchen stuff at the door to the stairs. He walked over to the box filled with his journals and the first draft of the novel.

Flipping through the manuscript, he noticed the section when Elaine called several months after their Christmas break-up to tell him that she was getting married, but not to the guy she was seeing then. As he flipped through the hundreds of hand written pages, he shrugged thinking about that marriage. He skimmed several pages about the follow-up call she made a year later, tracking him down from the rooming house, to a stone cottage he rented along the east side of the lake. She said she was getting divorced, and that she wanted to get back with him. "Elaine I'm flattered," he read, "but I don't think it's a good idea."

Shaking his head, he tossed the manuscript back into the box. He remembered her next phone call about ten months ago, a few weeks after he moved into this duplex downtown. "Danny, I'm getting married again. To my counselor. So, at least, he'll understand me. Wish me luck." He did. He hadn't heard from her since, and started working on the novel a few months after that conversation, the incredible journey of no distance took him six months to write, but it helped realign his emotions.

As he packed to leave Ithaca, he thought about the ten months since he'd talked with Elaine. He thought about the women since her that he'd met in Ithaca. He grabbed his most recent journal and opened it to the entry he wrote yesterday, while sitting on the balcony overlooking the street. He walked toward the balcony again, while reading it.

August 1, 1977
   A thunderstorm has cleansed the air... But always the memory of Elaine, Suzi, and Erin.

He rested the journal on the balcony banister and started to write.

August 2, 1977: 3 p.m.
   My views of love and lust changed during these three years. Dramatic change.
   With Suzi my heart opened, like it had with Erin. But Erin was my Catholic sweetheart. I loved her purely, innocently. I would not go beyond kissing with her. My innocence lasted several years after we broke-up. Oddly, that night after her birthday party, when I gave her the overlapping-hearts ankle bracelet, I stood outside her house after the party. It would have been the perfect Catholic marriage I believed, standing under the large maple across the street waiting for Frank and Tom my soccer buddies to walk home. I saw Erin and me married, both teachers. But there's something untamed in me that rebelled. I didn't understand it then, but now as I pack my car to leave Ithaca, I'm thinking about the loves and lusts of my life.
   I've got a box filled with journals and the first draft of this novel that I finished on my thirtieth birthday.
   My whole life is contained in this cardboard box.
   But I've lost my way with my theory about genuine teaching...it doesn't crystallize. Writing fiction is the impulse, and so I must pursue it. I need to leave academic philosophy. I need to live...

I'm off to direct a co-ed dorm in the Illinois cornfields as a Cornell philosopher drop-out. I'll need to revise <u>Commencement</u> about my relationship with Elaine. But time to get on the road. Ithaca abandoned!

He closed the journal, tossed it in the cardboard box. He carried it down stairs and placed it next to him in the front seat. He headed south toward Elmira and Route 17 West.

That autumn, *Commencement* was rejected by every publisher as "too introspective." In Illinois, he met a woman named Melissa, a high-energy Leo from Huston, who directed another dorm at the university, and was wilder than any woman he ever dated.

In the spring of 1978, he got a surprise call from Elaine. "Danny, I called your folks. They said you're directing a dorm in Illinois." "Yep," he said, groggily, feeling strange to hear her voice. "What's up?" he asked, cautiously. "I wanted to let you know that I got married again. And I'm pregnant!" "Congratulations," he said, happy for her, and figuring she wanted him to know she had gotten beyond the abortion.

A few weeks later, his residence hall contract ended. He was tired taking care of other people's children, especially the misguided ones from incompetent parents that had to be talked out of suicide or starting fires or assaulting others. He decided to see the country and look for a place he wanted to live. He started at Mount Rushmore and the mountain nearby, where an obsessed sculptor believed he would release Lone Eagle – the great Souix leader – from another granite mountain. He headed to Yellowstone then the Grand Tetons and on to the Rockies in Colorado, then from Santa Fe to the Grand Canyon, and up to Yosemite.

He arrived in Eugene, Oregon on his thirty-first birthday. He called his folks from a pay phone, "The Grand Canyon was spectacular. I loved Yosemite and the giant Sequoias, but I've decided to stay in Oregon." "Thanks for letting us know. It's God's Country out there," his dad said. "And happy birthday, Danny boy. We wish you the best," his mom added, and his folks sang "Happy Birthday" into the phone.

That night, he rented a studio apartment near the university. The next day, he started a novel about Wild Melissa called *Shattered Images*.

Chapter 9: The Far Horizon

A month later, Danny drove his Toyota cross-country to be best man at Antonio and Allison's wedding in Virginia. The ceremony was on the thirty-acre farm that Antonio and Allison just bought outside of town. Antonio was on the faculty at Thomas Jefferson University and Allison was a local attorney. The day before the wedding, Danny and Tony walked the hills on the farm.

"I love it here. The university is a great place to work. Allison and I have started a Center for Social Justice, based on my book *Justice Unveiled*. We really feel we can make a difference in people's lives."

"If anyone can make it happen, Antonio de la Montealto, it's you. I can see it rising above good old Thomas Jefferson's campus and pointing toward Monticello. Humble immigrant boy makes good. Antwan, you are the American dream."

"We'll see. But, back at State, I never thought I'd get this far. And with the wedding tomorrow, my life feels focused."

"Allison is a wonderful woman. And you two are great together. What did the midwife say back in Montealto when you were born? 'You will bring the world together.' You can do it, Antonio."

"Maybe, but will I ever see you hold a job?"

"Who knows?" Danny said. "But my Ithaca astrologer said that I had to follow that dream I had back in high school…about the budding tree… whatever it means."

"Only you, Danny boy. You took that Sixties poem 'Desiderata' seriously. But however the universe unfolds and whatever you believe are your rights here, the universe doesn't owe you a living, Danny boy."

"I'm a philosophy school drop-out. I'm just lookin' for minimum wage, Professor Marino," Danny said, smiling, and they looked at each other shaking their heads.

The day after the wedding, when Tony and Allison left for their honeymoon, Danny drove back to Eugene. He looked for work, but in 1978 there was a recession, and the job market was tight.

Unable to find a job, he consulted Estella, a Virgo astrologer with flaming red hair who appeared transported from the Italian Renaissance into a local book shop, The Book and Tea.

"You have a fabulous chart," Estella said, sketching the final astrological signs onto the page. Pisces rising, there's a mystic in you. Your moon exalted in Taurus, sensual and stubborn. I bet you have a green thumb."

"Huh?"

"A green thumb. You're good with plants."

"Pretty good," he said, puzzled, but the budding tree dream flashed into his mind.

"Anyway, you'd make an excellent teacher. Mercury is in Cancer. You're a writer sensitive to the human spirit. Uranus is conjunct the sun in Gemini, that's a sign of genius! There is so much balance in your chart!" she continued animatedly.

"Thomas Edison said genius was one per cent inspiration and ninety-nine percent perspiration," Danny said, chuckling.

"You have that kind of talent and endurance!"

"Somebody said talent does what it can, genius does what it must," he replied, seriously.

"They're right about you. And the universe will encourage you."

"Estella, what do you mean by 'the universe'?"

"How you treat yourself and others," she said, looking into his eyes. "What signs are your parents?"

"Both Aquarius. Why?" Danny asked skeptically but intrigued.

"A Gemini raised by parents who believe in justice and fairness. Uranus rules Aquarius. Uranus is conjunct the sun in your sign. You have great affinity to Aquarians. My guess is you have been disappointed by the reality of the world, but mostly, women who do not live up to your expectations, after the love you've seen between and from your parents."

"Home was a supportive place, yes. The world seems quite brutal. Women-wise, I've met some wonderful and not so wonderful ones," he said, feeling lured by what she said.

"You are naïve and vulnerable because of the trust you learned from your parents. You've got a warm heart, a sensual nature, and a brilliant mind. That Uranus Sun conjunction in Gemini is a rare romantic combination.

But untended, genius becomes erratic, unbalanced. You will have to learn to balance your sensuality with your intellect. But be careful in the world, especially with women. You believe in great love, but it is rare. I've never seen such a fabulous chart. Follow your dreams. You will do great things."

"Fabulous? So, why can't I find a job?" he asked, regaining his skepticism.

"You will create your own job in this world, Danny. If you're concerned about money, write yourself a check for a million dollars and sign it 'Abundance of the Universe.' Put it in your wallet. Born to genius, the universe needs you, wants you to be happy."

"If you say so," he said, and laughed. But finding her exuberance about his chart amusingly absurd, he wrote the check that night and put it in his wallet.

A few days later, when school started, he worked as a substitute teacher then he got a job through the federally funded Comprehensive Employment Training Act (CETA) in a sheltered workshop for mentally retarded adults. He met Molly, a singer at a local bar but the relationship never developed. Within a few months, he was fired from the CETA job for incompetence. He decided it was a sign to leave when all he had in the refrigerator was a wrinkled russet potato and a yellow box of Arm and Hammer baking soda as air freshener.

He drove back East in the summer of 1979 to visit Tony and Allison, who was pregnant. The day after he arrived, Antonio woke him in the predawn light to say they were going to the hospital. He saw the labored joy of birth on Allison's face in the hospital that evening. When he asked how she felt, she said, "Giving birth is the most natural and wonderful thing I've ever done. But thank God for drugs!"

"What's his name?" Danny asked, as she cradled the baby against her breast.

"Thomas."

"Because of Thomas Jefferson, an Aries like you Allison, who founded the university?"

"Nope," Tony said.

"Not Doubting Thomas like me?"

"We just like the name," Allison said.

"Thomas Marino would be a great name for a Supreme Court Judge. Or Tommie Marino could player centerfield for the Yankees. We've contributed to the next generation, that's what counts," Tony said.

"A moon child, born with the sun in Cancer, the month of America's birth," Danny said while sweeping his arms toward young Thomas.

"You're getting weirder by the year, Danny," Tony said, and they all laughed.

He stayed with Tony and Allison a few days and returned to Long Island. Financially bankrupt, he moved in with his folks in Litteltown. His life had collapsed at age thirty-two. Litteltown was the last place he wanted to be. The school district officials had even closed his high school – where he figured as a last resort he might teach. His friends had left Litteltown. He visited Frank's mom, who was living alone since her husband died, terribly lonely because Frank and Dawn remained exiled in Canada. Danny knew he had to leave and applied for jobs in colleges around the country.

Chapter 10: Paradise Dreamed

Within a few weeks, Danny was back taking care of other people's children. He applied for a job at Florida South University in Tampa, but somehow, the letter resulted in an offer to interview to be a dorm director at Gulf Coast University downtown. On campus, Danny stood near the river, surrounded by Canary Island date palms and an ancient oak that Ponce de Leon allegedly stood under, but the crescent moon topped silver minarets on the old Tampa Hotel, the main academic building, convinced him to take the job. The following semester, he started to teach in the philosophy department and began another novel, set in Oregon. It was about a soccer player and a singer that he titled, *The Final Season*.

He worked on the novel for two years. When he finished, he sent it to the president of Orion Pictures. The president, who happened to be a soccer fan, loved it. He wrote to Danny, "Write it for Chevy Chase and Goldie Hawn. It will make a great comedy!" Danny wrote back, "The soccer player loses his teammate from Africa and his leg in a car accident. It's about overcoming tragedy." The president wrote back, "Tragedy doesn't sell in America. A comedy or no deal." Danny replied, "No deal."

Frustrated by agents intent to commercialize his writing, he returned to Ithaca that summer to work on his dissertation.

July 4ᵗʰ 1982

Independence Day. Is independence freedom? Ah, how questions without answers appear and reappear. Ithaca again. The rooming house where I started in '74 in view from my apartment in grad student housing. The summer of '77 I left and I return in '82 seeking a PhD. The summer of turning 35. Ulysses returned to Ithaca for Penelope. For me it's a dissertation and a degree I will not let escape.

The struggle that wouldn't crystallize then was about the German philosopher Martin Heidegger's concept of authenticity in <u>Being and Time.</u> Now, I believe I can explain authenticity using fictional characters: the old Cuban fisherman in Hemingway's <u>The Old Man and the Sea</u> and the absurd Meursault in Albert Camus' <u>The Stranger.</u> I'm skeptical of the German's obsession with the concept of will – that led Heidegger to support Nazism as a philosophical descendant of Nietzsche's will to power embodied in his idea of the Superman.

I want to work out my own educational theory about personal development that connects authenticity to integration of thinking, feeling and acting within the ideals of American democracy. As mom used to say about us Germans, "Where there is a will there is a way. But don't let your will get in your way." Her parents left Germany as Nazism rose. Her family came to America with the will to build houses and apartments and paint murals and pictures. The Roarkes left Ireland to save people from burning buildings and crime as firemen and police. I need to blend art and action. I must understand and teach will to care.

That fall, Danny returned to Tampa to teach and write. The following spring, he met a free lance writer named Maureen Wilmar in his logic class at Gulf Coast University. Near the end of the semester, he gave her a photocopy of his manuscript *Shattered Images*, about a sculptor who has an affair with the beautiful wife of a prominent attorney and ends up killing her.

"Danny, not only are you an excellent teacher, but your novel is a minor masterpiece. I adore the way you describe the Colorado River in the Grand Canyon. My favorite sentence is, 'Rock carved and honed, worked and worked and smoothed, dispersing light and color, endlessly, endlessly, and to the depths that a turbulent river wrinkles along like a tiny chain of liquid silver and disappears behind a fold of massiveness.' Danny, that is brilliant writing."

"I'm glad you liked it. Weird being quoted like that. Great memory. No wonder you're so good in logic."

Danny leaned against the chalkboard in the Teddy Roosevelt Room as they stood together, after the other students left. He admired how her black dress accentuated her blond hair, and the way her green eyes sparkled as she spoke with an accent at times that sounded like an amalgam of British and American. She seemed taller up close, almost his height.

"Danny, you are a great writer. I've been thinking. I want you to collaborate on a novel. Set in Spain. I call it *Costa del Sol*. It's about a woman named Misty, who is often confused about romance, and gets pregnant after a series of affairs. She's torn between abortion and having the child on her own. I'll write the female character Misty. I want you to write an odd male character, who is her friend, but not her lover. He has to assess the moral implications of Misty's plan."

"My feeling is that Misty should have an abortion and get on with her life," Danny said flatly, flashing on Elaine.

"Abortion is immoral. And although Misty had no intention of marrying the father, readers would prefer to see her heroically accept the consequences of her actions and raise the child on her own."

"I wonder… Hawthorne wrote that story over a hundred years ago. He was a great writer, whether he gave Scarlet A's for adultery or abortion, but he let religion get in the way of ethics. Although I think he wanted the Puritans to accept Hester and her daughter Pearl. I've worked with all kinds of kids…those from wed and unwed mothers, and those from happy and miserable home lives. Good parents raise good kids. So I'm concerned about lack of mutual consent to have the child. That seems worse than abortion," he said slowly, flashing on his run through the woods back in Vermont, when he struggled with the choice.

Maureen said, "Abortion won't sell. Just make her friend weird so Misty looks more heroic."

A few months later, as Maureen and Danny discussed the book deal on the balcony of her condo, Danny noticed a bright green light far out in Tampa Bay.

"I'll give you twenty-five thousand to write the book. And I'll treat to a Hawaii vacation to seal the deal," she added then held her glass of Chivas Regal to his to clink glasses.

Suddenly the green light reminded Danny of the green light of the orgiastic future that Scott Fitzgerald described in *The Great Gatsby*. He wondered if he was the misguided Gatsby or the more balanced Nick. But Maureen was beautiful and talented and had money that seemed to stem from her success. He felt his muse finally discovered him. As he looked from the bay toward Maureen, after clinking glasses of Scotch, he thought he let Elaine's money get in the way of their relationship, but with Maureen, working together toward the creative birth of a novel, sharing her wealth was justifiable.

"You're making an offer that's hard to refuse. Throwing in Hawaii is quite a bonus. I gotta say yes."

"Oh, Danny, you make me so happy. We'll write a great novel," she said, hugging him against the balcony rail, spilling several ice cubes from her drink into the pool below.

Danny sits in his old rocking chair reading Maureen's novel *Utopia Means Nowhere.* His left leg is bent at the knee over the oak arm rest. Maureen's main character Belinda wants to go to Paris to paint, but her parents want her to stay with them in Edinburgh and go to medical school. In one of the waiting rooms in her parents' clinic, she is painting a ballet dancer in the style of Degas, with a banner across the top saying "Equalite. Liberte."

He likes her writing. He rocks back and forth for a while then closes the book. He looks at her pseudonym, Marianne Twines – which her parents insisted on because of the way the novel exposed the family – on the cover. Her book makes his unpublished writing pretentious. He looks at the opposite wall at the Winslow Homer poster of the Bahamas, which he framed after he bought it at the Metropolitan Museum last summer, and wonders about the artist's life. He puts her book down among the pile on the oak-slatted camp table next to the chair.

He picks-up the collection of Hemingway's letters. He looks at the index citations he's circled referring to *The Old Man and the Sea.* He reads the letter Hemingway wrote to his friend Bernard Berenson, the art critic, describing characters as what they are, claiming symbolism is "shit." He takes the novel and reads the first paragraph, then the next about the old man's cheerful eyes but couldn't understand how Hemingway could call skin cancer benevolent. He holds the book in his lap then looks at the pile of papers on his desk, which are his dissertation that he's been writing for two years. He reads the description of Santiago again.

As he rocks back and forth, his eyes begin to burn, tears form then flow. He pictures Santiago's sun beaten face and worn body.

His eyes continue to burn. His facial muscles tighten; the tension works down through his neck and chest. Tears flow down his face, along his cheeks, through his mustache, over his lips. He licks the salt, and reaches for the lamp on the table, feels for the switch, shuts it off and tilts his head back against the cushion. His tears flow in quiet darkness.

He pictures the north end of Fort DeSoto beach, where it curves into the inlet rimmed by palms and white powdery sand. He imagines floating in the Gulf's green water, its warmth like his own body. He drifts in its buoyancy and his own.

Slowly, he opens his eyes and sees dark shadows created by the flood lights on the art building outside his window. He looks at the sharp outlines the hanging plants project on the couch. There are no colors. The Homer print is barely visible. He looks at the bamboo palm Ronda gave him from her plant rental business. Moonlight comes through the screened window near his desk. That side of the palm is powdery silver. He leans forward to touch it. Then he wipes his face with his hands.

He kneels near the stereo and sorts through the loose albums to find the one of Hemingway. He puts on the Nobel Prize acceptance speech. Sitting against the couch, his tears flow again as he listens to Hemingway's laconic style, like admonitions of a stern uncle about the writer's lonely life.

When it finishes, he plays it again and sits with his eyes closed, listening to Hemingway's precise, sparse style. He starts it again and gets up, then walks to the window near his desk and looks out at the waning moon. He goes to the liquor cabinet in the kitchen, pours some Chivas in a glass, takes several ice cubes from the freezer, drops them in and returns to the rocking chair. He turns on the light and savors the oaken-cast of the Scotch.

The phone rings. He lets it ring several times. Finally he picks it up.

"Danny?"

"Ronda?"

"I'm in Tampa. I just finished installing a job at the Hyatt. I've got some plants I can't use, want them?"

"Sure. I've got your favorite, diet Shasta root beer."

"A deal. See you in a half-hour."

When he hangs-up he changes the sheets on his bed. He cleans the kitchen and living room quickly then goes into the bathroom to shave and shower. Closing the door, he is amused by the black-and-white poster of a man holding his trench coat open, facing a bronze female sculpture, with the caption, "Expose Yourself to Art."

Dressing quickly, he goes into the living room and sorts through his albums. He selects Bob Dylan, Emmy Lou Harris, Willie Nelson and Linda Ronstadt to put on the stereo. Back in the kitchen, he puts the dishes from the plastic drying rack into the cabinet. The pile of things on the work table, he pushes back toward the corner, then takes a brush to sweep up some potting soil. As he's doing that there's a knock on the kitchen door.

He opens the door to Ronda who is carrying a ficus tree.

"The Gemini Plant Lady. Let me help," he says, taking the tree and plopping it on the work table, where it almost reaches to the ceiling.

"There are two more in the van."

He gives her a hug. Her white Volkswagen van with the colorful, "Gemini Interiors" logo is parked in his reserved area. The side door is open and there is a bamboo palm and a large dracaena. While he takes in the two plants, Ronda gets a white paper Maas Brothers bag from the front seat. When he gets them in the kitchen near the refrigerator, he offers her a root beer and takes a can of Busch beer for himself.

"Thanks," she says, and drops the bag on the work table.

"Thanks for the plants."

"They're pretty ratty, I can't use them anymore, but you'll be able to revive them."

"Your favorite plant. One that's been rented into retirement."

"It's called business, Danny," she says, with a broad smile and flash of her dark brown eyes.

"Big job at the Hyatt?"

"Very. This is my first big one on this side of the bay. A few more this size and I can open another office in Tampa."

She takes the paper bag off the work table as they walk into the living room. She's about five-five, with curly black hair and a quick easy smile. He admired her courage to have cosmetic surgery a couple months ago that refined the misshaped Irish-Jewish nose that embarrassed her throughout childhood. The change enhanced her eyes, which are openly childlike and emphasizes her smile. The surgery, which Danny accompanied her to, was a gift she gave herself when her business started to make money.

She sits on the couch. Danny is in the rocking chair. Bob Dylan sings, "Black Diamond Bay" on the stereo. She rolls open the top of the bag then takes a drink of soda. She smiles as she looks at him and hands him the bag.

"Here's what I promised you for the cutting-board you made last month, when I had my kitchen redecorated. I never realized how much I hate sewing," she added, with a short laugh.

He takes the bag and looks at her quizzically, then looks into it. He sees black fabric with brightly colored jungle animals printed on it. He smirks and shakes his head. He lifts it high in front of him, turning it to look at the tigers, rhinos, monkeys, plants, and flowers distributed over it. He bites his lower lip, still shaking his head, holding back laughter. Twirling it in his left hand, hiding his face momentarily, he says, "It's me!"

"Look at the pocket, Danny," she says, excitedly, leaning toward him.

"A pocket too?"

She spreads the fabric and he sees the clear white button on the pocket.

"It's a purple rhino. I had to set the pocket just right to get it there."

"Purple rhino, yep."

"Danny, you don't like it?" she asks sounding hurt. "When I found that material I knew it was exactly right. That's you, Danny, a purple rhino."

He takes a deep breath, his eyes go wide and he lets air out of his mouth in a rush. He covers his face with his hand and lets out a long high pitched burst of laughter.

"I really like it. I really do! Why the rhino?"

"Don't you remember the story you told me?"

He has no idea what she means. He listens to Emmy Lou Harris' sensual voice sing about shoes of white leather. He looks back and forth between the shirt and her face, waiting. Then he notices Maureen's book on the table next to him, but Ronda knows about her.

"Remember when you finished at Cornell last summer, you went to the Bronx Zoo because you used to go there as a kid?"

"Yeah," he says, uncertainly.

"The rhino with the telescopic tube steak?"

"I never called it that. I might have said dick or cock or phallus or penis or weenus, but not tube steak."

She laughs. "You are such a prude. You know how much I like oral sex. You said telescopic!"

"Yeah, telescopic dick. Tube steak is crude!"

"OK, telescopic dick. You said he was mounting a female and his cock was rubbing in the dust. You said it was the biggest tube steak you'd ever seen. And you know how much I enjoy your tube steak."

He looks at her without saying anything. He shifts his eyes back and forth several times between her and the shirt, exaggerating his look, chewing on the side of his cheek making sucking noises. She looks at him with a broad smile, her eyes bright and alive. He shakes his head back and forth several times. He points his finger at the rhino on the pocket, then his crotch. Smirking, he holds his thumb and forefinger a few inches apart and she laughs.

"There's more, Danny, look."

"More?"

He reaches into the bag and finds another swatch of fabric with a purple rhino. He takes it out, looks to see if there is anything else in the bag then drops it to the floor. He holds up the fabric and sees the attached elastic band.

"It isn't?"

"What?"

"What I think it is? Ronda you worry me."

"What?" she asks again, as she leans forward on the arm of the couch.

"The women's pirate fantasies in *Psychology Today*, right?"

He holds onto the black elastic band with his left hand and slowly lifts the shirt and puts it on the chair back with his right. He puts the band around his head and tugs the patch over his left eye. Diving at her on the arm of the couch, he pulls her over onto the cushions. When he starts to tickle her, she lets out a scream. Willie Nelson sings, "A Whiter Shade of Pale."

"Rhinos and pirates, Ronda?" he says, as he tickles her. "At least Catherine the Great stopped with horses."

"Do you like the shirt, really?"

"I do. Actually, it is a really nice piece of work. With the patch, I can do Hanover shirt ads. I should try the shirt, huh?"

"Yes. Later, just the eye patch, and we can screw."

"Doesn't anybody make love anymore?" he says, tickling her as he gets up.

He tries on the shirt. It fits. He wears it into the bedroom. Ronda lies on the bed he made, watching the goldfish in the tank on the headboard, under the hanging plants. He lights two candles in brass holders on the dresser, then takes his jeans off, and leaves them on the bench at the end of the bed. He puts on the eye patch and climbs onto the bed next to her.

"Oh, a pirate! Take me," she says, pressing the back of her hand to her forehead in a swoon, then reaching between his legs to fondle him. "Feels stiff, Danny. As long as I don't call it a tubesteak, can I suck on it?" she says, with a warm giggle.

The following morning Danny makes omelettes for breakfast. They go back to Ronda's house to feed her two dogs and her cat. Then they go to the pink stucco Don Caesar Hotel on St. Petersburg beach. They lie by the pool, watching the tourists and listening to the steel band.

"Danny, here, use this sunblock. It'll cover your peeling nose," Ronda says, trying to hand him the tube of cream.

"Only the top layers peel. We have a lucky seven," he says, pushing it back.

"Philosophers!"

"Old lifeguards. Let's walk the beach."

They take a long walk along the beach until they find a quiet stretch in front of dunes filled with tall raspy grasses and swim in the Gulf. Early in the evening, as the porpoise and pelicans stroke past, they walk back on the powdery white sand along the water's edge.

"They're going to move students into the dorm next week," Danny says. He walks along the water's edge looking for shells.

"I thought you were off for the summer?"

"They had high registration for the second summer session, so they need more room. The crew coach is running a camp and wants to use the dorm too. They asked me to be the director, or move out."

"What will you do?"

"Direct!"

"Won't that ruin your chance to finish your dissertation?"

"Hemingway said all artists are gypsies. We move when we must. But I'm not teaching, so I'll have time, moving would waste that. And they asked me to help with the search committee for the new philosophy chairman. Some things to do, that's all."

He bends down and picks up a sand dollar which fills his palm, at Ronda and hands her the sand dollar. He remembers what Maureen said about him being a womanizer, that he enjoyed dating several women at a time, each for different qualities.

"Do you ever wonder if our relationship will go anywhere?" he asks.

"It would be nice. But I'm a realist."

"Realist?"

She looks at the sand dollar then back at him. "You appeal to women because of your vulnerability. But you're dangerous because you haven't focused your life yet. You're a romantic."

Surprised by the emotional sting of what he knows is true, he says, "Soon my parents will be happily married fifty years. Other than that and their children, what more is there? I think Carl Sandburg had it right when he said that the lovers win in the tombs. Without love neither life nor death are worth it."

She looks at him sympathetically, familiar with his sporadic quoting.

"In my marriage, I thought love would overcome lifestyle differences. It's always compromise, never perfect. But the credits have to outweigh the debits in a relationship."

"Can't realists understand what e.e. cummings said about feeling being first?"

"Maybe not. But you have to get your life focused before you can love a woman completely."

"I guess Romantics are slow learners. It's taken years to make the transition from scientist to artist. Being an artist is tough in this country. I miss that connection with you. You're driven by business. Like all America... where poets are banished to an occasional line in the travel section... No offense, just realism," he says, but feels an edge in his voice.

"You're right. But seems you want a woman to focus you."

"Why not? I'm writing a dissertation about authenticity... Isn't life about caring for others? Loving some? It seems loving the right woman is key."

He feels confused by Ronda. They walk along quietly. Danny looks at the pink stucco of the Don Caesar Hotel and the people playing volleyball on the beach. The Gulf is warm as it slides up the wet sand with a gentle swish. He continues to pick through shells. When they approach the front of the hotel, he thinks about Maureen and Hawaii.

Friday evening Maureen meets Danny with a cab at his apartment. They both have on straw hats. Danny helps the cab driver put his canvas suitcase and camera bag in the trunk then he gets into the back seat next to Maureen.

"Honey, I'm so glad you agreed to come. Here's some travel money." She hands him a wad of hundred dollar bills, which he pushes back to her. "This is my treat," she says, and pushes the money back into his hand.

He looks into her insistent green eyes, then bows his head and says, "Thanks." He tucks the money into the front pocket of his jeans. The driver starts along the brick road which separates the dorm from the art building, then past the swimming pool and on to the airport.

High above the undulating west Texas hills, Danny takes his journal out of his camera bag and records his reaction, next to a sketch he made of the intricate alluvial delta at New Orleans. "Maybe I should write travel pieces," he mumbles, but he is sucked back into the trap of considering his dissertation.

"What are you writing?" Maureen asks, leaning against him.

"Just notes. Callahan, my dissertation chairman, hasn't responded to the draft I sent. It's been a month."

"You think he'll accept it?"

"Unless he's using it as puppy training paper."

She lets out a burst of laughter then composes herself. "Have you heard from my agent Stan Rutledge about your novel?"

Enjoying the vein of bleak thought, he says, "Maybe Callahan's worked a deal with Rutledge for the manuscript to train his puppy."

"Oh, Danny! But you keep writing. How long have you kept a journal?"

He thinks for a moment then looks inside to see number fourteen in Roman numerals. "About fifteen years."

He remembers the impulse to write started during his junior year in college, when he was rooming with his closest friend Tony. The need was an outgrowth of a junior high school exercise his English teacher Miss Bradley called an "observation notebook" and a challenge Emerson posed to Thoreau to keep a journal. It's been his most intimate companion since.

"Maureen, why don't we try some writing? I'll start," he says, and begins to write.

Oct. 14, 1983
When Oedipus read the message that
his mother called, he thought
about telephoning her. But he was
farming jojoba in New Mexico...

He hands Maureen the journal and laughs. She reads it and continues without hesitation.

> *Outside of the jojoba, there was*
> *the grocery, the cantina, and after*
> *the harvest and pressing of the dry*
> *wrinkled beans, the profit made and*
> *divided, there was Maria Verdad...*

She returns the book. He notices the difference between his minuscule scrawl and the large flowing letters of her handwriting. He feels a surge of competition as he responds to her entry.

> *But Oedipus seemed destined for the solitary*
> *life. The farm gave him a place, a purpose,*
> *but had he violated some cosmic law that*
> *forced him on an unending quest...*

He doesn't speak as he passes the book. But he feels uneasy as he wonders what she is really saying to him, or what he is saying to her. She reads what he's written and continues.

> *which led to the house of Maria*
> *Verdad. He came to taste and touch*
> *and feel in ways unusual for him.*
> *She knew he needed to tell what he*
> *kept hidden, to unlock his troubled*
> *heart to hers.*

As he finishes reading what she wrote, the flight attendant announces final preparation to land in Los Angeles. Danny puts the journal back into his camera bag and pushes it under the seat in front of him. He is excited by their exchange. He feels an intellectual and creative attraction to her that he's never experienced.

He has no idea what time it is when they finally land. In the airport, waiting for the connecting flight to Honolulu, Danny drags Maureen into a gift shop. He buys two "Los Angeles" T-shirts. He takes the money she gave him in the cab in Tampa and rolls it in the purple T-shirts, then stuffs them into her large purse. Maureen looks at the sizes on the tags.

"They're both small?" she says, questioning.

"They're the only two left."

"Who will they fit?"

"You? I want to remember we were here," he says.

Smiling, she shakes her head and pushes them into her purse. They hurry back to the plane. As it takes off, Maureen clutches his arm.

"You sure aren't calm for a world traveler."

"Landings and takeoffs bother me. The pilot is on his own."

"Everyone's on his own. Don't sweat the particulars."

Several hours of immense blackness outside the windows lead to a cluster of lights. But not until they get off the plane, when he sees the Honolulu sign, and a crowd of young women with flower leis, does he believe they are in Hawaii.

In the cab leaving the airport, the driver tells them about the island and the Kalika Hotel, where Maureen usually stays.

"I'm just glad to be back," Danny says, leaning over the driver's seat. He looks back at Maureen's startled face and grins.

"You from Hawaii?" the driver asks.

"Born here," he says, looking at the driver from the side and then at Maureen in the rear view mirror.

The cabby reminds him of the Hawaiian police inspector on the "Magnum P.I." television show. That and Hawaiian print shirts are the closest he's ever been to the islands, he thinks. Then he remembers the night he let his students talk him into a local Tom Selleck look alike contest. A car, which he needed desperately to replace his deteriorating white Toyota, was first prize. He got no closer than the final five, but wondered if a Detroit Tigers cap and straight teeth would have changed the results.

"Where you live now, man?" the cabby asks.

"We're getting back from an African photographic safari."

"You a photographer?"

"Yep, Ansel Adams Roarke."

Danny looks at Maureen very oddly. He feels an unusual giddiness, which he attributes to sudden mellowness in the air, and her willingness to let him play. He's relaxed and amused. His mouth goes.

"Maureen's writing a movie script to end elephant and rhino slaughter. We must reverse Hemingway's adulation of the hunt in 'Snows of Kilimanjaro.' We must identify with the frozen snow leopard."

"I've had movie people in my cab. Had Burt Reynolds once."

Danny wonders if it was the real one, then asks, "You from here?"

"My whole life. It's home."

"Robert Frost said home is where they always take you in because they love you," Danny says, struggling to remember Frost's poem, but knowing he's botched the quote.

Maureen rolls her eyes upward and laughs. Danny hugs her.

When they reach the circular drive in front of the hotel, the cab driver gets out and helps them into the lobby with their luggage. Danny takes money from his wallet to pay, then adds a ten dollar tip, as apology.

Maureen registers. Danny stops a few feet from the desk. He remembers the scene from *The Graduate*, where Dustin Hoffman tells the desk clerk about his toothbrush and pats his jacket pocket. He feels awkward that she controls the finances as she chats with the desk clerk, then walks toward him.

He looks at his canvas bag and remembers he got it with stamps from Publix. He takes it and Maureen's Vuitton suitcase and carries them into the elevator. Maureen cuddles into him on the way up, and he puts his arm around her.

In the room, he drops the bags on one of the beds then walks out to the balcony to look out over Waikiki. Maureen follows him.

"Glad to be *home*, Honey?" she says, laughing.

He rubs his hand on the balcony rail and smirks. "I understand the snow leopard. Wow! I haven't pulled that kind of bullshit in years. I really appreciate you going along with me," he says, hugging her and kissing her on the cheek.

"He enjoyed it. Deception doesn't hurt. It adds intrigue. Like dressing well. Oh, you wouldn't know."

"Wait a minute, Bucko. My wardrobe oozes sincerity," he says, holding his arms out, rotating side to side.

"Is that what it oozes?"

"So this is Waikiki?" he says, pointing to the expanse of beach below them and out to the jetty which moored expensive boats.

"Waikiki welcomes you, Danny! "

"Then that shadow is Diamond Head?"

"Tourism *is* your life, Ansel."

He pushes her playfully and goes inside quickly to get his camera. In front of them the beach curves outward on both sides. In the faint light, the ocean is calm. Waves break delicately as light runs along their curling edge before they splash onto the sand then scrape in retreat. Water and sand mix in a soothing audible rush.

Danny snaps a picture of Diamond Head, admiring its volcanic texture. His hesitancy disappears. He feels close to Maureen.

"I'm sorry I've been a pain in the ass about the trip. I've wanted to see Hawaii ever since I was a kid. Thanks."

"You're welcome. I know it's been hard for you."

"Now what?" he says, realizing they will be together for the longest time since they've met.

"You're not tired?"

"No. You?"

"I'm on holiday," she says with a broad smile.

"I saw an ad in the lobby about their disco. Probably Don Ho and a million people in polyester from Minnesota drinking Mai Tais. Up for it?"

"You dance?"

"Actually, I've never had a Mai Tai with a little umbrella."

The nightclub is crowded. The band is squeezed against the edge of a parquet floor. People filled tables along the windows which overlook the beach. When a couple leaves, Danny pulls Maureen toward the vacant table. To hear each other, they need to lean forward. He enjoys the scent of Maureen's perfume as they order Mai Tais. Danny insists on an umbrella – the waitress brings him two.

The band plays rock and roll oldies, mostly Beatles and Rolling Stones. The time warp it creates filters perfectly into the one Danny feels. He comes alive as he hears the stormy early bars of the Stones, "Satisfaction," a high school favorite.

"Gotta dance, Maureen."

He takes her hand and an umbrella from his drink. They walk out to the dance floor. There are several other couples already on the floor. Danny moves to his own beat and enjoys Maureen's rhythmic sensuality.

Danny offers his hand and tries to Lindy with her. As she begins to adjust to his rhythm, he gyrates his hips quickly.

Unable to follow his movements, she asks, "Danny, are we partners?"

"Can't follow good dancing?" he teases, and Maureen laughs. "The pattern's printed on the floor. See?" he says, pointing at imaginary footprints.

She laughs again. He holds her close. As the song ends, he shakes his hips rapidly, like a penguin skidding down ice. He bows from the waist and escorts her from the floor.

"Thank you, Danny. I understand primitive tribesmen better."

They walk back to their table and sit down. He hears another Rolling Stones song a few minutes later and pulls her back on the floor as the band sings, "Get off my cloud." They dance to several more songs before returning to their room.

It's past four o'clock. Slowly, they undress each other. They toss the clothes a piece at a time onto the other bed. They embrace and kiss for a long time, then make love slowly in predawn light.

After several hours of sleep, they call room service for breakfast. Afterwards, they walk a few blocks to find a rental car. Maureen asks for a Datsun Z and signs for it with her American Express card. She hands him the keys. He tosses them up and catches them several times, trying to adjust to her extravagance.

He drives east along Kalakaua Avenue to Diamond Head. He takes her picture in front of the lighthouse, overlooking the pale blue Pacific and thirty foot palms. They continue north around the island's rim. Dazzled by the colors, Danny stops at a rock formation called "Chinaman's Hat" in Kaneohe Bay's green, blue, and turquoise shoals, and photographs her again. In each shot he admires the intensity of her eyes and smile as she draws him in through the lens.

He stops along the road to take pictures of moss covered lava mountains, like folds of a giant accordion a thousand feet high, impregnable black stones lost in clouds and mist. Each bend of the road exhilarates him. He chatters excitedly with Maureen between abrupt roadside stops. They continue to the north side of the island to Sunset Beach and Waimea Bay. They buy sandwiches at a small delicatessen and go to watch the surfers.

Danny is enchanted by the easy going style of the surfing town. During the summers he spent as a lifeguard on the Atlantic beaches agonizing about the meaning of life, he envied the carefree attitude of guards who spent their winters on Oahu surfing.

They stay for a few hours, lying on the wide white sand beach, watching the surfers a few hundred yards out along the sand bar. Waves slap quietly against the beach in front of them as he applies suntan oil to Maureen, immersed in sensuality. Afterwards, he runs in to body surf. He rides the waves until he's exhausted then plops down next to Maureen, lazily sniffing her coconut scent.

When they start to pull out of the parking lot to drive back to Honolulu, two bearded men with bright headbands approach them.

"How much?" Danny asks the taller one.

"Forty, man. This is Kona."

"And I'm the Pope."

The taller one hands a plastic bag in through the window. Danny looks at the swollen green buds and rolls them between his fingers. He feels the resin and sniffs to enjoy the musky scent.

"Ten bucks," Danny says.

"Forty, man. This is Kona."

"Kona has red buds."

They look at him. The tall one pulls out another bag. "OK, two bags for forty."

"I'm not an entrepreneur. I want a few Kona buds."

"These are, man," the short one says.

"Nice, but not Kona."

"OK, how much?" the tall one asks.

"Twenty." Danny takes the money from his wallet and hands it to the taller one who hands him both bags. "One's plenty. Thanks, guys. Need a ride?"

"No, Man!" the short one insists.

Danny smiles, understanding why they don't want to get into the car. He thanks them again and stuffs the plastic bag into the back pocket of his jeans.

"How did you know what they were selling?" Maureen asks, after watching the transaction silently.

"What would you sell a guy with sunglasses and a flowered shirt in a rented Z?"

"You have more street smarts than I thought. What is Kona?"

"You're the journalist."

"I've never heard of it."

"I think it's part of the big island. They grow coffee. Probably the main cash crop is Kona buds. In Oregon, my next door neighbor was an Asian guy from Hawaii. He always had plenty. It's a resinous bud with a bright red sepal. A few tokes of a bud in his bong moved me into another dimension."

"You think they sold you Kona?"

"Who knows? But it smells good," he says, getting back on the highway.

As they reach the hotel lobby, he sees the newspaper headline in one of the machines. At first it doesn't register. But he looks into the red metal box and reads in large black letters across the front page, HURRICANE. He shakes his head and laughs. He gets out of the car and walks over to the box to buy a paper.

"Story of my life, Maureen. In Hawaii one day and there's a hurricane!"

He holds the newspaper out to her. A satellite picture of the Hawaiian Islands on the front page shows a huge circle of clouds to the east, dwarfing the small chain.

"They're calling it Raymond. It's a couple hundred miles off shore. They figure it for Oahu in the next few days."

Maureen looks at the paper. Her eyes seem to fissure. She is silent for a long time as they sit looking at the newspaper. She puts her hand on Danny's wrist and pushes herself back in the seat. She begins to speak very slowly and quietly.

"It may miss us."

"With my luck, it'll start in our room."

"We've got at least twenty-four hours."

Danny looks at the newspaper again, amazed by the size of the swirling cloud mass in relationship to tiny islands in expanse of ocean. He feels trapped. He hadn't checked the weather before they left Tampa. He folds the newspaper in half, hands it to Maureen, then pulls out of the circular drive into the parking lot.

In the lobby he says, "Let's stop in the gift shop. I'd at least like a T-shirt to wear to the hurricane."

They go in and he finds an XL with turquoise flowers on it. At the counter, while he pays for the shirt, he sees packages of cigarette papers and buys one.

In their room they listen for weather reports. The radio and television are filled with special announcements. Danny sits in the chair next to the television, turns the dials to see pictures of the huge storm.

In the meantime, he takes out the plastic bag, and dumps it onto the front page of the newspaper. He removes the seeds. He rolls a joint, looks at it and takes it apart. He rolls several more, undoing each until he gets one that he likes. He lights it, takes a puff and hands it to Maureen.

"Nice stuff," he says.

She takes a toke, passes it back to him. They pass it back and forth.

"What do you want to do, Maureen?"

"I've been in storms here. They are never as bad as they advertise. You know journalists exaggerate," she adds, with a Cheshire cat grin.

Danny looks at the huge swirl on the front page of the newspaper. He starts reading the article out loud. "One of the biggest and most intense storms to threaten Hawaii closed in on the island chain today as Civil Defense officials urged residents to begin preparing for the worst."

It is several times the width of the entire chain of islands, a tightly packed mass of white, rotating counter clockwise, with two broad spirals emanating from it, like a photograph of an approaching galaxy.

"Couldn't be a regular storm. No, gotta be a big mother hurricane. It's Saturday, right?"

"That's what the newspaper says."

"Oh, right. If that hits tomorrow, the airport will be closed until it blows over."

Maureen sits in a chair facing him. She sounds animated but tired. "We should start our novel. And you'll have to go to Spain to research it. When we get back, start planning. I'll pay for it. You have to go to Gibraltar. Near Algeciras. And see a bullfight. That will help you with your dissertation about Hemingway. He loved Spain."

"We writing a best seller or literature?"

"Would you know the difference?"

Feigning a condescending look, he says, "People keep their clothes on in literature, and don't use contractions."

"Then let's write a best seller," she says, and pulls off her shirt, to expose her breasts.

"But the next one's literature," he says, diving at her, knocking the chair, and them both to the floor.

He feels an explosion of light in his chest. A broad grin expands across his face. Lying on the floor in a Hawaiian hotel undressing a woman with whom he is falling in love, as they wait for a hurricane, feels like a perfect beginning.

"The thought of being linked with you forever in print scares me to death," Maureen says.

"Don't read it," he replies, and kisses between her breasts.

"I'll have my lawyer draw up a contract when we get back to Tampa. We split fifty-fifty."

"Literature fifty-fifty. I only want twenty-five percent on a best seller. I'm terrible with money."

"I got an advance from Scribner's. That's where I got the twenty-five grand. But I don't want that in the contract."

"Fine. Just help me get our clothes off."

"You are so mad, I love you," she says, and hugs him.

"Then you'll be delirious when you really get to know me," he says, and tugs off her jeans.

After they make love, as the afternoon moves to evening, they talk about the novel. The sky thickens with gray clouds. They go out along the beach for a walk in the cool damp air. They are the only ones on the windy patio of an outdoor café overlooking the beach when they have dinner.

Chapter 11: Entering Hades

Oct. 8, 1984

> *Is this your Spain, Mr. Hemingway? The Madrid airport below...after several bumpy hours in the air from JFK... And so, Gibraltar, bullfights and to write a response to Maureen's first draft of* Costa de Sol

"No es...my...ticketa," Danny says to the man behind the airport counter. "I want to go to Malaga in Spain, not Majorca."

Again the man smiles and says, "Majorca, Señor Anderson?"

Danny leans on the counter and yells, "Ayudo, por favor. Yo hablo Ingles, solamente! I speak American!"

His high school Spanish and the few hours of cramming on the plane with the *Berlitz Spanish for Travellers*, now stuffed in his camera bag, don't make this easy. Nor can he understand how he got the wrong ticket.

A thin young dark-haired woman hurries down the aisle behind the counter. As she approaches, Danny steps back. He bumps into a soldier in green khaki. The soldier's eyes are the same shiny black as the gun barrel across his chest. Danny steps sideways to give him room. But the soldier takes a step toward him and says, "Alto. Stop!"

"Mr. Anderson, may I help you?" the dark-haired woman asks.

"I'm not Anderson. I'm Danny Roarke. That's not my ticket."

"You do not want to go to Majorca?"

"I want to go to Malaga." Danny eyes the soldier, who seems un-amused as he slow dances with his machine gun.

"This ticket says Majorca, Mr. Anderson."

"It's not mine," Danny says, again. Suddenly he remembers the flight attendant took his ticket and passport as they were preparing to land in Madrid and thinks she must have switched the tickets. Frightened, he reaches to zip open his camera bag, but the soldier grabs his wrist.

"My passport," Danny says nervously.

Immobile, the soldier stares at him.

Danny turns to the woman. "Tell him I'm looking for my passport."

She says something too fast for Danny to understand, but the soldier lets go of his wrist. Slowly, Danny zips open the camera bag and pulls out a passport. He flips it open and sees his picture. Relieved, he holds it up to the soldier, who is unimpressed. Then he shows it to the agent.

"This is me," he says, pointing at his picture. "I'm not Anderson. I think our tickets got switched on the plane. Can you page him?"

She looks at the passport and reads the name. Then re-reads the ticket. She smiles. "Mr. Roar...key? Sorry. I will announce for Mr. Anderson."

"Gracias," he says. He turns to the soldier and says, "Gracias," but sees no change of expression.

The soldier stands next to him for what seems like an incredibly long time. Danny looks at the departure board and sees that his flight to Malaga is boarding. Then he looks at the soldier; framed by white suspenders and white canvas belt, over the breast pocket of his green shirt is a small rectangular yellow badge trimmed with red. The blue letters read "Todo por la patria." "Everything for the fatherland?" Danny guesses. As he waits for the elusive Mr. Anderson, he wonders if that includes shooting tourists.

Eventually, a man comes shuffling through the arcade. His shoulder bag bangs against his side. He turns to the woman agent and announces his name. She asks for his passport then exchanges the tickets.

Anderson glares at Danny. "You almost screwed up my vacation!"

Startled, Danny looks at Anderson. The attendant hands Danny the exchanged ticket. He reads his name on it, then turns to Anderson and says, "Very gracious, Andy. I see the Nobel Peace Prize in your future!"

The agent directs Danny toward where his flight is boarding. He waves to the soldier and says, "Adios!" then breaks into a sprint toward the gate.

Finally in Malaga, with the rental car keys in his hand, he tosses his suitcase and camera bag in the trunk of the little white Fiat. He starts it and aims toward Algeciras and Gibraltar, one hundred and fifty kilometers south along the coast road. When he sees the blue water of the Mediterranean from the highway, the sun is high in a clear sky. He bangs out a rhythm on the steering wheel.

"Oh, Ms. Barraclough, we're not destined to be household names, but how right you are," he says, and starts to sing her song "Covered up in Aces."

He remembers the days in Oregon that were the result of no plan, which Barraclough sings is the best plan because it tends to be exact. He just believed it was a great place to live, until he had to move on to survive, and now, he had no plan, just excitement about traveling.

The road weaves in and out between sandy beaches and hilly towns. Assorted flowers in orange-brown clay pots clutter wrought iron balconies. Terra-cotta tiled roofs over white stucco abound. Construction is everywhere, as new villas spill onto beaches or cluster in olive-green hills.

About forty kilometers south of Malaga, he passes through Fuengirola. Posters announce a fiesta and bullfight for Sunday. He looks at the map to see that he is about sixty miles from Algeciras. He stops to take a picture of a poster. It will work he thinks, a bullfight. He jumps back into the car excitedly.

Somewhere south of a chic beach town called Marbella, he sees Gibraltar. Abruptly, he stops on a sandy brown beach strewn with bright yellow, green, and red rowboats. He hops out of the car and grabs his camera. The water is turquoise, blue, and gray. Through the camera lens the sky is diffuse, but the water sparkles. Gibraltar is black in shadows and silver everywhere else. It dominates the viewfinder as if superimposed. He clicks several pictures, then extends his arms to the sky with joy, the way he did when he scored in soccer.

Suddenly, an elderly weathered man appears. He's unshaven, with thick black and gray hair. He has the brim of his plaid cap pulled down over his eyes and is wearing a dark sport coat over his gray sport shirt. "La playa esta muy bonita," he says.

"Sí," Danny replies, assuming the fellow likes the place.

Pointing to the camera, the man indicates he wants Danny to take his picture. Danny nods. Through the lens, the man appears with dignity as Danny snaps his picture. The man extends his hand to Danny. It feels coarse and strong when they shake. After Danny thanks him with an unknown denomination of brightly colored Spanish money and turns to walk toward the car, the man says, "Vaya con Dios, Señor."

"Gracias Señor, Y usted."

Danny opens the car door and swings his leather bag into the front seat by its shoulder strap. He turns to look at the man then gets into the car. He backs out onto the road and waves to the man as he passes.

Gibraltar becomes an increasingly larger presence as he approaches the little seaport of Algeciras. He finds the Hotel Regina, where the novel is to be set, and registers at the desk. He is embarrassed when the desk clerk formally dispatches a bellhop to carry his bags. But when he gets to the room, Danny is amused by the colorful money he got at the exchange in Malaga, and unsure of the denomination, he hands the boy a color which elicits a smile and bow.

Danny walks to the window which overlooks a brick courtyard. He pushes open the green shutters then spreads open the lattice windows. The garden below has palm and cypress trees. There are rhododendron bushes and a huge azalea with large pink blooms. Two shiny young cats play in the sun along the whitewashed wall of the flower bed. He watches them for a while then takes his camera to explore the hotel.

It is more elegant than he imagined. He is in jeans and flowered shirt. Most women are in formal dresses and the men in suits. The male staff is in tuxedos. It makes sense to him why Maureen selected this place. It will allow for interesting movement of characters as Maureen's main character Misty navigates a series of affairs with hotel guests and ends up pregnant. Out the front entrance, Gibraltar dominates the bay. Beyond a beach filled with palm trees and a broad expanse of sand there is a huge rock jetty with a red light at the end.

He walks along the beach then circles to the road into Algeciras. He stops at an outdoor café and sits down on the patio. A waiter, with a white shirt and black bow tie, approaches the table.

"Cerveza, por favor," Danny says.

"Sí, Señor."

The waiter returns promptly and places a glass of beer on the table, with a white saucer under it. Danny takes a drink then looks across the road to where a line of fishing boats is moored. He takes his journal out of his camera bag.

The harbor water is like a blue nylon ski jacket. The brightly colored fishing boats along the seawall are strung with crimson, maroon, cerise, and pink nets. Men in groups stand along the dock. Occasionally, he hears a voice carried on the lightly salted breeze. He writes in his journal:

Oct. 9, 1984

> *For now, I'll call pregnant Misty's child Zygote…a fertilized egg. And my character, the weird scientist friend of hers: Quark… the mysterious energy in the atom. Quark will take pregnant Misty to the corrida – the bullfight on Sunday. They'll watch red capes wave as an animal is slaughtered for pagan ritual, in the shadow of the Invincible Rock. Here she and Quark can talk about her options.*

When he finishes the beer, he puts his journal back into the camera bag and walks toward the fishing boats. He takes out his camera after he crosses the street.

In the congestion of small fishing boats, with cabins barely larger than a telephone booth, a man in a green sweater is crouched in a wooden dory. He is the only one in any of the boats. A fringe of gray hair frames his tanned head. Deliberate in his movements, he guts a fish.

When Danny centers the fisherman in his viewfinder, he notices that the rowboat is attached to a larger boat by rope. He follows the line of attachment. On the white cabin of the larger boat, *Dios te Salve* is painted in bright orange letters. If not God, then we must save ourselves, he thinks, but this is a country of religion and ceremony. He snaps the picture and stands to watch the fisherman for a time, thinking about Santiago in *The Old Man and the Sea,* then moves on.

As the sky darkens after sunset, Danny crosses the road toward town. Past the café, he turns into a side street. A man calls to him. He sees a short, stocky man leaning in the door frame of a stucco building.

"Señor, hashish?"

Danny stops and feels a surge of fear. He takes a deep breath and faces the man. In the shadows, he watches aluminum foil peeled back from a golf ball of something dark brown and shiny. Danny looks at the salesman as he holds the resinous ball into better light and peels back more foil. He has black hair combed straight across and dark eyes. He looks like a self-portrait of young Picasso.

"Señor. Hashish. Excellent."

"How much?"

"Twenty dollars American."

Danny looks at the ball. He has never seen that much hashish. He leans forward to look at it in the uneven light. He looks toward the lighted street. He guesses he isn't a hundred yards from the outdoor café.

"From Turkey. You will not find better," the man says.

Danny remembers the scene from *Midnight Express,* where Turkish soldiers pushed machine guns into the young American's face, then pulled open his shirt to find bricks of hashish taped around his waist. He takes several steps backward.

"Mañana, Señor. Vaya con Dios," Danny says, and thinks of the man with the plaid cap on the beach in Marbella.

He walks several blocks and turns onto a cobblestone street, so well lighted that it looks like a movie set. People walk in all directions, talking loudly. He takes his camera out of his bag and checks the light meter. He tosses the shoulder strap over his head and holds the camera by the zoom lens. He snaps a picture of a man and brightly dressed woman as they cross the street. That ends the roll. He rewinds the canister, takes it out and puts in a new roll.

He walks on and takes several pictures. As he sets himself for another shot, he hears someone say, "Alto." But he pays no attention. He focuses on another brightly dressed woman and a man in a dark suit.

He feels something hard jabbed into his back. He stops and lowers his camera.

"Alto. No picturas."

Danny doesn't move. A soldier, dressed like the one in the airport, circles in front of him, the machine gun tilted toward the ground.

"Camara, por favor!" he demands, and thrusts out his hand.

Danny takes the strap from around his neck and hands the camera to the soldier. The soldier snaps open the back and pulls out the film, then returns the camera.

"Pasaporte, por favor."

Danny starts to unzip the camera bag, but the soldier takes it from him. Cradling the gun in his arm, the soldier unzips each compartment to look then search through with his hand. He takes out the passport and looks at it. He returns the camera bag. Danny wonders what would happen had the soldier found the golf ball of hashish the dealer held in the doorway and breaks a sweat.

"Por qué no picturas?" Danny asks, his voice trembling.

The soldier slaps the closed passport back into Danny's hand. "No picturas," he says, and walks on.

Shaking, Danny takes a deep breath. He looks at the brightly lit street. Maybe the women are a bit too professionally friendly for the town fathers to want in tourists' photographs, he thinks, and starts back to the hotel.

On Sunday morning, Danny checks out of the Hotel Regina and drives the coast road to Fuengirola. Gibraltar is majestic in the blue haze. When he arrives in Fuengirola the streets are crowded for the festival parade. The Spanish women wear bright frilly lace dresses of reds, yellows, and greens, their dark hair adorned with bright ribbons and flowers. Men with wide brimmed hats and tight riding clothes carry them on sleek black horses. The church bells ring and music is pumped from loudspeakers onto street corners. In a town surrounded by palms, century plants, aloe, geraniums and white plumed pampas grass, sun burned tourists gather on café patios.

Danny drives around the arena to find a space to park. He grabs his camera bag and walks toward the cluster of cafés. He finds a table under an umbrella, sits, and reads the menu.

"Cerveza y calamare fritos," he says.

The waiter brings him a bottle of beer and fried squid rings. He takes out his journal and looks at the arena. When he begins to write, a cat jumps on the chair next to him.

Oct. 10, 1984

After the Christian, now the pagan Sunday sacrifice… A tiger cat sits meowing Spanish, pale green eyes insistent, with a bandit's thin face. The easy sensuality of a cat anywhere, who accepts my offer of calamare fritos… Everyone in traditional costume where tradition gives stability. La corrida. As Hemingway said about war in Farewell to Arms, *death had no more meaning than cattle slaughter in a stockyard. But we are a generation seeking meaning. A generation that's decided war is not a sport. But bullfights are death sport. How will it affect Quark's advice to Misty? How will it affect me?*

He finishes the fried squid and beer and follows the swelling crowd to the arena. The most talked about matador is José Galan. Danny finds his seat about halfway up the stands, and takes out his camera. He puts the strap over his head then pulls out his Gulf Coast University baseball hat.

As the first picador lance plunges into the hump of muscle behind the bull's head, and blood swells up around it and spreads across the huge black back, Danny knows whose side he is on. He clicks several pictures. He remains for the second match and similar result. Galan is the third matador. He is short and trim, like a lightweight boxer, in blue tights above pink socks in black shoes, and a blue jacket covered with gold.

Danny watches through his zoom lens as Galan works the bull. Galan moves and spins like a diver rips water without splash. With sword hidden by sweep of red cape, he turns the bull's lowered head, and lets the green and white bandelleros pass. Finally, he exposes the sword to the bull with a gesture of defiance. He sights along the blade, snaps the cape, and with an arching stab high above the oncoming horns, he plunges the sword to the hilt as Danny snaps the shutter.

The bull stumbles forward and falls to his knees gasping. Blood pours over his outstretched tongue onto the hard packed brown sand. Three brightly uniformed assistants gather around with large pink capes. Galan, with his red cape in front of him, faces the stunned bull.

The bull is stationary on his knees. Two men in blue jeans and white sport shirts approach cautiously. The younger one moves from the rear and stabs a small knife behind the bull's head. The bull collapses instantly, its massive head like the profile of Gibraltar. When it rolls to his bloodied side, two draft horses are brought into the ring. Harnessed to the bull, they drag him from the arena, to the crowd's cheers. When the horses reach the exit, Danny clicks a final picture of the bull's upturned hooves, his bushy black tail brushes a faint line in the clay.

Repulsed, Danny starts toward the exit. When the trumpets announce the next matador, he turns to look. But emotions in his stomach tell him to leave this sport of futility.

When he gets to the car and looks at the map in the front seat, depression permeates him. He traces his finger along the Costa del Sol, looking for a place to go.

He decides that the Alhambra in Granada may relieve his distress. He remembers that Maureen never heard of it, but it is a place he has always wanted to see.

He aims toward the coast highway, then onto a twisting mountain road. The interior land is steep, rolling, and barren. Olive trees predominate along reddish clay fields focused by huge white haciendas. Small towns cluster on hills in the distance. They remind him of Italian towns he and Antonio traveled on their way to the one where Antonio was born. Granada is spread out across the plains, backed by mountains. But it is built up on three large hills, one of which contains the Alhambra, the ancient Moorish fortress and palace.

As he arrives, the blue sky shows signs of sunset. He finds a way up the steep hill to the citadel. When he gets to the top, he drives around the Alhambra. He races through the narrow streets to find a place to get perspective for a photograph. Finally he finds a huge field to the east. As the sun turns the sky mauve, umber, and indigo, he focuses on the ancient earthen building and mountains silhouetted in a double range to the west. Excitedly, he snaps pictures until the mountains turn black and the sky turns mustard above darkening clouds that are black underneath and tipped with orange. Finally, when there is too little light, he leaves to find a hotel.

It is odd to see the name "Washington Irving" in neon on a Spanish hotel. He parks the car and looks at the entrance through the windshield. He thinks about cowardly Ichabod Crane from "The Legend of Sleepy Hollow" then of Irving's house in Tarrytown, near the Tappan Zee Bridge, that he visited with his family as a kid. He stays there for the night.

The following morning he walks to the Alhambra. In the Myrtle Garden, he sniffs the warm air scented by aromatic purple flowers, a tropical incense, richness like gardenia and lilac. He sits on a marble bench next to the reflecting pool to watch huge goldfish feed lazily among blooming water lilies. The quiet elegance of the huge garden is a tranquilizer. He hears Spanish reflect off the water. In the window arch above the fountain spray, he sees a young Spanish couple. They are seated cross-legged facing each other. He cannot understand what they are saying, but he takes their picture as they kiss. He picks several purple flowers to press in his journal then walks into the Court of the Lions. In view of the fountain surrounded by carved lions, he writes:

Oct. 11, 1984

What meaning is there for Quark, the dying scientist, in Spanish sounds reflected from Casa Real's arches by myrtle rimmed water? Near death Quark realizes that words are watery sounds. Meaning is soundless; it is the earthen arch that connects us to others with a kiss. For me, to kiss Maureen in the arch. The first woman who inspires me to explore, to write, to live and appreciate the lions.

He sits for a time enjoying feelings about Maureen and to steep in the seven hundred year old craftsmanship of carved lions. Eventually, he returns to the car for the drive to Malaga.

When he reaches the city, the sun has set. He finds a hotel along the beach, within a few miles of the airport from which he is to leave in the morning. As the moon rises orange and full over the Mediterranean, he watches flat white curls on waves as they slide noiselessly up the sand at high tide. Impulsively, he tosses his topsiders, shirt and shorts off. He runs naked into the moon's reflection, then dives, submerging himself in cool salt water. When he returns to the surface, he thinks fondly about Maureen, as he immerses in the sensual feel of arms slowly stroking dark water, drawing his body effortlessly toward moonlight.

Three weeks later, back in his Tampa apartment, Danny woke groggily. At the left of his dresser he saw a dark object. Rolling left, looking at the doorway to the kitchen, the dark object became a Black man. He couldn't make sense as he vaguely remembered last night was Halloween. As students partied, he went to bed, but this was neither a dream nor prank. Feeling threatened, he moved slowly, as if rolling in his sleep.

But as he moved, the Black man dove onto the bed, straddling Danny, stabbing the mattress repeatedly.

"Don't do nothin' stupid, Whitey," the guy said forcefully, sprawled over Danny. He grabbed Danny's arm into a hammer lock, then pushed the blade into his neck.

His arm bent up hard, Danny felt pain stab into his shoulder. He saw the guy grab the electric cord from the reading lamp clamped to the bed frame. Pinning Danny's bent arm with his knee, the Black guy cut the lamp cord. He grabbed Danny's other arm and wound the cord around both wrists quickly, like a rodeo rider binds the feet of calf with a rope. Danny lay face down with a knife pressed against his neck, expecting it to plunge into him.

Ripping the comforter and sheet off the bed, the guy said, "Ya ain't got no undawear!" He laughed as he tossed everything on the floor.

Danny saw the guy from the corner of his eye. He sounded high on something, probably cocaine.

"Get me a White woman."

"Do what?"

"Don't play dumb, Whitey!" he said, and stabbed the mattress repeatedly. Then he pushed the knife under Danny's chin. "You know White women. Get me one."

It was an absurd demand. Startled, faces of women he'd slept with in this bed flashed in his mind. Expecting to die, he kept thinking had the guy stabbed him instead of the mattress, he'd be a dead bloody mess. But submitting a woman to rape to save his life seemed like a bizarre compromise.

"Keepin' quiet's only gonna get you killed. So get me a woman, Whitey. I killed a guy last week a few blocks from here," he said, bragging. He jerked Danny's bound wrists shooting pain into both shoulders.

"Kill me an' you won't get laid," Danny said, trying to control his fear.

"Look man, I'm startin' to come down. So don't fuck around."

"Coke?"

"Yeah. So you betta call quick. Or I'll kill you."

The guy grabbed the electric cord binding Danny's wrists and pulled it, but Danny controlled his pain. Naked, except for his T-shirt, Danny's butt was exposed, but he was more worried about his genitals.

"That your phone?"

Danny's head was turned to the left, so he couldn't see the phone attached to the headboard to his right. He kept thinking about the women he knew, but he didn't want to call.

"You listen'n? You better find me a White woman," he repeated, poking Danny with the knife.

Danny rotated his head toward the guy's voice. Straining his neck as he turned toward the phone, he felt the guy's weight dig into him. When he looked up, he saw a guy about his own age with a thin dark face and close cropped curly black hair. His bulging eyes darted place to place.

When the guy grabbed Danny's wrists and pulled him up, shoulder pain jerked him to attention. But when Danny felt his knees shake uncontrollably, he realized he'd never been this terrified.

With the knife still to his throat, he looked at the phone and thought about women he could call. But a few moments later, his knees stopped shaking, and his head began to clear.

"Since you ain't talkin', you betta be thinkin' about what White pussy's gonna save your ass."

The guy pushed the knife blade against Danny's throat, then grabbed the receiver and cracked his head.

Angrily, Danny tried to free his hands. The electric cord cut into his wrists. His skull aching, women flashed in his head. Alexandra, the beautiful flight attendant was back in Philadelphia. Ronda, with whom two nights ago he played their pirate fantasy, wearing the eye patch she made, would have been with him now, he realized, but luckily, she was installing plants at the Don Cesar in St. Petersburg. Maureen was in San Francisco. Nancy, the psychology professor, was closest in Hyde Park.

"Shit, man. You don't say much. This knife i'd cut you an' you'd be dead for you hit the bed. Gimme a number, Whitey. Or this knife's gonna start cuttin'."

"I don't know any women to call," Danny said, calmly.

"You gotta know White pussy."

"No one who's gonna come here now."

"Even if you tell 'em I'll cut your balls off if they don't?"

The guy hit him with the receiver then held the phone to Danny's ear.

"Who should I call, Whitey?"

"I don't know any women."

"Shit, man, you're an asshole," he said, then slashed Danny's stomach.

Blood beaded up along the blade line. Angry, Danny knew he wasn't going to call.

"Mutha fucka, get me a White bitch or I'm gonna fuck you up the ass."

The horrible image of the rolly polly guy in *Deliverance* getting raped in the woods flashed in Danny's mind.

"I'm telling you man, no woman I know is gonna come over now," he insisted, worried by the threat.

The guy cracked him hard with the receiver and put it back on the phone. He pulled hard on the electric cord several times until Danny let out a groan.

"Whitey. I'm lovin' this. You ain't gonna let me fuck your women, I'm gonna fuck wit you. Let me slap that white ass. Yeah, maybe I should fuck it."

The sting of the guys hand flashed the rape image in Danny's head.

"OK, Whitey. I'm here to get a White woman free. Or you gonna be dead! But first, shit man, you got money? I needs more coke."

"Look, man. Why don't you just leave," Danny said, angrily, but feeling subservient, like a hostage.

"You gonna be dead when I leave."

The guy grabbed Danny by the electric cord and pulled him back to his wallet on the dresser. He took the cash, about twenty dollars, and threw the wallet on the floor. He pulled Danny through the small kitchen into the living room, to his desk.

"Anything in here?" he asked, then after pulling out several drawers, he saw the silver pocket watch on the desk corner. "This worth anything?"

"Some... My uncle gave it to me...leave it alone."

"How much?" he asked, slicing again on Danny's stomach, pulling out another desk drawer.

"Fifty. Maybe a hundred," Danny said, noticing the guy was coming down from the cocaine.

"Thanks, Whitey. And in this box?"

The guy popped open the metal cash box from the main desk that had about fifty dollars. Danny kept thinking that the more the guy touched the more fingerprints there would be.

"Take it. Just get out before you crash."

"OK, Whitey. I'm not gonna fuck that tight white ass a'yours. You just bought me mo' coke," the guy said, and stuffed the cash and watch into his pants and left.

Standing at the open door in his T-shirt, his wrists still bound, oddly, Danny felt sorry for the Black man, amazed to be alive. He was thankful there was no woman with him tonight, as he pictured women he'd come to know during his journey several times around the Zodiac in search of one great love.

Several weeks after the assault, while shaving, Danny notices a white patch on his nose. The skin patch is round and translucent, like sautéed onion, the diameter of the razor handle.

His hand is unsteady. He scrapes his face with rapid, uneven strokes. He shifts his eyes to the patch. His head tingles.

He's obsessed by the patch, and pushes his face close to the mirror. Anxiety floods him as he denies what scares him.

He studies the whitish patch, rubbing his finger over it until the skin around it turns red. But the patch remains a whitish gray. This is how it starts, he thinks. He feels trapped in his body.

He gets the phone book from his desk drawer. He opens the *Yellow Pages* to physicians, then drops the book onto the desk and goes back to the bathroom mirror. His stomach is queasy and he starts to perspire. He goes to his closet for a shirt. He looks at the shirt that Ronda made. He pulls it out then sickened by irony, he returns it. He takes a solid blue short sleeve shirt out. He goes to the bathroom and rubs deodorant under his arms. He looks at his nose in the mirror.

"Welcome to the *Costa del Sol*," he says, cringing at the Spanish word for sun.

He goes into the living room and opens the *Yellow Pages* to dermatologists. His hands shake. He recites names out loud. Perspiration accumulates in his armpits. He settles on a name and calls. It rings twice and he hangs up. He hurries back into the bathroom.

He looks into the mirror. He tells himself to be rational, be rational. It may not be what he thinks. But he doesn't want to say the word.

He goes back to his desk. He looks at the first page of *Old Man and the Sea* and sees the words "skin cancer" but then he repeats the word, "benevolent", wondering how Hemingway could call skin cancer benevolent. He slaps the book face down on the desk and opens the phone book. He looks at the list of dermatologists again, and recites the names. He stops at the same name. It sounds the best. He dials the number, but waits until someone answers.

"Does the doctor have an opening?" he blurts out.

"One, a patient cancelled. Today at three. Is that OK?"

"Yes," he says haltingly.

"May I ask what it's about?"

He fumbles through explanations in his head, then says, "There's something strange on my nose I want him to look at," and feels foolish.

In a calm, quiet voice, she replies, "OK. See you at three."

When he hangs up, he says, "That's it. Just matter of fact."

He picks up the novel and looks at the first page again. He reads the words about skin cancer, but can't say them. Feeling trapped, he decides that getting out of his apartment will help

In the street, he looks up at the sun in the cloudless blue sky. He remembers Camus' novel *The Stranger*, when Meursault explained to the magistrate that he killed the Arab because the sun was in his eyes at the beach. As he walks across the brick road toward the post office, he recites words from Camus' notebooks about the sun's dark side. He thinks about his dissertation and Hemingway, who pondered the struggle if one tried to destroy the sun. The irony coalesces in his chest with a thud as he walks past the mango tree to the post office.

He has no mail. He leaves by the side door and walks toward the pool. There are students sunning in lounge chairs surrounding the clear blue water.

He continues around into the main lobby and goes to the Rough Rider Room, where he teaches. He looks at the picture of Teddy Roosevelt on the back wall. Roosevelt is seated in a leather chair with brass tacks. His left hand is on the knee of his jodhpurs, which are tucked into his leather riding boots. His tie and mid-section are contained by a buttoned vest. His right hand, closed in a fist, is on a dark table. A pince-nez over intense eyes and bushy mustache enhance the confrontational face.

Danny thinks about the animal trophies at Roosevelt's house in Sagamore Hill, on Long Island, which he toured as a kid. He felt a connection between that childhood memory and teaching in this room. He has no idea about Roosevelt's politics. He likes that Roosevelt overcame asthma, which he had as a child also. We have to overcome whatever impedes us, he thinks. How well is what counts.

He realizes the room feels cool because the sun has already passed to the west, something he's never thought about. He looks at several wooden student desks. One desk has an ongoing argument about sexual encounter, with challenges and denials. On another desk, he rubs his fingers over the name of a student he recognizes and the boyfriend she "loves."

Somewhat settled, and more optimistic, he heads to his car and drives Tampa Bay's arc along Bayshore Boulevard past Maureen's condo in the Monte Carlo, to the turnoff road. A couple blocks up on Euclid, he stops at the dermatologist's office. Across the street there are outdoor tables surrounded by a wrought iron fence in Café Parisian's lush garden, where bougainvilleas hang from the awning. He and Maureen ate escargot and drank wine there a few weeks ago.

"Small world," he says, shaking his head as he parks.

He reads the sign outside the office; the word surgeon under the dermatologist's name bothers him. He walks into the waiting room. The receptionist greets him and hands him a medical history form on a clipboard.

He takes it back to a seat. He completes the information about his address and then reads through the list of illnesses. He stops to look around. The glass table in front of him has a pile of *National Geographic* and *Smithsonian* magazines. He returns to the list. When he comes to the word cancer, he stops. His hand shakes as he checks "no." He rushes through the remainder of the list, signs the bottom, returns it to the receptionist, and sits.

An older woman emerges from behind the door to the clinical rooms, and he glances up. Suddenly, in the back of his head, like his brain focusing a camera, he recalls the white gauze patch covering part of her face. He closes his eyes and submerges into the hollow of his stomach.

He shoots a look at her face and looks away. Then he thinks about skin cancer on Santiago's face. He tries to imagine the old fisherman's worn skin. But he's drawn back to the gauze patch on the older woman. She passes in profile, then stops and looks directly at him before she walks out.

He feels he is going to throw up. In profile, where the patch was, her face was flat. Full face, the white gauze patch replaced her nose.

He looks at the white ceiling and tries to resist nausea. He grabs his nose with his left hand and massages it. He looks at the closing door. He grabs a *National Geographic*. He turns the pages rapidly. In an article about an archaeological dig in Greece, he sees a marble bust. The man's nose is broken off. He drops the magazine onto the glass table. He stares across the room at a large philodendron plant. His entire body shakes.

A nurse opens the door to the clinical rooms and calls his name. She leads him past several closed doors into a room.

"Please take off your shirt. The doctor will be with you shortly," she says.

She closes the door as she leaves. At first he sits in a chair. Then he gets up. He takes his shirt off and hangs it on the hook attached to the door. He sits down. Then he sits on the operating table, the paper over it crackles. He stands. He looks at the beige walls. He reads a small certificate thanking the doctor for his contribution to the community.

After what seems like hours, the doctor enters with his nurse, and extends his hand. Danny shakes the hand, which feels firm. As the doctor ends the handshake, he asks Danny to sit on the table.

"Mr. Roarke, you have sun damage you want me to see?"

The idea sounds absurd to Danny. He wonders how the sun could do damage, but he nods. "My nose," he says, overwhelmed by the image of the lady with the gauze patch.

"Sit on the table please," the doctor says, and turns on the large lamp over it.

Danny watches his hands. The doctor turns to the counter behind him to get a magnifying glass.

"This?" he says.

"Yeah," Danny says, desperately trying to read something into the sound of the doctor's voice. "What is it?"

"Sun damage," the doctor says, exploring the rest of Danny's face with the magnifying glass. "How long has that been there?"

"I just noticed it," he says, but he doesn't want to call it anything.

The doctor studies the patch with the magnifying glass. He rubs his thumb over it. He turns to the nurse, saying quietly, "We'll need to set up." She nods, then slips quietly out the door.

"Set up for what?" Danny asks, alarmed.

The doctor looks directly at him and is quiet for what seems a long time to Danny. "You spend a lot of time in the sun?" he asks.

"I was a lifeguard."

"Where?"

"Long Island. On the ocean."

"That's better than here. How long?"

"When I was in college. What do you see?"

"That patch concerns me."

"Skin cancer?" Danny blurts out.

The doctor seems to sense Danny's fear. "I'll clip it off and we can test it. This isn't like cancer in the body. It doesn't metastasize – doesn't move. I'll clip it off, and that'll be it. It's not a big deal."

"It's not your face," Danny says, forcing a laugh.

"Think of it as a mole."

"I don't have any moles."

"You do now. And soon you won't. Leave it at that."

The nurse returns with gauze, scalpels, and a hypodermic needle. Danny tries to control his anxiety. It's absurd to walk into a windowless room, where a stranger cuts-off a part of my face, he thinks.

The doctor lies him down on the table, adjusts the light over his face, and injects something that numbs his nose then takes out the scalpel.

"I hope you have good hands," Danny says.

"Pretty good," he says.

He carves a piece off Danny's nose and puts it in a Petri dish on the tray. He cauterizes the cut with a small drill like tool and then covers it with a circular bandage. Danny sits up on the end of the table and looks at the slice of skin sitting in the dish. The doctor follows Danny's eyes.

"Is Irish skin thinner?" Danny asks. "I thought we had seven layers of skin to protect against the sun."

"But they're connected, and sun damages all of them."

"Is it a skin cancer?"

"A fifty-fifty chance. But it's not a melanoma, those are deadly."

"Didn't the Reggae singer Bob Marley die from a melanoma?" Danny asks suddenly.

"I don't know that name. But I'll know about this after the biopsy."

Danny's gut constricts at that word. He feels the bandage then sees his face in the metal towel holder. The dime size bandage covers the tip of his nose.

"Start using sunscreen. And avoid exposure to the sun."

"I never thought the sun was the enemy."

"Life is compromise. Moderation is the key. You can't indulge yourself anymore. That's all."

"It's a tough life to give up... I've always loved the sun."

The doctor nods his head then leads him to the receptionist. Danny writes her a check and walks out into bright sunshine, which is suddenly dangerous.

Dejected, he drives along Bayshore Boulevard to say goodbye forever to a lifestyle he loved, but he keeps reminding himself that it could have been worse. Picturing the woman with the gauze patch that replaced her nose, he remembers his mom's phrase, "When you hear other people's troubles, grab yours and run."

Several days later, Danny sits in his rocking chair reading *Utopia Means Nowhere.* Maureen has Belinda leave art school in Paris and become a journalist for Reuters News Agency to cover the Viet Nam War. He admires Maureen's guts and her sense of political responsibility, which she's translated from her personal biography to fiction. He hears a knock on the kitchen door and puts the book face down on the oak camp table, then walks nervously to the door. When he opens the door, Ronda looks at him and laughs.

"I'm sorry Danny. I didn't mean to," she says, and hugs him around the waist.

"Thanks," he says sarcastically. He rubs the scab on his nose and takes a deep breath which he lets out slowly.

"I was surprised. But it doesn't look that bad. Really."

"Forget it. C'mon in."

He walks with her into the living room and sits down in the rocking chair. She sits in the couch. For a long time he doesn't look at her. He remembers Maureen said Ronda couldn't understand his sensitivity, that he had a hard time accepting his own sensitivity.

"Danny, I know you're upset. But it doesn't look bad."

"OK, Ronda," he says, holding up his hand. "Can I get you a diet Shasta?"

"Thanks."

He gets up to go into the kitchen. He tugs on the bamboo palm as he passes. He gets a soda and a can of beer out of the refrigerator.

"Can I have a glass?"

He looks at her, frowns then walks to the kitchen. When he returns, he has a glass filled with ice, which he hands to her, then rubs the scab on his nose.

"Thanks," she says. "You're upset about it?"

"I hate it."

"You were a sun bunny. I told you to use sunblock."

"I know. But I never thought I could over do the sun."

"Lots of people get it in Florida."

"I still hate it. I guess I understand why Ulysses never defied Zeus, the sun god. You can't defy the sun."

"You just have to stay out of it."

"Doesn't it seem crazy to have to stay out of the sun? It's ninety three million miles away. It's in the sky every day. How do I avoid it?"

"I mean you can't worship it the way you did."

"Maybe I'll start getting a moon glow," he says, and laughs.

"You'll get over it."

"Or it'll eat my face away," he says, and the image of the woman with the gauze patch flashed in his mind. "Hemingway's old man Santiago said it was lucky we didn't have to kill the sun…but ultimately, we get killed by it."

"Danny, you're exaggerating."

"Maybe so, I overreact," he says, impatient with the conversation, remembering Maureen's read of Ronda.

"You got it early and now you know you have to be careful. You've learned something."

"You've become quite the philosopher."

"When you're not being a crank, you say some bright things. I listen. Some of what you've said about people and running an organization have helped in my business."

"I should get consulting fees."

She looks at him and smiles impishly. She takes a sip of her soda. "Only you don't know what you've said that's helped."

"Story of my life."

"What you don't do is listen well to yourself."

"You're on a roll."

"No, seriously, Danny. You've changed since you started that book with Maureen. I worry about you."

"How so?"

"You're impressed by her wealth and power. She wants you, but I don't think she loves you."

"She's the most exciting person I've ever met."

"Are you confusing excitement with love?

"C'mon, Ronda. Look what she's done for me."

"What, really? She took you to Hawaii. She paid for your trip to Spain. That's because there's something in it for her."

"She appreciates my writing. She showed *Shattered Images* to her agent."

"Nothing came of it."

"That wasn't her fault. I told the agent I wouldn't revise it. She's offered some of her advance money. That'll get me back to school. The dean at Cornell said I have to go back for a year of residency or I can't get my degree."

"You have to go back?" she asked, her voice wavering.

"Yep. Or no PhD. That's why I said yes to the book. I need the money. Maureen said she would pay me a thousand a month."

"I'll miss you Danny," Ronda said sadly.

"Thanks. I'll miss you too. But I gotta go back. I want that degree," he said, realizing how important it was to him.

"I understand that. But what do you really know about Maureen?"

"I'm impressed by her talent. By her lifestyle. I think she really cares about me."

"Danny, I care about you too. Say it's a hunch, but I think you're a challenge to her. When she gets you, I don't know what she'll do. Maybe I am jealous. I don't know. That's all I'll say about it."

"I appreciate your concern, Ronda. She's going to San Francisco to finish the novel. I have to go back to Ithaca. We'll see what happens."

Suddenly, through the living room windows, Danny sees an explosion of colors from the art building next door. He runs to the phone on the kitchen wall and bangs out the numbers to the university police.

"This is Danny Roarke, the Mackenzie director. The art building's on fire."

"I'll call it in right away," the operator says.

Flames slash across the sky with color and ash. Smoke billows out black, blown toward his apartment. He goes into his bedroom to grab his camera. He runs out the kitchen door toward the fire. The roof of the wooden building is eaten through by flames. There is a small knot of students near the edge of the dorm facing the river. He snaps several pictures, but it is too dark to see anyone clearly through the smoke.

Soon after, the sirens of the approaching fire engines echo off the old brick hotel. He hears tires vibrate on the cobblestones near the pool in the warm night air. A breeze from the north blows flames toward the residence hall. Staccato radio broadcasting catches Danny's attention as one of the university police comes around the north end of the old building. Danny watches him jog across the lawn, breathing heavily.

"Sergeant Rich, I'm gonna evacuate the dorm."

"I'll call for back-up, Mr. Roarke. That's out of control."

Danny yells across the courtyard to his resident assistants Karl and Vinnie who are running toward him. "Vinnie, Karl, get everyone out of the dorm, toward the river. Check every room!"

Feeling heat from the fire on his face, Danny looks toward the river. In the darkness and smoke he cannot see much, but someone is in the city art museum parking lot across the bridge watching. Oddly, as he snaps a picture, he thinks it's Maureen, then he looks back at the fire. Exploding paint containers add color. Danny looks at his car but it's too close to the flames to move. He looks at Ronda's van, which is between his car and apartment.

"Ronda, got your keys?"

"They're in the van. Under the seat," she says excitedly, looking from her van to the fire.

He hops into the van and backs it out toward the fountain. When he runs back toward his car, the roof of the art building collapses, the side wall falls out toward them. Danny back peddles as wooden siding slaps against his car.

After they both back away from the flames, Danny turns toward Sergeant Rich, "You think it's somebody from the dorm?"

Sergeant Rich shrugs, "You think it's that jerk Madden?"

"Madden threatened his roommate with a SCUBA spear. But this is even too crazy for him. We got a real psycho."

As the fire consumes the building, a television news crew arrives in a van. A third fire engine arrives. The two trucks already there spray water into the flaming cavern in the center of the building. The spray from the third truck, using the hydrant at the pool, combines with the others. The three arching sprays are like a ceremonial tugboat at a Fourth of July fireworks show. Danny watches the flames spread up the side of his car along the plastic rocker panels.

"Hey, man!" he yells to the fireman with the closest hose, "Do my car!"

The fireman turns, then soaks the car and sprays Danny's apartment roof. Errant sparks float on the wind but flicker out as they pass over the dorm. Eventually black billows of smoke begin to rise from the collapsed building, as the dorm residents gather to watch. Danny helps the police keep them at a distance.

The flames die as the firemen flood the charred pile of wood that was the art building. People stand around looking at the rubble. Danny walks back to Ronda.

"You can tell it's finals week," he says, facetiously.

"You think Madden did it?" she asks worriedly

"He's flunking out. He's never gotten this crazy, but this might be his farewell to arms. You can never tell what will set someone off."

"Did you get any pictures?"

"Yeah, but they just show who got here after me."

"I bet you'll be happy to leave."

"To leave this, yeah. This is crazy."

"Danny, I have to go home. Walk me to my van?"

They walk hand in hand toward the van which he parked near the fountain. Danny's mind is still on the fire, but saying goodbye to Ronda seems equally unreal. He looks at the fountain, then across to the silver minarets shining in spotlights. He puts his arm around her shoulder.

When they get to the van, Ronda leans against the door. She looks up at him and caresses his face. Tears form in her eyes. Again, she caresses his jaw with her fingertips.

"It's so sad," she says. "I'm sorry you're leaving."

He hugs her and feels her tears against his neck. He holds her for a long time, then slowly eases his grip and steps back to look at her face. He kisses her softly.

"I'll miss you," he says, quietly.

"Danny, be good to your self," she says, as tears flow down her cheeks.

She turns abruptly and pulls open the door to hop into the seat of the van. She rolls down the window and leans out as she starts the engine.

"It's so sad. Danny, can I have another kiss?"

He leans toward the window. She grabs him around the neck. He kisses her as she presses against him.

"Goodbye," she says, "Take good care of your self."

"You too, Ronda. I'll miss you."

He watches as she smiles amidst tears. She races the engine then starts toward the exit. She stops at the red light at Kennedy Boulevard. Her directional signal indicates her right turn. As she pulls away, he reads "Gemini Interiors" stenciled across the back doors.

He thinks that's a contradiction. The only interior he's ever felt as a Gemini has been in flux. His eyes fill with tears as he watches the van disappear behind the stand of oaks. He feels no interior just emptiness of loss. He looks up at the silver minaret near the Roosevelt Room, then turns and walks toward the burnt art building.

One fire truck remains and a few students stand around looking, but the police and firemen have blocked off the entire area. The building is now a pile of rubble. Random pockets of steam and smoke hiss from it.

He looks at his car. The rocker panels and fender, which he formed from plastic body compound, melted; stalactites hang from the driver's door. The paint is blistered like sunburned skin. He tries to pull the door open but can't. He tries again, with the same result. In disgust, he walks back to his apartment.

Inside, he hears his phone ring. He looks at the clock radio on his headboard and sees that it's almost midnight.

"Hello?"

"Danny, are you all right?"

"Maureen? Yeah, why?"

"I saw the fire on the news. It was near you!"

"The art building. Burnt to the ground."

"Are you safe?"

"I'm fine. Burnt the shit out of my car though."

"That can be replaced. But you were unharmed?"

"Relax, Maureen, I'm fine."

"Oh, Honey, I was so worried. I saw Ronda's van on the tellie. Is she still there?"

"No, she left."

"Oh, good. I'm glad you're both safe."

"Thanks."

"You think it was that Madden boy?"

"No idea. The police and firemen will handle it from here. I'm just glad we close in the next few days."

"And you'll be leaving then, right?"

"The art building torched…after I almost get raped on Halloween, then get carved for skin cancer for defying the sun, I think it's time for Ulysses to leave Hades to return to Ithaca."

"You do live dramatically, Danny. I'm so relieved you are safe. I've made arrangements to sell my condo. Movers will take my things to San Francisco. I fly out tomorrow."

"So soon?"

"I must finish *Costa del Sol.*"

"You move quickly."

"Journalism training," she responds, with a short laugh. "My life fits in two suitcases."

"I'll take you to the airport."

"That would be wonderful. What about your car?"

"If it doesn't work, I'll call you."

"Even if it does work, I insist you take my car. Your car is so unsafe. I shall get another in San Francisco. My flight is at 3 o'clock. Should I get you a ticket?"

"Thanks for the offer, but no. Remember, my Ivy League future."

"Your talent is your future," Maureen insists. "Until you get that degree, you will not understand it is worthless. But you know I'll support whatever you want to do."

"I want to be a certified philosopher. I'll have a diploma to put up in my bathroom, next to the *Expose Yourself to Art* poster. An Authentic Renaissance Man!"

"Danny, you are so mad. That's your charm."

"Now, if only I could write."

"You write exquisitely. I must pack. See you tomorrow."

"I'll meet you for lunch around one, my treat."

Chapter 12: Siren Call

Before leaving for the Ithaca airport, Danny grabs his journal to write:

Jan. 5, 1986

Ulysses returned to Ithaca to face the challenge. As have I. Now, at the dean's insistence and Callahan's control, I've been captive a year already since leaving Tampa. I must finish my dissertation. But I'm excited that Maureen is coming so we can complete Costa del Sol. Ulysses and Penelope united in Ithaca. How strange the journey... My life taking shape around the woman I've begun to love arriving today.

Danny stands expectantly at the large glass window in the Ithaca airport. Waiting for the plane to taxi to the gate, he sees snow blow off drifts surrounding the runway. When Maureen steps out of the plane onto the stairs, she is more enticing than he remembers.

He feels protective when her blond hair is caught by the wind, and she snuggles into the upturned collar of her mink coat. Others plod down the metal stairs in drab coats or ski jackets, hats pulled tightly onto their heads. She moves fluidly as others hurry to protect themselves from the cold.

When she reaches an open space in the lobby, he maneuvers through the crowd with a surprise hug. Her mink is cold. Her lips are cold to his kiss. But she feels good through his leather jacket.

"Cold and snow. I warned you about Ithaca," he says, and kisses warmer lips.

"It's like a lovely Christmas card," she says, returning his kiss.

He puts his arm around her. They walk toward the luggage drop-off, where bags are already unloaded. Unable to restrain his hands, he feels like a zoo monkey grooming a friend. Finally, her Vuitton suitcases appear. Danny grabs them. They walk out together to the car.

Suddenly, the snow, which falls daily from low clouds in sullen skies, that he's hated while brooding about his banishment from Tampa's sun, feels magical. He puts her luggage in the trunk, then hurries around to open the door for her. Once in the car, he hugs her again, to convince himself that she is real.

"Danny, I'm pleased you accepted this car. And it's still working. Last year, I worried your stubborn Irish pride would interfere."

"It did. But when my car was trashed in the fire, I really appreciated your offer."

"You were going through Hell then. It was the least I could do."

"No, it was very generous... I really thank you."

He drives out the side entrance of the airport to cross Route 13. He goes back roads, which are poorly plowed and filled with drifting snow, past Sapsucker Woods to Freese Road. He crosses the little bridge over Fall Creek onto Ryden Road, near the Varna church, then past Buddy's Homestyle Café into the snow covered parking lot of his apartment.

He carries her suitcases into the bedroom and goes to the fireplace. He takes kindling he's collected from the woods behind the house. Crumpling newspapers around the kindling, he arranges oak logs he's split, and tosses in a lighted match. He puts an Eric Clapton album on the stereo and fans the fire with the cover.

"Is it started yet, Danny Boy?" Maureen calls from the hallway.

"Yep. Call me Mountain Man Roarke."

When he turns toward her, she has on her mink coat. She holds out a round glass jar to him. He motions her to toss it to him. He catches it and reads the label. It's black caviar. When he looks up, she pulls back her coat. She is naked. He laughs and feels a surge of interest in his jeans.

"You have a bit of your main character Misty in you Maureen?"

"Remember, I have ideas too. *Research*, as you call it."

"Hang on."

He gets up and kisses her on the cheek, returning the jar. He hurries into the kitchen. He takes a bottle of Taylor champagne out of the refrigerator and grabs a glass from the cabinet. On the way back to the living room, he removes the wire basket around the cork. He hands her the glass, then pops the cork and fills her glass.

"Let the research begin," he says.

"OK, Mountain Man. Take off your clothes."

He does. He fans the fire rapidly with the album cover, then sits on the rug in front of the fire.

"No. Put this under you," she says, removing her coat.

"You have a plan?"

"Yes. Now sit Indian style."

"American Indian or Indian Indian...Lotus style?"

"Philosophers! Either way. Now let me put caviar on your cock."

He laughs, excited by her intensity. He leans back, supporting himself with his hands. She kneels in front of him. He looks at her eyes, but they are intent on her fingers, which she dips into the jar of caviar. He looks at her breasts, which are honey colored in flickering firelight. Her stomach is firm and tight above the curly blond hair in her crotch, which contrasts with the caviar. It tickles when she fondles him and rolls his erection between her hands, then cups caviar onto his erection.

"Danny, this is getting me wet."

"And me filled with caviar."

She puts a large dollop of caviar on the tip of his penis, then leans down to take him into her mouth. Slowly, she rides him up and down.

He reaches to caress the lips of her vagina. Feeling them soft and wet, he reaches his fingers in gently to rub her clitoris.

She continues to stroke him up and down in her mouth. The tiny spheres of caviar add slippery texture to the warmth of her lips around him. The mink feels cool and soft on his bare skin. The caviar's salty aroma mixes with the scent of burning oak, during her foray into research.

She looks up to offer him caviar from her fingers, then a sip of champagne. They kiss warmly.

He pulls her toward him in an embrace. He rolls her slowly to her side, away from the fire. When he enters, she feels incredibly warm and supple. They blend together in fluid intimacy. When he feels her come, he rises toward climax then diffuses into warm waves, their bodies pressed tightly together. They lay quietly embraced listening to the fire pop.

"Danny, I have such passion for you," she whispers.

He holds her tightly. Slowly, he lifts his head to look into her eyes. He studies their deep green color, like Chinese celadon glaze. Her lips ease to a smile. He cannot comprehend how completely lovable she is. He kisses her long, but softly.

"I love you, Maureen. I love you. I've never felt this way."

They look at each other quietly then as he rolls to his side, he looks at the fire, which crackles loudly when an oak log breaks through the burned kindling.

"I hope you can stay," he says.

"Until we finish editing *Costa del Sol*. It will take a good fortnight."

"That's two weeks American isn't it?"

"Yes, Honey. With what you've done with Quark and the unborn Zygo, we'll need every day."

"Quark's kinda weird, huh?"

"Very."

"That's what you wanted."

"I had no idea how imaginative you can get."

"Do you think his S-E-X theory makes sense?"

"Oddly, it does. Where did it come from?"

"S for sperm. E for egg. And X for consciousness. Sperm is the male part of the contract. Egg, is obviously female. But when Elaine got pregnant back in Vermont, she planned it without me. I don't believe we should bring new consciousness into this world without agreement of the man and woman…a unity of consciousness, because they are responsible for the child."

"That justifies abortion. But I believe the reader will want Misty to have the baby."

"The single parent route bothers me. Misty seems selfish, wanting the child without a marriage commitment to the father, doesn't even seem interested in who the father is. Given her lifestyle, she can't take care of a kid."

"It's not an ideal family, Danny. But I'm choosing life over death," she says earnestly.

"Quark is concerned about Zygo's quality of life since the father and mother don't consciously plan to have a child. His quest to build the solar powered water skis before he dies lets Misty smuggle out the salvaged treasure to help others. Why does she need the kid?"

"Emotionally, it's more satisfying to the reader."

"I'd rather tell them what's true," he replies, poking the fire with the stick.

"As the novel stands, I have interest from Swifty Lazar, the movie agent in LA, for a screenplay. That would be a large chunk of cash. With my money tied up with the bloody lawsuit over the condo sale, we can use it."

"I don't feel good about going commercial."

"Quark will maintain your integrity."

"Unless we edit him to death."

"I won't do that. But I am unable to free any cash to help you financially."

"I'll cope. I told you that Linda Valenti agreed to be on my dissertation committee. Surprise of all surprises, Callahan accepted her. If I teach at

State this winter and rewrite the whole thing to the committee's approval, I'm free."

"But how will you pay for next semester?"

"Callahan won't let me substitute teach. I'll have to get a student loan."

"When the lawsuit resolves, I can give you the money I promised from the advance. The movie rights may be as much as fifty to a hundred grand. We would split that."

"By summer I'll be into debt. Money would help."

"I promise you a best seller. We will be rich!"

"How about a shower with your co-author, then editing? Later, tonight, I want to show you sunset over Lake Cayuga from Panache, on top of the Ramada Inn downtown. I did some research to find your kind of place in Ithaca."

Two weeks later, standing on a chair, Danny spreads lights around the spruce they cut from the woods that afternoon for a belated Christmas. He looks at Maureen. She has on a thick red sweater and blue jeans as she sits on the couch stringing popcorn. Then he looks at their final editing of *Costa del Sol* on the glass topped table in the dining room. It looks secure with the thick blue rubber band around it in the uncovered typing paper box. He hopes that the timing is a good omen after the long days of revising.

Maureen runs the large needle carefully through each popped kernel. Her attention to detail shows everywhere, he thinks. He recalls that the hours of revision and discussion never wore her down, never made her impatient. She impressed him continually with her intelligence, sense of humor, and perseverance. Time after time, she eased his frustration during the hours of writing. As she sits quietly pushing the needle through each piece of popcorn, then slides it along the string to the previous kernel, she seems completely absorbed.

When the arrangement of lights looks right, he hops off the chair and turns them on. She doesn't look up.

"Maureen, look."

"Prometheus brings fire to mortals. They are lovely."

"You finished with Orville Redenbacher's contribution?"

"Almost," she says, adjusting the popcorn coil on the couch.

"I want to make a toast. Tequila this time."

He goes into the dining room and takes a bottle of Jose Cuervo Tequila and two shot glasses from the liquor cabinet he made. He puts them on the wooden table in front of her. He gets a lemon from the refrigerator, a small serrated knife, a cutting-board and a salt shaker. He slices the lemon on the cutting-board then fills the shot glasses with tequila. He licks his hand, then shakes salt on it, and motions her to do the same. He hands her the tequila and lemon.

"Maureen, I've never enjoyed anything more than these past two weeks doing that book with you."

"You griped, grimaced, belched and farted all the way through."

"And you never complained. That's why I loved it. You're the classiest woman I've ever known. I love you."

They each finish the tequila and put the lemon slices in their mouths then place the rinds on the cutting-board.

"Maureen, let's put the popcorn up. I have a present for you."

"I thought we were calling tomorrow Christmas."

"In my family, we always do it on Christmas Eve, after we finish decorating the tree."

She gets up from the couch and hands him an end of the popcorn. They walk together toward the tree. He climbs back onto the chair to lay the strand across the sturdy top branches. She weaves it side to side around the front of the tree. When they finish, he goes into the bedroom and pulls a package wrapped in brown grocery bag paper from under the bed. Next to the tree, he hands it to her.

"An artful wrapping job, Danny," she says, laughing. "Wait, let me get my present for you."

When she returns, she hands him a box covered with shiny silver and red paper. It is wrapped with silver ribbon and topped with a huge silver bow.

"C'mon Maureen, open mine."

"Should I save the wrapping?"

He frowns impatiently. She removes the bow and attaches it to the tree, near the top. She undoes the end and folds the paper back.

"Oh, Danny, what a magnificent cutting-board."

"Guess what it's made from?"

"It's like your liquor cabinet. Redwood. And maple?"

"But where'd I get the wood?"

She looks at him with surprise.

"I wondered what you did with your goalpost. This?"

"You got it. When I read *Costa del Sol,* I realized how much what you called my goalpost – where I hung plants – bothered you. You described how Misty loved the guy who just happened to have a bed similar to mine, but that she hated she was one of his several lovers. Not only did I learn how writers steal from real life, but I realized how much it hurt you that I slept with other women. Since I've been in Ithaca, I've had no interest in other women. I realize I love you. So, I took the goalpost down and made a cutting-board."

"When did you make it?"

"I started before you got here. Then when you were at the gym or around town, I finished it."

"It's gorgeous."

"My cutting-board arrangement is no goalpost. No other women."

"Do you mean that?"

"These two weeks convinced me of that.

"Danny, this is the best present ever. Thanks," she says, and hugs him. "Now open mine."

"Should I save the paper?" he teases.

She scowls, and he rips it open. In a box from Neiman Marcus, wrapped in several layers of tissue paper, is a purple cashmere sweater.

"I thought it would keep you warm when I wasn't here."

"I'd prefer you. But it's beautiful. Thanks."

"I wish I didn't have to leave. But I'll have to retype that whole manuscript. With that done, I will be able to concentrate entirely on you."

"Do it here."

"I need the money from the Chronicle to keep me afloat during this lawsuit. I'll return as soon as I can."

"That will be a great present," he says, and embraces her.

The day after Maureen left, Danny feels excitement build as students arrive to his first class. But it feels odd to return to State to teach. He writes his name on the board and thinks about Professor Hager, still chairman, who arranged this course for him to do his dissertation research.

Professor Hager ended Danny's desire to teach science by opening him to the journey of philosophy. As he arranges his tape recorder to tape the sessions for Callahan, he looks at the pages he's photocopied and thinks about Linda Valenti, the only female committee member. Long and enjoyable discussions with her about Carol Gilligan's *In a Different Voice* and the ethic of care helped him revise his dissertation for these students. It helped clarify the book *On Caring* that Professor Mayeroff was writing fifteen years ago, when Danny was an undergraduate at State. Ideas he began thinking about then were finally taking shape.

"I'm Mr. Danny Roarke. I did my undergraduate degree here during that aberration called the Sixties. This course is called Philosophy of Literature. We'll read a few novels and talk about them."

Danny distributes the syllabus and copies of chapters from his dissertation to the nine students.

"There will be several quizzes, a short research paper about the novel you choose, reaction papers, and I want you to keep a journal."

"What's a reaction paper?" a tall, thin boy with a sparse mustache asks.

"A paper that tells me how you feel about what you're reading."

"How will you grade that?" he asks, skeptically.

"You get full credit for doing it, my appreciation when you do it well."

There's a wave of nervous laughter. When he has circled the table to give each student the materials, he returns to his seat at the table.

"We'll read Ernest Hemingway's *The Old Man and the Sea*, Albert Camus' *The Stranger*, Kate Chopin's *The Awakening* and Eudora Welty's *The Optimist's Daughter*. The syllabus gives the dates. That other wad of paper is my dissertation. It's an attempt to describe these writers' philosophy by analyzing their characters. In a good novel, an artful writer shows how characters confront their lives honestly. The word I use is *authenticity*. To be authentic, one must think about fairness and equality, feel care for and intimacy with others, and act through dialogue and reciprocity, to treat others as well as one is capable. We'll see if men and women view their lives differently. There's clever work being written by Carol Gilligan and others that says they do. When I was an undergraduate here, Professor Milton Mayeroff was writing his book *On Caring*. The last time I saw him was in Ithaca, back in the Seventies, shortly before he died in a car accident. I'd like to keep his memory and work alive. That's the philosophic part of the course. The practical part is for you to consider your own authenticity. That's where your journal comes in."

A round faced girl with curly brown hair raises her hand tentatively.

"What do we write in our journals?" she asks.

"Good question. What year are you?"

"A junior," she says, more confidently.

"Do you know what you'll do when you graduate?"

"I don't know what I'm going to do this summer," she says, giggling. "My boyfriend, who's in the Navy, wants to get married, but I want to finish my degree."

"That'll fill up your journal."

She smiles then rolls her eyes and nods, "How many volumes can we write?"

"*Walden* kept Thoreau busy his whole life."

"How can you tell if we're authentic?" the thin boy with the mustache asks.

"I don't have an authenticity meter, if that's what you mean. But we all have issues to resolve in our lives. You'll see what I mean as we read the novels. But we write the scripts of our lives."

A dark eyed girl with long black hair raises her hand.

"Are you saying how things we read affect our lives is what this class is about?" she asks.

"Strange, huh?"

"No one's asked me that in school. Sounds far out."

"You folks will help decide if that's possible or worthwhile. The final chapters of my dissertation will be based on this course."

Grateful for the enthusiastic comments about genuine teaching from the students in the final class for the semester, Danny drove down the hill from campus toward State's athletic fields. All semester he had mixed feelings about seeing the old soccer field. But since this was the last class, he wanted to say goodbye to that part of his life forever. He passed his freshman dorm and looked in the window of his room twenty years ago.

He stopped for the traffic light at the bottom of the hill and looked through the pine trees that border the gravel path that he jogged to the field for practice. He drove around the football stands, along the macadam road leading to the soccer field. He stopped the car across from the goal. He walked out on the field, where several players were kicking a ball. He looked up at the broadcast booth above the stands, which wasn't there when he was a player. He read the name Prof Galsworthy painted on it in large red block letters.

The players referred to Galsworthy as "Prof." He heard Prof died, but this was eerie confirmation. Danny looked at his leather topsiders and thought about the soccer shoes Prof issued. That's when the name seemed most ironic.

Galsworthy, the English writer, wrote a story called "Quality" about an old shoemaker. Danny thought about the old shoemaker, who couldn't make a living because manufactured shoes were so cheap. Prof used to say, "Practice makes perfect. But if you don't practice quality, you'll become perfectly lousy." Danny looked at the letters again, admiring the man.

He looked from the goal across the field, toward the hills in the distance. Dairy cows grazed like they did when he was a player. He remembered how the maple trees exploded with color on the hills each fall. The air was crisp and tart in his nose when he ran, and a cool energetic sting in his lungs created a mysterious second wind that carried him through the game.

He zigzagged back toward the net. The air felt cool but damp in his lungs, the ground soft. He stopped at the top of the penalty area and looked at the net. He remembered the award ceremony his senior year when Prof said, "Danny is obsessed by the margin between performance and perfection." Motionless for a long time, he ran diagonally toward the car. As the net's yellow mesh appeared larger, he flashed on a goal he scored into it, feeling twenty years fuse together.

On his way toward the exit, he passed the athletic complex, which was built after he left. He went inside. He walked through the lobby filled by a large trophy case. In the section devoted to soccer, he was surprised by a picture of his African teammate Dobu, whose smile was a dramatic contrast of brilliant white teeth and rich black skin. Danny enjoyed memories of their friendship. Next to Dobu's picture was one of him, the year they were voted to the All State team.

His face was young and serious, his eyes intent on something in the distance, the fuzz on his lip barely hinted at a mustache. He felt weird to be sealed in glass. As he turned to leave, he felt reattached to Dobu, who returned to Uganda after Idi Amin's dictatorship collapsed. He heard Dobu ran for the Uganda Parliament, intent to create a new vision for the troubled country. Encouraged by the photos and students' comments about the course, Danny felt his vision of genuine teaching had value for a troubled education system.

When he got back to his apartment, from the parking lot he saw Maureen through the kitchen window.

When he opened the door, he yelled "I'm home from philosophizing dear..." He continued into the kitchen. "What's all this?"

"To celebrate your freedom from the classroom. I got lobster. I made strawberry shortcake for desert. Let me give you your present," she says, and kisses him. She walks to the bedroom. She returns to hand him a large, brightly wrapped package.

"Free at last," I guess. As he opens it he says, "No wonder I went to the old soccer field today."

"Your college soccer field?"

"Yeah, oh wow, Maureen, a VCR," he says, opening the package. "Thanks," he says, and hugs her.

"It will replace that antique of yours."

"I guess… Maybe we should make adult movies?" he says, and kisses her.

"Tell me about the soccer field," she says, amused.

"I felt my life was going to take longer to work out when I didn't take the scholarship to Brown. Strange… I told you about that dream…of the budding tree."

"What do you mean?"

"I started at State twenty years ago. Now I'm back there to finish what I started twelve years ago at Cornell… They dedicated the field to Prof Galsworthy. He was my coach, and coached my high school soccer coach.

Strange how State affects my life… I met Antonio there – still my closest friend. And my African teammate Dobu. Two great guys. If not for my Italian high school coach who knows what my life would be? But the students really enjoyed the course. They say that genuine teaching helps make sense of their lives. I was amazed… Maybe going to State *was* following the dream that I have to go my own way in life."

"With your talent, of course you do. Plus, all that Irish superstition in you, I find it lovable."

"I'm getting really weird lately. With the dissertation shit, our novel going nowhere, and you coming and going all the time, I'm about over the edge. Lately because of the stress, I don't sleep."

"You have a vivid imagination, but I've never seen you at its mercy. It's almost as if your imagination is controlling you. That worries me."

"I need some stability. I finished teaching today. So I can write my dissertation. If I get Callahan off my case, I may not snap."

"Writing for others is horrible. But what you showed me looks good. Even that bugger Callahan should be satisfied."

"I've got three weeks to make the graduation deadline."

"I'll do what I can to help."

"I'd appreciate that. If only you'd settle in."

"Honey, I'm here to help. But I also have to keep Mr. Swifty happy in L.A. But I had my mail forwarded this time. And that house I saw near the lake was darling."

"Why would we want it now?"

"Your lease ends this month. If you got a post at State or Cornell after graduation, we would have a place to live."

"The chances of either of those happening are like me getting elected to the Baseball Hall of Fame."

"You never played baseball."

"You are quick."

"You bugger. Anyway if Mr. Swifty comes through with the screenplay option, even if we don't live there, it would be a good investment."

"Keep wheelin' and dealin' Maureen, that's what you're good at."

"Are you ready to open the champagne?"

"May as well celebrate. My parents used to have a great sign in the bathroom. `We get too soon oldt and too late schmart.' Whadda think?"

"Have some champagne, Honey. Too much philosophy causes headaches," she says, and hugs him.

A few days after taking Maureen to the airport, alone again, with his dissertation stagnated and unable to sleep, Danny felt he was losing control of himself. He called his closest friend, Antonio.

"Tony, I called for you to help me sort things out. Maureen's back in L.A. or in Mexico."

"What do you think she's doing?"

"She says she's trying to sell that screenplay to Swifty Lazar. But it never seems to go anywhere. I think she might be bullshitting about it. And her condo sale getting tied up in a lawsuit. Sounds weird. Then she started some weird stuff about her ex-husband's business, where he thinks employees are smuggling cocaine from Mexico. The whole thing's getting pretty crazy. And I'm getting pretty crazy. I started looking through some old pictures."

"You do sound hyper, Danny. Pictures of what?"

"Remember that fire in the art building I told you about?"

"In Tampa?"

"Yeah. I think she might have set it. Somehow she knew Ronda's van was at my house that night. I'm looking at pictures of the fire. I think she might have been standing across the river, in the Art Museum parking lot. I'm going to get the negative blown up to poster size."

"Danny, it sounds like you're starting to lose it."

"I know, but it's her coming and going and suddenly all her stories. Today I was in the newspaper section of library looking at job listings in *The Chronicle of Higher Education*. I applied to a couple teaching jobs in Florida, and San Francisco – in case we go back there. She said she wrote an article about the Space Shuttle disaster. I checked *The San Francisco Chronicle*, there was no article."

"So?"

"She said they didn't print it."

"That happens all the time. You sound hyper. You getting any sleep? Or exercise?"

"Not much of either. I think she might be dangerous. She's got a real temper. I asked her to marry me when she was here...even gave her a small ring. But when I got pissed about her leaving, she got cold and distant."

"Danny, she's a strong woman. You're under a lot of stress. You say you aren't sleeping. That's not good. But make sure you protect yourself."

"I'm worried, Tony. She might be violent. Maybe I should call the police."

"What are you going to tell them, that your fiancé went to L.A.? That's not a criminal offense. But start putting the pieces together."

"What about the fire in Tampa?"

"What evidence do you have?"

"This photo," he says, looking at the solitary figure in the dark parking lot.

"Listen Danny, get some sleep. Call a psychologist in town, or at the university. Call me if it will help. I'm starting to worry about you."

"OK, Antonio. Maybe I am overreacting, but I'll do my homework," he says, and hangs up.

Still agitated, he calls the university counseling center, but feeling embarrassed, he hangs up before they answer.

He drives to the camera shop with the negative from the art building fire to be enlarged. In the stereo shop around the corner, he buys an adapter for the telephone which will jack into his tape recorder. He goes back to his apartment to wait for Maureen's call. When the phone finally rings late in the afternoon, he attaches the adapter to the receiver and turns on the tape recorder.

"I may be able to finish up in a couple of days. Then I'll be back, Danny."

"Good," he says, but he feels like his emotions are insulated in Styrofoam.

"I may be able to help my ex-husband keep this from a federal case."

"Who's smuggling cocaine?"

"Donald believes workers on the off shore platforms. You sound strange, Danny. Are you still angry?"

"No," he lies. "I just haven't slept in three days."

"I'll be back soon. I love you."

"See you soon," he says.

He hangs up mechanically, then shuts off the tape recorder and puts it in the desk. Distracted, he turns on the television. The national news describes a huge fire in L.A. He watches in horror.

A couple weeks latter Maureen returns. When they reach the apartment, Danny takes letters from his mailbox near the road. He sorts through them as they walk up the stairs.

"A rejection from Berkeley," he says, with disappointment. Guess we won't be living in San Francisco. Metropolitan University in Detroit is inviting me to interview. Detroit's the last resort. But this letter from University of Florida apologizes for delays in their selection process. They want to know if I'm still interested."

"A post in Florida, what about the sun?"

"Like Dr. Carve says, there's sun everywhere. Life is compromise. Just be careful. I'll tell them a delay is fine, I took a month off to kiss Callahan's butt to have him sign off on my dissertation, anyway."

"I'm glad to see you have a sense of humor about it."

"How else can I take becoming a certified philosopher? Oh, you gotta love this, 'Congratulations on successful completion of your degree.' American Express sent me a credit card. Being a jobless philosopher entitles me to an American credit card!"

After they go into the apartment, Maureen goes to the grocery store. When she pulls out of the driveway, Danny calls Metropolitan University to arrange an interview date. Next he calls the University of Florida to tell them he's interested. Then he notices her phone bill and steams it open, nervously. Apart from calls to him, there are two other numbers with multiple calls. He checks the dates and looks at his pocket calendar. One of the numbers looks familiar. He looks back on his calendar. It's the number she gave as the airport phone booth the day she said she had to fly to Los Angeles to meet the movie agent Swifty Lazar, when she couldn't make his parents' anniversary. He gets out his tape recorder and the phone adaptor. He calls but gets no answer. The other place is a small town in Washington named Treetorn.

Nervously, he dials the number and waits as the phone rings. On the fifth ring a woman's voice answers.

"Hello," he says, anxiously. "Is Maureen Wilmar there?"

"No," an older woman replies.

"This is Danny Roarke, a friend of Maureen's. To whom am I speaking?"

"This is Maureen's mother."

Shock rushes through him like a storm wave hits a beach. He is lost in its reverberation as he struggles to speak to a woman that Maureen said died over a year ago in Scotland.

"Do you expect her soon?"

"No. She's in San Francisco with her husband."

He hangs up then snaps out of the chair. He spins several times. He gasps deeply for air as his heart races. Electric in his brain turns to hot salty tears.

Crying, he goes to the window and looks at the hill filled with evergreens behind the house. He remembers her plan for them to go as journalists to see Halley's Comet and get married in Chile. She emphasized that Mark Twain was born during the first and died in Elmira during the second of Halley's previous visits to Earth. They drove to Elmira and he bought her a wedding ring. No wonder the Chile trip never materialized, he thinks.

He remembers a picture of him in front of the obelisk marking Mark Twain's grave in Elmira. He let's out a tortured laugh. As he searches through his desk to find the photo, he recites Twain's quote that we are each like the moon, with our own dark side that we hide from others. Maureen caught

136

his impish look when he dropped his jeans spontaneously to expose the white cheeks of his butt to moon the camera, a picture that Mark Twain would appreciate.

Holding the picture, he calls the first number again but gets no answer. He calls information in San Francisco but cannot locate her number. He looks at his United States road map and locates the small town of Treetorn, Washington. He thinks he may be able to find out something from her high school.

He calls the high school and says he's writing an article for a San Francisco newspaper about successful women from small American towns. He asks if there are any teachers who knew her. The secretary finds Jim Corrigan, currently a social studies teacher who went to school with Maureen.

"I knew she'd be successful. She was so full of life and so bright," he says, excited by the opportunity to talk with a journalist about his high school friend.

"What did her parents do?" Danny asks eager to understand her real life.

"Her mom stayed home. Her dad was a mechanic at the Air Force base. She hated him. Rumor was that he abused her as a teenager. She closed herself off from the family and drifted out of town after high school. Her dad died a few years ago."

"Did she ever get married?"

"A few years later. I think she was in San Francisco then."

"Did she ever go to college?"

"She was smart and had a great imagination, but wasn't much for school. I heard she was in Tampa working on a degree. I don't know if she finished. But you say she wrote a novel. That's great."

"Thanks, Mr. Corrigan, this will help."

He hangs up and snaps off the recorder. Stunned, he feels limp. He is dizzy as he breathes deeply several times. Her actual life sounds tragic. But Corrigan's affirmation about Maureen causes her disintegration for him. His interest suddenly feels voyeuristic. The woman he thought he knew is gone, which astounds him, but he needs to know more.

He calls information for *The San Francisco Chronicle* number. They never heard of her. He calls Swifty Lazar's office in L.A. Swifty Lazar rejected the manuscript in February, but never heard of him or Quark. She submitted the novel under her name, without his part. He's startled by the realization that he never doubted any of her stories before.

He calls Scribner's to ask about the advance. They don't know her. Then he goes into the dining room to get *Utopia Means Nowhere*. He calls the publisher in London, but it is too late to get an answer.

Worried that she may return soon, he takes the phone with him into the kitchen so he can watch out the window for the car. He tries the San Francisco number again. He shakes nervously as the phone rings. Finally someone answers.

"Mr. Wilmar?"

"Yes"

"Do you know where your wife goes when she flies off?"

"Who is this?"

"This is Danny Roarke. I'm engaged to your wife."

"I can take a message for Maureen Wilmar."

"Did you hear what I said?"

"Yes, but in San Francisco cranks call occasionally."

"You're too rich to be stupid. I said do you know where your wife is?"

"And I said I can take a message. Or I'll hang up."

"You're as weird as she is. Don't you care about your marriage?" he asks, but the line goes dead.

When she pulls into the parking lot, he's scared. He flashes on the poster enlargement of the person in the museum parking lot the night of the art building fire in Tampa, which should be finished at the camera shop downtown. He's afraid he may be right about her. Standing in the kitchen with the tape recorder, he watches as she crosses the gravel lot carrying a bag of groceries. He puts the recorder in a drawer next to the window.

"I'm back, Honey."

"In the kitchen."

"I missed you," she says. "What have you been doing?"

"Making phone calls. I arranged an interview at last resort Detroit. I told University of Florida I'm interested. They said they're down to three candidates. They'll interview soon. How suddenly the world changes," he says, sarcastically

He takes the grocery bag and puts it on the counter.

"Ithaca is such a wonderful town. I got trout at that little market, and vegetables for a salad. I'll start dinner."

"Can I help?" he asks, feeling his voice strain.

"You could pour some wine and keep me company."

He takes the wine out of the bag and gets a corkscrew from a drawer. Maureen washes the vegetables then takes a large serrated knife from the silverware drawer to slice them. After he hands her the glass of wine, he takes the recorder out of the drawer next to the window and rewinds the tape.

"I had a surprising time when you were gone. I talked to a man named *Mr.* Wilmar," he says, his heart racing.

She looks at him sideways but remains intent on slicing celery. "Oh really," she says.

"Listen, '*Mr. Wilmar?*' '*Yes.*' '*Do you know where your wife goes when she flies off?*'" Danny watches Maureen's face, which stays fixed on the celery.

"Now you're checking up on me?" she says calmly

"That's the phone booth you called from at the airport on your way to see Mr. Swifty in L.A. Strange that your husband answered in San Francisco."

"Did he really?"

"He says so."

"So that makes me married? Danny, did you ever think it might be my answering service?"

"C'mon Maureen," he says caustically and rewinds the tape. "Ever hear of somebody named Jim Corrigan from Treetorn High School in Treetorn, Washington?"

She stops cutting, but holds the knife tightly. She turns toward him and says, "What are you talking about?"

"Here. '*...Her dad was a mechanic at the Air Force base. She hated him. Rumor was that he abused her as a teenager.*' Sound familiar?" he asks, stopping the tape.

"You bastard. How dare you!"

He stands glaring at her. "Your dead Scottish heart-surgeon mother? Alive in Treetorn, Washington. Listen, kind of like the TV show *This Is Your Life*. '*She's in San Francisco with her husband.*' You must have forgotten to tell her about me and our engagement. Ain't that a kicker, Maureen," he says, tensely, but suddenly feeling sadistic, he clicks off the tape recorder.

"You bastard!" she screams, thrusting the knife at him.

"Did I hit a nerve?" he says, his eyes on the blade.

"How dare you invade my privacy."

"Your privacy? We've seen a counselor for your fucking privacy."

"That's because you're mentally weak," she says, shaking the knife, threateningly.

"No. It's because I've tried to adapt to your craziness."

"Stay out of my private life. I'll cut your balls off like I should have that pig of a father."

"C'mon, stop wallowing in a dead man's shit. All men aren't your father."

"How dare you!" she screams, jabbing the blade at him.

"Maureen, you're married!"

"Am I really? You've proved nothing. But I swear, if you don't stay out of my private life I'll kill you," she says, and lunges at him with the knife, slashing across his open palm.

He sidesteps quickly then grabs her wrist with both hands. He slams her wrist on the counter, shooting vegetables everywhere. She screams and the knife falls free. He kicks it away then pulls her out of the kitchen. He grabs both of her wrists and holds tightly.

"Maureen you're married. You're not a journalist for the Chronicle. There's no movie option with Swifty Lazar. There's no advance from Scribner's. It's all bullshit."

"Is it really?" she says coldly

"Maureen," he says, controlling his anger. "It's all in your imagination. You sucked me into *your fantasy*. Let it go!"

"How dare you!"

"Maureen, grow up."

"Look who's talking, the man who whines about a little skin cancer. You know nothing about suffering. It's the hidden inner life that's torment."

"Then don't hide it! Lying is bullshit!"

"Who are you to judge!" she screams. "I demand that you take me to the airport."

"Fine!" he says, letting go of her wrists, glaring at her, then at his bloody hand, which he wipes on his jeans. He grabs a dish towel and wraps it around his hand, then says, "Get packed."

She looks at him through narrow fierce eyes, but doesn't move. She remains stationary for a long time then slowly withdraws. He follows her into the bedroom. She gathers things into her suitcase. He stands in the doorway, watching. When she finishes, he follows her as she carries the suitcase into the hall, aware that she may go for the knife.

At the apartment door, she says coldly, "Don't touch me. I'll get a cab."

"No way lady. Get in the car. I want you on the next flight out."

He reaches for her hand but she slaps the dish towel. He follows her down the stairs into the dark parking lot. He's too angry to think of anything but getting her to leave. Finally, she gets into the car. They drive Freese Road across Route 13 to the airport in intense silence.

She is congenial with the ticket agent as she checks her luggage and gets her boarding pass. Her face is inscrutable when she passes through the metal detector to the exit.

He is numb as he watches her board. She climbs the stairs without looking back. He stands near the huge window, his cut hand pressed against the glass until it feels cold. It leaves a red stain when he removes it. He watches the rotating blue light on the top of the plane as it taxis onto the runway, then the flashing red lights under it.

Out in the parking lot, he watches the plane's lights until they disappear into the clouds above the lake. He feels cold and empty as he drives back to his apartment, stunned, wondering what's next.

After a night guarding against Maureen's return, Danny is relieved when the moon is replaced by sunrise. A shower and change of clothes feels like a symbolic beginning, which turns ironic when he calls the publisher of *Utopia Means Nowhere*. He talks a secretary into giving him the phone number of the author, Marianne Twines, who he calls. Twines tells him about growing up with parents who were famous doctors in Edinburgh, Scotland. Danny realizes that Maureen created her identity from Twine's sister, the character Belinda.

Later, he drives to the camera shop for the poster of the person in the art museum parking lot the night of the fire. But even with that much enlargement, he can't tell conclusively that it is Maureen. That afternoon, he calls the counselor with whom he and Maureen met, wanting to sort the chaos of the last night.

"Elizabeth, Maureen lied about everything. She's the product of American child abuse."

"I thought her accent was contrived. When she felt in control, she had it. When she got upset, it left her. It's usually the opposite."

"I never even noticed that," he says, embarrassed.

"Now that you say she was abused as a child, it makes sense why she would create that fantastic personality."

"How so?" he asked, amazed by how naïve he was.

"You said she divorced her husband partly because he was impotent. That may be her way to say she loved you but couldn't fit you into her life. She needs his money. You being a professor and writer confirmed what she valued in herself. She couldn't admit the book's failure to you. She needed a best seller for freedom from him and self-respect."

"I'm still having a hard time believing this is real."

"I'm sure you are. She's in turmoil. She needs extensive therapy. You must have felt that on some level?"

"Not really," he said apologetically. "I saw fulfillment of predictions, college dreams of love. Someone who valued my writing. Book contracts and movie options. I was sucked in completely."

"Not completely. You're lucky you went through this. If you cornered her it could have gotten dangerous."

"Yesterday, she slashed me with a knife because I violated her privacy. Last night I thought she might come back. I was afraid she might be an arsonist."

"She's capable of violence. Especially to protect herself. You made her confront herself."

"I can't believe anyone could lie like that."

"I'm sure it's complex if she were abused as a child."

"Her life sounds tragic. I feel bad for her. You remember that dream I told you about me climbing naked in the maple tree surrounded by granite and snow?"

"Yes. Why?"

"Could that explain my fascination with Maureen?"

"What you did for Maureen, she did for you. At least her fantasy did. You want the granite certainty of tradition, but also, confidence in your talent to climb in your own direction. You need to blend those. You loved her. But you were vulnerable to her deceit. It will take time to understand that."

"I never even saw it," he says, distressed by his gullibility. "At least Ulysses had enough sense to plug his ears with wax when the Sirens called. An astrologer in Oregon told me I was naïve and trusting. My friend Tony was skeptical of her. I got sucked in completely."

"At some level you knew," Elizabeth says encouragingly.

"I've always been a slow learner," he says, with a self-deprecating laugh. "It takes time for things to get from my mind to my heart."

"You're too hard on yourself. Danny, you've got to accept that you are sensitive in ways that you may not want to be. You're more than that macho image you like to cultivate at times."

He shrugs then says, "I remember a book called *The Velveteen Rabbit*. There was a Skin Horse who was worn out, then tossed aside by the child. The Skin Horse explained to the new Velveteen Rabbit that we become real only after we are worn."

"To lose the woman you love and a book that you counted on is wear. But remember *you* finished your doctorate."

"That feels like little consolation, Elizabeth, but thanks for reminding me. I really loved her..."

After the phone conversation, Danny took out his journal and started to write.

August of a new life, 1986

Like a person scribbling in wet cement or on a dry cave wall, we each want to note our presence and want to believe it matters to others. Lucky it does. It does! Aloha, Maureen... Let me climb the budding maple above the snow covered granite!

In the mailbox he finds a letter from Florida University notifying him they hired another candidate. Heartbroken, he calls Metropolitan University to confirm the interview date. He calls the local Pontiac dealer to get an estimate on the value of the car Maureen gave him. He advertises it in the *Ithaca Journal* for half the price.

He drives to pick up his dissertation from the word processor and chuckles as he pays for it with his American Express card, knowing that the car must sell before he can pay the bill. He gives a photocopy of the dissertation to each of his committee members. If they sign off, he thinks, as he jogs back from Roberts Hall across the soccer field to the car, he can present it to the thesis secretary within the week to finish his degree.

He flies to Detroit to interview at Metropolitan University. He has good feelings about the people he meets, but Detroit is bleaker than he imagined. Two days after the interview, the director of the learning center makes the only offer he has. With no other options, he accepts the job as her assistant.

He rents a truck with money from the car sale to a retiring Cornell professor. After he loads the truck, he celebrates his final day in Varna with dinner at Buddy's Homestyle Café. He signs for it with his credit card, amazed that he has money to pay the bill.

On his last trip through the apartment, he takes the manuscript of *Costa del Sol* and his bound dissertation and stands on the deck.

"Money? Fame? Who cares! *Doctor* Roarke prescribes granite and maple!" he yells, to the stand of pines on the hill, then bounds down the stairs.

He tosses the manuscript into the dumpster and walks toward the truck. When he reaches the truck, and opens the door, he puts the dissertation on the seat. He begins to climb in then stops. He walks back to the dumpster and looks into the pile of things that he's thrown away. He reaches in to grab *Costa del Sol*. He extracts the part he wrote and tosses the rest into the pile of junk.

"You're the only one who made sense in this whole thing, Quark. Who knows, maybe you're the writer."

He tucks his part of the manuscript under his arm and walks back to the truck slowly, looking around as if emerging from a dream.

He drives Varna Road through town and up the incline past the cattle barns and orchards. When he sees the "No Stopping" sign he's passed so often, he laughs, feeling liberated from a macabre journey.

He turns onto Holly Hill for a final view of Lake Cayuga. The disc jockey on Q104FM cranks out Rod Stewart's "Maggie May." He draws strength from Stewart's voice and starts to sing along. He lets the lyrics seep into him as Stewart's bittersweet song about love and deception tumbles over in his mind with memories of Maureen.

When he sees the lake, he lights a cigar on Route 333.

"Let me not curse the darkness I anticipate in Detroit. Somehow, it's the next step of my cosmic odyssey. Ole!"

Chapter 13: Cutting-board Arrangement

June 16, 1989 Detroit Institute of Art, Ye Olde DIA.

Happy 42ⁿᵈ Birthday! Three years in Detroit ending!

What is it about technique that gives one a world view? What is it about world view that gives one technique?

Sitting in the Detroit Institute of Art looking at Seurat's "Looking at Crotoy from Upstream". I have mixed feelings about what is there. To my right is Van Gogh's self portrait with a straw hat. He looks out through dark, uncoordinated eyes, concealing and revealing hysteria below the surface.

Points of color, slaps of color. Haze in Seurat. Intensity in Van Gogh. Two world views, two techniques. Emotions withheld, emotions indulged. Give me the full brush strokes of Van Gogh's emotion indulged.

The DIA, where I revive myself. And today is my birthday. Ten years ago today in Oregon. Ten years before in Litteltown. And ten years from now? Who could have imagined any previous decade? And who can imagine the subsequent decade? But ten years is a long time. Ten years. Imagine one! I turned forty in Detroit. Will I turn fifty? Where? Two very different questions.

Certainly the wheel was the greatest invention, but ah, the arch. What can rival either? Practical Beauty. And the beauty is in being, not in being-resolved. Hmmm...

Talked with Astrologer Tim about me taking the job at Palm City University. Pluto square Pluto aspects my return to Florida. Return means learn political lines and refrain from rebellion. The return to the past is to a place I've been burned before – how literal. This is a time of living the life of the humanist not the rebel...not the iconoclast...no more <u>Shattered Images</u>...

He says revise <u>Cutting-board Arrangement</u> to make my relationship with Maureen more believable, more about how I succumbed to the Siren's call. It is started, not complete. I gotta make it believable that she sued me in Federal Court in San Francisco for palimony, claiming I fleeced her out of money. It was great to hear the judge remind her that I wrote <u>Costa del Sol</u> and made arrangements for our wedding. I'll always remember Maureen's line when the judge asked her if she was married and she said, "Yes, but I don't sleep with my husband." Lucky it was a female judge, cause her response was classic when she said, "Welcome to America. Lots of women don't sleep with their husbands." And so, it cost thousands, but it was worth it.

I am going among Evangelicals concerned that I carry the torch of Palm City University and its founder John Palmer – named for John the Divine who wrote Revelations, the last part of the Bible. Oddly coincidental, good old Johnny Palmer left Michigan with a vision of founding a "Heavenly Earth" — a place where each would become all one can be. He founded Palm City along the Sunrise River and built a university.

It is now my liberation from three years in Detroit, where I was again the only white boy. Born in Harlem, it seems somehow my fate is to pursue the life of a white man advocating liberation and education of all people.

How weird to meet Rodernick Hawkins, a Black guy my age who did time in Joliet Prison for armed robbery in Dearborn bars. Finally out, trying to finish his bachelor's degree in art, and I have to get him through the university's writing proficiency exam. He told amazing stories about being a pimp and terrorizing White folks in bars and how distressed he was now about kids these days with automatic weapons selling crack cocaine and killing people for no reason. But it took forever to get him to write a coherent sentence. It was a great celebration when he finally passed the exam. And he made me realize how lucky I was to avoid getting raped by that guy in Tampa and not getting AIDS.

Palm City sets me free to be a professor for the first time. The only offer in three years. So, I take it and feel the Fates are once again involved. When there is one choice to make it is either/or. But all choices are that.

After publishing several articles about genuine teaching, I accepted an invitation to present a paper at a national conference in Washington and saw Bob Anzione's name carved into the black granite wall of the Vietnam Memorial…our high school goalie, who Charlie went to avenge but returned home without a leg to declare Vietnam was a foolish war. When will the world finally outlaw war? When will everyone realize diplomacy trumps deployment?

After reading one of my articles, my Gemini friend Mike asks me over the phone last night as he wishes me a happy birthday, "Why is authenticity so important?" My answer, "Mike, simply, I see no other way worth going. It's my search for an ethical common denominator…to transcend religion…or at least offer common ground among religions." And so, I need to advocate against oppression and war. What more could anyone aspire to, but to be part of a "Heavenly Earth"? Off to Palm City.

And so, the bright side of Detroit was several years with Charlie and watching his marriage flourish and my nieces grow... A wonderful experience. Family here traveling to be with family on the Island. Detroit was a place to teach...with students to care about. Several cycles around the Zodiac; every sign now accounted for, several signs becoming favorites with delightful moments of love and lust, but still the search for one great love. So, time to move on to become a professor of genuine teaching.

A new life to craft toward perfection. Aloha, Detroit.

Chapter 14: Copper Moon

When Danny passed the huge old brick cigar factories of Ybor City on I-4, he noticed the Tampa skyline against a bright blue January sky. The buildings clustered like giant mirrored chess pieces in a busier city than he left ten years before. The press of traffic veering off I-4 toward I-275 was frantic. He accelerated to change lanes to make the sharp left curve, then cut right quickly to the first exit.

After he began around the exit's long curve, he glimpsed the crescent moon topped silver minarets at Gulf Coast University. He saw them again near the Tampa Art Museum as he continued south. Lantan Hall, with silver turbans sculpted above windowed brick minarets, was still the most fascinating building he'd seen in America, and the reason he took the job there fifteen years ago.

He crossed Kennedy Boulevard, but got lost amidst a tangle of unfamiliar streets. Finally, after circling back from Bayshore Boulevard, past the tourist ship from *Mutiny on the Bounty*, he took the Platt Street Bridge that led to Harbor Island Hotel. When he reached the entrance along the circular drive, he left his car with the valet. He carried his bags up the wide stairway in the bright atrium filled with elegant Kentia palms and broad leafed giant birds of paradise.

When he got to the room, there was a note on one of the beds. "Roomie, Welcome. Don't do anything criminal. I'll meet you here at five." He thought Tony's signature had flourished over the years.

Danny opened his garment bag and took his suit to the closet, but it was already filled with several of Tony's suits and shirts. So, he hung it from the rack opposite. He checked his pocket watch, felt some change, pulled out three quarters. He shook them in his closed hand, thinking about his game of "Where & When." He opened his hand and looked at their dates. One quarter was dated 1978, the year he lived in Oregon. Another was 1989, the year he started at Palm City University. The third was dated this year 1994. He realized he was in Palm City longer than any place he lived since he left Litteltown in 1965. He jiggled the coins in his hand, smiling. He took his camera bag and walked to the elevator. Outside he walked toward the bridge and the convention center.

From the bridge he saw two minarets on the south end of Lantan Hall. He stopped. He aimed the zoom lens of his Nikon camera at a silver minaret against the cloudless blue sky. After snapping the picture, he pulled out the quarters. He flipped the 1978 coin several times and mused about the sixteen years between. No plan brought him to Tampa. It was a surprise offer for job he hadn't applied to, after getting fired from the CETA job in Oregon. And he had picked Eugene, Oregon, because it felt like the best place to live after his drive around the country looking for a home.

Staring at the minaret as it gleamed in the sun, he started to recite Elizabeth Barraclough's song, "Covered up in Aces" about planning versus letting life unfold. As he adjusted the lens the years disappeared in the shutter's click. He cranked the film forward and focused again. He thought about those aimless years on the road, but as he concentrated on pressing the shutter, he projected ahead – fifteen years would put him near retirement. The thought scared him, thirty years compressed in two clicks of the shutter. He couldn't imagine what he'd be like in fifteen years.

He put the camera back in his bag and walked to the convention center. He registered and looked at the exhibit booths and circled several presentations in the program for the following day. By the time he walked back to the hotel, Tony was in the room.

"Good to see you, Antonio" he said, and they hugged.

"Chairman Mao, if only Prof Galsworthy could see you now."

"Department Chair is such bullshit. I feel like used furniture. There's so much competition. The religious wars raged over the university's separation from the Evangelicals. So many talk Southern charm in public and plot privately. Unbelievable!"

"Welcome to America, Danny boy. You're lucky the Evangelicals bailed out. They would have gone after you at some point. Nobody likes pagans. Especially liberal Northern pagans."

"They were starting to dictate curriculum, believing their read of the Bible held the truth in their purse strings. I'm glad we're free. But I'm not doing the chair thing for long. I did it because the dean asked. She's this tough minded chemistry professor who faculty wanted to play hard ball during the transition to become a great university. She said the department was self destructing. If I wanted tenure, I'd have to be chair. Otherwise she wouldn't support me for tenure and I'd be gone. Ah, the joys of indentured servitude. The plantation worker mentality of the South."

"What a nightmare for a philosopher who believes in authenticity. But now that you got the hardware off your teeth, you can smile about it."

"Oh, the braces? Yeah, three years is a long time to endure the public announcement that my teeth bothered me. When I bought my house, my folks gave me a thousand dollars to do with what I wanted, since they'd given my brothers the same amount for bedroom furniture when they got married. They figured there was no chance I'd get married, so I put the money toward braces, and several additional thousands. They came off a few months ago."

"I know how much your teeth bothered you. But you realize no one else really cared?"

"I realize that. How like life. We are overly sensitive to our imperfections. And no one else cares. But just like life, I had to do it for myself. That simple."

"I'm glad you did. It's good to see you smile."

"Well, I'll never be the International Ipana Smiling Handshaker that you are, but thanks. I'm glad I did it. It's nice to smile. Let's head to dinner… My car is outside."

Danny drove them to the Colonnade Restaurant on Bayshore Boulevard. He enjoyed how familiar the crowded bar felt as they waited for a table. They were seated at a booth by the window that looked onto Tampa Bay.

"I'm impressed that nobody remembers you here, Danny," Tony said, a gracious smile easing across his face.

"Anonymity has its advantages. I'm not an international celebrity like you, Antonio. Ever since your book *Justice Unveiled* hit so big, and you and Allison expanded the original center to the International Center for Social Justice, you've become a movement in education. I'm really impressed," Danny said, handing Tony the basket of rolls.

"Now that you're Chair of Palm City *and* Renaissance City that will change. How's that going?"

"They just call it Renaissance. The developers think it will be the size of Palm City in ten years. And they want us to develop the school system. When he was chairman, Stan Sandler got us involved. He talked big about his new ideas in education, but especially after we faculty dumped him as chair, he's kept at it because he sees there's a lot of money involved. He told the dean I was slowing him down on the project. Dean Thomas called me yesterday."

"Are you?"

"No way. You met Sandler. We agree he's not competent. And his big ideas don't amount to much."

"Tell the dean to replace him."

"I did. Now she wants me to monitor Sandler. Like I'm a dorm director. She's afraid he'll ruin our public image."

"Unbelievable. But you're good at that stuff when you want to be."

"Welcome to the South, Antonio. Polite in public, lethal in private."

"Danny, this ain't rocket science. Tell the dean you've thought about it, you'll cooperate. If she's holding tenure over your head, don't mess with her."

"As my guru that's your suggestion? I at least wanted to play hard to get."

"Playing hard to get will get you fired. Anyway, you have no bargaining chips. She knows that. But she wants you. That's what counts. Just don't screw up.'

"My international friend, you power lovers drive me bat shit."

Antonio shook his head slowly and smiled. "You've avoided responsibility your whole life. It's time to grow up. If you don't get tenure, you'll be homeless and back on the streets of Detroit with all the other artist-philosophers. Remember, people only like you artists after you're dead."

"Thanks, Sage. I may have to buy another suit."

"You *have* a suit? When did you sell out?"

"I wanted to see what the attraction was…not much. It's hanging in our hotel room."

"Congrats. There is hope for you. But don't go dancing along the highway alone. At least until you understand all the political bullshit. Or at least until you get tenure," Antonio added, toasting his wine glass.

"I guess you're right. We'll see."

After dinner, Danny drove them back to the hotel. Then they walked downtown to the Hyatt, where several nationally known experts were having parties. Tony introduced Danny to several speakers whose presentations he'd circled on the program. They chatted in the hot crowded noisy rooms and moved on to another party, where another well known expert was surrounded by an equally hot and noisy crowd. Noticed immediately, Tony extracted himself graciously from the various crowds, and he and Danny found the elevator to the main lobby and went back to the street.

As they started to walk toward Kennedy Boulevard, Danny took a Macanudo cigar from the inside pocket of his leather jacket. He unwrapped it, clipped the tip with his cutter and handed it to Tony. He turned his back to the brisk wind and cupped the small Bic lighter in his hands as Tony leaned toward him to light his cigar. Then he lighted his own.

"Now it's *official*. The cigars are lit! Good to see you, Anthony. But how is Cleopatra? And your buddy, Caesar? Everyone keeps asking."

"Antonio, remember? Not Mark Antony. No interest in Cleopatra. I'm happily married. And Caesar had issues. And like Danny boy, he needed good counsel."

They smoked cigars as they walked along Kennedy Boulevard and stopped on the draw bridge over the Hillsborough River. They faced north, toward Gulf Coast University on the west bank. The minarets shined silver in the spotlights; the river flowed black beneath them. Danny stared at the reflection of the red light under the bridge arch in the moving water.

"You've come a long way since our roomie days, Antonio. Those people in the Hyatt think you're hot shit. Everybody's talking about your work with the International Center for Social Justice. Who would have thought you'd be a guru in international education. Folks at Tommie Jefferson U. must be impressed?"

"After twenty years at the university, I still love it. I'm thankful they're supportive."

"They let you and Allison run the Center the way you want?"

"Like our own business."

"What's completely mind numbing to me is that my roomie, exiled from a one room school in the mountains of Italy because the teacher wept at your stupidity, comes to America and ends up with a PhD and law degree teaching at Thomas Jefferson University as an international advocate for social justice through education."

"Hey, my folks wanted a second opinion."

"You don't see that as a little odd?"

"Having you as my friend is odd. But for some unfathomable reason, the universe compensates me well to be your friend, because it acknowledges my burden. I see our friendship as great luck for each of us."

"Having me as a friend Thor is certainly a huge burden. But you keep me alive. Except when you tried to kill us in that Vermont canoe. Your Libra balance keeps my Gemini duality under control. You remember that *B.C.* cartoon, with the two cavemen, Thor and his buddy, waxing eloquent about the sunset? Impressed by each other's class?"

"Yep."

"Well, Thor, I continue to be impressed by your class."

"Our friendship puts all things in perspective. I would never trade it. Your craziness makes my life interesting."

"Agreed. The blind poet Homer wrote *The Odyssey*. At times I feel like a blind poet writing my own odyssey. Who would have guessed it back at State thirty years ago, unbelievable, a great friendship. And you are doing a great job building an empire worth building."

"We're doing good things for students. Ideas you could use at Palm City. Or you might end up teaching back in Italy."

"Seriously, Tony, I'm proud of you. You've got a great marriage with Allison. You love your son. You've busted your ass to be successful. I'd love to use your ideas with the Renaissance project or with my summer program for kids."

"And you with a PhD from Cornell, publishing articles about genuine teaching, and presenting at the conference. Impressive."

"But not a keynote speaker, like my internationally esteemed friend. You really do have class, Thor."

Danny looked at Tony. He had aged well. He was still trim, muscled, handsome, the gray in his black hair softening his youthful good looks to good character. Danny turned slowly to look at the minarets and drew in on the cigar. He held it out over the bridge and flicked the long ash into the river below and watched it hit the water then dissolve in the flow. He leaned his elbows on the bridge and watched the red light shimmer on the rippling water. Then he looked toward the bridge north of them, where crews spray painted their university's names.

"I was thinking before, I started working here at Gulf Coast fifteen years ago. Fifteen fucking years. Tony, I've been on the road forever... You think I'll ever settle down?"

"Face it. Vietnam ended soccer for you. And breaking up with Suzi hurt you. You're still an artist at heart. I thought you'd straighten out because you were excited about Cornell, but when you blew out of there over Elaine, the Tampa job saved your butt after you collapsed in Oregon. Only you'd go across country to live somewhere because you liked the town. When you started to lose it with Maureen here, the best thing that happened was that you went back to Cornell to finish your doctorate. Without that you'd never have gotten to Palm City. I think you're finally settling down."

"I guess so. But I meant with a woman? You went through the Suzi disaster. Then Elaine. And finally, Maureen. You think I'll find a woman, or am jinxed?"

"I think you're ready. After Suzi, you went after sprinters. You need a long distance runner. That was the difference for me back in Vermont, that's why I left Jody for Allison. Jody was a beautiful cheerleader, but as I moved through my doctorate and on to the law degree, I wanted a woman who would appreciate those things. Jody couldn't, but Allison has been great. Making a marriage work day to day and running the Center together is hard, but worth it."

"What about Dawn once she and Frank split?"

Danny was still leaning over the bridge looking at the reflection of the red light in the water, but then turned to look at Tony. Tony took a long slow draw on his cigar. Then he flicked the ash into the water. He rotated the cigar several times back and forth in his fingers then put it in his mouth.

"That's not an option, Danny."

"Not an option? Why not?"

"She's your friend's wife."

"*Ex*-wife when they're divorced."

"Bad idea. Plus Frank's friendship is ruined."

"Then talk about a rendezvous in Bermuda is dumb?"

"C'mon, Danny, that's absurd."

"I know it's crazy. I don't know if I'd do it. But we've been talking as the divorce is finalized."

"Of all women in the world, your friend's wife?"

"I know. I was best man at their wedding…then they went into exile in Canada. Since Carter granted amnesty to draft dodgers, they've been back in the country. Outrageous coincidence. Had I met her first, I wonder what would have happened. But it went the other way around. I would never have met her without Frank. Who we meet in life is so weird. But she is such a loving and lovable woman. An Aquarius. But I agree it's crazy. And I've been there with the Sagittarius knifer Maureen," he said, and flicked another ash into the red light rippling on the black water.

"Trust me. Bad idea. Even for you. Especially for you. You'll want them to all love you, and they'll end hating you."

"No matter how I look at their divorce, it's going to cost me one of them. I'm sure of that. The real question is which one?"

March 6, 1996

How clearly life focuses. Took mom and dad back to the airport today. They cut their visit short. Dad felt sick, blood in his urine. He fears the colon cancer has erupted again since surgery in the Fall. He wanted to head home.

But before they left, they surprised me by attaching a leprechaun to the bathroom light pull chain.

"For good luck now that your braces are off and that you'll earn tenure!" Mom said. "We expect great things from you," Dad added.

What worries me though is the night perching and hooting of an owl in the backyard water oak their last few days… With the dean on my case and dad feeling sick, I wonder what's next.

A few days after that journal entry, Danny was grading papers when his mom called.

"They took your father to the hospital today. We should donate more money to emergency fire services, Daniel, they were wonderful."

"Are you OK, Mom?"

"The emergency people came right away."

"How is Dad?"

"He's at Nassau Hospital. They're keeping him for observation. He complained about pain in his back when he was taking groceries out of the car."

"Well maybe rest will help. I'll call him," he said, pacing the floor.

"Do that Daniel," she said, and gave him the number.

He called his dad after he got off the phone with his mom. His dad said that the pain in his back made it too hard to walk. Now they were starting to do tests on him.

The next several days were calls back and forth to his mom and brother to find out about his dad and the tests. Finally the accumulation of results pointed toward a diagnosis.

"It looks like the cancer may have returned," Rich said, over the phone.

"What will they do?" Danny asked, his insides going numb.

"It took several days before the increasing number of doctors agreed on a diagnosis. Dad keeps hearing they were still testing. Finally, I interrogated the oncologist to demand a diagnosis. He said that the CAT scans and MRI's and blood work indicated that the back pain wasn't from muscle, but from a fracture in the vertebrae. The tests confirmed that cancer had spread throughout his body."

"Why did they take so long to decide?"

"They don't want to rush. But there are tough choices."

Danny felt nauseous as they talked about the possibilities.

"If we do nothing, he may live six months, Danny."

"With radiation and chemotherapy, how long, Rich?"

"No one knows for sure, but it could go into remission."

"That could mean a few years?"

"It could, Danny. I don't know how optimistic they are."

"Chemotherapy is nasty. Couldn't it make him sicker?"

"If he gets sick, we stop."

"I agree. Let's do it. Dad understands?"

"He knows it's cancer. He knows he can stop treatment."

"I'll get a plane tomorrow."

When Danny got to the hospital the next day, his dad looked like he'd aged years in the two weeks since he saw him. His hair seemed wispy, sticking up, uncombed. Danny never saw his dad with several days beard growth. The white stubble made him look more fragile. His handshake was still firm, but he had lost a lot of weight and his legs looked fragile as they extended out from under his white gown, and tubes ran from an IV into his arm. An oxygen hose hung around his neck and a urine bag and colostomy bag hung over the side of the bed near the floor. The thought startled Danny that the bags of yellow and brown were symbols of life being drained from his father.

After they shook hands, Danny handed his dad a Palm City baseball hat, like the one he was wearing. His dad put it on. There were tears in his eyes as he thanked Danny. Danny sat in the chair next to him.

"Dad, how about I give you a shave?"

"That would be great. They don't seem to have the time."

Danny grabbed his father's razor from the chest of drawers. He got a face cloth and went to the bathroom to heat it. He put the damp cloth on his father's face. Then he applied shaving cream from the can.

"You're looking better already, Dad."

"Thanks. Ryan is due back from his voyage around the world. I'd like to look clean shaved when he gets here."

"Amazing, my nephew spent the semester on a ship traveling around the world."

"We have a great family Danny boy. Everyone went to college. And you, you have doctorate from Cornell. Your mother and I never finished high school."

"Different times, Dad," Danny said, as he looked at the scar on the bridge of his dad's nose that never healed after he scraped it kissing the Blarney Stone several years before. As he continued, he noticed the chip out of his dad's ear from frostbite when he was a young man. Danny finished shaving the foam off his dad's face and applied the warm cloth again. "Now you're looking smooth. How about some pinochle?"

"That would be fun. I feel lucky," he said. "The Lord has let me make it to eighty-six and to see my grandson marry a great girl. I've lived a great life Danny. I'm glad to see you."

"Thanks, Dad. Great to see you too. I'm sorry you had to cut your vacation short. I look forward to you and Mom coming down next year."

"It's in the Lord's hands, Daniel. Just start dealing those pinochle cards. Right Lil, we've had great lives? Let's play cards."

As Danny dealt the cards to his mom and dad and to himself, it was hard not to cry.

He took his mom to the hospital twice a day for the next week. The three of them played pinochle and talked. His dad could stand only with great effort. Danny lifted him under both arms to move him from the bed to the chair, and felt his infirmity. The doctors insisted they were succeeding, but Danny realized they flooded his dad with steroids and morphine. He returned to Palm City with the understanding that his dad had at least six months to live.

Two days later, the hospital released his dad to home care. The next day he went into a coma. He died sometime that night.

The wake brought out people Danny hadn't seen in years: Hibernians, Knights of Columbus, and the Rosary Society. Father Jerry, the family priest who said Rich's son Ron and Jennifer's wedding mass, prayed at the wake. Leaving the wake that night, Danny noticed the sun set behind vapor trails turning orange as a crescent moon rose. Danny slept in the room where his dad died, next to the plaque of the Sacred Heart of Jesus. On the other wall was a picture of his mom and dad's fiftieth wedding anniversary that he took at Rich's house overlooking the Sound, and a picture of his dad sitting on the patio in Litteltown smiling. The night before the funeral, writing in his black bound journal, he cried often, feeling he had to put his feelings into words, had to share his feelings with the family, as he struggled to write a eulogy.

The day of the funeral was bright blue and cool. After helping to carry the coffin from the hearse, he walked in with his mother and Rich's and Charlie's families to the first row as the coffin was rolled into the church, draped with a red cross on the white cloth.

He listened to readings by Father Jerry but thought about what he had to say as he sat in his dark suit, waiting to read the eulogy. When Father Jerry signaled him, he walked to the pulpit. He carried the black bound journal in which he struggled to write the eulogy. He had carried it with him during the wake and back again at home, trying to finish the eulogy before saying his last goodbye in front of his dad's open casket in the funeral home earlier that morning. He continued working on it since. He adjusted the microphone on the pulpit and started to read.

Dad

Dedicated to Maurice Roarke: Feb. 19, 1910 - May 27, 1996

What can I say about such a likable guy? That he loved golf. Pinochle. Bridge. Traveling. The Saturday night lottery. A good used car. Trips to Atlantic City. Beefeater martinis at long lunches with friends and family. That he cared deeply about the success of his family. That he enjoyed being called dad, grandpa, poppi... He was a Hibernian who cherished the Irish legacy in his blood, and the blood of his descendants. And he felt blessed by a great family.

He was educated in the school of hard knocks. He said often that "America is the greatest country in the world and anyone who works hard can succeed, but in this day and age you need an education to succeed." So he was proud his sons graduated from college and that his grandchildren went to college to become professionals.

I remember when I was a kid. He said three great men were born in February. He mentioned Lincoln and Washington. I knew his birthday came between theirs, on February 19th. And he knew I understood what "blarney" meant. But he kept a straight face, so I've kept it in mind all these years.

When mom and dad were visiting me in February, I found a smiling leprechaun suspended from the pull chain on my bathroom light. They laughed when I asked how it got there. With a straight face, Dad said, "We have no idea." But he reminded me that leprechauns are a sign of good luck. This wisdom from a man who scraped his nose kissing the Blarney Stone in Ireland, who had great good luck because the scrape never healed, which gave him undeniable proof of his Blarney Stone encounter – the gift of gab.

He's a man who respected hard work and loved to watch it. And he knew how much fun life can be. He worked for Republic Bank his entire career. He commuted from Litteltown for twenty of those years, then introduced Rich into the bank and retired. He watched Rich commute for twenty years, while he painted, traveled, philosophized, and gloried in his family's hard work and success.

About this time last year he was eagerly anticipating Ron and Jennifer's wedding, excited about a family celebration – a man who knew how to party. Proud of another generation starting new lives with marriage – something he was great at. Incidentally, don't think he didn't realize this marriage guaranteed the next generation would have to call him great grand pa and great poppi!

Today we are here to celebrate the man who gave our family life. When he and mom left the airport in March, he shook my hand and wished me "Good Luck." I thought about the smiling leprechaun still suspended on the pull chain to my bathroom light. In the hospital last week, he had a tear in his eye as he shook my hand to say good-bye and wished me "Good Luck," happy that Ryan returned safely from his voyage around the world. I thought about the smiling leprechaun.

I think about the smiling leprechaun now, Dad. You have blessed us with a great family, and have shown us what we need to do from here. Your work is done, relax, enjoy, your luck is good. Next February I'll be looking forward to celebrating the birthdays of three great men. Dad, only you can say you've met Lincoln and Washington now. But we can all say we knew you when you were on Earth. I'll miss you. We'll all miss you. But now, on your behalf, I'd like to ask everyone to share a handshake or kiss to wish good luck, while thinking about the smiling leprechaun.

As he finished, he closed the black journal. He stood looking at his brothers, then his mom, who had a tissue in her hand, but was smiling. He was glad he had written it and was relieved he had read it without losing control of himself. He felt it come from his heart and was glad he said what he did. He stood for a moment as if floating then started to walk off the altar. Father Jerry started to walk toward him and extended his hand, as a reflex he offered his hand, but was surprised when Father Jerry said "To wish good luck," as they shook hands.

· He realized it was the request he'd made in his eulogy, but as Father Jerry said it, he was startled as he continued across the altar. The animosity he'd held toward the Church for so many years fell away. Suddenly Father Jerry became a person not a priest and the rebuilt church, where the mass was offered facing the people felt genuine. He continued across the altar and returned to the pew next to his mom and kissed her cheek.

"Daniel, you were wonderful. Your father would be proud," she said, as she held his hands between hers and thanked him.

The ride to the cemetery and putting the body in the ground was difficult. But he remembered how positive his dad was in the hospital the day he shaved him, saying that he had a great life. His sadness gave way to a great love and respect he had come to feel for his father. His dad had gone to the end heroically, knowing when it was time, leaving a proud legacy.

Danny flew back to Palm City a few days later. From the time he got on the plane, he stared out the window. Toward the end of the flight he started to write in his journal:

June 2, 1996

All blur and fantasy. Casket. Flowers. Hibernians, Knights of Columbus, Rosarians. Dad with the casket open. Like Pharaoh. Mummified. Eaten from the inside. Nose prominent. A death mask. Drawn. Boney. Wisps of white hair. Hands folded around a rosary. The K. of C. pin. The diamond chip tie bar. The A.O.H. pin. Striped shirt. Navy blue suit and floral tie. Maurice Roarke, May 27, 1996 in bronze on the coffin. This is death. Absolute calm and stillness. To the right amidst the pictures of family "Dad on the Estate" smiling in the webbed aluminum chair on the patio. He is my father. In the casket what remains after the unwinable battle with death. An 86 year old man...

I'm adrift. Life goes on within grief. Everyone working hard... He is a man greatly missed. Impossible to replace. His protection removed. The mass, funeral, dinner after...all of it. This is the life after. It's hard...

I hate the finality of death. I would like to see it undone. It would be good to see dad again. The photo in the bedroom is all that's left. Horrible. Unfair.

A full copper moon rises over the Atlantic during the last lap of my flight home. A full moon. Copper orange above black below. Stratus clouds stretched above. Silver. And so this is it. An orphan in the sky. A man clearly lost in the loss of a father. The disk of moon rich and bright. In the eastern night sky it is all. The sun is down, set. The moon silent, quiet, supportive, marks no destination, only journey. Not pale or silver but luxurious in its glow. The nearest celestial orb. Two hundred and forty thousand miles. Ten times around the Earth. It is what is left to me now. A moon child. Son of the night sky, of a golden light in the darkness. I am about the moon's quiet beauty, an orphan drawn to the night sky.

It is sheer, utter silence of ascension that lures me. Orbital elegance. Below the shoreline appears in green and yellow lights. The barrier island linked to the mainland by yellow lighted bridges. As we turn toward home the moon disappears below the wing and then behind. The golden moon at my back. This is what is left. This is what counts.

The moon exalted. The moon above the city, the peninsula. Full and quiet and complete in the black sky. Attentive to Earth. Empathic. The ebb and flow of waters. As we circle and descend and aim and re-aim to the airport it disappears. But I know it's there. Somehow this is comforting as the pressure squeezes my ears. The sun gone, what's left is the waxing and waning comfort of the moon. In the black sky it disappears, but I know it's out there somewhere. How strange to exist at all and now how odd to re-chart my course as we hit the ground and slow. Earthbound again and mortal. Oh so mortal and slowed to stop. And so mortal life continues...

A few days after he returned to Palm City, he met with President Jackson to resolve the Stan Sandler fiasco. The president agreed to remove Sandler from the project and let Danny develop the Renaissance schools.

The next day, when he got home, he found a letter in his mail box from the President's office. It was official notification confirming tenure. As he stood with the letter in his hand, outside the porch, he looked into the Koi pond, and slowly shook his head from side to side. He finally had roots. He called Tony.

"Professor Marino, Danny Boy has tenure!"

"Well, even good universities make mistakes. Congratulations. You and Scarlett O'Hara will never go hungry again. From soccer player to philosopher in only thirty or so years."

"I couldn't have done it without your infernal vigilance. Thanks."

"No, seriously, Danny. This is great. You've remodeled your house into an art gallery, and now tenure. Congratulations!"

"You mean Danny Boy's Bed Breakfast & Grove? Yeah, really feels like home now. My dad would be proud. Oh, the Sandler thing is resolved. He's off the project. The politics wear me down."

"But you made it happen. And you did it fairly. Just get on with your own work."

"If you want to get involved in the Renaissance project, you're welcome."

"Thanks, well see. I'm doing a lot of consulting in Europe and Australia and soon in Asia. And I'm trying to finish my book called *Elevate the Republic*. But I'm proud of you Danny boy."

In a university meeting the following week, faculty and administrators discussed the future of the university.

With heartfelt confidence to keep the religious heritage as part of the university mission statement, Danny said, "Palm City is an excellent university. To abandon our heritage for some vague notion of political correctness would jeopardize that excellence. The Evangelicals wanted to stifle dialogue that invigorates a university, and so we moved on. Now we have the opposite extreme. Some people want to deny the university's roots. To abandon our Christian heritage would be to deny our psyche. Believe me, I've tried. It doesn't work. As my dear eighty-two year old mother – who just lost her husband of fifty plus years – says, 'God is Love.' Fundamentalists of any religion can't control the world. But the fundamentals of Christianity are to love one's neighbor as oneself. Most of us were raised Christian. Most of our students are Christian. What would we gain to deny that? John Palmer left Michigan with a vision to build a 'Heavenly Earth'. To build a city where each would become all one is capable of becoming. He tried to fulfill that vision by founding this university. I don't support removing reference to our Christian heritage. But I do support transcending religious heritages to seek common ground beyond particular religions. To be authentic is to believe that genuine virtue is its own reward. Believe that. Let the individual religious interpretations about life and afterlife tend to themselves. The university is a place where we should teach people to care and be fair. The common denominator is authenticity."

He was surprised by the applause.

He went back to his office, feeling that he had finally established roots. He was expecting a visit from Angie Harper, one of his graduate students, to continue planning her master's thesis project.

As usual, she arrived on time and smiling. "Dr. Danny how goes the philosopher's life?" she asked enthusiastically as she entered his office.

"Camus' mythological Sisyphus just had to roll a rock up an endless mountain. Why do I get the feeling I'm going to get a pitch for an endless Mark Twain project?"

Her reflex smile confirmed his guess as she replied, "No greater American writer. Even your buddy Hemingway thought American literature started with him. Yep, Mark Twain! It's the hundredth anniversary of his book, *Following the Equator*."

Danny smiled, appreciating her enthusiasm. She completed her undergraduate degree with him two years before and was now teaching elementary school, having returned to school years after she dropped out of high school, got married, and raised two children. He knew she divorced recently, and although she hadn't discussed it, Danny felt it was because her husband became abusive because he couldn't endure his wife to be better educated than him.

"I can't believe how much you love Mark Twain. How about an animated video of his works? Would your art teacher friend be interested?"

"That's the plan. We could work with third through sixth graders. He'd teach them cell and clay animation, and I'd teach about Mark Twain as they read *Following the Equator*."

"Sounds like fun," he said, and she looked ecstatic. "Then let's take the kids and parents on a riverboat cruise on John Palmer's Sunrise River to premiere the video. What do you think, Angie?"

"Sounds great!" she said, her face focused in a broad smile.

"Sketch out what we talked about today in your thesis. And let's invite some kids," he said, excited to work with her.

Chapter 15: Feathered Serpent

Several weeks after his dad's funeral, as his mom arrived through the airport gate, she looked disoriented. Danny rushed toward her.

"Good to see you, Mom," he said, and hugged her and kissed her on the cheek.

"Thanks, Danny. You're looking good."

They walked off together, his arm across her shoulders.

"Nice to be here. It's strange traveling without your father. But it's God's will after our long and happy life together. God was merciful to let him die first. He couldn't live alone. He couldn't even boil water," she added, with a sweet laugh.

"He was a wonderful man. You two were lucky."

"Yes. And we have a great family to show for it. So how's my youngest son – Doubting Thomas, our absent minded professor?"

"Good to see you have your sense of humor."

"I'm being serious. I understood what you did as a chemistry teacher. But I've never understood what you do as a doctor of philosophy!"

"You're right. I know you always wanted me to be Albert Schweitzer. But I'm not a real doctor. I can't prescribe drugs legally. I'm sort of a metaphysician. I watch the sky to try to figure out why it's there, and what to do about it."

She laughed then said, "I'm glad I love you, because sometimes I find it hard to follow you. Lucky Dr. Milani was there to remove the caul the night you were born and make such wonderful predictions."

"It has been a long and winding road from Harlem to here, Mom. So let's you and I have some fun."

The couple weeks that his mom stayed were difficult. She felt lost without her husband. The day she was to leave, they sat in the wicker rocking chairs on his porch talking before they left for the airport.

"Why would God make me suffer this much?"

"You have suffered, Mom. Breast cancer... Dad's death. But it's part of life."

"I wish God would let me die."

Danny looked at his mom and frowned. He looked at the citrus grove he planted when he bought the house five years ago, then back at his mom.

"I believe you should have that right, if you believe your life is over. Dad accepted his death. Felt his time had come. But Catholics say you can't choose, Mom. You have to keep faith that it will work out. You just have to endure Mom," he said, and put his arm on her shoulder and kissed her cheek. "Mom, you have to keep at it, your Catholicism requires it, and your growing family loves and wants you."

They continued the conversation in the car on the way to the airport.

"I know it's God's will, Danny. But it's hard alone. Your father was such a great guy."

"I know it's hard. But you can do it," he said, as he escorted her to the plane, hugged her then kissed her on the cheek. Thinking that aging and loss of loved ones is tragic, he was sad as he watched her walk slowly into the plane to be met by Rich at the other end. Soon after, she moved to a nursing home after she found it impossible to live in the Litteltown house alone.

June 30, 1996 3:33 a.m.

Up from a dream. The Mayan pyramids in Chichen Itza under a full moon. An elaborate ceremony to sacrifice the ball players. But unclear if the winners or losers are sacrificed... How strange.

Last night, on the paddle-wheeler Riverboat Sunrise with the kids and their parents to celebrate the success of the summer program, the moon rose full as we traveled up the Sunrise River. Angie will make a great teacher – Tony will love her as a doctoral candidate at Tommie Jefferson U. I'm so glad he offered her an assistantship to work with him. The doctorate will transform her life. She was ecstatic about the students' work – the animated video the kids made captured so much of Mark Twain's writing.

But now, I need to travel. Lured to Chichen Itza. That simple. Two weeks since my forty-ninth birthday. Twain has motivated me. Working with Angie – one of my best graduate students ever – and working with the kids has set me free in a new way... With dad dead and mom suffering to adjust, I feel I must explore in new ways. The summer program a success.

But called to the soccer like ball game. Fascinated by Mayan astronomy and astrology. I must go...to see the next full moon. To take pictures of the full moon over the dome shaped observatory and get away from the U.S. for a while... Twain went around the equator... I just need to see the moon rise over the Mayan ruins...

July 29, 1996

After flying into Cancun today, I sit on Las Perlas' terrace looking at the Gulf of Mexico...in Mexico. The Gulf... Turquoise on the horizon...the turquoise of cobalt and shine of flint. A glaze for pottery to bear the bones in the world's sarcophagi... The artist named or unnamed in every century to ornament the world. It is the artists...
Tomorrow off to Chichen Itza.

July 30, 1996 Chichen Itza

The intrigue of ruins and Mayan culture. Non-Christians obsessed by sacrifice. Their Christ-like hero Kukulcan, the Feathered Serpent – a mythical combination of god and man who offered them an ideal of justice. And the rain god Chaac Mool, who they appeased with blood and human hearts to keep the earth fertile.
A thousand years before Columbus, Mayan astronomers and priests watched planets transit the sky. Cleverly, they constructed a pyramid which at the equinox casts a shadow that undulates down the northern stairway to return the Feathered Serpent to the earth each year. I hope the photo of the full moon above the observatory works...the moon exalted.
I'm fascinated by ambiguity surrounding sacrifice of athletes in the ball game they called pok-ta-pok. According to the Mayan tour guide, the captain of the wining team was worthy of being sacrificed to the gods. But according to American anthropologists, the losers were sacrificed. I like the Mayan guide's story better. Sacrifice is perfection. Defeat requires courage to try again to achieve perfection. Christ allowed himself to be sacrificed to his father.

Under the palm trees on the terrace at the Mayaland Hotel at Chichen Itza, Danny sat writing in his journal. As he waited for the tour bus back to Cancun, he heard a young couple talking with the Mexican trio strolling among the tables. The woman asked, "Are you related?" The oldest one said proudly, "This is my son, and my son's son. What would you like to hear?" "A romantic song, for newlyweds," she said, and wrapped her husband's hand around hers. The oldest man started to sing "Guantanamera" in Spanish.

August 2, 1996 Chichen Itza

Ah, yes, the sincere man wanting to share his poetry in song. What a beautiful song. I write with tears in my eyes as I remember the Sandpipers singing "Guantanamera" years ago as Suzi and I would listen. My tears flow warm and salty. But I'm not sad… I'm happy for them. It makes sense of my trip to the Mayan ruins…much like when I saw the couple kiss in the arch at the Alhambra in Spain.

Back at the Book and Tea in Oregon, Estella said I would write about the human spirit… I can't overcome my sensitivity, so I must write. Tears flow under the palms… My destiny is to search but see others find love.

My brothers are happily married and I saw my parents happily married for years. As I listen to the trio, I realize I was lured here by the moon in my dream… Maybe I should write about family and friends who found love. A novel called <u>The Feathered Serpent</u>*. But a female main character this time…a psychic…or astrologer, exploring the mystery of love.*

At the Cancun Airport, Danny got bumped from his Tampa flight to a commuter flight to Miami. He sat alone in the back writing in his journal.

August 2, 1996

America, I hate our violence. It makes no difference to me whether you believe or don't believe in a Christian God, or what gods you do or don't believe in. We have to reconstruct America's psyche. As I learned from Professor Mayeroff, we are not at home in this world by dominating but through caring and being cared for.

Standing on the roof over love and lust one sees the importance of family and friends.

But I've grown to enjoy my single life. I realize mom and I are the only ones left from that wild ride down the Grand Concourse with mom and dad and Uncle Rudy to meet Dr. Milani in Harlem. It's humbling to know that my life could have ended then, or any time along the way since, or soon. But I can say honestly that Dr. Milani's prediction was right, I've had great luck.

I've gone beyond a Christian cosmos and Hawthorne's Scarlet A. I may be a crazy blasphemer, but finally, with my braces off, I can smile and say honestly, I'm a happy man. As Taj Mahal sings in "Giant Step" whether you win or lose at love, you gotta keep going, gotta take that next giant step… I wish others great luck and giant steps!

In the back of the plane, in the empty seat next to him, the flight attendant strapped herself in as the plane hit a thunderstorm over Cuba.

"Pretty turbulent," Danny said, unable to write in the bouncing journal.

"It'll be ok," she said.

Suddenly the plane dropped. The beverage cart missed them and smashed into the bathroom door and spewed everything onto the floor. The attendant went pale and clutched Danny's forearm.

The plane caromed to the left and dropped again. She screamed. Danny's chest tightened as she dug her nails into his arm. They rocked to the right. The plane pitched left, and she screamed again. She clutched him harder. He sat immobile as he stared at the pale flight attendant, thinking repeatedly that he wasn't scheduled for this flight.

"Seems to be leveling off..." he said, looking into her terrified eyes.

Danny felt his heart race, but put his hand over hers, clutching his forearm. He rubbed her hand gently.

Suddenly there was a cheer from the passengers as the plane stabilized. Danny removed her hand from his arm slowly and hugged her shoulder.

"Geez, this happen often?" he asked, forcing a laugh.

She looked at him with her mouth open.

Moments later, the pilot announced final approach to Miami; the passengers cheered wildly. The flight attendant hugged Danny.

"Thanks so much!" she said, and kissed his cheek.

"Thanks for being so friendly," he said, returning the kiss.

The flight from Miami was smooth and short, but while in the air, Danny felt rattled.

August 2, after almost dropping out of the sky...

Near death experiences do motivate...

A novel called The Coincidence of Death... *I could use our college séance with the picture from the old farm house of the woman we called Greta. Use Erin as a character...and Hester Prynne. Maybe connect in St. Augustine to explore notions of heaven and hell. America's oldest city. Named for a guy who, after a life of worldly excursions, became Bishop of Hippo in North Africa and wrote about the City of God – over fifteen hundred years ago. St. Augustine was founded four hundred years before Sally, Tom, Frank, Tony, Erin and I graduated from high school and years before the Puritans.*

I'll take my tripod at sunset. Plant myself at Castillo De San Marcos' tower, the old fort made from coquina stone. This time of year, the moon should rise north of the Bridge of Lions, over the bay. If I'm lucky, I should get sky, earth and water surrounding the sun's reflected fire off the moon and tower.

Although no mortals have walked the moon in almost twenty-five years, I'll consider the moon heaven and the sun hell. Although we bury our dead in the earth, Brother Charlie might be right, our spirits escape and actually choose their future on the sun or moon and keep tuned to earth. Or maybe mom and dad are correct, only the pure of heart will see god as spirits in heaven.

And if the moon is heaven, and if the Middle Ages maxim that an infinite amount of spirits can dance on the head of a pin, many more could fit on the moon. Like Shakespeare's Ariel in "The Tempest" – go dashing around the solar system. Or go out beyond Einstein's paradoxical saddle shaped universe that he claims to be relative, except for the constant speed of light. How the universe can be relative and light constant has never made sense... But then few relatives actually make sense... And so who knows about heaven and hell.

But the plane didn't fall out of the sky. So, who knows why I met Erin, Suzi, Elaine, Maureen or Frank or Dawn or Sally or Tom or Tony, and the others along the way... All I know for certain is that the spirits of my friends and family are alive. And I look forward to a July 4th Independence Day that celebrates everyone walking safely every street in America...and on Earth. Agreed, unhinged again, but smiling!

Chapter 16: Easter Lily

April 17, 2001

Lily died on Easter. Easter, the day they rolled back the stone for Christ. I know death, but have no understanding of resurrection. A myth is a myth. But my mother is dead. Her body is in the casket in front of me. A tired drained woman, not like dad – pharaoh at peace with death.

She suffered death.

Christ allegedly said, "Father forgive them for they know not what they do." But he suffered and asked at the end, "Father, why have you forsaken me?"

The oppression and empire building of the fundamentalists brings clashes of biblical interpretation into biblical proportion.

The zealots claimed a patch of dusty land on the southern Mediterranean as God's chosen land, and they his chosen people. Jews, Christians, Muslims. And so, the world endures interpretation of a small city called Jerusalem that three major religions claim. What foolishness, to let religious accounts make world policy.

Remember, there are a billion Chinese making shoes for Nike, cell phones for AT&T, ornaments for the world. Two billion Christians and Jews. Nearly a billion Muslims of various allegiances... A billion Hindus... A billion assorted communists and socialists and pagans west and east of the Caucuses and around the world seeking answers... Let us all outlaw war world wide...

With Mars at its closest in 60,000 years, it saw the evolution of homo sapiens in its previous passing. In its next approach it could see the passing of this self-important species. We have a cracked bell and a parchment document that claimed the sexist and racist view that women and Black skinned people did not deserve citizenship. It took a hundred years and battlefields of blood to edit the parchment to fairness, and it still requires editing.

It is all poker at the nuclear table. North Korea is hungry for a nuclear bomb. A neighbor on our block, Vernon got polio in Korea from a mosquito…and lived bitterly for the rest of his life over a battle for the 38th parallel. Why contend an imaginary line? I am sick of America's current fascination for empire… It is wrong headed and stupid…

Care about people…care about world citizenship. I would like to decide who lives and dies, but it is a private decision and a global vote.

But my mother is dead… in the casket in the front of the room. She moved off this mortal coil. And now, once again I'm an orphan of the sky. I must write a eulogy…say what I have to say.

Danny closed his journal, walked up to look in the casket again, then walked with Rich and Charlie into the lobby of the funeral home.

April 18, 2001

A cold gray wind rattles the windows and bare trees – gray upon gray outside – the winds of changes shift. But wind up early and hard. A gray breaking day. Mom dead. Her body unlike her in the casket last night. Drawn thin and tight around her skull…the curve of forehead strained and drained…not the round faced chubby Lil, but worn to death…quiet, exhausted. Death a nasty business – a getting through that must be gotten, but at the final price and all that's left is looking back. A mourning dove in the night and this morning the flight and caw of crows.

Breast cancer, more recently ovarian cancer and the brutality of electro-shock wore her down. I expect the gray and cold wind today – not the blue sky of dad's funeral. These are the pulleys of life, the clothes line upon which we are suspended – Alpha-Omega – birth-death. How we see the opposite and must say finally – it is both.

When I visited her at Christmas she saw trees dancing on the lawn outside. The daughter of artists. And so, the poet sees the world as it is and says it could be different. Let the poets among us sing and dance – the artistic life is the fullest life! She was a great mother. Has left me the comfort of hand crocheted Afghans…the encouragement of a loving Aquarius woman. But now to the funeral…

At the church, Rich, Charlie, Danny, Rich's two sons, and Charlie's two sons-in-law carried the casket to the altar. The altar was filled with yellow daffodils and white lilies as the organist accompanied singing of "Amazing Grace." Father Jerry, the family priest, invited Charlie's daughter to the altar to read from "Lamentations" and Rich's daughter to read from "Corinthians."

Danny's insides churned as he sat on the aisle, next to his mom's casket through the ceremony and sermon and songs. The incense the priest wafted over them felt hypnotic, as it reminded him of his fascination with High Mass and stained glass windows during his youthful allegiance to Catholicism. But, when Father Jerry signaled him to the altar he felt terror. His mouth went dry. The church was unfamiliar, the altar bigger than their Littletown church, the pulpit higher as he walked toward the microphone. But he felt he had to speak...for himself...and for the family.

As he walked to the pulpit, oddly, he remembered in fifth grade, when his mom told him there was a great writer named Daniel Maurice Roarke. He checked references in the library for days and told his mom he couldn't find him. "It will be you Daniel, when you write from your heart, not just your head," he heard her say as he reached the pulpit. He looked toward her casket and smiled. Then he looked at the crowd of family and friends. He swallowed hard several times as he adjusted the microphone. He wet his lips then started.

Mom
Lillian Roarke: Jan. 28, 1914 – April 15, 2001

Let's talk about love... Mom loved Dad throughout their fifty-seven years of marriage. She loved her three sons – happy to marry two off, wanting to let go of all three that way. She loved holding onto her five grandchildren, and one great grandchild, then letting them go back to their parents. She was happy to see three grandchildren already married...hoping for more marriages to come. And who knows how many great grandchildren...and beyond.

She met Dad at Rockaway Beach in 1932, when she was eighteen, on a blind date arranged by a friend with whom she worked at Gimbels. I wouldn't be telling this story, nor would you be listening, if she had not held onto Dad to marry in 1939.

Lily, as her mother called her, could be a stern teacher. I think partly, because she learned that life can be hard. She lost her father, a successful builder on Long Island, during her first year of life. Afterward, she saw hard times when her mother moved back to Ridgewood with three kids, to survive as a housekeeper, then an apartment manager. Mom also endured two World Wars and the Great Depression along the way. She learned it takes will to endure.

"Lily-babes", as Charlie used to call her, had a sense of humor, but was strong willed...qualities we Roarke's value. I remember a family hike to infamous Moffitt Beach from Lake Pleasant in the Adirondack Mountains, where our

family vacationed back in the Fifties. I think Rich and Charlie will agree that hike became a forced march as we kids whined about what felt like endless miles, spurred by the loving phrase, "Shut up and keep walking!" Afterward, that character building phrase became an amusing family slogan.

Mom showed her sense of humor and love often, but especially with our ill-tempered family dog, Spotty, who for years prowled under the kitchen table and attacked misplaced feet of three intimidated boys. All Mom would say is "Men!" and shake her head. But only Mom could love Spotty – whose legacy is three men unable to bond constructively with dogs. Charlie tried twice – with Pro and Nicko – but surrendered, and moved to cats. Seems like Ron and Jennifer can love a dog, but they have learned the dangers of letting Rich near Bailey. And, I suggest to Jeanne and Brad to monitor Charlie with Crackerboy, if you want a mentally healthy pet. My limit is turtles and fish.

The earthquake of Dad's death in '96 dazed Mom, but the after shocks wore her down. Eventually, she was unable to rebuild psychologically. I guess in great love, the Earth does move. The key is to ride the movements together, then learn to regain one's balance when love ends, and one must continue alone. This has been the lesson of Mom's past five years. Now she is free from the struggle.

I want to say thanks for Mom's love, hard work, and dedication during her life. These are noble qualities. I'll miss her intelligence, sense of humor, and her optimism from her belief that "If you put your mind to it, you can do anything." I'll miss the way she enjoyed sharing her excellent cooking and conversation with family and friends. But, also, I want to thank Rich and his wife Beth and their daughter Teri for their hard work, and especially Beth, for her dedication during the ever increasing challenges toward the end. These are measures of family love.

Now we can think of Mom and Dad together, because great lovers are inseparable. Love is the measure of one's life. Each love is independent, but both are more together. I think that knowing what to do after losing the love of her life was the problem Mom could not resolve, nor something anyone else could fully understand.

Mom struggled with holding on for five years since Dad died, confronting the overall that she could not grasp. But finally, after eighty-seven years, she has let go... We remain...as Mom's expanding family.

Clearly, Mom's life was her art. She dared and defied. But now it's time for us to move from holding on, to letting go. In Mom's memory, let's give each other a sign – a handshake or hug or kiss – to wish each other love on the new walk that starts here.

As Danny stepped down from the pulpit and walked across the altar, he saw people shaking hands, hugging and kissing. He walked to brother Rich and shook hands then kissed Beth on the cheek. He did the same with Charlie and Carol then patted his mother's casket as he returned to his seat. Afterwards, outside as they moved the casket into the hearse, Danny said, "We gotta go back to Moffitt Beach." Rich and Charlie agreed.

They planned the trip for the following summer, to mark the fiftieth anniversary of the Moffitt Beach hike. Rich drove Beth and Danny in his Mercedes from Long Island, up through Amsterdam to rendezvous with Charlie in Speculator. Danny brought a wad of black and white photos that his parents took during the trip that Beth found among their mom's belonging.

"It's the same road," Rich said, as they reached the center of Amsterdam.

"Pretty," Beth said.

"Scenic down town Amsterdam, Beth," Danny said, videotaping from the back seat.

"Speculator Department Store," Rich read from a sign north of town.

"How about stopping at the antique shop in that barn?" Danny asked.

"He doesn't stop," Beth replied, turning toward Danny.

"I know…just testing," Danny said, focusing the large wooden barn in his lens; then widening to include Rich intent on the road, he videoed the GPS screen.

The river was to their left on the two lane road as it weaved along side. The green hills elevating as they moved north.

"How did your Mom's sister meet Uncle Kent?" Beth asked.

"I think he came down to a wedding in New York," Rich answered. "This road is getting even windier."

"Yeah. Remember what Dad said, 'The guys who built this must have been following a snake.'"

As they passed through a cluster of buildings called Wells, Beth noticed a church. "Is there a Catholic church in Speculator?"

"Of course," Rich and Danny responded, "In Lake Pleasant."

"Then how can it be such a small town?"

"You wait," Danny added.

A while later Danny saw a red wooden sign with white letters, "Welcome to Speculator All Season Vacationland." The female GPS voice said, "Continue to follow the road." And within a few bends of the road, Beth read the sign, "Lake Pleasant."

"Oh, yeah, this is the lake," Rich said.

"Yep. There's the island."

A short way up the road, Rich pulled into Dreiser's, an old wooden hotel.

"Well...what are your first words?" Danny asked, focusing the camera.

Opening his door, Rich said, "It's just the way I always remember it."

As Rich and Beth got out, Danny videotaped the Dreiser's sign, "In Scenic Downtown Speculator." Charlie had arrived a short time before them. So the four of them got into Rich's car to find their aunt's house.

As they road along the west side of the lake Charlie said, "It's all tin roofs, so you know they get plenty of snow here. I was coming down this road, Route 8 for the last sixty miles."

"Route 8?" Rich asked.

"That's what we're on," Danny said.

"Oh, you came this way?" Rich said, a hand signal meaning from the opposite direction.

"Yeah. At *eighty* miles an hour! What a great road."

"It winds so much," Rich said, incredulously.

"That's what I loved about it. Great time. And Dreiser's is kinda nice."

"For what we need. It's only sixty a night, Charlie," Beth said.

"Oh, that's all? The owner, she kept saying, 'I'll keep this tab open'. I figured this'll cost me a million bucks when I leave."

"Sixty a night, Charlie," Beth repeated.

"Oh. OK. The owner, she's really nice. Oh, there's Moffitt Beach," Charlie said, pointing toward the sign. "So we walked to here?"

"From our cabin on the lake to Aunt Flo's house to that entrance," Danny said.

"We'll measure it on the way back," Rich added.

"But you don't know where Flo's house is?" Beth asked.

The brother's responded in unison, "We'll find it. Remember we walked all this."

As they continued on, Charlie said, "I don't believe we walked all this. No wonder we were ready to shoot them."

Suddenly the road ran unobstructed along the lake. Danny saw the white lodge at the south end. He grabbed the picture of them sitting together in the back seat of a rowboat, in height order Rich to Danny, as their mom rowed, the old lodge behind. He passed it around.

"This is the church," Rich said, pointing to his right.

"The Catholic church?" Beth asked.

"St. James Catholic Church," Rich said slowing to a stop. "Saturday four and five-thirty mass. Sunday at eight."

Charlie moaned, "We won't be there Sunday."

"No. Saturday," Rich replied.

"What else is there to do on a Saturday night?" Danny teased.

"We can go to dinner after church," Beth said, and the guys agreed.

"Yeah. And here's the golf course. I remember that," Rich said, pointing to his right.

"Golf courses he remembers. The rest of his life is meaningless. He has no clue where he's been," Danny teased.

"He doesn't remember me," Beth added. "He remembers golf courses."

Sounding hurt, Rich moaned, "Nooo."

As Rich continued on, Charlie and Danny noticed the old stone jail and the court house. Rich turned left onto South Shore Road.

"There's the court house. I remember the stone jail. Dad said if you're bad you go to jail," Danny said, excitedly.

"If you're mad you have to go to jail?" Charlie asked.

"No, *Bad*. Mad they bin you. Bad," he added, laughing.

"Dad always accused us that we were goin' to jail," Charlie added.

"Oh, that's the building where Uncle Kent worked on the trucks," Danny said, excitedly.

"How do you remember so much Danny?"

"Don't you Rich? Down on the right is Aunt Flo's house."

Watching through the windshield wipers under gray clouds and drizzle along the tree lined road, Danny said, "Uh, oh, here it is," as an old green wooden house with white trim appeared in a clearing. "That's it," he added, but was confused because it had no front porch, it's most endearing quality.

"No," Rich said, and kept driving.

"The prophet ignored...crying in the desert," Danny teased.

Danny handed Charlie a picture of his mom, dad, and uncle sitting on the back porch. Danny wore a horizontally striped shirt, holding a baseball glove above his head.

As they passed an upscale A-frame house, Beth pointed to it.

"No way," Charlie said. "They didn't have that kind of money. The biggest industry around here is poverty," he added, and everyone laughed.

Further down the road, Danny said, "I think that was it. We passed it. Oooh...wow...we *are* at the Bates Motel! The place without the porch is it. The one on blocks." A short distance later, on their left, a huge white wooden frame mansion appeared. "Yeah, we passed it," Danny added.

Charlie and Rich agreed as they recognized the huge white house, the biggest one on the lake, imposing from the small cabins around the lodge.

As Rich turned the car, the lake was visible through gray drizzle. In the distance, beyond the huge white house, the mountains appeared in layers of grays and muted greens.

"They move here in the Forties?" Charlie asked.

"Thirties," Rich replied.

"Well, your cousin Tommy was born in the early Forties," Beth said.

Danny tapped Charlie and said, "And so, Moffitt Beach – what you guys called a forced march in Nam, Charlie – must have been Fifty years ago."

"I guess."

"And so, I think we should call it parent abuse and sue the estate," Danny joked.

"He's the smart one," Rich said. "Sue the estate, what estate? We're still getting bills from doctors."

"Still getting bills? Unbelievable! Mom's been dead a year," Danny replied, surprised, still looking at the lake through the camera. "Oh, wow, look at the lake. The island at the north end. And the mountains in the background. Gorgeous! I guess this is the estate Mom and Dad left."

"This *is* gorgeous," Charlie said.

"Yeah. I remember that little island," Rich added.

Danny zoomed in toward the island as they moved. It sat tranquilly at the opposite end of the lake, a mile or so away, framed by calm gray water and layers of mountains. Danny remembered rowing with his brothers to the island as the group praised the beautiful setting.

"This must be the day we hiked," Danny said, and handed Charlie a photo of the family in front of the small cabin. Their mom and dad are standing behind them. Rich has a black cowboy hat on and Charlie is holding a long walking stick in one hand and a cowboy hat in the other. Danny has both hands around a walking stick.

Moments later, Rich pulled into the driveway of the old green house they passed.

"They removed the front porch. But here's the back porch," Danny said, as they all got out of the car.

"Yep. Remember when Aunt Flo warned us to watch out for the bears? There's the pump and the chicken coop," Charlie added, pointing.

"I remember the well and the chickens," Rich said, walking from the gravel driveway toward the thick grass in the back yard. The white wooden chicken coop, where Aunt Flo had them gather eggs in the morning, looked the same.

"Where's the big rock?" Beth asked, pointing to the picture of the three boys perched atop a boulder several times their height.

"Oh, no. That's at Moffitt Beach," Danny said.

"Look at that roof. Look at that roof. That wasn't like that," Charlie said, excitedly.

"No. That's a new tin roof," Rich answered.

Danny had Rich and Charlie in camera view. He widened the shot to include the worn old house, not much bigger than their parents' house in Litteltown. Paint was chipped from the old boards and the new boards near the cinder blocks were unpainted. The metal roof was a drab green in the overcast, but the house appeared to be in the process of being remodeled.

"What are your impressions, there, Rich?" Danny asked, laughing.

Rich walked toward him slowly, with his hands in his pockets, shaking his head, as he smiled. "All I can say is that we've come from humble beginnings."

"No doubt about that."

Surveying the back yard, his glasses set comfortably, his hands still in his pockets, he repeated, "This is unbelievable, unbelievable. Fifty years. Fifty years later!"

Danny handed him a photo of them near their apartment in the Bronx. Their mom, in sunglasses, is seated next to their dad's parents on a long wooden bench. Rich and Charlie in short pants with suspenders and long ties stand in front of Danny in a baby carriage. The next photo was the three boys in ties and sport coats wearing short pants. Their dad had Rich in one arm and Charlie in the other as Danny leaned back on his dad's lap. The next was of the three boys wearing baseball uniforms standing together with their hats and gloves.

Rich kept repeating, "Unbelievable," as he looked from the pictures to the house, as they walked toward the front.

With Rich, Beth and Charlie in the lens, Danny said, "That's where the porch was, but it's gone. It makes the house look so bare. Rich you were the *Monopoly* mogul on that porch. You used to always win."

"I was almost twice your age. Somebody had to do the math," he said, and laughed.

"This looks like my house," Charlie said. "The salt box look. I can see why we should add a porch. It makes the house," he added, taking a draw from his cigarette. "The metal roof must protect from the snow, just slides off. Wow, looks a lot smaller than fifty years ago."

"You guys are a lot bigger than you were fifty years ago," Beth said.

They stood in front of the house for a long time. As Danny videotaped them, he walked across the road toward the entrance to the lodge and cabins.

"Let's go to the McCarthy's. We want to see our friends the McCarthy's place," Danny said, and they returned to the car. "Go through here. That will take us down to the water."

The dirt road, which cut through an open hay field fifty years ago, had become tree filled. There were trailers mixed in with the old wooden cabins. But the lodge looked the same. They parked near the deck.

"Rich, this is private property," Beth said.

"They'll love Rich. He'll run for mayor. And we have all these photos, they're our *Get Out of Jail Free* pass," Danny said.

The rain stopped. It was still cool. As they walked onto the deck, Danny saw the raft, located where it was fifty years ago, then focused on Beth and Charlie.

"Why did they live here, Charlie?" she asked.

"They were just getting away. It must have taken a lot of *chutzpa*. They just said, fuck it, we're leavin', goin' to the mountains."

"It really is beautiful," she said, admiring the view.

Danny listened to them, but focused on the raft, then out to the mountains, feeling more comfortable here than any place on Earth. It amazed him how the years evaporated as he felt embraced by the mountains and lured to the island in the distance, images he loved as a kid. He felt Camus was right; suggesting this trip to his brothers was the "slow trek" to rediscover the few simple images that first opened his heart. He looked at the photo of their mom rowing the three boys, and one of them sitting on a boulder on the beach with their mom and dad, and one of Rich rowing the flat bottomed boat while Charlie and he sat.

"Well, Rich, what do you have to say about your trip to the mountains?" Danny asked.

"Just the way I remember it. Nothing changes in the mountains," Rich replied, hands in his pockets, enjoying the smile spreading across his face.

As the brothers laughed, Danny asked, "Charlie?"

"I'm amazed we're still alive," he said, a broad smile on his face. "Fifty years later. Fifty years later."

In the moment between the repeated number of years, Danny flashed on Charlie's Vietnam ordeal that cost him his leg, impressed with his brother's courage and endurance.

"And look, Adirondack chairs. But not as good as yours, Charlie," Danny said, sliding a chair toward him.

"Adirondack chairs all over the place!" Charlie said, lifting it by an arm.

His hands still in his pockets, Rich stood at the white wooden deck rail, "I remember swimming out to that raft many times."

Danny pulled out the photo of Charlie and him standing on the dock in jeans and T-shirts. Behind Charlie's cowboy hat, was the raft, where the mountains behind intersected.

"In those days it was a long way to the raft. And we have come a long way," Rich said.

Everyone laughed good-heartedly.

Charlie added, "The circle is not complete. The circle is not complete!"

"Let me get your picture?" Beth asked.

As they backed against the rail, Rich stood in the middle and put his arms on his brothers' shoulders. The three brothers smiled – in height order, from Danny to Charlie – the raft visible behind Charlie's shoulder.

As they walked to the lodge, Danny videotaped the raft in the distance, beyond the chairs and wooden rail. He extracted a photo of him and Charlie sitting on a bench against the rail, their mom smiling, wearing sandals and a dark blouse over dark slacks, her arms around them.

Inside the lodge, nothing changed. Danny was amazed that the bear was still on the piano in the back corner. The stone fireplace against the back wall had a fire in it, and the furniture looked like it had only gotten more comfortable over the years. The room looked smaller, but felt like a part of his life that would always be there, now that they'd come to see it and it remained as it had been when they were kids.

Back on the road, they headed toward Moffitt Beach.

"Tomorrow we'll walk it, Danny," Rich said as they approached the entrance.

"Yeah? I doubt it. But did Uncle Kent pick us up? I don't remember how we got back."

"I don't remember walking back," Charlie said.

"There it is. There's the turn off," Danny said. He handed Charlie a picture of the three of them next to their dad on the old dirt road to Moffitt Beach. They were wearing dungarees, horizontally striped T-shirts and black canvas sneakers. Each of them had a small pack over his shoulder. Their dad, in a collared short sleeve shirt and slacks stood between Danny and Rich next to Charlie.

"No wonder we grew up so tough," Charlie said, as they started down the road. "Holy cow! I can't believe we walked this."

"Yeah, we walked it," his brothers said in unison. "We still remember it."

"That was a long walk for little kids," Beth said, painfully.

"We're not gonna do it now, Beth. You think anybody in this car is gonna walk this tomorrow?"

"I jog five miles a day, Danny."

"But you were nine, Rich. I was five. Charlie was seven."

"It's a long walk. We're on three miles," Beth said.

"*Shut up and keep walking!*" Danny said, repeating the family phrase, and his brothers laughed.

"*It's just over this next hill. We're almost there,*" Rich said, recalling the encouraging phrases their parents repeated. "*Just over this hill.*"

"Oh, look, a caution sign. Caution, we got foot prints of three Roarke kids," Charlie said, laughing.

"Three point one miles," Rich said.

"They really made you walk?" Beth asked, with concern.

"*Shut up and keep walking!*" Charlie repeated.

"Why do you think we've turned out the way we have?" Danny teased.

"*We're almost there. Just over this hill,*" Rich repeated.

Danny handed Charlie the photo of the three of them on the boulder, with Rich in the middle. "That's a big boulder. Wimps couldn't climb it."

"I gotta believe, Danny boy."

"Three point five miles," Rich announced as they reached the beach. Rich parked the car. The Moffitt Beach Boys hurried down the beach to a wooden lifeguard stand at the water's edge. Rich climbed up toward the seat, while Charlie and Danny scrambled up the sides. Beth videotaped the cheers, saying into the camera, "They finally made it to Moffitt Beach, which hasn't changed much. They are really enjoying themselves. I've never seen them so happy."

Chapter 17: Bloom's Day

The following year, Danny videotaped the River Shannon as the plane descended to the airport. Below the clouds, in morning light, Ireland appeared as a patchwork of astounding greens. After landing, he realized he had no idea where he would go first.

He retrieved his luggage, hurried to the car rental counter and found the car in the small lot outside. The opposite placement of the steering wheel amused and confused him as he sat watching airport traffic pass by.

Eventually, after spreading the map on the seat to his left, he started the car. Beyond the airport, the countryside was stones piled in endless walls within walls, not random walls of Vermont, but centuries of rock collecting piled for huge distance and heights. Rolling hills became worn weathered mountains in the distance. A few miles from the airport he stopped along the highway to videotape a weathered castle overgrown by trees in a field crisscrossed with chest-high stone fences.

"Oh, Danny boy, pipes are calling," he yelled above passing traffic, as he panned the landscape with his camera and breathed cool air. Cars swished past him.

Back in the car, looking left to the map, he navigated roads for several hours. He was fascinated by the greens, not the chrome green of Oregon but deep varied greens in fields filled with sheep and cows contained within endless stone walls. He felt lured to Yeats' grave to see its famous view of Benbulben in Sligo County.

A narrow road wound to the cemetery. A huge Celtic cross marked a sight on the left, and the church to his right. He pulled into the small parking lot. In the distance, he saw the distinctive cleft of Bunbulben. He walked toward two men in the far corner digging a grave.

"What're you guys up to?" he asked.

"Ah, layin' another soul to rest tomorrow," one digger said.

"Dig well… Where's Yeats' grave?" he asked, as he videotaped them.

"Ah, the great poet. His grave's over there, son. And ya can see Benbulben as well from there," the other digger said, as he heaped a shovelful of dark earth onto the pile.

Danny walked toward the grave, looking back to watch the men dig, then focused his camera on the gray slab as he read the carved inscription:

> *"Cast a cold Eye*
> *On Life on Death.*
> *Horseman pass by"*
> *W B YEATS*
> *June 13ᵗʰ 1865*
> *January 28ᵗʰ 1939*

"No doubt, he's buried in sight of Benbulben," he said into the microphone, as he panned to his right over several graves and beyond the stone wall to the mountain.

He focused from Bunbulben to the grave diggers then Yeats' tombstone.

"I landed in Ireland a few hours ago. Suddenly I'm at Yeats' grave in Benbullben's shadow. The poet of Irish mythology and astrology. One of the world's greatest poets. Buried where he wanted to be, with the epitaph he wrote. But what does it mean? Is Yeats saying he lived and died, and so, the horseman must continue the journey? We all look for a father, a birth father or a spiritual father. He is definitely to be admired. And it's his birthday Friday. Another Gemini. It's 2003, if I got the math right, he'd be a hundred and thirty-eight, and three days later I turn fifty-six. Wow."

Danny reread the epitaph. He thought about his dad and mom's grave. He looked toward the gravediggers and thought about his own death. He wondered how he would be remembered.

Afterward, he continued on the winding road from the cemetery toward Lough Gill, to find the Isle of Innisfree. The narrow road twisted up several rises with cows in the meadows below. After several stops along the roadside to videotape the fields and stone walls and animals and small lakes, he stopped at a castle perched on Lough Gill. The cold wind white capped the lake surrounded by broad brazen mountains uninhabited under low hanging clouds, their gray underbellies pressed toward slate gray water churned by winds scented with open country.

Danny looked for the Isle of Innisfree as he surveyed the lake. It reminded him of Lake Pleasant in the Adirondacks, and the journey back to Moffitt Beach with Rich and Charlie last summer. He understood how Yeats would be drawn to the rugged land and water. With a castle turret to his right, he brought the small island in the distance into focus with his camera.

As the captain of the water bus advertising a poetic tour of the lake approached, Danny asked, "Where is Innisfree?"

"It's in one's imagination," the captain replied, and winked.

Danny looked at him and smiled. The Irish were enchanting, he thought, as he looked beyond the thin dark haired man to the water bus advertising the Yeats' tour.

"I coulda sworn Hemingway caught a marlin, and Camus knew the invincible sun. I believe Mark Twain sailed the Mississippi. You mean when Yeats said he would build a cabin on Innisfree, there was no island?"

"Ay there's an island. But he never built a cabin there. That was all imagining. He was paying homage to your American writer Henry David Thoreau, but Innisfree is down the lough," he said, and pointed west.

"Definitely bigger than Thoreau's Walden Pond. Thanks," Danny said, and the image of the island in Lake Pleasant popped into his mind.

Standing at this lake felt like a pilgrimage to feel kinship with his ancestors. Looking toward the small island, travel markers flashed in his mind. From New York to Vermont then to Ithaca. Illinois to Oregon, then Florida. Back to Ithaca. Then Michigan. Again to Florida. In a life of travel, he planned to turn fifty-six on Bloom's Day in Dublin. Here at Lough Gill, the guide said that Innisfree is in his imagination. He remembered Camus' quote about the slow trek to rediscover one's heart through art. Yeats' Lough Gill was his Lake Pleasant, that simple.

"Thanks for reminding me about my imagination, Captain."

"Keep it opened," he said, and saluted.

Danny waved then walked back to his little red Fiat to continue his journey.

A short distance after he made a turn south along the lake, he saw a sign that read:

WELCOME TO DROMAHAIR
Seat of the O'Rourkes
Lords of Breffne

Startled to see a variation of his family name at the entrance to a town he'd never heard of felt like being drawn further into a leprechaun inspired tale. Several pubs, shops, homes, a post office and hotel framed the narrow road into Dromahair. He parked under the Guinness sign in the small lot in front of Breffne Center Hotel. As he walked along the road, he read a variation of his family name highlighted on several historical markers. He walked the main street amazed and stopped into The Blue Devon for his first Guinness in Ireland. The female barkeep finished by carving a shamrock in the tan foam with the final flow from the tap before handing it to him.

"Where in America are you from?" she asked.

"You mean my brogue ain't so good, eh? Florida."

"I lived thirteen years in New York."

"I was born there. In Harlem," Danny added.

"I avoided that part," she responded, smiling.

"Small world indeed. I guess there aren't *six degrees of separation*. Maybe none."

"Separation is a terrible thing. How's the Guinness?"

"I love it, especially the shamrock. *Erin go Bragh*! How'd you do that?"

"A bit of Irish magic," she said, with a short laugh.

He stayed the night at the Breffne Center Hotel and had an Irish breakfast the following morning. Afterwards, he walked the main street and read the signs about the O'Rourkes. Along a narrow sidewalk on a small bridge that took the road out of town, Danny met a red haired woman in a black sweater. He asked about the O'Rourkes.

"Are you an O'Rourke?"

"I may be related," he said, "but who knows really. I just wanted to know more about them."

"Oh, right. Well, the O'Rourkes were the royal family of this area. The Kingdom of Breffne. And O'Meracoo was the King of Lenster in the east part of Ireland. And Dervogilla eloped with O'Meracoo, the King of Lenster. So this enraged her husband. And he got his army together. The local yokels. And they went across to Lenster to fight O'Meracoo. So O'Meracoo sought the help of the King of England. And so, that resulted in the Norman invasion of Ireland."

"Oh, wow," Danny said, as he continued to videotape her.

"So Dervogilla, who we are commemorating on this bridge," she said, gesturing toward the name carved on the small bridge, "was really the cause of all that," she added, with a whimsical smile.

"Certainly no Penelope. She sounds like Helen of Troy," Danny said, amazed.

The red haired woman nodded. "Well, a bit like her. Yes. And she was also the, ah, patron of the Abbey. There's a Franciscan Abbey in the village. The ruins," she said, pointing across the road as another car whooshed past over the bridge. "There were all little kingdoms at that time."

"Wow… Are you the town historian?"

"No. I have the craft and specialty shop up there," she said, pointing in the direction she'd been walking when Danny stopped her to ask about the O'Rourkes. "I finished walking three and a half miles that I do in the morning," she added.

"Well, I appreciate it. Thanks a lot."

"My pleasure," she said and continued her walk.

Standing on the bridge over the small river, Danny talked as he videotaped. "So look around. Build your castle, but choose your women wisely, for they run off with others. It happened before. It can happen to you. Welcome to Breffne," he said, then focused the camera on the name carved in stone on the bridge, DERVORGILLA 1152 A.D. "So, there's the tale at the O'Rourke's castle," he said, amused, as he videotaped the water running gently under the bridge from an expanse of farmland and mountains in the distance.

It felt weird to find a town he'd never heard of that was linked to his family name. His father knew only that his father and mother came from Ireland, but there was no connection to the history he just heard. No one could trace the name beyond his grandparents. Danny found it bizarre that suddenly the family name was linked to the English invasion of Ireland and the history of animosity between the nationalities, but it was also terribly exciting.

He continued around the lake looking for Innisfree and noticing how Benbulben dominated the landscape from above intruding over the rolling hills when the cover of trees gave way to views to the west. He found Innisfree through a cover of trees on the southeast side of the lake. He parked his little red Fiat next to a stone fence and walked back along the road through the trees. It was a small tree filled island at most a few hundred yards off shore. It reminded him of the island in Lake Pleasant at the north end of the lake. It amazed him how far he'd traveled to see it and the surprise was not seeing it, but hearing about Dervogilla and the O'Rourkes. Yeats dominated the lake country, but he got an insight into his family history and the beauty of Ireland and its people.

"Walking from Innisfree the left is right and the right is left," he said, as he videotaped the road on his way back to the car.

He looked at the map and decided to go to Connemara to see the marble, some of which his parents brought back as the handle of the letter opener he loved. Danny stopped the car along the open road and videotaped the fog and cloud shrouded mountains. Excitedly, he played Kate Smith singing "Danny Boy" and caught it on camera as he enjoyed the cool cloudy sky. "Sing it Kate. Ireland," he said, panning three hundred and sixty degrees around him,

"Ireland, can't see the mountains for the fog....but Danny boy...ah, yes, the pipes...and the mountains and glens and graves...and peace."

Several miles later, he laughed as he played Bob Dylan's "Don't Think Twice, It's Alright" and he stood in the drizzle to video ruins of an old stone house along the road. Further on, he was overwhelmed by the primitive beauty as he stopped opposite a fence surrounding sheep that dotted a mountain of barren rock and huge rhododendron bushes with red flowers.

Over the mountains, he was tense as he drove the single lane between rock outcroppings and sheer cliffs in cold windy rain. But he reveled in the whistle of wind and rain as he stood on a cliff to videotape small islands off the coast. In Clifden, he delighted in the feel of the green marble as he selected marble shamrock key chains he bought for gifts. He was fascinated by endless hills and rocks through the interior of brooding mountains and valleys filled with sheep. He loved the primitive and elemental way fog and mist shrouded land in grays and greens as it unwound in front of him.

He continued to Dingle through Galway and Limmerick as the rain cleared. He pressed on to Tralee because of the song "Rose of Tralee." He stayed at a hotel in Tralee that night and was on the road to Dingle the following morning.

He drove along the bay up into the mountains and stopped to videotape a gorgeous expanse of valley that ran to the bay carved by hedges and trees into wide fields with sheep and cattle in the distance. Excitedly, he drove over the hills along the two lane road with views to the bay to the south and the neighboring peninsula. Everywhere he looked and everything he saw exhilarated him. Stopping to view pastures, he saw an old stone castle along the southern tip of the Dingle peninsula open to the sea, as if a setting for a romantic novel.

He kept on toward Dingle, a fishing village with a quiet harbor surrounded by hills. He parked, suddenly lured into the aquarium. He was intrigued by the chestnut haired blue eyed hostess at the front desk. Flirting, he handed her the map.

"What should I see?"

"You should go to Puck Fair where the goat is king."

"You say Puck?" he asked, teasing then smiling broadly.

"No not from Shakespeare," she said, her eyes acknowledging his other meaning.

"You want me to see a goat fair?"

"Might be good for you," she said, and smiled. "OK, maybe not. Have you heard of the Great Skellings?" she asked, tracing her finger along the peninsulas on the map. "It's a beautiful area. You got out to Terrace Cevine and then Valencia Island. Then you go to Puffin Island. And out here is the Great Skellings."

"That's all water…are you kidding? Can I get there by car?"

"Americans. No, no, it's out in the ocean. It's gorgeous though." She shook her head and smiled. "Are you faint of heart?"

"No my heart's fine," he said, infatuated.

"Well, you do go out in a dinghy while waves rock you up and down," she continued, moving her hand up and down, smiling as she caught his eye several times.

"You've done it?"

"I haven't done it myself, personally," she said, and they both laughed, as she looked apologetic. "But people have and lived to tell. So it's do-able."

"I'm lookin' for land bound stuff," he said, catching her eye, smiling about her final words.

"Oh you coward."

"I'm trying to get to Cork where my people left hundreds of years ago. I got to get to Dublin by Saturday."

"Got to be in Dublin tomorrow? Then Dingle might be your only peninsula."

They both laughed.

"I'm no expert, but you don't have much of a brogue. What's your name? From Dingle?"

"No brogue, you're right. My name is Donna. I'm from L.A. I saw Dingle on a Rick Steves PBS travel show. I came on vacation three years ago. I've stayed."

"Dingle Donna. Gutsy move. Like it?"

"Love it."

"If not the Great Skelligs, where could I get lunch?"

"Lord Bakers. A great little restaurant around the corner. Think you can make it that far?"

"Yep… You are a wise ass from L.A. I'll try. Thanks. Great meeting you," he said, and they shook hands as she returned the map. He had lunch and thought about returning to meet her, but it felt better to leave it be and enjoy her courage and charm without forcing anything.

He traveled west of Dingle to an old stone fort. A young girl selling tickets to it in a small white shed told him that it was built to protect the people from the barbarians. As he walked out to the stone mounds on the sheer cliff a hundred feet above the water, he talked into the microphone as he videotaped.

"The people built the fort she said. To protect them from the barbarians. So, who are the barbarians? I'd like to know who I was walling in or walling out."

He stood and looked at thousands of rocks piled together dating back hundreds of years. Shaking his head sadly, he acknowledged it as the way of history. He stood for a while looking, then headed back toward Dingle. Passing through Dingle, he was drawn toward Dingle Donna, but decided to appreciate her memory and not stop. He went to Blarney.

He got to the Blarney Hotel by early afternoon. There was an enthusiastically monitored soccer match on television in the hotel pub. He smiled as he watched for a while, feeling at home in Ireland, nostalgic for his soccer career that never bloomed. He watched it for a while, chatting with several spectators, then went to unpack in his room. He was eager to go to Blarney Castle to kiss the stone.

The castle was old and worn. The tight winding stairs were a challenge. His breath was short by the time he reached the top, where people were looking over the walls and turrets or into the hollow core.

He stood admiring the view, then walked to where several people were being helped to kiss the stone, assisted by a wiry gray haired attendant.

"Get your help?" Danny asked, as he offered his camera to a fellow who had just kissed the stone. "Just push that button," he said then went to lay back and grab the vertical bars embedded in stone. He leaned back and kissed the darkened stone.

When he got up, the fellow handed him the camera.

"Didn't work," he said, apologetically.

"OK. Try again. Try this button."

"Oh, the red button, the one you pointed to."

"Never trust an Aussie," his friend said, and they all laughed.

Danny leaned back and kissed the stone a second time. When he stood up, the fellow returned the camera. The playback showed him in his green sweater being supported by the gray haired Irishman as he kissed the aged stone, like his father had years before, but no scraped nose for him.

"You guys feel any more eloquent since kissing the stone?" Danny asked.

"We came all the way from Australia. I hope it works."

"Only the Irish could pull off an international scam like this. Gotta love my people."

"You're Irish?"

"I am now…" he said, and shook each of their hands. "Thanks, guys. Good day, mates."

The old castle intrigued him. He photographed the tower and the stone and walked the grounds. Out by the stream, he was surprised by a sacrificial altar and wondered eerily what or who was sacrificed on it. Afterwards, he explored the winding narrow dungeon with the camera's macabre greenish night view light, happy to get out and head to the pub.

Outside the pub, he met several fellows talking about soccer. A young girl and boy were on the town square playing soccer with a younger boy. The older boy played keep away from both of them as Danny videotaped and a group of lads were standing outside the pub as the constable walked past. Everything felt charming. A guy who looked like Babe Ruth said, "Take my picture."

"This is going back to America. OK with that?"

"I love America," he slurred.

He put his arms around two guys flanking him.

"Alrighty, alrighty, alrighty," he repeated. "What's your name?"

"Danny... So you guys know each other?"

"He's our manager."

"Soccer players?"

"Yes. He was a great player," the light haired fellow said, and walked into the crowded pub.

Standing with a beer in his hand and squinting through his round face and puffy eyes, Babe Ruth put his arm around a woman walking by.

"Danny, meet Mrs. Conkie, she owns the restaurant across the street. She has five daughters."

"I have six daughters," she said, correcting him, with a quick pat to his face.

"Six daughters, no sons. She's my best fucking friend in the world. I was her butcher. She's known me since I was about six inches," he said, and they both laughed.

Danny imagined it meant something about sex, but he did not want to know more. "You kept him away from your daughters?" They laughed. Then Danny asked, "He a better butcher or soccer player?"

"Well he's like my son," she said, hugging him.

Babe Ruth interrupted saying, "She's like my mother. She took care of me. And she knows I had the most goals scored ever. Ninety goals in five games."

"What? Ninety goals in five games?" Danny repeated, thinking Blarney is the perfect town for this guy, and meeting him on Yeats' birthday was epic poetry.

As Mrs. Conkie excused herself, the light haired fellow returned through the crowd and put his arm around his coach.

"Danny. I just want to say, he's a great manager and he was a better player. I hate to use language. But as a player, he was a dirty bastard. And with that I will leave."

As the player laughed and turned to walk away, Danny pictured his red card for "language" that got him thrown out of his final Spartan game. He realized how he missed the excitement and camaraderie of soccer, and how much it was part of Ireland but not America, that difference bothered him.

The village green was still light after ten o'clock as the moon started to rise. Danny videotaped it. It was a small town and hotel, but he liked the international flavor from the castle tourists and the local people he met on the streets and in the pubs.

Around eleven thirty, he saw the moon rising full over the village square with the Blarney Hotel to his left. It felt like a good omen the night before his trip to Dublin for Bloom's Day.

Walking back to the hotel, he felt a hit on the back of his head, telling him to wake up, that there was far more to life than he was allowing himself to experience. This trip showed he needed to be out of the U.S. This mostly rural country was beautiful and friendly. As a member of the European Union they were happy. And as he heard often in the pubs, as soon as people recognized him as an American, "We're not involved in the Iraq War. Why do you people want to conquer the world?"

The next day he drove through County Cork to Dublin, through land more rural and affluent than he imagined. He felt connected to the beautiful land having expected potato famine poverty that brought his grandparents to New York a hundred years before.

Dublin was an intriguing twist of bustling old streets that confused him as he struggled to find his hotel. After checking in, he took the map with him to walk to St. Patrick's Cathedral. He sat in the church and videoed it as he wrote in his journal.

June 15, 2003

First stop St. Patrick's. Four Euros to enter. The architecture and stained glass that impressed me as a kid sitting in the first row of St. Brendan's in the Bronx impresses me here. The art and architecture and philosophy of truth…the grand design captured in a butterfly wing.

St. Patrick drove snakes out of Ireland. Their patron saint. And so, as I consider my main character for _My Block_ – a novel about everyone and everything I know – church and religion are key. This pilgrimage is to Dublin but Rome is on the horizon. The pagan temples of the Mayans and Druids and Apollonian temples of the Greeks all to sort life's mystery. But this is transcendent glory.

Dedicated sculptors and glass makers and masons. My meditation in St. Mary's back at State in '69 still haunts.

We each choose to go our own way in this cosmic odyssey. Hemingway declared the rule that it starts with a true sentence; everything develops from there. My main character will have to be the impatience of youth, the indulgence of passion, and the confusion of choice. But with at least one close friend. For me it's Antonio...the one person in the world who knows me so well he calls my stupidity and explains what to do. My character will have no judgment, only talent needing to be expressed, and passion to be directed...

As I leave, I find St. Pat's is Anglican. The ticket taker doesn't even know where the Catholic Church is. What a scam. And he doesn't even know if Jonathon Swift and his woman Stella ever married, although he insisted Swift was buried standing up, right near the ticket booth. Right!

St. Augustine's was the only Catholic church he found as he walked the streets enjoying the easy going friendly town and chatting with people. He videotaped fans leaving a soccer match and walked the Ha'Penny Bridge to see a mime out front of a pub. He walked through the Temple Bar that appeared in James Joyce's *Ulysses,* chatting with folks as he videotaped, feeling alive as if a scribe for everyman living in what he called the "cosmic odyssey." He continued on to Trinity College, impressed by the Henry Moore sculpture. As he videotaped the George Salmon provost sculpture dated 1904, he realized it was the year James Joyce set *Ulysses* to commemorate the date he met his great love. Time marked the buildings with dark water stains. But he was surprised to see the American sculptor Calder's huge metal piece on the green outside, as he felt lured into the Book of Kells exhibit.

Across from Trinity College, he started chatting with a bouncer standing in the doorway of a pub called Judge Roy Beans.

"How good is David Beckham?"

"Ay. He's the wealthiest sportsman in the U.K.. He captained the English World Cup team. Had ego problems with his coach Alex Ferguson. You've probably heard about the famous incident when Ferguson kicked a football boot and cut Beckham?"

"Yes... I guess every man is in competition with every other man in the world, since he won his first sperm contest in the womb, and wants to win them all," Danny said, testing the fellow.

"Interesting way to put it. But think about it. On the national team. An icon in the UK. And your coach kicks a boot at your head. He had to get steri-strips to close the wound. Might be disillusioned."

"I guess that's why he took the forty million to go to Milan... But is he worth it?"

"He's excellent skills. Doesn't produce a world beating goal every match, like Rinaldo."

"How does he compare to Eusebio and Pele?"

"Pele or Maradonna are that small clutch at the pinnacle of the profession."

Danny stood video taping as they spoke while people came and went from the pub.

"Ay, look over there. He plays for Blackburn Rovers. That's Daemean Duff, talisman for the Irish team."

Danny looked as the slightly built fellow walked across the street from the pub.

"He's the captain of the national team."

"Better than Beckham?" Danny asked, as the conversation about soccer players being national heroes and making millions of dollars continued to astound him.

"You never know. Give him a few years. But Beckham is brilliant at what he does and the boss kicks shoes at your head, surely he got disillusioned."

"Is he hyped...with all the stuff about his ex-Spice girlfriend?"

"Ah, certainly, he gets publicity, but watch him on the field."

"I will someday...thanks," Danny said and walked on, thinking about how different Europe was from America.

A few blocks later, Danny saw the Italian woman he met on the university campus walking in the street.

"How do you like Dublin?"

"I love Dublin."

"What will you do tonight?" he asked, the camera an invitation to talk with anyone, as if his life had become that of a video scribe.

"I will do shopping."

"And bring it home? Where are you from?"

"Florence, Italy. Then I will visit the pubs and discos."

Danny was tantalized by her dark eyes and long curly dark hair and her openness. They chatted for a while and he wished her luck and walked on. He passed a man in a turban at the entrance to an Indian restaurant.

"You have curry?"

"Yes, of course."

"Irish lamb?"

"Of course."

"I think tonight I'd like an Irish lamb sacrificed," Danny said, shaking the man's hand and walking in for dinner.

June 15, 2003 10:30 p.m.

And so I sit in the Khyber Restaurant after eating Irish lamb sacrificed in curry. This is life on the Emerald Isle. The lambs live a life of tending for sacrifice. And today, I was "paparazzi" photographing everyone everywhere and then some young Irish footballer near Trinity College. He is their World Cuppper…and bouncers talk about soccer and money… Like the T-shirt on a young woman on the Ha'Penny Bridge "Love Sex Money". That says it all.

My Block will soon write itself after much weeping and laughter. Joyce's wife said Jimmy used to sit in his room laughing about what he wrote. Let me be crude and gleeful. Let me enjoy the male for what we are and the female too… Yes – a scandal. Me, paparazzi…but a camera is so much easier than the hard flow of words that can never grasp the range of vision – but occasionally, the depth of emotion. Let that be my epiphany for the day, for this trip. I am international… In an hour and a half I will be fifty-six in Dublin.

Afterwards, he continued to walk the streets and videotape the street musicians and anyone interesting he passed. He chatted with a clarinet player about her travels through Europe. He felt the city alive with artists playing out their lives. He was fascinated. He followed a walking tour about the Irish Rebellion of 1916 for a while then continued back to the Central Hotel for the night.

The following morning was Bloom's Day, his birthday, June 16, 2003. He had breakfast at the hotel and walked to the Writer's Museum and then the James Joyce Museum. A crowd was gathered and a group of actors were performing on top of a double-decker bus next to a James Joyce look-alike, complete with eye patch and hat.

One fellow in a yellow terry cloth bathrobe kept anointing himself from the glass he held filled with dark brown Guinness. The other man on top of the bus wearing a suit kept swinging a sign that read "Censored" as the first one spoke.

"I could fly like the wind from the top of Mt. Olympus in Ithaca at the gateway of Ulysses' house," he continued, pushing away the "Censored" sign.

Inside a group was gathered around a man reading from *Ulysses*.

Danny videotaped as he listened and watched people drinking Guinness in the morning as the reader continued reading Joyce's exquisite work.

He wandered off after a while, exhilarated that the city was alive with James Joyce ninety-nine years after the novel was set. He walked around the block back to the Writer's Museum and chatted with a gray haired fellow welcoming people to the museum.

"What's the appeal of Guinness?"

"Some say it's because it's made from the Liffy water."

"You mean that river?" Danny asked, pointing back toward the bridge he just crossed. "Nobody drinks Harp?"

"Guinness is the favorite. We have a saying about Harp. Drink Guiness and clean paint brushes with Harp."

"I guess that says it all. I'll try some more Guinness. Thanks."

Danny walked back toward the bridge, past the Charles Steward Parnell Memorial. There was a James Joyce sculpture on a side street, complete with hat and cane where folks were taking pictures.

He walked and videoed and chatted with anyone who caught his attention. A young couple from America told him they just came from Portugal. The blond girl said, "We loved the Algave Coast. You should see it."

Danny agreed, "I should."

As they parted, he continued on, past the Trinity Theatre and soccer shops and street musicians. An old man near the sculpture of Molly Malone sang, "Cockles and mussels alive alive oh." Smiling as he sang along while videotaping the musician, the whole town and day and his own life felt alive since the smack he felt at the back of his head that night in Blarney.

He found a garden shop and asked about shamrocks.

"We have them," the fellow behind the counter said.

"Can I take them to America?"

"As long as there's no Ert," the older heavy set man next to Danny said.

"No Ert?" Danny asked.

"No Ert. No Ert," he repeated, insistently.

"Oh, Earth? No Earth? What conditions do they need?"

The man behind the counter said, "We plant in June and July for following March."

Danny bought several packets of seeds with a bright green shamrock on them, smiling as he left, repeating the word "Ert!"

On the way back to the hotel, he stopped in a gallery displaying a painting of James Joyce in the window.

"The painter is saying James Joyce is still important in Dublin?" Danny asked the gallery owner as he entered.

"Everyone's saying it. He's a great writer."

"Where is the tower where *Ulysses* starts?"

"Head out to Sandy Cove. James Joyce lived in one of the Martello towers built to protect against Napoleon invading Ireland. They made it into a museum. You'll have a good time out there."

Danny found a cab and headed out.

After asking the cabbie to take him to the Joyce Museum at Sandy Cove, Danny asked, "What do you think about the Beckham trade?"

"Well, Barcelona offered him 40 million."

"To play soccer...wow," Danny said, amazed by the amount, thinking back to his contract with the Spartans that would have paid him a hundred dollars a game. "So he's that good?"

"Well, Real Madrid matched it. They think so. You are interested in James Joyce?"

"I love a town that celebrates a writer. And *Ulysses* was considered by the literati as the greatest novel of the Twentieth Century. The century is over.... So, I guess he won."

"He was a great writer. Yes. I've read it. You came to Ireland for Bloom's Day?"

"I came to see Ireland. My grandparents came from Ireland. But I timed it for my birthday, which happens to be Bloom's Day."

"Today is your birthday! Great luck to be born on Bloom's Day, especially if you're a writer."

"Well, I write..." Danny said, humbly. "I wrote my dissertation on Hemingway and Camus. I like a plot and characters...action... *Ulysses* is hundreds of pages of brilliant writing. But I can't tell what's going on. Homer's *Odyssey* I follow a lot easier. Actually, I think *The Great Gatsby* is a better read. It came in second on the literati's list. I can see the characters and houses and action. With *Ulysses*, no idea... But clearly brilliant. Joyce's *Portrait of the Artist* came in third...two in the top three. Great writer. But being a Catholic boy, I understand *Portrait...*"

"Have you ever read *To Kill a Mockingbird*? A great American novel."

"Yes... I agree... Atticus Finch is a wonderful character. Gregory Peck, who played him in the movie, just died, since I've been in Ireland. Great actor."

When they got to cove around ten-thirty, the sun was descending into a massive gray cloud above calm water in the huge bay. People were swimming in the cove. He asked the cabbie to wait and walked toward the round stone tower where the novel started. He looked from the massive tower to the water and sky, listening to the sea gulls, some floating on the breeze others scouring the shoals below.

June 16, 2003 10:30 p.m.

Today I am fifty-six. I hear the gulls cry. I am home.

June 16, 1904 was Bloom's Day. But I have come to Ireland to free my soul, to arouse my voice – the gulls speak in the voice of gull, but the writer must speak in his own voice. Ulysses must travel his own journey.

I am a man on a journey around the world – through the universe. I do not speak gull, but I hear their voice…

Ninety-nine years ago, Bloom was a second Ulysses…the wandering Jew… And Joyce, the wandering Catholic, on a day's journey… We are each Ulysses. My Block will be a third Ulysses…by the third child of a third child…born when mom was thirty-three. My Irish roots, my wild Irish eyes and soul. Begorra!

His bladder full, Danny stood next to the bushes near the locked gate and gravel driveway of the museum and relieved himself. He felt it was fitting tribute to a great writer and something Joyce would appreciate, having written about it in *Ulysses*. It was spontaneous, but it reminded him of when he mooned Mark Twain's grave as Maureen snapped his jokester grin and bare butt back in 1985.

Afterwards, he headed to another pub celebrating Bloom's Day with claret and gorgonzola. Everything Irish enchanted him. When he flew out the next day, he packed the shamrock seeds and piece of sod he dug from Blarney Castle in his camera bag, thinking about the leprechaun his parents gave him, smiling.

When he got home, he contracted to put an emerald green metal roof over his quaint Cape Cod in Palm City. He admired the workers' craftsmanship on the steeply pitched roof. It completed the transformation inside to earn being called Dr. Danny Boy's Bed Breakfast & Grove. A week after it was finished, he went, with his video-camera, to his niece Teri's wedding in New York. When he returned, Danny was convinced that the green roof confirmed he was over lust, content to write about others finding love.

Chapter 18: Newport Wedding

June 17, 2004

A plane leveling toward New York. Yesterday I turned 57 on the hundredth anniversary of Joyce's Ulysses and celebrated with close friends. Now off to Ryan and Diane's wedding Saturday, June 19th. The second family wedding in a year. Twenty-nine hundred years after Homer's Ulysses returned home to Penelope. The Roarke's must rely on this final marriage. Ryan, my favorite of this generation, is now the last one able to continue the family name...

I wanted a woman I cared about enough to take to this wedding... Caroline's erotic Scorpio magnetism attracted me after niece Teri's wedding to Sean last year. And so, with my new green metal roof, I've got a roof over love & lust, but mostly lust in my first sexual encounter since the previous Millennium. Sad it never developed to love, but a woman who believes a great relationship requires separate bedrooms and bathrooms cannot be Penelope.

I will see love and that must be enough. I must accept that I will never marry. This is the final wedding of my brothers' children and I remain uncle... Oh, Danny Boy the pipes are calling...

It's time to start that novel I thought about back in Tampa, when Maureen and I were writing Costa del Sol. This one has to be about everything and everyone I know. I like the title My Block. I just gotta start it and change the characters' names when I get it finished. For now, I'm gonna be Danny Roarke and everyone else can be who they are until I get through it...

MY BLOCK
Chapter 1: Wedding Anyone?

Worried about setting off the alarm, I asked a security guy about my camera and belt. He said, "Put the camera on the conveyer. Don't worry about your belt." But I took it off, along with my pocket watch, keys, wallet, cell phone and shoes and piled them in the plastic bin…basically, I was all but strip-searched, knowing I get one chance through.

We got out on time. Unable to nap, I'm in my journal…

At my birthday party last night, I so enjoyed Tyrella perking up to say "Jimmy!" as James Galway's "Danny Boy" started on the stereo as we all sat in my living room. An amazing Leo woman, whose father discovered James Galway and helped develop his talent. There are no degrees of separation unless we make them.

Now sketching pond planters and a pedestal for a table. But really starting My Block. I'm writing this novel because maybe a woman who truly understands me will read it and we'll meet. I believe that artists make things to be loved but do it because we must.

First a list of numbers corresponding to each chapter. Across the top of the page the astrological signs. Slowly, recording the important women in my life and their signs. Results of my research about love and lust. I've had encounters with women of every sign. That simple. And the ending "one works and hopes…" I see no other way to end it…

The guy next to me is reading USA Today and drinking Skyy vodka – definitely the right in-flight drink, because the name makes more sense through blurred vision.

"I had enough to drink last night, but I haven't seen a USA Today in a long time. Could I see it after you finish?"

He stared at me for a while and finally said, "OK."

I paged through it lackadaisically, until I saw a picture of the Pope. It was about the controversy over whether priests can refuse communion to politicians who support abortion rights. But what really caught my attention were statistics they quoted. The writer claimed twenty-five percent of Americans called themselves Roman Catholics. That translated to about sixty-four million, which seemed low, since there are over three hundred million in the U.S., but, whatever.

More interesting was that ninety percent approved abortion and only ten percent opposed it, which is the Church's stand. Reading it, I'm thinking I would be part of the ten percent. But when my beliefs didn't fit the religion, I gave up the religion. Seems most American Catholics disagree with the Pope but still call themselves Catholics. I guess we each interpret the world our way!

It all seemed very confusing to me, that's why I keep at this authenticity stuff. I mean, if one doesn't agree with the Pope about abortion or capital punishment or birth control or euthanasia or homosexuality, why stay Catholic? Is it because people need a place to celebrate birth, death and marriage?

The short of it was that ninety percent favor abortion, seventy percent favor capital punishment, two-thirds favored euthanasia, and two-thirds favored birth control. A third said homosexuality was "not wrong at all." The Church condemns it, but has priests demonstrating it. My feeling is that the Catholic Church needs help.

That's not to say Luther and his Protestant Reformation ever actually reformed things. But I'll complain about that throughout My Block. *As I finished the article, we hit turbulence and the Skyy guy looked seriously concerned.*

"OK if I tear out this article?"

He frowned. "You Catholic?"

"I used to be."

"You fish eaters never made sense to me. Take it," he said, then finished his drink as the plane groaned.

As the turbulence increased, tensely, the flight attendant repeated that the captain had the seat belt sign on. I ripped out the article, folded it then tucked it in my journal.

Mulling it over, I realized that I agreed with a majority of Catholics on everything but being Catholic.

I smiled as I closed my journal and put it in my camera bag. I thought about meeting the priest who would say the wedding mass Saturday. For years I felt Catholicism got to me unmercifully, but I guess it got to everyone.

As the plane rattled violently, I looked out to the gray sky then back to the guy next to me. His drink splashed over his hand.

"Worried we're going down?" I asked.

"Yeah!"

"Just the gods reminding us to take life seriously. They do it to me all the time... Must amuse them..."

I had my usual mixed reaction, like I had coming back from Cancun, figuring the only thing I'd miss about life was I wouldn't finish another un-publishable novel. But after several minutes anticipating death, there was a great cheer when we bounced down safely on the runway.

When Rich met Danny at the baggage claim he said, "Your plane was the last to land. They closed the airport because of thunder and lightning."

"Good timing," Danny said and they shook hands.

They waited for Danny's suitcase and headed out into the rain. Danny got out his umbrella and covered them as they walked together for a while.

Then Rich ran off toward his car. It made no sense to Danny, who kept walking carrying his camera bag and suitcase, until Rich came back with the car. He couldn't understand why he would hurry in the rain, but figured that's how Rich got somewhere in life.

In the car, as they talked about the wedding, Danny remembered the article tucked in his journal. He was confident that Rich's views sided with the pope, and that was fine, because Rich was an honest Catholic who believed the mystery. The next night, alone in the hotel room, Danny continued writing.

June 18, 2004

MY BLOCK
Chapter 1: Wedding, Anyone?

The famous I.Q. researcher Arthur Jensen wrote about a "zone of tolerance." He said that people need to be within ten I.Q. points of each other to make a relationship work. Watching Rich and Beth today, I believe it's a factor, but great marriages rely on chemistry…and chemistry, even according to Heisenberg's Uncertainty Principle and Quantum Mechanics relies on atomic forces.

The grand design that scientists call Unified Field Theory continues to evade, but the forces are gravity, magnetism, weak and strong molecular forces. The most powerful forces in the solar system are the Earth and the moon and beyond to the sun. One second without the sun would destroy the planet. A small asteroid smashed into the earth near Cancun millions of years ago and changed evolution.

Love has something to do with when people are born. Rich and Beth are compatible…born, as Thoreau said, the right time and place. I believe astrology has a say in why people are compatible. I saw it as they navigated the map. Rich ignored the GPS girl and Beth let him, but together they enjoyed the journey and found Ocean Cliff.

I told Beth on the ferry coming over, "I remember when you and Rich started dating when I was in high school. You both drove tan Pontiac LeMans convertibles. I mean was that a coincidence? That's why Aristotle and his Greek buddies got into Fate. I mean when you meet somebody and you feel you know them, it feels like fate. When Antonio and I met back at State, suddenly roommates as resident advisors, I felt we connected. You feel it or you don't. It's chemistry and astrology," I said, to finish, as Beth looked at me with amused concern.

And when we got to Newport, it was apparent that the Gilded Age of the Vanderbilts and Carnegies was luxury filled. When Rich passed Rosecliff, where the reception would be, protected by a wall and gardens and set back far from

Bellevue Avenue, he would not listen to the GPS girl in his Mercedes, so Beth kept explaining the map she had in her lap.

"If you go right at the next corner that should take us around to Ocean Cliff."

Rich missed the turn then took the next turn. Beth struggled to rethink the map and get him on track. I listened as they negotiated, impressed neither got ruffled. Rich's Capricorn practicality to push ahead and her Scorpio desire to plan while he plodded paid off. If it were me and Caroline, it would have gotten wild. I'd babble with Gemini impatience against her Scorpio insistence to go her way. Marriages last when couples coalesce.

At Ocean Cliff the entourage emerged. Teri and Sean met us.

"Happy Wedding," Teri said, as she hugged me.

"How's the happy bride after a year?" I asked.

"Happier than ever."

"What a great place for a wedding. I'm glad they're not getting married in the church where JFK and Jackie got married."

"Have to be a parishioner," she replied, with a frown.

"They can start out on their own... Great!"

A half-hour later, while the group sat under the awning on the bar at the back porch, boats sailing in the bay, Diane and Ryan arrived, moving among the group hugging and kissing and laughing and talking.

For me, surrounded by family, I'm involved. But with the video camera, I'm doing something. I'm the weird uncle. That's why this novel will expose me in ways no one ever knew. But I'm telling my story about everyone and everything I know.

There comes a time in everyman's life for confession. Back in St. Mary's at State thirty-five years ago it poured out. But I agree with mom, that life boils down to "Love." Last year I was drawn to Dublin for the ninety-ninth celebration of Bloom's Day. I came home in love with Ireland and put a green metal roof on my house to signal a new viewpoint in my never ending fascination with love and lust.

I'm glad this year for Bloom's Day hundredth anniversary I'm at a family wedding. Angie and I celebrated the hundredth anniversary of Mark Twain's writing with an animated video by elementary kids. I celebrated the hundredth anniversary of Hemingway's birth with my summer program for gifted elementary students. The kids performed The Old Man and the Sea *.*

Jim was Santiago and Tanesha the struggling marlin, connected by the rope. A white boy and a black girl fighting... But in rehearsal, I told her to stand during the fight, make the struggle noble, the way Hemingway intended it. In front of parents and friends she did. "You better be strong yourself old man," she said. The talking black marlin, the brother that Santiago so valued and felt he betrayed because he couldn't save it from the shark attacks.

That's what I want to teach. In conversations with Teri, who teaches elementary school and Jennifer who teaches middle school we talk about that. But that's for the book about genuine teaching, not this novel.

The family gathered for lunch on the hotel patio; as ships sailed on sparkling water under a translucent sky, Danny looked at the bridge onto Newport. He thought his way up Narragansett Bay to Providence and back forty years to Brown. With Rich calling the shots, he would have taken the offer to Ivy back in Sixty-five. But today, Rich took hectic Interstate 95; had Danny been driving, he would have taken the scenic and historic Boston Post Road. As he videotaped the bridge and the little house on the rocks under it, and panned back to get three generations of Roarkes in the lens, he smiled about his choice to go to State and that he couldn't know what his life would be otherwise.

He enjoyed catching the happy chatter among family on the terrace. But he refocused on the bridge and he thought that John F. Kennedy's son John went to Brown instead of going to Harvard, in the Kennedy family tradition. A few years ago, on his way to a family wedding John John plunged his plane through fog into the ocean, a few miles short of Martha's Vineyard. He killed himself, his wife and her sister. One can never know the path one did not take.

By evening, Charlie, his wife and daughters arrived with their husbands; the entire Roarke clan was assembled. When Charlie found Danny on the terrace, talking with Diane's dad, he handed Danny a bag.

"Happy Birthday, Danny boy," he said, as they shook hands.

"Thanks," Danny said, reaching to pull out a T-shirt that had a cartoon dog image with the words "Lucky Dog" and a book called *Danny Boy*, about the song. "I guess this says it all, Charlie, thanks."

Danny recalled that after he discovered Dromahair, he mentioned it to Charlie. They tried to trace the family name on the internet through the Ellis Island website, but they couldn't even find their grandmother and grandfather. It was absurd to think they were heirs to the Dervagilla fiasco that led to the invasion of Ireland, but, he heard about it after seeing Yeats' gravesite and Lough Gill's Isle of Innisfree. It was mythology, but he met women like Dervagilla. He attracted them. But that was part of the journey he wanted to write about.

As they talked outside the reception tent, Diane approached.

"Go right to the heart of the matter. Why?" Charlie asked.

Diane laughed and looked from Charlie to her dad. She tried to respond but her dad interrupted. Still smiling, she listened.

Danny kept the camera on her as her dad started.

"If you can't have fun… if you can't have fun…"

Danny focused on Diane. As her dad struggled, she smiled at him; then suddenly a skeptical look wrinkled between her eyebrows. Danny focused on him. Danny liked his gutsy style and that Diane was amused, and deferential, but she flashed a look of skepticism that drew Danny to her. She was waiting for his comment, but she would also judge it.

"If you can't have fun along the way… Why make the trip?" he got out.

"Yeah. Right," she said, nodding and smiling.

Danny caught her dad in the camera as he reiterated his comment with his right hand open, holding whiskey in his left.

Diane nodded approvingly. "I'm going to get a non-alcoholic drink," she said. "I've got to last."

She flashed an embracing smile from her dad to Charlie and Danny. Danny saw a woman who could build an empire.

"Oh, you're gonna last," Charlie said.

"Yeah, I need to last," she said, and they all laughed as she continued on her way.

Ron, Ryan's older brother, pulled Danny over to meet Father McKenzie, the piece of the puzzle he wanted. That morning Danny read a speech Father McKenzie made to the university trustees about the Jesuit tradition. They shook hands. He was short and wiry with close-cropped gray hair, glasses, and an ingratiating smile.

Danny asked, "Father McKenzie, what do you think of Ryan's business degree?"

"The finance stuff is going to help him."

"Of course! He's a Roarke," Danny said, teasing.

"But it's the philosophy that's going to stand him," Father McKenzie continued, emphasizing his point with his right index finger. He held what looked like water with lime in a wine glass in his left. His white collar showed through his black shirt and jacket. "Diane will be the beneficiary of all this philosophy. Remember, I was his philosophy professor. Trust me," he said, laughing.

"Did he get above a C?" Danny asked, enjoying the priest's graciousness.

Father McKenzie stepped back to formulate his answer, holding his glass with both hands.

Ron said, "Probably not."

McKenzie stepped forward and leaned into the camera, "No comment," he said, and everyone laughed.

"Ah, confidentiality. I can see why he appreciates you so much," Danny said enthusiastically.

A short time later, everyone assembled under the tent for the rehearsal dinner.

"We'd like to welcome Diane to the Roarke family," Rich said, walking from where he sat with his wife, Charlie and his wife, and Danny toward their table, toasting his wine glass as family and friends applauded. "We are absolutely delighted you're joining us, because you are such a special person. Very attractive, very bright, very athletic, and in fact, Diane knows more about sports than my son Ryan." Rich turned from their table towards the others, working the room well, enjoying the crowd's laughter. "So at least I have someone to have a normal conversation with when they come to my house," he added, as he walked toward Diane and Ryan's table.

Ryan, seated between Diane and Father McKenzie, looked up with a smile saying, "Thanks, Dad."

As the laughter waned, Rich continued, "It also gives us pause because not only that, but you're very organized and that's something we need in our family of two boys and our daughter. Two examples about how disorganized they are and why Diane is a good addition. Where is Sean?" he asked, looking around the room. "Sean and Teri who are part of our family," he continued, walking toward them as they raised their hands. "Everybody know Sean and Teri? They were married a year ago. They've been planning this wedding also for a long time. So they made reservations on the ferry for last evening. They were going to get here early. They drove all the way out to Orient Point to catch the ferry. And they got there five minutes after the ferry left," he said. He waited for the laughter and moans to subside. "So, what did they have to do? They drove all the way back to New York, all the way to the Throgs Neck Bridge, all the way up I-95 and took longer than Josephine took from Florida, seven hours. So that's the kind of family you're going into," he said, smiling, walking slowly as he faced each table and enjoyed their reactions.

As the laughter subsided, he continued, "I've got one better than that. This family is so organized, and is ready for this wedding and planned it so well, that, Ron...where's Ron?" he asked turning from his wife as she pointed behind him toward Ron's raised hand. "Ron and Jennifer have been married eight years now..."

Beth corrected him, "Nine!"

"Nine years," he said, looking from her back to their table.

Beth repeated to Danny, "Yes, nine years. Nine years this month."

"Nine years," he continued, raising his glass in toast. "Ron's the best man. He's been preparing his speech for tomorrow for probably thirty-two years."

Rich again waited to appreciate the laughter. Ron called out, "I thought this covered that."

"And he also has a tuxedo that he has to wear that he had all pressed. And he organized himself and put it in his car to come up to this beautiful wedding. And they get into the van this morning and get five minutes from Orient Point this morning, when we're taking the nine o'clock ferry to this magnificent place on Newport, RI, with amazing sunsets." He spread his arms wide and leaned to face west and look through the clear panels on the sides of the tent toward the gray overcast sky. "It's about to happen anytime this sunset. So, Ron gets five minutes from Orient Point and," putting his hand to his forehead, he continued, "Goes Oh, My God, I put my tuxedo in the other car!" Enjoying everyone's applause and laughter, Rich smiled then sipped his drink.

Sitting next to Danny, Charlie yelled "All right, Ron!" as folks continued to applaud.

Turning toward Diane and Ryan, Rich raised his wine glass. "So, Diane, God bless you. Welcome to our family."

After the applause slowed, Rich took a few steps then turned toward Diane, Ryan and Father McKenzie.

"Father McKenzie is here to say the mass tomorrow and marry Diane and Ryan. And he is a very unique man. Ryan met him at Trinity. He has a PhD in philosophy and was Ryan's professor."

Charlie cleared his throat a few times reacting to what Rich said about the priest. Danny leaned toward him thinking their dad would have been impressed with McKenzie's credentials, but Charlie's guttural check mixed skepticism with admiration. Without words, Danny sensed Charlie assessed the man's guts and spine through the filter of the hell he had endured.

"Not only a professor, but a good friend of Ryan's during school and after school, and they've stayed in touch over the years. And I think he's been very instrumental in helping Ryan become the kind of person he is today. So, I'm absolutely delighted that Father McKenzie was able to join us for this evening."

After the applause, Rich returned to the table.

"Nice work, Rich," Danny said, as Rich sat down next to him.

Danny thought about *My Block* as he congratulated Rich. He enjoyed the happy rustle of the hundred or so folks under the tent as Father McKenzie started to talk.

"As I was driving down from Boston, I was reminded of the first time I met Ryan. He walked into my class as a senior. He was smart enough to avoid me for three years. He had just come back from that fabulous experience of a semester at sea, where he basically went all over the world on a boat and had a great education there. But I was thinking tonight, having met Diane that his ship has finally come in," he finished, his hands clasped in front of his chest, smiling toward Diane and Ryan to rousing applause.

Charlie leaned toward Danny, saying quietly, "He's good."

"Yeah, I met him outside…"

June 19, 3 a.m. Wedding Day

Up, unable to sleep, looking at the bay outside my window. Against a clear black sky, the bridge lit like an elegant pearl necklace. Mulling over the day, still thinking about My Block.

Rich loves an audience the way Frankie Odono did back on the Spartans. He fed off the crowd and loved to see himself in their reflected laughter and applause. He sacrificed his children to the audience, but in the gentle way he had for years. He told what he saw people do and knew its humor.

Our whole lives he held my choices in the mirror of his worldview, but we never saw the same world. When I wanted to take a day off work to go to the county finals in the pole vault, he said, "Your medal won't bring much money if you lose your job." When I played soccer professionally, he asked, "What happens if you get injured?" When I started teaching, he said, "You're never going to make much money."

The banker graciously works the room for an honest five per cent. The artist alone is compelled to risk everything on his next passionate imagining.

And so, over the years I've established a truce. We've learned to appreciate each other. He's good. Very good, and so, he is always there as a measure of myself, as is Charlie, who cannot understand why I do what I do, but who seems to appreciate me more. Oldest children love the spotlight, and hate to lose it to a younger sibling. But Rich established himself through a solid marriage, successful career and wonderful kids. He is the financial success dad never experienced, but hoped for his kids. Charlie, once a Viking warrior, mellowed since Vietnam and has achieved harmony with a good family.

I follow my own path, buffeted by the gods or fates but primarily by my choices against unquestioned tradition. After years of voyage, content to appreciate my family, without one of my own, I accept the world that says I am an uncle, an itinerant teacher, whose Penelope is the muse that forces me to write about life.

I believe that Fitzgerald was wrong ending The Great Gatsby *with the idea that we are doomed to struggle against the current and lost in our past. We must make sense of our past by taking the two or three great and simple images on our slow trek and integrating them into our lives. Like Hemingway ending* The Old Man in the Sea *with Santiago home after his great struggle with the marlin and sharks, alone sleeping on his cot, immersed in a dream about lions. Images that inspire...*

When Hemingway wrote to Fitzgerald that novels could be from things a writer overhears or his own life wrecked and reconstructed, he seems closer to the truth. But Fitzgerald ended killing himself with alcohol and Hemingway with a shotgun. So the solution must be to overcome the torment of our past to embrace the present and transform our future.

I left the "Lucky Dog" T-shirt that Charlie gave me for my birthday near the tent. It's in the bag with the <u>Danny Boy</u> book he gave me also... I hope they are still there in the morning...but how could they not?

The following morning at the church, Danny videotaped the ceremony as people filed in.

"How do you feel about your sister and Ryan's wedding this morning?" Danny asked.

"I'm Michael, the eldest brother of the O'Donnell's. And I'm testifying that Diane is a fantastic sister, and we couldn't have wished for anything better in a husband."

Then Rich and Beth preceded the bridesmaids. Blake, their adopted Korean grandson, started, but panicked with the rings and had to be consoled, letting out a wail as he was guided into a pew. Then the first notes of the bridal entry sounded and Diane appeared escorted by her father. Elegant, smiling confidently as she passed each pew filled with friends and family. She flowed toward the altar. Her dad pulled back the veil, kissed her on the cheek and turned to shake hands with Ryan.

Watching, Danny thought that all Catholic weddings were similar, but this was the last for this generation of Roarkes.

Father McKenzie started with, "What a pleasure it is to welcome you to this beautiful church on this happy occasion in the life of Diane and Ryan. Their love brings them to the altar today. And as they do so, they are surrounded by family and friends who are totally happy for them. And share in their joy. Gracious God you have made the bond of matrimony a holy mystery. A symbol of Christ's love for his Church. May their lives always bear witness to the reality of that love."

From the pulpit, he said "Weddings are love's promise for yet another generation. I might note how fitting it is for Diane and Ryan to exchange their vows in the context of faith. They have truly learned well from their Jesuit education that all true knowledge eventually leads one to God. Little did they know that their Jesuit education would lead not only to new heights of knowledge, but to each other. For the past twenty-five years, Father Bernard, Trinity's president delivered the same address of welcome every year to the freshman class on their very first night on campus. His opening line never changed. I want you to look to your right, now to your left, look behind you, and now look down front. You are six hundred strangers, but little did you know you probably had a glimpse of your future spouse. Sometimes he gets it right. Today we rejoice that he got it very right. When marriages start out on a base this solid there is indeed cause for great hope."

Danny smiled, near tears at times as he videotaped, mumbling, "Gracious sales pitch for God and his university," as Father McKenzie blessed the rings and sealed the marriage amidst glowing smiles and photographers and friends and family. From the testimony of Diane's brother and the best friends and brothers at his side, Ryan was well loved. As they turned from the altar and held hands, Danny was proud to know him and was impressed with Diane. As the couple walked hand in hand down the aisle, they were a match of quiet confidence, a couple clearly in love and able to epitomize family success.

Outside the church, the bag piper started again. The receiving line stretched down the steps along the walkway to the sidewalk where the piper paraded. Behind the happy couple, the flag was at half-staff for President Reagan's recent death and a red EMT vehicle passed. Life goes on, Danny thought as he videotaped the celebration. Bubbles floated out from behind them, lifted by the breeze into a cloudless blue sky, as they hugged and kissed friends and relatives and posed for pictures.

Bellevue Avenue, built in the Gilded Age still dazzled in the new millennium, as it led to the reception at Rosecliff. Rosecliff was the dream child of Theresa Fair Oelrichs, the daughter of an Irish immigrant James Graham Fair, who made a fortune by discovering Nevada's Comstock silver lode. Legend had it that Theresa met Hermann Oelrichs on the tennis courts at the Newport Casino in 1899 and they married a year later. They bought the property from the fellow who developed the American Beauty rose, George Bancroft and commissioned the famous architect Stanford White to replace the original mansion with one that emulated a residence of the French kings. It had the powdery white marble design and finish of an elegant wedding cake.

Danny remembered that Scott Fitzgerald's *The Great Gatsby* was filmed there. It was Robert Redford's mansion as imaginary Jazz Age character Gatsby. In a tuxedo, Danny wanted to see if the green light that portended the orgiastic future that so tantalized Gatsby and his author still hung from the dock. But the expansive back lawn opened to a wide view of the ocean and the Breakers, the Vanderbilt family's major attraction. As the tour guide said about the Isle of Innisfree, "It's in one's imagination," he remembered, as both blessing and curse.

Soon after, the wedding party arrived in a white Rolls Royce. As Beth checked with the caterers, Rich wandered off toward the wedding party. Danny toured the house quickly and went outside to watch the photographers orchestrate the wedding pictures.

The sailing yacht cruise the following morning, Diane and Ryan arrived and looked like heirs to the Kennedys. The newest Roarkes. He felt that if there is a chance for greatness in the next generation, it would be with their children.

The following day, at Rich's house overlooking the Sound, as they watched the sunset, Danny turned to Beth and Rich standing in the doorway to the porch,

"Any words of wisdom for the new married couple?"

Beth smiled, put her arm around Rich, and looked into the camera. The setting sun put soft golden light on them. "They'll be very happy. They're a wonderful couple. They're on their way to Cabo San Lucas. They're going to catch a marlin. Who could have a better life?" she said, and Rich nodded approval.

"There you go," Danny said, feeling a journey had come to an end and another was starting.

He turned back toward the sun. He heard Beth behind him say, "Look at that beautiful purple sky." And it was orange and purple and majestic; and as he panned back the sun was white hot in the center and yellow on the edge, and shot out three bright orange spikes over the water. Several minutes later, as he stood watching the sun slide below the horizon, leaving a layer of orange afterglow and deepening blue above, he noticed a crescent moon rising to accent the new beginning.

The next day, while Beth was out doing errands, he videotaped photos on the piano in the game room. He clicked pictures of Ryan, Ron and Teri as kids, then his mom's and dad's parents, and his mom and dad, and Beth and Rich and Beth's mom and dad. Four generations. This, the final wedding until the next generation, unless something unimaginable, that some day he would get married.

Chapter 19: Pond Prince

August 15, 2004

My Block
Chapter 2: The Devious Duo Attack

Scooping water lettuce from the pond with the net, I dumped it into the clay pot for the compost pile. I stepped back over the white picket fence and grabbed the Koi pellets.

Once they see the net, they hide under the plants and watch.

Last night as Sherry left, I scooped water lettuce that was overgrowing the pond. She asked, "Daniel, how come you don't feed the fish on a regular schedule?"

"I don't want them dependent on me."

She's such a sweetheart, like that old song "Five foot two and eyes of blue". A school counselor concerned about the future of the planet.

"What do they eat?" she asked, concerned.

"Algae, plant roots, whatever they can find. They're independent. I just help out. You know, like the Christians believe God intervenes for their benefit."

"I was raised Jewish. Our God paid more attention to his people."

"Seems the folks in Sodom and Gomorra thought God used the net on them..."

"I'm not a Bible scholar. Sorry. I lean toward Buddhism these days."

"Well as Pond Prince, I have to keep the fish and turtles away from the water lilies. So I made these planters that let water flow through but keep fish and turtles out. I'm no god, that's for sure, but I like to see reptiles, fish and plants live in harmony..."

213

"Danny, you're SUCH a philosopher," she said, with a cute laugh.

"Oh, that the gods were as fair," I said, facetiously.

Eventually, the big yellow came back to graze, eating slowly, followed by the others. I knew we'd reconnected, so I pressed upward through the strain in my legs, no longer the energy of a young soccer player, but a guy aging.

I backed my car out of the garage and headed to campus. Sunday morning there's rarely anybody around. Anyway, I went toward my office and was surprised to see Angie Harper, my Mark Twain fanatic grad student now colleague, whom we hired back to Palm City after she finished her PhD with Antonio at Tommie Jefferson U. But she works constantly. We talked, and she said that the Devious Duo – Terry Rheames and Lorrence Slutski – were not supporting her for tenure.

Dr. Rheames is Orphan Annie on steroids: tall, big-boned, raggedy red hair, unattractive, unmarried and angry about it. And Dr. Slutski is a gay guy who won't go public, so the Duo is going after a talented warm-hearted woman because she's good. Unbelievable! But Angie was terribly upset, so we talked for a while, to figure out a plan. I reassured her that everyone else in the department supported her because we see her as a Palm City U success story. But she reminded me that the Devious Duo hate to see others succeed.

So, like with Brother Charlie, when tragedy hits everyone endures it. Life is like that. Those who care have to confront the tragedies of those they care about.

But like Randy April used to say when he was department chair, "The battles in academia are so fierce because there is so little at stake."

Randy was our best chair. He was a no bullshit kind of guy. But he saw the infighting and knew that he didn't want to deal with it. Randy endured Tweedle Dumb and Tweedle Nasty for a few years and bailed out to a public university.

The day before he left, we went to Pub Central for a drink. He said, "The bullshit's different in public universities, but at least it's public. I won't have to deal with the incessant whining of self-indulgent intellectuals behind closed doors. It's easier herding cats."

"Thanks, Randy, now Dean Thomas will stick me with chair."

"You deserve it Danny boy. You've been too happy here."

Taking the job got me tenure, but my dad died that semester and that was tough. The following semester I took a sabbatical to work on a book, so Thomas appointed someone else chair. When I returned, I knew ex-chemistry professor Thomas didn't like liberal White boys from the North; so it was a matter of days before she told me to resign. Randy was right about the fierce battles, but Angie's career isn't little stakes.

I gladly resigned as chair, but rumor had it that Thomas started to irritate other faculty also. Eventually, she was voted out as dean during discussions that said the university had to embrace diversity, had to live up to the mission Johnny Palmer set of a "Heavenly Earth", where all God's children were valued equally.

That led to the appointment of Clarissa White as dean, a Southern Black who apparently learned politeness means promotion.

But according to Angie, Tweedle Nasty and Tweedle Dumb – the Devious Duo – seem to be plotting against her tenure. I mean when a woman isn't happy about herself and a guy confused about his gender identity endures sadism, both get unbelievably venomous. My hope is they come to terms with whom they are and why they want to hurt others. The playground gets unbelievably vicious without a good referee. So, I told Angie I'd do whatever I can to help. She was thankful, but still worried.

As I was leaving, in one of my desk drawers, I noticed the picture of Caroline and me at the <u>Skyline Magazine</u> award ceremony honoring Kajaw Carribe as the magazine's "Man of the Year." Her wig really got to me that night. In a crowd of hundreds of formally dressed African Americans, Caroline looked happy. But my wan smile was not because of crooked teeth anymore, but because we didn't coalesce. She had a great body and a thing she did that was euphoric when we made love.

"You should do workshops with that technique," I said one night after making love.

"It amazes me that women don't use their vaginas more during sex," she said, with that magnetic smile.

"You've discovered something no woman I've ever known knows."

But a magnetic Scorpio smile and sexual magic can't make lust love… I mean we had outrageous arguments about wooden and plastic cutting-boards, and what you can cook in a microwave. With Maureen the cutting-board argument was about me giving up other women – although she forgot to mention her husband. But Caroline harangued about germs running rampant in the wood and killing us… Gemini guys don't do well with Scorpio drama. Scorpio Brother Charlie had a temper, but I never lusted to sleep with him. Caroline will do better with a less mercurial guy.

But I found blank DVDs that I wanted and left. I drove to the studio. It looked cleaner, comfortable. A few of my bowls and vases were on a table with the birdbath stands and platters I made for Tony and Allison. They still weren't the way I wanted them, but I took a bowl with a glaze combination that finally worked after months of trying, and walked back to my car.

The whole trip around my block was under a mile. I parked my car, closed the garage with the remote. As the door closed, I put the DVDs in the bowl. I remembered the day I boarded up my house for Hurricane Lloyd and left town. I realized that one's life's work can be summed easily. The bowl and the Wedding DVD for Diane and Ryan could be my measure.

My sister-in-law Beth asked about the day I boarded up to leave town. "That must have been scary. What did you take?"

"You really streamline your life. I took my journals, my novels on disk, some clothes, one of my pots with an orchid and a little marble sculpture I made when I taught on the Island."

"I wonder what I would take in a situation like that?"

"Pictures..."

Holding the DVDs in the bowl, I was content to think what I held in my hands that moment was sufficient testimony for my life.

As I walked toward the pond, I thought about John Keats' "Ode to a Grecian Urn". Keats coughed his lungs out with tuberculosis and was dead at twenty-six...but Ode is still a great poem. I watched the fish and turtles crowd together for food, and I remembered talking with the poet Archie Ammons the day I showed him my poem about the bullfight I saw in Spain. Often I think about what he said about his own writing, *"When my poems were getting rejected, I kept saying I like them. Then when I started getting awards for them years later, I wondered what had changed."*

I tossed some pellets to the fish. I'd told Tony dozens of times my limit is fish and turtles. As pond prince I have to keep harmony between the turtles and fish and keep them away from the water lilies with the pond planters I've made. My life is best kept simple.

It all seems like metaphor for God, no matter how I conceive of him or them. Homer's gods intervened in human lives all the time. Joyce wanted out of the god stuff. I don't know for sure. But if the Christians are correct, I don't think God is intervening sufficiently in his pond. Tweedle Dumb and Tweedle Nasty should be better people. And Politically Correct U would be a better place if all the Christians actually lived up to Christ's teaching.

After I watched the fish and turtles eat, I went into the house. I took the DVDs up to my office and copied the Wedding DVD I made for Diane and Ryan. I fought with Hewlett-Packard CEO Carlie Fiorina for months to replace the old DVD burner, but finally she acquiesced and sent a new burner and it worked. Like I said, I believe life is endurance.

I walked out to the citrus grove filled with young fruit. My astrologer in Ithaca said, *"I see you tending trees when you are older."* That connected with my forty year old dream about the budding tree. My astrologer was right, I'm tending trees. But the buds on my dream tree suddenly made sense as my students. That hit me, not as some ecstatic revelation, or Joycean epiphany, but nodding recognition that I am a teacher. I teach and my opinion is that authenticity is the key. I don't know how long I'll last, but if I have anything to teach, it's my belief in the dream tree bearing fruit. I believe in that, all else is beyond comprehension. So I know I have to help Angie overcome the Devious Duo.

Within a week, Hurricane Brandi hit and took down an oak tree in the backyard. A week later, when Huricane Genny was clocked at 150 mph winds, Danny boarded the large triple hung windows with plywood. It blew into Palm City at 90 mph, splattered rain against the wood, beat on the metal roof, and cut the electricity. The morning of the storm Danny heard a knock on his front door. He was surprised to see his colleague from the art department and pottery mentor Dan.

"You got to be crazy Dan. There's a hurricane out there," Danny said, extending his hand and pulling his friend into the living room.

"Come on Danny boy, what else are you going to do? There's no electricity, we have to do something."

"So this is the Zen of kiln building, do it in the eye of the storm?"

"Exactly. I got my van. Get your back brace. Let's get started."

Danny got a jug of ice tea from the refrigerator and followed Dan out the door to his van.

"May as well get killed in a hurricane," Danny said, hopping into the front seat. "I just got a flood of rejections on *Genuine Teaching*: Cambridge, Columbia, and Harvard. They say no one wants education to be *genuine*. What I've been doing for twenty years means nothing to them. My best students understand. Many say it changed their lives. But America still isn't ready."

"You can't give up. Someone will want it. You still want me to do the graphics for the cover?"

"May as well, *Danny-boy*. But it's such bullshit to call a gray-haired Scandinavian guy from Minnesota *Danny-boy*. I should be the only Danny-boy," he said, teasing, enjoying the banter they'd developed about their names over a decade of friendship.

"Well, you're not the only Daniel in the world. But you gotta keep writing."

"I guess. Maybe I should get back to my novel, *My Block*. Maybe if I use my journals. Write from the heart. This time I have to use my journals. Sum up all I know about life."

"Make sure there's plenty of sex. And find a new woman. You're ready, Danny boy."

"Maybe I can write about my primal people and the acrobatics of Internet dating, eh?"

"Sex sells. Write about it. And make me handsome and irresistible to women."

"Geez, it'll really have to be fiction for that. I want to sell philosophy, and everybody wants drugs, sex and rock and roll!"

As they built the kiln in the turbulent winds and rain, Danny wondered about the astrological prediction that he would find a woman this year. Afterwards, as he sat on the porch watching the hurricane winds and rains blow sporadically through the front yard, his friend Dan's optimism gave him hope that he would find a woman.

The day after the hurricane blew through Danny mowed the front lawn and trimmed the gardenia and hibiscus bushes along the driveway. As he went out to tend the citrus trees in the front yard, he got a call from his African-American colleague Kajaw Carribe. So they met for dinner at a local restaurant.

"Doctors Roarke and Carribe, so nice you come to my restaurant," Sing said.

"So glad *Le Fleur* is still here, Sing," Danny responded.

"No hurricane will destroy us. We survive Viet Nam," she said, and the three laughed. "Now what I get for you smart men?"

"Whatever your talented husband Pierre thinks best on the menu."

"OK. Trust me, we treat you well tonight," she said and walked toward the kitchen.

"So why the urgency, Kajaw?"

"My closest friend from graduate school has cancer."

Danny groaned, momentarily thought about his father then said, "Sorry to hear that. Hopefully they've caught it early."

"He doesn't know yet. His father died of it a few years ago. He's in the Cancer Institute in New York. So I'll have to travel. But it's the best place."

"So sad my friend. Sorry to hear. But I've heard great things about the institute. Hopefully they can cure him. I'd be happy to cover your classes if you need me," he said, thinking about his father. Looking at Kajaw's round face, expressive eyes and full lips, Danny pictured an Olmec stone head sculpture, whose powerful presence fascinated him and evoked mystery as the earliest artifacts in the Americas. It was a lineage to which his close friend traced his ancestry and name, Kajaw, which meant "jaguar", and the family name Carribe, linked to the Native Americans after whom the Caribbean was named. Danny admired Kajaw, who not only had to struggle as an immigrant, but had to endure racism still prevalent in America. "Let me know what I can do."

"Thanks, I appreciate your help. The rest is in God's hands."

"You have to believe that you are doing the best you can. And we survived the hurricanes," Danny added encouragingly.

"You men ready to be treated well?" Sing said, returning and handing them a plate of Imperial rolls. "Dr. Carribe, you and Dr. Roarke are such funny men. So smart and so nice. That's why we love you."

Kajaw smiled warm-heartedly as she turned to walk toward the kitchen then they each dipped an Imperial roll into the sauce.

"She's a sweetheart," Danny said, savoring the crispy roll.

"They are good people," Kajaw said, as he finished his roll hurriedly. "Let's not talk about me. You heard my story. It will work out. So, how is your pond?"

"The morning after the hurricane passed, I found five of my largest Koi belly up. The cement Buddha still smiled. The lilies may contain Christ, but death consumed the pond. The small Koi survived without the pump, but the large ones smelled. They were so rancid I almost puked as I buried them under Monument Rock in the back yard, near Blueberry Hill. The courageous turtle, the only young one to survive the winter, was on top of the two large turtles on the rocks in the sun contemplating Buddha. Losing the fish was sad… But nothing like losing a close friend to cancer. You gonna be OK?"

"I'll survive. I have to do everything I can for him."

"Let me know what I can do to help."

The next morning in the office talking with Angie, Danny said, "Sometimes Brother Charlie has it right about women. Says, you can't live with them and you can't kill them."

"I know what you were saying," Angie said, with a short chuckle.

"But you're one of them. You have gender affinity."

"No. I am one of you guys. Some women are high maintenance."

"Well, whatever. Sherry called a couple days ago. Making excuses about why she hadn't called. But it was all whining about her family and her two daughters and her three ex-husbands. It's not a life I want. All I said at the end was since she didn't call, I felt she dismissed me. I told her there's no future in this relationship. But I'm still hopeful. Today I e-mailed a woman called Carpe Vita at an online dating service in Orlando called Sunshine Connections. A five-nine blond blue eyed Gemini woman with a master's degree."

"Danny, you'll find someone. You will. You're ready."

"Well the hurricanes passed and the plywood's off my windows. Lucky I cut the oaks over my garage and bedroom before we put the roof over when I came back from Ireland last summer. I mean the house is ready. And so am I. You get your tenure portfolio finished yet?"

Sitting behind her cluttered desk, she held up a large binder, "Just about finished."

"That looks thick enough. Tenure. Amazing."

"But Lorrence and Terry told me they won't support me."

"That's bullshit. Tweedle Dumb is a gay guy who won't go public and Tweedle Nasty is Orphan Annie on steroids aspiring to be an Amazon. Who cares. Everyone else will. You'll be fine."

"I hope so."

"Has to go your way. Especially after all the hurricane bullshit. I lost a tree to Hurricane Kelly. Luckily, fell along the property line. I'm just gonna leave it to become part of natural Florida. Tweedle Dumb and Nasty will fall. They have to. You'll be fine. Just finish your portfolio."

"I should be done next week. And you keep at your love life."

"Actually, I got a call from Ann, the Leo teacher down in Sarasota. I thought that might have worked. But she wants a sailor and Danny boy has skin cancer. Ugh. She was a sweetheart. But she's looking for a Christian missionary and sailor. Anyway, she called during the hurricane. Good to talk with her. She was telling me about doing missionary work in Haiti. She is a warm-hearted woman."

"You'll find the right one when the time is right."

"We'll see. My brothers have done it. Both happily married," Danny said, then felt like rambling on about his brothers and their lives. "Good old Rich keeps playing *Monopoly* with Florida real estate. Like when we were kids on my aunt's porch in the Adirondacks. He was the banker. But he's good-hearted, believes in the Christian God and hard work. The warm handshake and ready smile. Rich epitomizes Tony's motto, 'Sincerity is eye contact leaning forward with an Ipana smile.' Not like Willie Loman in *Death of a Salesman,* who was unsure of himself and twisted his family. Rich has the warm-hearted good-natured handshake like our dad, but with a college education and connections. Rich was disappointed he couldn't go to Notre Dame because our folks couldn't afford it, but he got over it. He told me how much that hurt him the night he told me he owned his house outright, a several million dollar house overlooking Long Island Sound. He said owning the house free and clear and a good wife with traditional values who loved him and kept the family together and all three good kids that was what life was about for him. And Brother Charlie happily married. Carol is a good wife, a dedicated nurse. Their two daughters are happily married, good parents, well educated, caring about how others feel. I've seen it."

"You do have an amazing family."

"Only Uncle Danny doesn't fit. The only one unmarried. And Tony, he and Allison married since 1978, a great marriage. And now he's in *Time* magazine for his new book. Sherry gave me a copy of the magazine the last time I saw her."

"Why didn't that work out with her?"

"She got into a lot of Zen stuff and then whining about her kids and ex-husbands. But really, it was three marriages. I mean, I'm really a sensitive and traditional guy. I love to watch Doris Day and Audrey Hepburn on Turner Classic Movies. I like a woman I can trust, who likes her life and wants to stay married."

"Audrey used to think we would have made a good pair."

"I know, she told me. You know I really like you. But for me, it's best as friends. Romance would have ruined it. We work well together, but feels best as friends for me."

"I agree. I thought about it the other way. But I think you're right."

"Elaine was a Taurus also. We never really could make it work. Never enough compromise. And then, when she got pregnant to try to get me to marry her that blew it apart."

"I remember you telling me that. That was weird."

"Abortion never sits comfortably, but that's not the way to get married and have kids. Lucky Roe V. Wade passed that year. Otherwise I don't know what we'd have done. I'm just glad the Supreme Court saw it our way. Otherwise, who knows. So, no, I'm not lucky in love. Maureen was another weirdo. Forgets to tell me she's married. Let's me plan a family wedding. Then sues me."

"You definitely paid your dues. You must be ready."

Danny was leaning against the Mark Twain carving that Angie's kids gave her as a birthday present. The wooden bust, of roughly carved cedar, was up to his belt. Danny was running his hands along the grooves of the hair. "I guess I should rub Mark's head for luck."

"Good idea," she said, chuckling. "He's an American charm, especially for a writer."

"OK, Bucko, I mooned your grave. And the moon rose full last night. This morning it seemed to balance on the peak of my roof. My brother put a man on the moon, but it seemed to be encouraging me to go beyond lust to love. The hurricanes are past and town is still here. Millions are getting electricity back. And Tony is in *Time*. What's this world coming to? I saw Halley's Comet with Maureen in 1986 as we planned a wedding. You got to arrive and leave with the comet. I won't see it again. Mr. Twain, think I'm ready for real love?"

"Let's see what happens," Angie laughed. "I'm sure he would have appreciated the moon. I know I loved the look on your face in that photo you showed me on the way to Tony's conference. Mark would have loved it too."

That night, with electricity back, and his computer reconnected he sent a third e-mail to Carpe Vita.

On that Sunday, after filling the dead mower with gas to bring it to life, he mowed the yard and trimmed the banana trees cut up by the hurricanes. He checked his e-mail, one from Carpe Vita, Joy Perkins. She included her phone number and he called immediately.

"I wondered why you didn't respond?"

"Oh, with the hurricanes, I wasn't paying much attention. But you were adorable in your e-mail. Sorry I didn't respond sooner."

"I love that photo of you, with the blue top and pearls. What a smile."

"That was at my daughter's college graduation. I was a happy mom."

"Magnetic. And why *Carpe Vita*?"

"*Dead Poet's Society*, with Robin Williams as a teacher, is one of my favorite. But I don't want to *Carpe Diem* – seize the day – I want to seize life. So, I thought *Carpe Vita* worked. Not a lot of guys get it."

"I get it. I like it. What do you do?"

"I teach social studies in middle school."

"So your master's is in education?"

"Yes, I love teaching."

"That's work. I taught seventh grade science."

"I teach seventh grade. It is work. But my daughter is going to law school. I thought about law after my divorce took so long. But my undergraduate degree is in psychology. When my divorce was final, I looked at my psyche. I love kids and social studies and travel, so I got a master's in teaching. And I love it. Plus, I get time to travel. I went to Asia the past two summers."

"Wow...exciting. Where you from originally?"

"Near Cincinnati. That's where I went to college. Then got married and eventually moved to Florida. I've been divorced ten years. So, getting my daughter graduated from college was great relief. That's why such a big smile in that picture."

They talked for a couple hours about their travels and relationships in a breezy stream of chatter and laughter, even when she mentioned her blind dog Bubba.

"Let's get together. How about Pebbles? That's near you."

"That sounds like fun. I'll look forward to meeting you."

"Wednesday night around 6?"

"Sure."

That night, he wrote in his journal.

Oct. 3, 2004

A rendezvous. The astrologer said this may be the month. I'm so ready. How bizarre if we suddenly hit it off. A twelve year drought, according to the astrology reading, but I haven't been in love since Maureen in '86. Suddenly, a five foot nine slender blue-eyed fifty year old blond with a master's, sounding like her self-proclaimed "Well educated, well traveled."

Simply the most intriguing woman in months. Would that she be the most intriguing woman in years. And of course the most intriguing in my life. Who knows – the astrological read says it is possible. How bizarre, that would be. To love again...

So after dinner Friday with Kajaw Carribe, Angie and Peter at Cristo's complaining there are no women. Weeks of feeling lost by Sherry and frustrated with women online. Only Joy looked good. Suddenly, today, she responds. A Gemini with a graduate degree. A dog owner. Not like Sherry and Caroline and June and Winter Park Linda with cats to which I'm allergic, a woman with a blind dog named Bubba.

And so we talked for hours. Joy Perkins, chair of the social studies department at Verana Middle School. One marriage, her husband 10 years older. "We should never have had children. He wanted a girl and I gave him one but even that didn't make him happy. I learned a lot from marriage and raising my daughter alone."

And so, she's the girl with an older brother. Her dad a German disciplinarian. The brother, a lawyer. Her in Florida, everyone else in Ohio, a Midwest sweetheart. Raising a child on her own and teaching middle school for ten years. Wow... She sounded like a sweetie. We covered a lot of ground. Will we excite each other? I'm looking for love, no longer just lust. I want to expand into another through another and reciprocate. Love. That's the word...connection... completion.

We're set for Pebbles, where I've met so many women. I remember June and Linda and the Vegetarian and Blondie and the Jewish girl with braces, and the one that taught at Rollins and ran the meeting the day I got the speeding ticket, but Joy seems different. I mentioned Leo Erin, and Capricorn Suzi. But I avoided Taurus Elaine, and Sagittarius Maureen.

But how could I ever explain June and Ann recent Leos, Aquarius Sharon, Suzanne the sweet sensitive Cancer, and Caroline the lusty Scorpio...Ronda, the Tampa Gemini, Sherry the local Gemini, Alexandra the Tampa-Phillie Aquarian flight attendant. And others. Liz the artsy Libra at Cornell and Anne the economist Virgo at Cornell. Lynn the mystical Pisces and Susan the energetic Aries... I've been around the Zodiac with women...who could understand? But I'm ready to try again... I want to love and be loved...that simple.

After exiting the interstate, he saw the sign at Pebbles now read The Plumed Parrot. As he parked, he chuckled to think she would not be on the list of women he'd met at Pebbles. She was the first woman he'd ever meet at The Plumed Parrot.

He told the hostess that he was expecting a tall blond, and picked a booth he'd never been in, by the front window. Joy arrived a few minutes later.

He stood as she approached the table. "Ms. Carpe Vita, nice to meet you," he said, extending his hand.

"Professor Roarke, I presume?"

She wore a black jacket over a gold blouse and heels that leveled their eye contact. He heard the gold bracelets on her wrists as he noticed clear polish on manicured nails and enjoyed her firm handshake.

"Yes. Great to meet you. Have a seat?"

"You are a gentleman. Thanks."

"How about champagne? Danny asked, signaling the waiter.

"Great."

"What do you like?"

"For really special occasions? White Star."

"Could we have a bottle of White Star champagne?" Danny asked, looking at the waiter, then back to Joy.

Red lipstick accented her full lips. Her blue eyes reminded him of a shiny rutile glaze when they flashed as she talked. Blond hair that rested on her shoulders framed her softly angled face that lured him in as they chatted.

The waiter returned and said, "Sorry, Sir. We are so new, we don't have that. Let me see what we have."

The waiter returned with a dark haired woman.

"I'm Tonya Harrolds, the owner," she said, extending her hand to shake Danny's. "Sorry, we have some splits of champagne. But not White Star."

"Then you pick, Tonya," he said. Turning to Joy, he said, "Maybe we'll start a trend."

They sat and talked and laughed and Danny grew more intrigued. By the time they shared a piece of chocolate cake with vanilla ice cream and strawberries, they'd been together four hours.

"To our future!" Danny said, toasting the champagne glass.

"What do you want for the future, Danny?" Joy asked, leaning toward him as their glasses clicked.

"I want to love and be loved," he said. "Here's to what you learned from sixteen years of marriage and your daughter graduating from college."

"And to you finding the love of your life, *Danny boy!*"

"I'm rooting for both of us. I couldn't take Caroline to my nephew's wedding. It was lust that never moved to love, and weddings are for lovers. She ended my several years of celibacy, but never reached the feeling I had for Elaine…or Maureen."

"I can't believe you were celibate for four years."

"Wasn't worth it to get in a relationship just for sex. When I was younger, but not now. But Caroline had that Scorpio magnetism. And really, was a very nice woman. We just didn't click. We argued over wood versus plastic cutting-boards and what you could cook in a microwave. With Maureen, I made a cutting-board to assure her I was faithful. Caroline knew I was faithful, but she complained that wooden cutting-boards breed bacteria. Not a great way to keep a relationship going."

"I like to cook. But I love when a man cooks. I won't mess with your cutting-board," she said, laughing graciously.

"How nice. Well, let's toast left-handed Gemini's. You have such pretty hands."

"Thanks. But they're pretty beat up from swimming and playing basketball in school."

"Geez, you're smart and funny *and* an athlete. Wow! To us."

Afterward, they walked to her car. They chatted for a while as cars passed along the highway. Finally, he hugged her and kissed her gently on her cheek. "See you again?"

"Soon, I hope," she said, looking into his eyes.

"I'll call. Let's plan for this weekend."

As he walked back to his car, he kept the scent of her perfume in mind and her easy going style. Driving home, he felt light hearted for the first time in years.

The doorbell woke Danny on Saturday morning, a few days later. When he got to the porch, in jeans and a T-shirt, he saw Kajaw, dressed as usual, in a dark suit with a bold tie.

"Kajaw, come in. What's up?" Danny asked, worried.

"I was on my way to my office, but wanted to let you know my friend looks like he'll pull through."

"Great to hear. You deserve good news. Let me make you some tea."

"Thanks, but I have to get ready for class. I have to hurry. I just wanted to let you know they say it will take time, but they are optimistic. A tremendous relief. Now I have some time to worry about your bad relationships. I've been praying you will find a woman," he added, with a warm laugh.

"My bad relationships? Good luck! Hopefully, I'm about due for a good relationship. But great to hear about your friend. You are always good-hearted. The cancer thing has to go your way."

"Thanks, Danny. I appreciate your encouragement. You are a great friend."

225

"My man, you have suffered. I admire your strength. You'll get through."

"Thanks, Danny. It's good to hear you say it. I wanted to let you know some good news."

They hugged. Then Danny put his arm around Kajaw's shoulder.

"You're a good man, Dr. Carribe. A close friend. Anything I can do, let me know," Danny said, admiring his friend's courage. They talked for a few minutes then walked through the porch to the pond. "Consider the fish and turtles Dr. Carribe. See, reptiles on the rocks contemplating Buddha. Fish swimming among the lilies."

"Alright! Alright! I'll stay optimistic, Danny."

"Here feed them. You gotta believe your friend will recover. Buddha smiles near the sundial. Christ is in the lilies. Who knows about the other gods? But you must be strong."

Kajaw threw some pellets into the water. The orange and white Koi, now leading the remaining five fish since the hurricane deaths, swam slowly and started to feed.

"Thanks, Danny. You philosophers!"

Danny followed Kajaw out to his car parked on the driveway. They hugged again and Kajaw got into his car. Danny waved goodbye, concerned about his close friend, but optimistic as he walked back to the pond.

A short while later, Joy called to confirm their rendezvous to the beach.

"Maybe we can go to Argo too?" Danny asked.

"The spiritualist community? I've never been there. Would be fun."

"It's a small town of psychics and astrologers. I set my novel *The Feathered Serpent* there, about Pearl, a psychic whose clients were getting killed mysteriously. Anyway, see you around noon Sunday."

A few minutes after Danny ended the call with Joy, Tyrella Bishop called and invited him to dinner with their artist friends Raiz and Nicole.

At the large wooden table in the dining room, Tyrella and Nicole were surrounded by curry chicken and shrimp and chutney and relish as they wrapped the ingredients in rice paper and handed the spring rolls around.

"Well done, Ms. Bishop," Danny said, toasting her with a spring roll. "Some talented women here, eh Raiz?"

"Absolutely," Raiz replied, and filled Danny's wine glass.

"Did you see the Bush Kerry debate, Daniel?" Tyrella asked.

"Unfortunately. Bush sounded frightening. All isolationism and nationalism. He's obsessed with safety, not leading the world."

"Well, we all favor Kerry," she said enthusiastically.

"Lesser of two evils, I guess. When I was in Ireland last summer, everyone was asking why America wants to conquer the world. Frightening really. The EU folks seem pretty happy, but worried about the U.S."

"We'll see what happens with the election," Tyrella said. "But the good news is Nicole and Raiz are planning to open a gallery in town."

"Really? Great idea."

"Raiz will do the photography. I'll sell ceramics. We want you and Tyrella to sell ceramics too," Nicole said, as she handed him another spring roll.

"Works for me," Danny said. "When do you plan to open?"

"We're hoping to open early in December," Raiz said.

"Count me in. Dan and I just finished the kiln. So we should be able to fire things soon. Looking for the mystical green flame. It just amazes me at the end of a firing, when that green flame licks its way out of the spy hole when the firing is going well."

"Oh, I love when the green flame shows up at night," Tyrella said.

"That's when it's the best. So, I'm ready for some night firings. I just love seeing that flame at the end. I mean the chemistry of it has to do with copper oxidizing in the kiln, but it's the mystical green flame to me...with Irish implications of lucky leprechauns."

"Then you're in, Dr. Danny?"

"Definitely, Nicole. Great idea. Maybe it's time for me to get into the arts. Ever read Howard Gardner's book *Creating Minds*? He talked about Stravinsky, Picasso, Eliot, Einstein, Martha Graham, Freud, and Gandhi. He believes that brains are wired for certain arts. Maybe it's time for me to get into clay. Shakespeare's right, the stars shine, so we have to shine in response or remain underlings.

"Daniel, I can't imagine you as an underling."

"Thanks, Tyrella. That's because around you I feel inspired. We gotta get back to the studio soon."

On Sunday, Danny drove Joy to the beach for lunch. The dunes were eaten away by the barrage of hurricanes. Part of the beachside restaurant Sand Dollars had fallen into the ocean.

"Look at the exposed beams. The concrete just fell away."

"Those storms caused a lot more damage than I thought," she said, sadly.

Joy and Danny were standing on the ramp down to the beach, next to Sand Dollars. People were standing on the car ramp that dropped off into the water. The seawall was cracked in several places. The entire beach was chewed away.

got lucky. The beach is beat. I heard that near my Brother Rich's
here Kelly and Genny hit, there was lots of damage."

it's really sad to see this."

"Well, at least we should have lunch at The Blue Heron. I called, they said the deck is still there. They just lost the stairs to the beach."

The beach was eroded there too, but Joy and Danny used the beach access near where they parked to walk along the sand. Walking the beach always reminded him of his lifeguard days on Jones Beach. But today, as they walked hand in hand along the beach, Danny felt closer to Joy than he'd felt toward a woman in years.

The next day, Danny stopped in to see Angie. He stood near the Twain sculpture. "In the fifteen years I've been here, Tweedle Nasty has gotten more bitter. And much more dangerous. My first week she said, 'Be careful, you're future is in my hands.' I asked, my future? In a hateful whisper I still remember, she said, 'Remember, I've got your balls in my hands, pretty boy.' Unbelievable hostility."

"I heard they wrote letters against my tenure," Angie said, shaking her head. "And now Terry is on the Tenure Committee. She hates me. But they really hate you. You and Kajaw. Their only satisfaction is making others miserable."

"Angie, we just have to get you tenure. We've been listening to them for years. They've tormented you since you got here. Yep, being Kajaw's and my friend makes them hate you. But remember. You have support from all the other faculty. And Tony in Virginia."

"I hope so. But I think they got to Doreen Hopp too. And she's our Chair. I just want it to be over," she said, near tears.

That night, around three in the morning, he heard an owl hoot. Up in the dark, he thought about his mother and father. He went into the living room, turned the lights on over the fireplace mantel. He walked to the center of the room, next to the couch he built, near the planter he made to hold the palm that towered over him. Under the vaulted ceiling, feeling strange, he looked up to the balcony. He walked up to his office and looked out the back window, but he couldn't see the owl. He looked for a while, then walked to the balcony and looked into the living room.

He loved the house since remodeling it to create the balcony. But the green metal roof transformed the quaint Cape Cod into what he called Dr. Danny's BB&G. He heard the owl hoot again, but kept his attention toward the palm tree below in the large planter he made. "I hear you owl. I've lived here fifteen years. I heard you hoot my mom and dad's deaths. But I'm not gonna let Tweedle Dumb and Tweedle Nasty destroy my favorite student. So go hoot somewhere else."

Tony flew in the next Friday. Danny picked him up at the airport. They drove to the Marriott Hotel where the conference was scheduled. Tony was carrying his black leather briefcase. They checked in the main desk and went to the room. It smelled of cigarettes, so they went back to the main desk and asked for another room. They found one just over the pool.

They hadn't seen each other since the great conference Tony ran in Virginia that spring. They had dinner on the hotel patio under a warm sky.

The following morning, Tony gave the keynote speech for the conference sponsored by the International Center for Social Justice that he and Allison founded. He started by saying, "My Italian Catholic mother used to say whenever we did something wrong, that God would punish us. So what ever you people in this state have been doing, I hope you stop it, because those hurricanes were really bad. My next comment is that I know people don't let facts get in the way of what they believe, but the title of my new book, that some of you may have seen in *Time* magazine, is *Elevate the Republic*. It's about teaching children to improve the world they will inherit."

The applause was often and loud as Tony continued. Danny sat smiling as he watched his closest friend work.

That night they went to Danny's place. They had dinner downtown and talked. Danny drove Tony to the airport the following morning.

The night Joy came to dinner Danny cooked Dungeness crab and opened a bottle of White Star champagne. After dinner they hugged and kissed playfully while dancing as Dean Martin sang "Amore," amused they both really liked him. Then he showed her the Ryan and Diane wedding video. Afterward, he offered her the pearl earrings he'd bought when he was writing *The Feathered Serpent*.

"Danny, we don't know each other that well yet."

"Well, at least consider them," he said, disappointed.

"I will, but not yet. When we know each other better," she said, and hugged him near the fireplace, where he returned the pearl earrings to the scallop shell on the mantle.

"At least take the bowl. The rutile glaze is so like your eyes. Look how the blue shines, and the white sparkles. Your eyes have that shade of blue, and such an intense shine."

"Wow! You're going a bit overboard Danny boy. But thanks, no one's ever told me that. The glaze is beautiful. And I'm so impressed that you made it. Thanks," she said, and hugged him again.

He kissed her softly on the lips and extended their embrace.

"So Joy Perkins…social studies teacher…ex-Girl Scout leader…ex-Pop Warner cheerleader coach, a rah, rah girl, with rutile blue eyes – iridescent white splattered over sky blue, I think I'm falling in love with you."

"Why thank you. And you are adorable Danny," she added, and grabbed his butt. "Firm," she said.

"For an old man." Danny laughed, laying his hand on hers. "Used to be hard, but I got up the morning of my thirty-fifth birthday and realized my body moved out on me. This is all that's left at fifty-seven."

"Don't be so hard on yourself. Very nice," she said, and kissed him.

Nov. 3, 2004   3:33 a.m.

A few days ago, Boston won the World Series, during a lunar eclipse. 3:33 a.m. and so the eclipse of the moon moves above and over the house. In a minute, the deed is done, but the moments moment is 333. Ohio contested by Bush looking for votes. New England, the conscience of the country voted Kerry. The remaining states in the fundamentalist camp.   Political Correctness runs rampant.   During the Halloween tour with Joy through the Palm City Cemetery, a huge Ku Klux Klan headstone that pays homage to the Grand Wizard, a car dealer owner in town… Absurd…   How will America ever overcome our racist sexist ways?

The trip to assess the storm damage and visit Rich who believes in God, Church and country.   But I have a business deal for him.   I want to start Palm City University Press.   And so, I want to publish <u>My Block</u> and the book about education.   This white boy from Harlem must be about a mission…

November 10, 2004

My Block
Don Quixote Lives

Talking with Don Quixote as I sat on the curb next to him in his wheelchair outside Winslow Hall.   A professor with guts, his face contorted with the irony of life.   The moist breeze flapped his pants legs below the two amputations.   We talked about the future of PCU.   Don Q said, "Sometimes this place feels like a bad novel, all plot and no character.   But remember, honesty and openness spell hope," and he finished with a Cheshire cat grin.   I looked at him skeptically and asked, "Did you just make that up?" He replied quickly, "I've always been a good speller," and we both enjoyed the laugh and the sentiment equally.   Sitting next to him on the ground, I mentioned Hemingway's line about writers facing eternity. Don Q agreed, and he is a man who has suffered.

As mom said, "Take your troubles and run, Danny." But Don Q is heroic, so I sat on the curb and looked up to him as he talked about his novel <u>Drag Bunt</u>. He looked at me and said, "Write what you know Danny boy. My book is about a minor league baseball player who lost his legs in a car accident. And so, one writes about one's own struggles."

"Don Q, <u>My Block</u> is about everyone and everything I know."

"Well, an impossible but enviable task. Like Sisyphus rolling the rock endlessly. It will keep you busy, Danny boy. I'll root for you."

And so, a few days later in the Hutchins Grill, Danny and Rich talk about benefits and priorities.

"What do you want the book to do?" Rich asked, as they toasted Beefeater martinis to their dad.

"To transform American education."

"That's a pretty grand plan. Got anything more realistic?"

"To become a full professor and sell a book."

"I'd be happy to pay for producing it. Just acknowledge our support."

"I will."

"I was in the Plaza Hotel in Manhattan for lunch and Jim Watson was there. I went to say hello, then back and told my bosses that was Jim Watson of Watson and Crick, the guys that discovered DNA." Rich laughed. "Couldn't have been a better coincidence. I think you've got talent of his caliber."

"Would be nice to think so."

"I think you do. So, I'd be happy to help on the education book. But you are on your own with the novel."

"I haven't applied for full professor because it's an issue of integrity. I published a few articles, but I am 0 for 9 on novels. I don't even mention them on my annual report. Tony just published a book that *Time* magazine wrote an article about."

"You can do it too, Danny. You gotta believe in yourself. You're due."

Chapter 20: Arts Desire

Danny wrote his mom's Irish soda bread recipe on a piece of paper and packed the ingredients in his canvas bag with green handles. He bought a cast iron skillet at the Winn Dixie before heading the back way over the Sunrise River to Joy's house in Verana. He sang along with John Denver's *Greatest Hits* on the CD player as he drove the two lane highway though rural Florida.

"Sweetie, so good to see you," Danny said, when Joy met him at the door. They hugged long and tight.

"You brought gifts?"

"Just what you've always wanted…a cast iron skillet…and the recipe for Irish soda bread."

"So that's a skillet. I've heard of them," she said teasing. "I'd love to help you make Irish soda bread, Danny-boy."

"Glad to hear it," he said, and hugged her again, luxuriating in their embrace.

With his arm around her, they passed the gold fabric furniture. Asian prints hung in the living room to the left. The formal dining room to the right had a glass breakfront and wood dining table surrounded by eight chairs. Walking through the TV room, with the beige couch and love seat facing the big screen TV, Danny looked through the sliding glass doors to the pool and tree filled park beyond. He put the canvas bag on the kitchen counter and the skillet on the stove.

"Why don't we take a bike ride first?" Joy suggested.

"Great idea," he said, and hugged her again.

He pumped the tires on each of the bikes and they peddled out of the garage. Joy led up the small hill to the bike path. Danny followed, enjoying how the wind caught her ponytail from under her baseball cap.

"Let's take the path along the golf course, Danny."

"I see why you like Verana. Great view."

"That's where Julia went to school," she said, pointing toward the building in the distance. "I wanted her to be able to walk or bike to school."

"I've got to meet her. What's she doing these days?"

"Working for a law firm. She started law school."

"Must feel good to be a successful mom."

She smiled, then peddled on past the school to a narrow path behind wooden privacy fences as they alternated speeding up and peddling slowly to chat.

Back at the house, Danny opened the buttermilk. Joy unpacked the flour, salt, baking soda, baking powder, raisins, caraway seeds and safflower oil.

"You even brought an egg?" she said, and unwrapped it from the paper towel in the Ziploc bag.

"My mom would be impressed," Danny said. "She'd love the German woman in you. Both her parents came from Germany."

"She sounds like a good woman."

"Yes. Very. Her dad died when she was one. She was the youngest of three kids. Her mom was a house keeper then became the *Super* – superintendent for the apartment building they lived in. Resourceful Germans. A lot like you. I mean raising your daughter on your own...getting a master's...doing all the stuff you do. I'm impressed."

"Well, thank you. But remember, I'm half Scotch. And the Scotch and the Irish are like twins separated at birth. When my parents got divorced it was tough. I lived with my mom for a while. But she became intolerable. She started a wild lifestyle in the Sixties. I moved back with my dad. But he was into control and angry about the divorce. I had a lot of insecurity to overcome. I think that's what led me to my first marriage, but I learned a lot from that. So, I appreciate that you see me as a good person. I think you're pretty special too."

He mixed the dry ingredients with the beaten egg and buttermilk with his hands.

"I'm ready for a special relationship. I've told you about Elaine and Maureen."

"Yes. Maureen sounds very odd. And Elaine, was she frigid when you started dating?"

"Pretty much. Said she never had an orgasm. We worked on that for months, and she finally started to have orgasms. Then she started to share her new talent. I remember the morning I saw this metal watering can next to her bed, with a bright sun painted on it. Seemed very weird. When I asked about it, she admitted the carpenter who was remodeling her house gave it to her. Eventually, she acknowledged what she gave him in return."

"That's amazing. I've never been able to have just a sexual relationship with anyone. I have to feel intimacy. My husband used to go around cheating on me. But I could never cheat on him. I didn't have a sexual relationship with anyone until Julia was in college. It bothered me that my ex had women around when Julia was visiting him."

"Man, you have been through a lot. But you seem so positive."

"A lot of counseling and hard emotional work. Glad it shows. Tell me more about Elaine."

Danny kneaded the bread as Joy leaned against the counter next to him.

"I talked to her a few years ago, around the time her daughter was getting married in Portland. She tracked me down through my parents. Coincidentally, I was presenting at Tony's World Conference for Social Justice in Seattle that weekend. We talked about getting together. I hadn't seen her for twenty years. It was funny, she said 'I became a sex addict after you cured my frigidity. You got the best of my virginity. Now my pussy is turning gray, but I want to thank you for getting it to work.'"

"She actually admitted to being a sex addict?"

"That's what she said. But I loved the line about her pussy turning gray."

"Did you see her?"

"No, Tony said, 'What's the point?' And I agreed. Instead I went to see my third grade teacher who just retired from teaching at a university in Vancouver."

"Good decision. And Maureen sounds even weirder. Not telling you she was married. That is sick."

"No doubt. But I loved both of them, and learned a lot. Breaking up with Elaine, the incredible journey of no distance took six months. Emotional work is the hardest. But writing about it helps resolve things for me," he said. He shaped the dough in the greased skillet and put it in the oven. "Irish soda bread in forty minutes, Sweetie."

"Danny-boy you are an artist."

"Have a dress picked out for the gallery opening?"

"Want to look?"

He followed her through the TV room to the bedrooms at the north end of the house. Bubba, the blind Yorkie followed him as he scuffled his feet and kept slapping his thigh to keep her attention.

"I think Bubba's gonna be my spirit guide. Homer to Odysseus. She is such a happy soul. Ever since I turned down that soccer scholarship to Brown, I felt I needed a spirit guide. Meeting Tony at State has become my greatest male friendship. But a blind female dog, I think that's what I really need."

"She likes you. I can tell a lot about a guy by how Bubba responds."

Joy stood at her open closet filled with formal dresses. Danny led Bubba into the room, and looked at where her left eye had been cut out and healed over with fur and the translucent gray right eye. It was sad and heroic to him.

"She likes you. It might work for both of you," she teased, and laughed gently. "Well, here are some formal gowns," she said running her hand across them.

"Geez...they're some gorgeous outfits."

He rolled out the soccer ball he saw at the bottom of the closet.

"I got that ball in Korea, during the World Cup. Which ones do you like?" she asked, sliding several on the closet pole.

He saw a red dress with crystals on the bodice, an elegant piece. There was a three stone constellation at the waist of the short black dress that she showed him as he juggled the black and white soccer ball from foot to foot as she talked.

"Did you see the World Cup, Danny? I saw a game in Korea."

She took another red dress and held it toward him.

Danny juggled the ball on his feet. Then he kicked it gently against the molding.

"I wish I played in the World Cup. Think about it, guys are born for competition. The winner in a flood of sperm frantic to connect. Millions of sperm in search of one egg. The egg patient, sometimes looking to find the right Y chromosome to become a guy or looking to connect with another X chromosome to continue the monthly cycle aligned with the elegantly changing moon. For men it's always competition. For women it's selection. A closet full of dresses...how about that red one?" he said, pointing, still juggling the ball.

"It's cut too tight. It wouldn't fit."

"Hold it up."

She did. She was elegant, bright red against her gorgeous blue eyes and thick blond hair. She was beautiful, but with a rare compassion, he thought. Her astrology chart showed an Aquarian moon which made her a defender of rights and children, his mother's sign. He kicked the ball gently against the wall several time and looked at her in the gorgeous red dress.

"Geez, you are beautiful."

"Oh, Danny. I'm glad you find me beautiful. But what does it mean? It's just physical. Some belief people have about some imaginary ideal. It's what's inside that counts. I see my students, the pretty girls get all the attention. Silly. As a teacher, I have to explain to my students we are each valuable for who we are."

"I agree. It's part of who somebody is. I left soccer to teach. The crowd's applause meant nothing. As a kid, I pole vaulted. It took a whole season to move the bar a foot. It made no difference if anyone watched. I needed to do it. I'd set it at the world record, the way one looks at the moon and out to the stars and beyond. It's aspiration that counts, what one wants to become, what self one wants to achieve. I miss that I didn't go farther in soccer. But I always follow my interests. I think you understand that too. Look at all you've done."

"I agree one has to follow one's interests. I love what I do. I love to teach and I love to travel. To experience the real world that I teach about in geography. I want to share that with a man."

"You are a sweetheart. I love what you're saying," he said, and hugged her, squeezing the red dress between them. Kissing her, he said, "I hope this works between us."

Looking at a shelf to the right behind her he saw several pictures.

"What are these?"

"My trip to Chichen Itza."

"Who's the guy you're kissing?"

"My boyfriend then, who became my husband. Julia's father, my EX. A painful experience. Sixteen years, three of which were in court to get my share of what we worked for all those years, and to get past all the open-heart surgery Julia went through. And the son I lost in a miscarriage because I wanted a sibling for Julia."

"That must have been terrible," he said, and hugged her again.

"Painful, yes. But I've gotten over it. I loved Mexico and especially Chichen Itza. It seems so mystical and magical."

"I know. Back in the '90s I had a feeling I needed to see it. I loved it. I wrote a novel called *The Feathered Serpent* about it. Seems we see similar things in the world, Sweetie. And you have been through hell. I hope you are enjoying yourself these days."

"With you I am, thanks Danny. Let me read your novel?"

"Sure, thanks. Let's celebrate. The Irish soda bread must be ready. And the champagne cold."

That night as he drove home, a gorgeous golden globe moon rose as if moving up the lines of a musical staff as it glowed through the power lines along the interstate. He watched it along the scrub oak and pine and palms. As he passed Argo, he realized that his life was once again full, the feeling that if he were to die tomorrow, his life would be complete.

He drove to the studio to check the bisque kiln. He moved several bowls and vases from the kiln shed to the table in his studio. He went in to look at the high fire kiln to plan his next firing. He kept thinking about Joy, feeling he was moving toward love, a wonderful feeling percolating mysteriously in his chest. When he got home, he put on some music he bought in Ireland and called her.

"The gallery opening is at six. Friday traffic means you gotta leave early."

"You still wearing your tuxedo?"

"Absolutely! This will be fun. We'll serve the wine. So have fun picking a dress."

After they talked, Danny walked out along the driveway to the road. The moon appeared as a lucky pearl over Palm City. He stood watching it silently, smiling, thinking about Joy.

As morning light appeared through the bedroom shutters, Danny opened them. The moon was above over the water oaks draped with Spanish moss. He opened his journal on the nightstand and wrote.

Nov. 29, 2004

Life is the sun and moon waxing and waning. How did our ancestors determine what moved? The stable firmament and all others moved around it. To see the sun rise each day and set each evening and the moon's elegant passage. How did anyone decipher it?

The moon 240,000 miles away. Brother Rich helped put a man on it. The tides related, but how and why the empty rock with a mirror image of the American continent. The moon always facing, so no one saw the dark side. How did Galileo determine the moon was a sphere? These are the questions that the Egyptians built pyramids to consider.

The Mayans built pyramids and temples and observatories for the same reason. The Mayan pyramids in The Feathered Serpent explore the mystery of the summer solstice cascading down the pyramid steps in homage to the return of their god Kukulcan. Did they sacrifice the winners or the losers in the ball game? How glorious to sacrifice the winners…to win and to be offered to the gods… Amazing.

Life isn't acquisition…like Columbus and Isabel and Ferdinand conquering the New World. In <u>Ulysses</u> Molly Bloom made love sound arbitrary. But it's not…to find love and live it to the fullest.

Rich got a man to the moon with the simple rule that "F=MA". We learned in high school physics that Force is equal to Mass times Acceleration. I love to watch Rich recite the formula as a plane flies overhead. We know it's what got man to the moon. But the Mayans splattered their temples with blood under full moons and solstice sunsets. Then Bishop Landa burned the Mayans' scrolls and destroyed their history during the Spanish Inquisition.

Joy and I've been to the Mayan ruins… She survived her daughter's open heart surgeries and the miscarriage… She has seen the blood gore and sacrifice. I've seen my parents die and my brothers marry and have their children marry… That is life, beyond blood sacrifice to love completely and fully.

That morning Danny drove through Tampa to the state education meeting in St. Petersburg. The twenty-five years since he arrived in Tampa had changed the skyline. It went from sleepy town to overcrowded city. He drove through Gulf Coast University campus and admired the minarets.

He continued on to St. Petersburg. That evening, he called Joy from the beach, walking out under the moonlight, watching the waves lapping in from the Gulf. The next morning, he called Joy from his room as the sun rose above the power lines.

"Sweetie. It's time to leave this country. Let's think about Europe or Asia or South America. I'm sick of America. I'm sick of its fundamentalist attitudes. I loved Ireland last summer. I know you study world religions. It seems to me if I started a religion, it would be one where women would be allowed to do what they want."

"In the Koran, even before that Taliban and Osama, women were second-class citizens. They couldn't go anywhere without a male escort. They had to cover their faces. In Buddhism, women have no choices. I told the kids that women have three choices in America: Mrs. means married. Miss means unmarried. Ms. means it's none of your business!"

"I knew I liked you. Well done. Let's plan an escape after the gallery opening."

"Danny, you are adorable, but weird. I think that's why I like you."

Danny went to the meeting and listened to nonsense. During a break he talked with a friend of Kajaw Carribe. As they talked and joked about their antipathy toward the Bush brothers, Danny recited a line from a woman he dated, "If I can't have my way, at least I'll have my say."

During the meeting nobody acknowledged that Florida was one of the worst states in the country for education. During a question-answer period,

Danny asked the national director, "Why do you allow this state to do as poorly as we are?"

She smiled wanly.

He persisted. "I moved to Tampa in '79. I just drove over from Palm City yesterday. The roads have deteriorated in twenty-five years. It's still two lanes from Orlando to Lakeland. The state hasn't improved the road in 25 years. The speed limit is 55 miles an hour and two lanes. What makes you think the government can improve the schools?"

"That's why we are all here. We can make a difference."

"And so the national standards board makes a living selling nonsense? Its curriculum and assessment people force teachers to make kids perform on standardized tests. Teachers are leaving the field, even the state predicts teacher shortages."

"We have to cooperate with the state officials," she said, walking in another direction.

"Florida is in the bottom five states in the country on any measurement. The state tests haven't changed that. Teachers are still under paid. New schools can't be built until the old ones are overcrowded. So third world portables pop up near parking lots and kids get squeezed in. That's got to change."

Danny heard scattered applause but decided to stop. He sat through the hours of meeting dedicated to completing a workbook that the State developed to train teachers. It all seemed mindlessly futile and motivation for him to develop genuine teaching.

Friday night, Danny walked out in his tuxedo with a glass of chardonnay as Joy pulled into the crescent shaped parking area in front of his house. She stepped out in a long-sleeved black sequined dress, gorgeous and classy. Her silver earrings flashed as they hugged.

"You are elegant."

"Why thank you. Glad you like it," she said, with an engaging smile.

They drove to the gallery in his old white sports cars. The gallery was already filled with people. He walked to Nick the Tailor and put his arm around him, "Thanks for coming, Nick. Since you have the major shop in town, it'll mean a lot to Raiz."

"Glad to do it, Danny. Nice tuxedo!"

"You're Nick the Tailor," Danny said, bowing. "This tux made it to Rosecliff in Newport. Now the Hamid opening."

"You have good taste, Danny. And who's this beautiful woman?"

"My friend Joy. We are the wine servers tonight."

"Now I get the tuxedo. Let me walk you to the bar?" he asked Joy, looking up to her, extending his hand.

People were talking and drinking, browsing the paintings on the wall, and pottery and sculpture on shelves in the middle. Danny pointed to several tall textured vases with green glaze and two large rutile glazed bowls of his on the shelves as they passed through the crowd. Then he pointed to a large vase with his frolicking primal people, naked in amorous acrobatic positions.

"You are an artist, Danny," Nick said, touching the vase, as he walked Joy to the bar.

"As are you Nick. Let me pour you a glass of wine, so we can both toast Joy."

Danny opened several bottles of white and red wine that Nicole had on the floor behind the counter in the back corner of the gallery.

"This reminds me of being beer man at Jones Beach. The drunks would wander up from the beach Sunday morning waiting for the one o'clock starting time," Danny said, as he filled several glasses.

"They look eager," Joy said, touching him gently on the shoulder.

They served until they were able to fill extra glasses for the crowd. Then Joy walked off to talk with Raiz and Nicole and Dan. Danny poured several more glasses then found her near the front door. They went next door to the Black Market, a fashionable clothing store.

"What do you think, Danny?" Joy asked, holding up an elaborate copper necklace and earrings."

"I like it...the copper against your skin and eyes...great. My treat."

They went back to the gallery and helped serve wine until the gallery closed.

Afterward, they went back to Danny's house. He opened a bottle of White Star champagne and said, "To a successful opening!"

They toasted then danced playfully to Dean Martin singing "Amore." As Dean Martin sang, they undressed each other slowly during each dance, tossing clothes on the couch. Finally, naked, they went into the bedroom. Danny lit a candle in the old brass floor lamp he used as a candle holder. They started to make love as Dean Martin sang "Volare."

"Oh, I love when he sings in Italian. Oh, that gets to me," Joy said.

They kissed softly then more passionately. Joy sucked his tongue and he caressed her thighs and breasts. Then he sucked gently on her nipples and felt her wetness. Slowly, he entered her and they kissed deeply as their bodies moved to the rhythm of the song.

Excited, Danny moved more dramatically. The headboard filled with books started to shake. As they sped up, books scattered from the shelf to the bed and onto the floor.

"All literature falls at your feet, Joy," Danny said laughing, as he saw *The Odyssey, Ulysses, Women in Love, The Old Man and the Sea, The Great Gatsby,* and others scattered around them.

"Dean Martin does it to me. But you, Danny, O'Boy! I love the way you just do me!"

"Well, thanks. Maybe we should do research for a series of vases with my primal people called *Just Do Me!*"

"What a great idea," she said. "You're even perspiring. Having fun?"

"I remember after my first soccer game for the Spartans. I was sitting at my locker, actually sweating joyfully about our first victory. But I never imagined this is what *Sweating Joy-fully* really means. You are incredible!"

"We do fit together well, don't we, Danny Boy!"

Danny rolled to his side and helped her on top of him, fondling her breasts as she straddled him.

"Not only are you beautiful, and a sweetheart, you're athletic. Let's just keep as this, you're wonderful."

Pushing books onto the floor, they continued to make love.

Chapter 21: Bridge of Lions

The next morning while Joy slept, Danny made Irish soda bread and picked fresh oranges from the trees in the front yard. He juiced them while the bread was baking and mixed champagne from last night. He brought everything to her in bed as she woke.

"Here, Sweetie."

"Mimosas and Irish soda bread. I knew there was something about you I loved. Thanks."

They ate and chatted for a while, then made love again. This time the kisses were deep and warm. Danny delighted in the soft texture of each of Joy's nipples, playfully sucking one then the other as their bodies fit together as if designed for each other.

Much later after they lay caressing each other and gently kissing, Danny said, "I have to go to the kiln. Nicole and Tyrella are doing a high fire today. I told them I would help. We're trying to get everything ready for the Christmas sale now that the gallery is open."

"Why don't you bring them some Irish soda bread."

"Good, idea. You want to come?"

"No, I'll see you later."

After giving Irish soda bread to Tyrella and Nicole as they tended the kiln, Danny found Dan in the studio working.

"Danny-boy," Dan said, looking up from where he was surrounded by brightly colored broom handles.

"See, you know I'm Danny-boy. You gotta be Dan. Or Great Whitehead, or whoever that Viking ancestor of yours was."

"OK. I guess you're right."

"Well thanks. I mean you don't even know who the singer Kate Smith is. And you sure as hell ain't Irish. What are you doing, anyway?"

"Sanding these mop and broom handles."

"How many you got?"

"About three hundred," he said, pointing to various barrels into which he had sorted them by color.

"And I guess you painted them red, blue, green and yellow?"

"Yes. I've been collecting them for thirty years. I want to use them in a sculpture. See the telephone pole?"

"Yeah. What's your idea?"

"I'm calling it 'Forces of Nature.' After the hurricanes, so many things were blown down I thought using the telephone pole and colored handles would show how nature rebuilds."

"That Jimmy Buffet song 'Piece of Work' works for you. You are who the hell you are! Dan, you gotta be Great Whitehead, America's Great sculptor! Can I help?"

"I need to drill holes to insert the handles. Think you can help me lift the telephone pole onto the drill press?"

"It's ten feet long!" Danny said, as he measured it with his shoes toe to heel, like he measured the runway when he pole vaulted. "It must weigh as much as you."

"That's why I'm lucky you're here, Danny Boy!"

"Let's try, oh Great Whitehead."

"Let's roll it as far as we can, then lift from the same side, onto the work table," Dan suggested.

They rolled it then lifted it onto the table to support its weight.

"You are an artist Great Whitehead. Nice work. We can stabilize it with these wooden wedges and you can start drilling."

Dan set the drill and they slid the pole onto the drill press.

"Thanks, Danny-boy. I heard from Audrey Hechsher that Terry Rheames and Lorrence Slutski won't support Angie Harper for tenure."

"Audrey said that? Angie heard it too. I can't see how Tweedle Dumb and Nasty can get away with it."

"They're saying Angie doesn't have passion for the stuff she's supposed to do for the department."

"Neither of them knows what passion is. I've never seen them in a relationship. Rheames is into control and Slutski likes to be controlled. That is not healthy. Rheames could fit Jung's witch archetype. Like a female mosquito looking for blood. Hopefully, we have enough tenured faculty to support Angie."

"I wish you luck."

"We'll see…"

That Friday, Danny drove Joy to Disney's Grand Floridian Hotel. They danced to Christmas music from the small band near the lavishly decorated tree. Then they walked through the Swan and Dolphin Hotels.

"When I was going through my divorce, I brought my daughter Julia here. She loved it, especially the pools outside."

They held hands, and kissed and hugged as they walked.

"I'm so happy you survived all that."

"And now I have you. It was worth it."

"Well, *thank you,*" he said, playfully mimicking his favorite phrase of hers then hugging her.

They drove to Joy's house. They undressed each other on the bed.

"I think this is my favorite," he said, sucking her nipple playfully. Then going to the other, he said, "No, this one. Oh, such nice texture."

Eventually, he helped move Joy on top so he could fondle her breasts and nibble and suck them as she rode slowly at first, then athletically up and down on him, each of them moaning and sighing, connected emotionally and physically. She moaned as she reached climax and he climaxed and she lay gently on him, immobile for a long time. He embraced her and stroked her hair gently.

After they lay quietly embracing for a long time, Danny said, "Such a lovely face in an exquisite body, complemented with a gorgeous mind."

She looked in his eyes and said, "And you're such a blarney artist, but I'm falling in love with you."

"The falling in love part is mutual," he said, and kissed her softly.

The next morning he drove back to load the high fire kiln with things he'd made as Christmas presents for his family that he needed to get done quickly to send them. He told Joy he'd call around noon to confirm the time for her neighbor's party that evening, but forgot until about three.

When Joy answered, she sounded angry. She said, "Danny, you were supposed to call by noon. It's too late. I called them to cancel."

"I forgot. I'm sorry," he said, surprised by her tone.

"I want to be important. But I feel you fit me in around your projects."

"I'm sorry… but with the opening, the pottery sale, and now Christmas, I've had to get these things made. I love you. It's been twenty years since I've felt this way."

"You're not showing it."

"I'm sorry. I love your passion for teaching. Your independence. Your assertiveness. You're a great mind in a great body," he said, unraveling.

"I think you're letting the outside keep you from getting to know me inside. Communicating our inner selves is what counts. I don't feel that from you, Danny, I'm sorry. You've been so absorbed in all the pottery. Bottom line, I don't feel you make me a priority. We aren't communicating as well as I want to, and that feels like hell. I'm sorry, Danny. I hate how I feel. I don't want to hurt you. But, please, don't come over tonight."

"Joy.... No... Please."

"I think it's best, Danny. We need time to decide if we're good for each other. Goodbye," she said, and the phone went dead.

Devastated by the phone conversation, he spent the night in the studio, glazing pots, and loading the kiln, listening to Mozart on his CD player. Tyrella stopped by around six, as he was near finished loading the kiln, and had placed the cone pack to monitor the kiln temperature.

"Danny, I told Emma we'd get these two busts into the kiln," Tyrella said, pointing toward two busts on the rolling rack near the kiln.

"This one of a child doesn't seem to have a large enough hole in it to let the air out as it heats in the kiln, and the smudge under its nose makes it look like Hitler."

"It does rather. But it would be so nice to get it done. She is such a sweet woman."

Danny put them into the kiln and finished bricking up the front door. He told Tyrella about the sudden disaster in his relationship with Joy as he started the first two burners. They walked back to the studio where he had been glazing and Tyrella helped clean up. Then they went back to the kiln to start the final two burners and stood talking. Suddenly he heard a loud pop. He removed the brick from the fire hole to look into the kiln. The cone pack was shattered, scattering the temperature cones like broken teeth, and he could hear clay crackling.

"Something exploded. I gotta stop the kiln," Danny said, grabbing a flashlight.

Looking in the hole as Danny held the flashlight, Tyrella said, "If it's just the cone pack can't we slide another in?"

"I have to see what happened."

"If we take the other brick out, we can see."

"Well done, I can see why I like you." He removed the brick she indicated, but it exposed more shards and each brick they removed exposed more broken pottery. Every shelf was filled with debris.

"The curse of Hitler!" she said. "When I was a child in London we suffered his bombings."

"I figured it wouldn't work. Emma didn't put a big enough hole in that bust to let the heat out. Damn! I gotta unbrick the whole thing. I didn't need this," he said, overwhelmed with frustration.

Four of his original twelve pots didn't make it through the bisque because he rushed them. They were already in the dumpster. Now this, and Tyrella was in a hurry to get to a Christmas party. Her insistence that he include the heads caused the disaster, but he wasn't angry with her. How different friendship was, he thought. Joy had abandoned him and now he would have to go north alone with whatever pots he could salvage from this kiln when he re-fired it through the night. As Tyrella formed clay to make another cone pack to measure the kiln temperature during the firing, Danny interrupted.

"I prefer a coil."

"I like this."

"Work with me today," he said, but felt uncomfortable about the edge in his voice.

"Maybe I should withdraw completely?"

"No... I respect your work, but let it be my Irish superstition," he said, trying not to let his heartache over Joy interfere.

"I don't care what you call it. Do what makes you feel best," she said, graciously.

And so, Danny rolled a coil. Sensing Tyrella felt badly because the two busts were her suggestion, Danny put his arm around her shoulder and said, "Thanks for being here...let me take it from here...you have your party...and you've listened to me complain all night about Joy."

"Danny, I'm sorry about Joy. Maybe you should have stayed with Caroline."

"That was lust."

"Yes. But you enjoyed it," she said, with a reflex smile.

"But I felt smothered," he said, and shrugged.

"I know. You are a difficult man Daniel Roarke. But I believe Joy will see that you are also one of the rare good men."

"Thanks, Tyrella," he said, and hugged her. "Caroline was so clearly lust and suddenly Joy is love. So bizarre. I never thought it would ever happen again. And now she feels rejected because of all the kiln firings I've been doing. It's been so long since I've been in love. It's hard to focus on her exclusively. She sees that, thinks I'm in love with her because she's beautiful... why so many guys chase her. She wants me to focus on who she is not how she looks. I'm so overwhelmed by the whole thing. I never thought I'd fall in love again."

"It's a woman thing to focus her life completely on a man."

"And to tell her I'm off to the kiln makes no sense to her. She must feel I'm just using her."

"Daniel, she'll see that you are a good man. Mark my words."

"Tyrella, you are such a big sister to me. Thanks. I really appreciate it," he said, and hugged her.

After she left, Danny tended the kiln in the darkness. Things tumbled in his head as he struggled to keep going, considering the irony of the exploding pots and his decimated relationship, and the exploded Hitler bust made by an Evangelical woman. It took five hours to unpack, clean and repack the kiln with Joy's small bowls he taught her to make, his vases, and student work. He was tired and sweaty from the kiln heat and the cold night.

After tending the burners, he walked out to the field beyond the kiln and looked at the crescent moon. When he sighted the Big Dipper, he thought about ancient cultures that identified and mythologized this and other constellations in the night sky. He noticed Cassiopeia and Orion all named and with stories. He walked back to the kiln and opened his journal.

Dec. 20ᵗʰ, 2004: 1:33 a.m.

Tending the kiln. A pagan vigil – transforming clay and chemicals to art. Is this my religion now? Without Joy… The kiln starting to glow. The random stars arranged in constellations that made Walt Whitman wonder and walk out in silence to look up at the stars when he heard the learned astronomer in the auditorium. Five a.m. Mozart on CD and me contemplating the kiln against the night sky. Flames, heat, oxidation and reduction, the fires of Hades and the eternal torment. But I built this kiln brick by brick with Dan during the hurricane. And so we built the sacred fire to offer sacrifice to art – practical and beautiful pottery. It is work that gives meaning under the night sky and a chance to look up in silence and wonder. But art cannot replace a woman… Oh, to have both…but writing is elegant torment. Throughout the night compelled to write a poem as I tend the kiln:

Torment

Anguish in my head and chest – call it agony of heart.
When you asked me to write a poem
I thought it would be a happy one
about the ecstasy I feel with you
when sharing Irish soda bread or playing in the grove or dancing on the rug
or making love in bed.
You know I love you and that extreme has been more with
you than anyone I've known.
But now you ask about the other side, the agony.
I'm here with you and hate it just as much.

You call it hell and I agree because we're out of touch; I prefer our
joyful touching hands and lips and favorite body parts in artful research
for "Just Do Me" the series you suggested, that I started today.
Alone, I work for what? It's just pottery…
But love you say and I agree is what we must resolve.
A writer writes because he must…
And so, I've written pages in my journal
to answer the question that you ask, "Are we good for each other?"

Poets write of love. Carl Sandburg wondered about lovers
and Yeats, who I've read to you in bed while we loved,
pondered love false and true;
And so I sit with tears down my face;
I keep at this with my left hand that we share so sweetly
in bed and other places to move the poem on. But only to tell you
not to move on, but reconsider.

Thoughtful Emily Dickinson pondered pain of parting.
You say now for you is hell and me too
because being away from you is all the hell I can endure.
You've made my life a joy of late and for that I thank you.
But this side of it I hate and doubly worse
because I've done it to myself and you.
The "bottom line" you say is my failure to communicate.
And so, the torment drives me to focus on our love –
that has never been love and hate,
but love and failure to communicate.

But you ask if we are good for each other.
That's our major issue. Is my failure to communicate
a symptom of a deeper problem that we can't resolve?
This is the torment that drives me to write
and the question I need your help to answer.
We are not in this alone, or certainly, alone we'll be;
and that's not what I want and I want you to agree.
You need me to be supportive and consistent and to tell
you how I feel; I need and want the same. Let's work at that;
let's promise each other that, and keep at
this love we've created so we can do away with hell.

Having tended the kiln all night as he wrote, he unbricked it in the morning as the sun rose pink at dawn, the heat distorting the air as it escaped. He had gloves on but could feel the heat. He opened the top layer of bricks and walked away. He came back a while later and kept removing layer after layer of brick. He shined the flashlight into the dark kiln and saw other pots cracked.

This final firing was a disaster. He salvaged four of the dozen vases he started with three days before. He packed up the small bowls he helped Joy make and then he took the vases to the UPS store and shipped them off to Brother Rich and Charlie's families. He called Joy when he got back to the house.

"I sent everything UPS. I won't go to New York tomorrow."

"I want you to go."

"But I want to be with you for Christmas."

"I don't feel good that now you're done with everything else, you have time for me. That's not the sort of love I want."

"I'll tell my family I'm not coming."

"I don't want to come between you and your family."

"They'll understand."

"No, Danny. You made plans. Have a good Christmas, goodbye."

Listening to her phone go dead, Danny felt his heart twisted and pulled from his chest.

Standing in his living room, before he left for the airport, as he passed the Norfolk Island pine with the Mr. and Mrs. Santa ornaments, he swung the Mrs. Santa doll.

"Mrs. Santa, Caroline and Joy are the only women I've slept with this Millennium. What can I expect for next year? Remember, my astrologer says 2005 is gonna be my year to meet the one."

Mrs. Santa smiled silently and swayed gently back and forth on the branch in her plaid coat. Danny hurried upstairs to his office and e-mailed Joy the poem he wrote at the kiln then hurried out to meet his plane.

After the security labyrinth where Danny stripped off his shoes, belt, keys, wallet, cell phone and pocket watch, he managed to get through with his *Genuine Teaching* manuscript and his journal and video-camera. The flight was bumpy at the end. Rich met him at the airport wearing a camel hair topcoat and carrying a red umbrella.

That night, in the upstairs guest room in Rich's house, Danny lay awake in bed obsessed about Joy. It was impossible for him to sleep or forget her; he wrote in his journal.

Dec. 22, 2004: 1:47 a.m..

Ulysses returned to defend Penelope... Bloom returned to make breakfast for Molly. I'm adrift watching clock hands move silently next to an empty bed, as the year winds down and the woman I love is more than a thousand miles away...

That morning, Beth sat at her work table, finishing the final gift boxes. Danny handed her the Florida hat for his grand nephew Blake and the luminescent fish for his grand niece Sadie that he got at the airport yesterday.

"Oh, she'll like it. I like the way it sparkles."

"And the pouch to hold her secret things," Danny said, pointing to the zipper along the back.

Beth sat surrounded by brightly wrapped boxes. Danny gathered the boxes with bows and stars and started to carry them down to the pool room.

"I finished the *The DaVinci Code* last night. The ending was kinda disappointing," she said.

"Where the grandparents talk about the kids?"

"Yes, that they are the bloodline from Christ and Mary Magdalene."

"Interesting idea, although I have a hard time buying it. But DaVinci must have been quite a guy. He may have forged the Shroud of Turin. I'd like to see that mystery solved."

"What's the Shroud of Turin?"

"Supposedly, Christ's burial shroud. So, with the Last Supper supposedly showing Mary Magdalene and Christ and the Shroud, DaVinci may be a key player in the history of Christianity."

Danny carried the pile of boxes downstairs and placed them around the tree. He continued shuttling presents from the work table to the pool room as Beth hurriedly wrapped them.

That night, after all the presents were given and everyone went to bed, Danny walked outside to look up at the night sky. He called Joy.

"Merry Christmas. I'm calling you from a windy deck overlooking Long Island Sound. Connecticut looks well decorated."

"Wait a moment. I have some friends over. Let me go to my room."

"Did you have a good Christmas, Joy?"

"It's been enjoyable. But I miss you terribly. I'm sorry I've been so difficult. I really over reacted. I guess all the mistrust I had from my marriage got in the way. I'm sorry."

When they ended the call, he stood in the snow and looked up at the full moon overhead. He couldn't wait to get back to Florida.

The following morning, Danny sat on the couch in the pool room with the *Genuine Teaching* manuscript as Rich explained a business plan to sell Danny's book.

Rich played older brother, saying "Money counts, that's the measure. You don't want to have a bunch of PhDs sitting around saying I disagree with what you said on page 51."

"So, if I'm gonna sell this book, I'll have to market it?"

"Yes. If you want it to sell. You can do it. I'll back you."

"Well, since life is a team sport, I guess there's no promotion like self promotion," Danny said, smiling, shaking his head in disbelief over what felt like arrogance.

As he sat surrounded by the presents and tree with his brother, he kept thinking that it was great to share Christmas with family, and he felt hopeful about Joy. It looked like he would sell the book about educating, but he wanted to love and be loved.

While driving Danny to the airport the next day, Beth said, "Maybe you should send Joy roses?"

"And how about adding a trip to St. Augustine?"

"Ooh! That sounds very romantic. Yes, do that, Danny."

On his way back from the airport that evening, he stopped at a florist. He ordered a dozen roses and attached a card that said:

Dear Joy,

> *I think of you often,*
> *you ignited my heart to love…*

> *Danny*

That night, the ringing phone woke him up.

"Joy?" he asked eagerly.

"Danny, yes. Were you asleep?"

"Yeah…what's up?"

"I want to invite you to a come as you are party?"

"It's one a.m."

"Yes. I know. I have a good idea how you are dressed, too. I want you to come as you are."

"OK, Sweetie. I'll be there as soon as I can."

He was on the road in a few minutes. The moon was bright, having been full on Christmas. When he got to her house, she met him at the door. He saw the roses in the vase on the table in the family room. They hugged and kissed at the door, then went into her bedroom and made love.

The following morning, as they woke and Danny caressed her, he said, "Remember, you called me."

He watched as she averted her eyes as if astounded by what she did last night and that he was in bed with her this morning. The look was of astonishment, as if looking back and forward at the same time, amazed that she called and he came.

"I'd love to know what just happened during that look," Danny said, and laughed, deeply and richly.

They both laughed. Eventually she returned his look. They gazed at each other, reconnected. They made love again.

As they kissed, Danny started to fondle her. "I know you don't like me to think about you as a sex object, but you are the best object I've ever had sex with."

"Why thank you, Dr. Roarke. And you're just what I need. I'm sorry I was so negative. Wow, it was like a flashback to my marriage. I really had to work to get past it. I'm sorry. And I know you don't think of me as a sex object, but I love the way we fit together."

"I love the way we fit together, too. Your parts are exactly where my parts want to go. But what I really like is how our hearts are fitting together. I think the separation made me realize how much I care about you. Astounding, Ms. Perkins...astounding!"

On New Year's Eve they watched the ball drop at Times Square on her big screen television, then walked outside with champagne and heard fireworks in the neighborhood and watched several sky rockets explode above them. In the morning, they went to her Korean friends' restaurant for breakfast. Then they met with a psychic at Argo who told Joy this year would transform her. They went back to Verana and had dinner with Joy's daughter Julia and her boyfriend.

The next night he made dinner from the Fresh Grocers and they watched a George Carlin movie. And so, Thursday, Friday, Saturday and Sunday night was the longest together ever. Danny offered her the pearls for New Years, and she accepted them graciously as they walked and talked in the lush park behind her house.

They made reservations at the Casablanca Inn in St. Augustine for the following weekend. They drove from Palm City to Amelia Island to Fort Clinch and Fernadina Beach ending at the porch overlooking the bay at the Casablanca Inn, where they watched horses and carriages framing the Bridge of Lions against a crimson sky at sunset. They had *tapas* at the Columbia Restaurant, enjoying elegant dark rooms filled with people. They chatted and laughed among the people at the crowded shiny wood bar as they shared lamb and squid and crab dip. Joy shimmered in a dark top and black pants and small heeled sandals.

They walked from Columbia to Tradewinds to dance in the crowded room of happy people. Two women applauded as they danced, offering their seats when they finished, and suddenly a cherubic dark haired man offered them drinks and introduced his wife. And so, they made people happy with their presence. Joy announced that they were going steady, hugging a biker at the bar, who toasted, "To a happy marriage."

And so they danced again then walked the long Bridge of Lions to Allison's on the other side.

Joy hugged Pat, the heavy leprechaun lead singer in the small band, as they discovered they were both from Ohio when the band took a break. Danny and Joy were the only ones on the dance floor when the band resumed. Joy barefoot with red toe nails. And so they danced and drank and walked back toward the Casablanca. On the way back, Joy hopped onto the bridge.

"Hey, Danny boy, want to see me jump?"

"No!"

"I can't hear you, Danny boy. Communicate. Why did you make me go over the bridge?"

"It's the Bridge of Lions. You know, roar, roar, Roarke. You wanted to see it."

"I see it right under my feet. Could we have seen it without having to walk over it back and forth?"

"You wanted to dance at Allison's. You met somebody from Ohio. That was cool."

"Don't ever push me like that again. Promise? Or I'm gonna jump."

"Relax... I promise," Danny said, as Joy slipped out of her shoes and started to walk the bridge like a gymnast on a balance beam.

"You better promise so I believe you," she said, as she continued to walk ahead of him.

"Com'on Joy, this isn't funny. It's a long drop to the water and you have no idea what's down there."

"I can swim, Danny-boy. And remember, I was a diver."

"Joy, diving would be crazy... Jumping would be crazy," he said, reaching for her hand as she stood on the bridge.

"Don't ever tell me what to do Danny. Please, ask."

"OK. *Please*, just take my hand."

"Tell me you love me, and you'll never tell me what to do."

"OK, OK. I promise," he said, feeling her lean toward the water, but afraid to pull her back. "You are beyond all women... I've never loved anyone more." He held her hand firmly, his heart racing.

"I can see the Casablanca. Maybe I'll swim back."

Danny stood motionless as cars swished past them in opposite directions on the bridge. He looked at the black water below and Joy's feet with red toenail polish on the course white texture of the bridge.

"How about we walk together?"

"Oh, Danny, you need to get out more. You need some excitement in your life," she said, and leaned toward him.

He eased her off the bridge and back onto the sidewalk.

"Thanks, Danny. I had to see what you'd do. I grew up in a military family. My father was into control and my mother wouldn't submit and left. I know I was being a pain in the butt. But I just had to see how you'd react. You are the first man I've ever met who let's me be me. You're into cooperation, not competition. You passed the test. I love you."

"I'm glad! Life is a team sport, Sweetie. Camus didn't want anyone walking in front or behind him... He wanted neither to follow nor lead... He wanted someone to walk beside as friends."

"Bright man. I've wanted that all my life. You were really worried I'd jump, that's great. I wanted to see how much you care. You really do. I love you. I won't ever have to be a pain in the ass again. Thanks, Danny. You are the first man I've ever trusted completely. It's a great feeling. Great!"

"Great to hear. You had me worried. But I'm glad you did it. To be tested on the Bridge of Lions...what more could I want?"

Holding hands, they walked back over the bridge to the Casablanca and put Dean Martin on the CD player as they opened a bottle of champagne and took a warm bubble bath in the Jacuzzi.

They played "Amore" over and over, Dean Martin their favorite singer, another Gemini. Danny was a man in love. Ulysses returned to find love in America's oldest city.

The following morning on the front porch overlooking the bay, watching horse drawn carriages line up for tourists, Danny wrote a postcard to Beth as he waited for Joy to share breakfast.

Beth,

Roses got me invited to New Year's, where Joy accepted lucky pearl earrings to announce we're going steady. So, we're spending this weekend at the Casablanca Inn, St. Augustine. Thanks for your advice,

Love, Danny

Chapter 22: Scylla & Charybdis

"Ever see D. H. Lawrence's *Women in Love?*" Danny asked.

"No," Joy said, sitting next to him on the couch after they cleared away the dinner dishes from the dining room table.

"Great movie. I have it on DVD." He walked to the pile of videos next to the TV and sorted through them. "I saw it in college. It was pretty racy then. About two sisters, Ursula and Gudrun, and their relationships with two guys, Rupert and Gerald, who are friends. Rupert is D.H. Lawrence. He has a great line about Ursula as all women to him."

"You mean your comment on the bridge about me being beyond all women? I thought you made that up?"

"I did make it up. But it's a variation on his theme. Guess I forgot to footnote D. H. Lawrence that night on the bridge. I was a bit preoccupied with your balancing act. But I believe it. And you are. Want to see the movie?"

"Sure. If you'll cuddle on the couch."

"Great idea, Butch. Keep thinking, that's what you're good at. We have to watch *Butch Cassidy and the Sundance Kid* too. I love Redford's line about the woman for him, 'She's beautiful, smart, warm' whatever – Katherine Ross, the school teacher."

"You have that too?"

"One of my favorites. OK, here's *Women in Love.*

Towards the end, they all get to Switzerland, at the Mattehorn. Tony and I skied it when we went to Europe in grad school."

As the movie started, they lay on the couch kissing. Danny fondled Joy's breasts through her blouse. When Rupert and Ursula were in the forest having a picnic, Joy helped Danny remove her blouse. She removed his shirt and jeans and started to fondle him. As the movie showed the two couples in Switzerland at the Matterhorn, he took off her panties. Fondling his erection, she straddled him on the couch, moaning as she rode up and down with increasing intensity. Responding to her passionate athletics, he massaged her breasts as elegant warm sculptures and sucked each nipple until she reached an exuberant climax, then exhaled dramatically and lay on top of him sighing gently as rippling contractions from her climax made him come. They embraced silently as Gerald wandered into the massive snow field below the Matterhorn's sheer peak.

"I want you like no other woman I've ever known," Danny whispered after a warm silence.

"Want me how?"

"I wanted you when we moved your furniture last week. While we walked through the grocery store today. When I'm with you or not. Not just sexually. I think my life is a quest for a great love. Ulysses wanted to return to Penelope but was stranded for ten years. The seven years stranded with Calypso was torture inflicted by the gods. Homer emphasized that even a goddess couldn't replace Penelope. Penelope doing and undoing the tapestry to remain faithful and keep the suitors at bay. I've wanted that since my first love Erin. A woman I dated my first year of teaching called me Sage: Such A Gigantic Ego. She said I was in love with being in love."

"Do you think you're on a quest more than seeking a great love?" she asked, kissing him gently.

"I don't think so. In counseling with Elaine at Cornell, she called me a perfectionist, said I was looking for the perfect woman. But a woman who sleeps with other guys or gets pregnant to trap a man is no great love. A married woman who lies about it, like Maureen did is worthless. Nor is the perfect mama-san one who averts her eyes and is compliant. I don't want that. You on the Bridge of Lions testing me, that counted," he said, and stroked her hair.

"I felt I had to that night. I want to be equal and honest. We make love and we have a great time doing it. I like it both ways because I trust you. But I've really come to love your sensitivity. You are like no other man I've ever known. You really care about the world, your friends, your students. I really respect that. I think our dedication to teaching connects us. I want to work with you on you're genuine teaching ideas. I think they're great. I really love you Danny."

"Thanks, Sweetie. Those weekends I was doing pottery and you felt ignored, when you got pissed, and told me to ask if we are good for each other, I understood how important you are. That night tending the kiln writing that poem 'Torment' I felt it. Writing is pouring your heart through the particulars. Penelope was Homer's image of the classic Greek woman – faithful, resourceful – in contrast to self-indulgent Helen, who returned to her husband after the war, still beautiful, but unfaithful. You overcame your parents' divorce, the way they shuttled you between them and didn't let you pursue swimming and diving. My parents were always supportive. But you overcame your folk's resistance. That's impressive."

"I realized in college I had a terrible childhood, but that couldn't be helped. I had to tend my own psyche. I got married naively. I thought a man could complete me. I was young, but the time married and raising Julia helped me get my priorities together. I think my husband married me because I was pretty and he wanted a mother for the children from his first marriage. But he didn't want to be a father. I saw a lot those years. But after the divorce, I got my priorities straight. Getting my master's helped me understand that I wasn't just a pretty airhead. And teaching and being department chair makes me feel like I'm doing something with my life. I'm not just another pretty face."

"Men pursued Helen and she loved it. Penelope had to find ways to keep men away. I want that kind of relationship. A mutual relationship, I think we're getting there," he said, looking into her eyes and occasionally keeping track of the movie.

"I'm so happy to hear you say that. I agree. You are self absorbed as an artist. I'm beginning to understand that. You're very different from the men I've known. But if I give you that space, I see how you make it up to me."

"I think it has something to do with our German roots. You feel like my female counterpart. You're beautiful and physically we match so well, but emotionally you complete me. Weird, but I feel we fuse into a whole, and I've never felt that. It's wonderful. Oh, here's the line, the two teachers – Ursula and Rupert – sitting in their cottage after Gerald committed suicide in the snow and Gudrun went off to Germany to live the life of the artist. Listen to what Rupert says," Danny said, pointing at the screen. "A little different from my line to you. But he wanted a male friend also, but Ursula thinks that's perverse."

"Am I really beyond all women to you?"

"Of all the women in my life, yes, and I love you for it."

"Did Rupert want a homosexual relationship with Gerald?"

"I think he wanted an intimate friendship, not a sexual relationship. Tony is my closest friend; he understands me better than anyone on the planet. We are great friends, but I have no interest in a sexual relationship. I want a great male friend and a great woman love. I think that's what Lawrence was getting at."

"I think you're doing great getting this woman in love."

"Why, thank you," he said, and kissed her.

The following week, at the faculty show, Danny and Joy walked into the gallery past the tables of hors d'oeuvres to Dan at the gallery doors.

Danny extended his hand and put his arm around Dan's shoulder.

"Nice Zoot suit, Great Whitehead. I love the spiked hair. Old Viking Whitehead would be proud."

"Glad you guys made it," Dan responded then hugged Joy.

"The sculpture's wild. It's huge," Danny said, looking to where it dominated the gallery, attracting a group of onlookers. They walked over to the ten foot brown telephone pole sprouting hundreds of red, blue, yellow and green handles that seemed to Danny like a brightly colored twenty foot pin cushion or a fantastic multi-colored sea anemone.

"Impressive, Great Whitehead! I told you he was my mentor, Joy."

"Let's get a picture. Where's your wife, Dan?" Joy asked.

"In the lobby," he said, and frowned. "She said she'd be back soon."

A few minutes later, Mallory walked in wearing a black and white zigzag blouse, black pants and pointed black shoes.

Danny hugged her and said, "You look great."

Mallory, Dan and Danny posed in front of the sculpture while Joy focused her camera.

"Get closer everyone," Joy said.

When Joy took the photo, Dan leaned his head on Danny's shoulder. Danny was surprised, sensing that Dan and Mallory seemed distant from each other, especially when she walked away after the photo.

After Mallory left, Angie and Tim walked up to Joy, Danny and Dan standing near the sculpture.

"Talk about a recycling project," Tim said, joking.

"I've been collecting these for thirty years. So, you're right. And after the hurricanes, seemed like the right thing to do."

"Don't mind Tim, Dan. He's getting nervous about the wedding," Angie said, putting her arm on Tim's shoulder.

"Everything set for Groundhog Day, Angie?"

"Yes, Danny. You and Joy gonna be there?"

"Of course," Joy replied. "Sounds like it will be a wonderful time. Danny and I had breakfast at the Old Mill last week. It's a beautiful setting for a wedding."

"And Kajaw Carribe's doing the ceremony. You gotta love it, Pastor Carribe," Danny teased.

"He's a minister too?" Joy asked, surprised.

Danny shrugged, playfully, "Who knows, Joy? Maybe rolling the chicken bones got him into some cult growing up in Trinidad, but as a notary he can perform weddings in Florida, right Angie?"

"Yes. We're gonna read from *Tom Sawyer,*" Angie said, excitedly.

"Think you can handle it, Tim?" Danny asked.

Tim's eyes went wide and he smiled broadly. Angie hugged him, but he just nodded his head.

"I'm a high school English teacher not an actor, but I'm sure I can pull it off," he said, and threw his arms around her.

"Angie, where is Kajaw this weekend?" Danny asked.

"New York, visiting his friend."

"Joy, I told you the man is unbelievable. His friend has cancer, so, he's traveling to the hospital in New York. I don't know how he does it. He's a classy guy."

"He is a classy guy, Danny. Like you. That's why I love you both," Angie said.

"You inviting the Devious Duo?" Danny asked.

Angie went stiff and frowned.

"I invited all faculty in our department, even those two."

"They still screwing with your tenure?"

"We'll see. All my stuff is in. Now it goes to the college committee, then it goes to the dean, and then to the university committee. I'll hear in March, around Spring Break."

"The Devious Duo can't keep you from getting tenure," Danny said, and put his arm around Angie.

"Everything I hear sounds positive. But you can bet those two will try something," Dan said.

"We have to stop them. When will the world advocate diplomacy not deployment?"

"Watch it Danny. Dean White is over there," Dan said, pointing toward a tall, thin Black woman.

"Good old Dean Whitegloves. Dean Thomas was a bully. I'm so glad President Jackson agreed with faculty to remove her. But Whitegloves is the opposite swing of the pendulum, a tall thin wisp. Growing up a Black woman in the South seems like she had to sacrifice her soul to please her way to the top. Even her name, Clarissa White? What's that about? A bit ironic that White is Black. Man, when slavery is mixed in a country's history, life is tough for everyone. I wonder if she could trace hers roots back to the Thomas

Jefferson fiasco with Sally Hemings? Anyway, she shouldn't allow Rheames on that committee."

"Danny, I'd much rather have a guy after me any time. My ex-boyfriend Crazy Steve just broke into my house and wrecked it. I have no idea what Terry will say. Women against women are nasty."

"You've got that right, Angie," Joy said. "An angry woman can be relentless."

"Well, Dan, thanks for the party. Everyone's happy now."

"Danny. It's gotta work out, trust me. You have to think positive."

"See Joy, that's why Dan's my guru. Only man on the planet I'd build a kiln with during a hurricane. Great Whitehead, you should write *Zen and the Art of Universe Maintenance.*"

Danny spent the week on the phone with Andrew's Pottery trying to get cracked kiln shelves replaced. When he called the factory, after being moved from one person to another, he eventually got to the owner.

Danny said, "I'm no rocket scientist. But I do have a chemistry degree. The shelves were faulty."

"We stand behind them. Those are our top line shelves."

"I write with a Cross pen, when it breaks, they replace it. That's standing behind their work. Don't you think you ought to do the same?"

"OK, Dr. Roarke. We understand. We'll have them to you immediately."

"Thanks."

The dozen shelves arrived in time for the next firing.

In the meantime, Danny had his teacher survey put online so his graduate student could complete her thesis about teacher's attitudes. Faculty around the state participated with their students, but the Florida legislators ignored repeated requests to participate. The day the governor's staff member called about the results, Danny had just come back from a frustrating meeting about national accreditation with several colleagues.

"Professor Roarke, the governor is interested in the results of your survey of teachers and legislators," the staff member said.

"I appreciate the call, but tell Governor Bush that the results will not make him happy."

"Can you be more specific, Dr. Roarke?"

"More specific? It's impossible to tell if he or his brother, President Bush, has hurt education more. But be assured, they won't attract enough teachers to Florida, regardless of how they insist the beaches are irresistible. And current teachers will leave in bigger numbers if the legislators keep at what they are doing."

"Are you sure?"

"You think the sun's gonna set in the west today?"

On Groundhog's Day, Danny said, "Angie, Punxsutawney Phil saw his shadow today. So, tell the camera how you feel on your wedding day."

"That's a good sign," she said, laughing.

Tim walked up and put his arm around her.

"Say something from Mark Twain," Danny insisted.

Angie smiled, "Oh, you know the one about drinking. But wait, you love the one about the right word and lightning versus lightning bugs, although you did tell me about your clay making episode with the lightning bugs. Hmm, Twain would like that story as much as the photo of you at his grave," she said.

"There you go," Danny said, surprised.

Tim looked into the camera and Angie looked away with a tight lipped smile, then looking at Danny she added, "We'll say the right words today," and her eyes sparkled to enhance her smile.

They walked toward the crowd surrounding the water wheel. Kajaw Carribe stood in his white robe with a brightly colored scarf draped over his shoulders and hanging down in front. He had papers stuffed in a black leather folder. Danny videotaped the sheet cake with pictures of Tim and Angie in the icing that read "and they lived happily ever after."

Tweedle Nasty, with her poorly dyed curly red hair fluttering in the breeze, marched through the pavilion escorted by Tweedle Dumb; they continued onto the path to the ceremony. Angie and Tim greeted folks as they proceeded along the narrow path toward the Old Mill's water wheel. Then holding hands they walked with the group. Tim held a small bouquet of daisies.

Angie looked back and said, "Danny has his camera on. So don't say any bad words or anything."

The group approached the old wooden building whose weathered gray beams enclosed the exposed wheel's thirty foot diameter; they opened umbrellas to protect them from the light rain. People formed a semicircle on the path and lawn around the wheel. Angie's son and daughter stood with her on the path near the old mill's waterwheel, covering her with an umbrella. Kajaw stood at the wheel, Tim and his daughter stood next to him as Angie and her children approached.

Dr. Carribe started, "Please turn your cell phones off first," which was received with laughter.

Laughing and jumping up and down, Angie said to him, "You especially!"

He nodded and bowed slightly, then started, "Let me welcome you to this double celebration of the anniversary of Olivia Langdon and Samuel Clemens also known as Mark Twain, and the wedding of this beautiful couple, Angie Harper, and Timothy Adams, also known as Tim. As you know, Angie and Tim have selected Feburary 2nd, not because it is Groundhog Day, but because they are inspired by the long and happy life shared by Mr. and Mrs. Clemens. Thirty-six years of happiness. It is their wish and our wish for them that they will enjoy at least that many happy years together. In lieu of traditional vows, they've elected to read selected passages in celebration of this marriage.

Holding the daisies Tim handed her in one hand and a script in the other, Angie started, "My introduction to Mark Twain, like most of you here was through Tom Sawyer. Tom and Becky had this classic American love story. So we want to read some passages from *The Adventures of Tom Sawyer* where Tom met Becky the first day she was in school and he kinda made a move on her."

She held the daises toward Tim and nodded.

Tim started talking about Tom's first meeting with Becky.

Angie was swaying side to side in her burgundy print dress that matched Tim's wine colored crew neck sweater and winked as he spoke.

When Tim stopped to look at Angie, she pointed the daisies, "Keep going!"

Tim continued about Tom and Becky meeting in the classroom and how they started to talk.

Tim and Angie recited their lines excitedly as Danny videotaped the ceremony.

Danny smiled as he watched her swoon with the final phrase about kissing.

"Now to get to the part with the kissing," Kajaw interrupted, "We have a few formalities that must be taken care of. According to the state of Florida I must ask this very important question. Does any one have any reason why this couple should not be joined in marriage, besides the fact that she'll drive him crazy with all this Mark Twain stuff? Speak now or forever hold your tongue and your peace."

"He is a trip," Danny said, hugging Joy.

"It's such a sweet ceremony. I love it," she responded, putting her hand on his shoulder. "Thanks for inviting me."

"A bit different than the Rosecliff in Newport, but such Americana. I love it too. Glad you're having fun," he added, kissing her cheek.

"Hearing no response, Tim, do you take Angie to be your wife to have and to hold from this day forward and in spite of the fact you are about to get a crash course of a lifetime in the writings of Mark Twain?" Kajaw asked, staring intently through his glasses.

Danny zoomed in then out on the bright green, orange, and red horizontal stripes decorating the long black scarf over Kajaw's white robe.

"I do," Tim said.

"And Angie, do you take Tim in sickness and health for richer or poorer whether rock climbing or kayaking regardless of how many frogs you find in his pocket?"

"I sure do!"

Angie's son handed Kajaw the rings. As Kajaw had the couple exchange rings, Angie hi-fived Tim and kissed him quickly.

"No kissing yet. First finish the reading from *Tom Sawyer*." When they finished, Kajaw said, "Tim you may kiss the bride."

After Tim kissed Angie, she let out a squeal as they hugged, and she kissed Tim quickly several times.

Kajaw pronounced them man and wife to a crescendo of applause and cheers. A few minutes later everyone walked back to the shelter of the pavilion. Danny videotaped Angie, Tim and Kajaw as their colleague Audrey approached.

"Danny told me he was next, Dr. Carribe," Audrey said, smiling.

Looking from Joy to Audrey, Danny said, "I'm ready to volunteer." Everyone laughed. But Danny added, "Only if Dr. Carribe will do the ceremony."

"I'll have to charge you," Kajaw said seriously.

"What? Hasn't my friendship been fee enough?"

"No, we have to charge you for this. Otherwise, you would be exploiting me," Kajaw said and laughed.

Enjoying the undercurrent of racism in the banter, Danny teased back, "Yeah right, like my people the artists and philosophers have for centuries." Continuing to laugh, Kajaw embraced Joy and Danny.

"I doubt Hemingway would be impressed. It's not exactly the running of the bulls in Pamplona, but Canine Carnevale is fun," Danny said, as he and Joy walked hand in hand into the crowd along Main Street. "See the banner stretched across the telephone poles up there?" he asked pointing, "*Welcome to Canine Carnevale on Main Street*."

As they looked for a space to stand, a white bull dog with a purple and yellow jester hat, a dachshund in a green and purple wreath, a poodle with green fur and a cape, followed by a woman in a Viking outfit holding a spear being led by two black cocker spaniels with tusk-like spears attached to their vests paraded past.

"The dogs are dressed to parade. I thought you were joking," she said. "Look at the beads and the outfits!"

"Oh no, look! It's Tweedle Dumb with his dog in a skirt."

"Say hi, Danny," Joy said, laughing.

"Unbelievable. He has got to get his gender issues resolved. But to dress your dog in a skirt to parade. Ugh. Too bad he didn't bring Tweedle Nasty, with that mane of curly red hair and her Amazon wanna be features, she'd fit today's parade. Nasty is even taller than you, and at least fifty pounds heavier. Dumb and Nasty could put collars on and parade each other, maybe use the leash for a little S&M."

"Oh, Danny, isn't that a bit crude?" she asked, laughing.

"Sorry. But Nasty seems so lonely. She revels in tormenting others to avoid tending her own unhappy garden. I've never seen her with a date, other than Tweedle Dumb. Mary Mary quite contrary. Geezez, Joy, look at the way Tweedle Dumb struts. What is he thinking? No wonder the Devious Duo hate Angie, especially now that she's so happily married," he said, angrily, as he continued to videotape the parade.

"Both of them seem unhappy about their lives. And Angie is clearly very happy these days. She's wonderful."

"The French philosopher Jean Paul Sartre spent over seven hundred pages writing about *Being and Nothingness*. He said all relationships were sado-masochistic. But he was a wall-eyed pudgy little guy who had a relationship with Simone deBeauvoir, one of the most brilliant women of the Twentieth Century. She wrote *The Second Sex*, about women's lives that helped launch the Feminist Movement. Sartre probably felt intimidated by her and so blamed her for his insecurities. Even winning the Nobel Prize, he was still insecure about himself."

"That seems so strange. But I know it took me years to overcome my insecurities from childhood. Growing up is hard."

"I know the feeling. I could have hated Charlie for busting my horns about my crooked teeth. But I realized I had to straighten them. Whether God does it to us or not, everybody has an Achilles heel. So, Tweedle Dumb and Nasty have to take care of what's tormenting them. That simple. But they seem to be playing Sartre's game that Hell is other people. Life is being or nothingness. You're either being good or being nothing but Hell to others."

"I understand what you're saying. I spent years coming to terms with my childhood. But it was worth the effort. So, I agree, makes sense that they'd go after Angie even more now but, c'mon Danny, lighten up, let's have fun," she said, moving in front of the camera to smile into the lens.

"Oh, wow, hi Cutie! But look behind you. Little Yorkie Bubbas. Maybe we should parade with Bubba next year. She'd love it. Since she's my spirit guide, maybe I should. It might offset Tweedle Dumb's bad karma."

"Sure, Danny, whatever you say. Let me buy you a glass of wine at Pub Central," Joy said, handing him the green plastic Pellegrino bottle filled with sparkling water.

"Good idea," he said, taking a drink. "Check out the Great Danes with the hats and the one with blond hair. Very Hamlet and Ophelia, no? Apollo and Zeus?"

"One has a blond wig, go for Hamlet and Ophelia. This is really fun. I understand why you love this town, Danny. I'm getting to know a whole new side of you."

"Whatever you say, Dear. And check out the black couple all in red in the red convertible. Rex Royale and Lady Divine. What a town. Remember the Ku Klux Klan monument to the Grand Knight we saw in the Palm City Cemetery on Halloween, the guy who owned the car dealership? I think they're riding in one of his cars. We've come a long way, baby. Of course they aren't riding on a float with white people, but hey, a king's a king and a lady's divine."

"Danny, let it go, you can't change the world. Although, I've told you together we can or at least we can try."

"All I know is that Kajaw says there are lots of places in town he wouldn't go. We at the university have to do more."

"Then keep at it. If you really believe in your theory about teaching, you two with some guidance from a decent woman can change the world."

He videotaped her waving to Rex Royale and Lady Divine as she caught beads they tossed her way. Danny videotaped others videotaping the parade and taking pictures as he panned the crowd up and down Main Street. He focused on Joy often. Her blond ponytail bounced through her black baseball cap. Her dark glasses, black T-shirt and blue jeans contrasted with the beautiful dresses she'd worn. But her statuesque elegance as she interacted with folks along the street and in the parade made him feel complete and in love as she added brightly colored beads around her neck and his.

The flamboyantly dressed dogs escorted by their owners, or in cars, or on the elaborate floats of winter snowflakes and castles and pirates and palm trees and gowned princesses backed by peacock feather displays accompanied by local school marching bands, dance groups, and military marchers flowed past as people lined the street and filled the restaurants and bars. Occasionally a dog would squat and leave a dump to the chagrin of its owner, but the parade continued around it.

"Joy, check the sign over there, 'The reason dogs have so many friends is because they wag their tails and not their tongues.' Tweedle Dumb and Nasty ought to take that advice. But isn't this town so America? "

"You really love Palm City, don't you, Danny?"

"Great town and an excellent university, all within walking distance. And now with you, Joy what more can I want?"

"Why, thank you. If only you could get a few books in print, then I think you'd be really happy."

"Well, with Bubba as my spirit guide, maybe I'm due."

"I hope so. Here's some gold beads," she said, placing them around his neck.

"Thanks, Sweetie."

"Oh, wow! There's Stephanie, President Jackson's wife. Stephanie wearing a tiara. She's tossing beads from the Committee Float."

"She's one of the organizers?"

"Small town, yep. She is a sweetheart, and all for the arts and artists. I really love her. In this town, she stands for the best we can be, both as a city and university. I hope her hubby steps up if Angie needs him for tenure."

"She's that influential? Wow! If you're impressed, I'm sure she is wonderful. I remember at the wedding, Terry and Lorrence didn't look like they were having a good time. I have a feeling they are going after Angie."

"I have that feeling too. They haven't met with tenured faculty to discuss it. The Devious Duo must have a plan, but they are not sharing it. We have five tenured faculty to support her, so if those two oppose, she should get it. But we don't know about Doreen, the department chair."

"The sweet little woman with the lisp who had the Christmas party?" Joy asked, putting another strand of beads on Danny.

"Yep. But she only lisps when she's intimidated. When I introduced you to her that night she panicked. You are tall, beautiful and competent. You dealt with your baggage. She hasn't. We are our life's work. That's the game. If we don't become all we are capable of, then we only hurt the team. For me, I thought soccer was me at my best. But I realize as a teacher I can help others realize that life is a team sport, and we have to train to become the best we can be. That's what I love about PCU. Good old Johnny Palmer's vision to make a 'Heavenly Earth' works for me, but making a 'Heavenly Earth' is hard. So many people believe the pay off is Heaven. But I believe Earth is as far as we get. And, so why make it Hell for others? Just play fair, care and share. What else is there?"

"You really are passionate about teaching. I knew I loved you. You really are a philosopher poet," she said, and hugged him.

"Well, thanks," he said, and kissed her. "But we still have to get Angie tenure. Who knows how the Devious Duo will manipulate Clarissa's insecurities. I hope she doesn't side with them. Oh, more beads. Wave!"

Joy jumped up and down waving, her ponytail bouncing from her baseball cap that she got during her visit to Vietnam the previous summer. Danny admired her enthusiasm and poise. He loved her broad shoulders and fluid motion as she snagged several necklaces tossed from the open float.

"Thanks, Stephanie!" Danny yelled to President Jackson's wife.

"Enjoy them Danny!" Stephanie yelled back, as she waved and winked.

"This is fun," Joy said, and put a purple and a green strand of beads around Danny's neck. "I can see living here. I understand why you love it."

"A great little town and lots of wonderful people. Just a few players who should get red cards and escorted off the field. Oh, the final float. Heeeere's Rex! All in white with his white princess all in white surrounded by white spires topped with crosses. Ah, yes America, we still need some work."

Joy waved. Rex noticed and tossed beads to her. She caught them while Danny videoed.

Turning toward Danny, she placed the beads over his cap and around his neck, "Maybe you'll be Rex next year Danny-boy."

As the parade ended, they walked in and out of several bars. They stopped at Pub Central where Joy ordered two glasses of wine. They continued on to the Café de Arts where Danny put his arm around Joy after he found seats at the bar.

"Danny, can you make that dinner with my Asian friends on Thursday?" she asked, as she snuggled toward him.

"Yeah, sounds like fun. It will get you in the mood for presenting at the Hawaii conference at the East West Center."

"You'll like them. I really liked traveling to Vietnam with them. But I ended up going to Japan myself. That was scary and wonderful."

"That was gutsy traveling alone. You do have *chutzpa*."

"*Chutzpa?*" she asked, quizzically.

"Oh, Yiddish for *courage*. That's what I like about you," he said. "Handsome or beautiful gets noticed, but heart gets loved."

He signaled the bar tender who worked his way toward them while tending the packed bar.

"I got a call from the director of the center yesterday. She offered me a job," Joy said.

Startled, Danny repeated, "A job?"

"She offered me a job as assistant director. I would coordinate exchanges between American and Asian teachers. She sponsored my trip to Vietnam and to the conference. I told her when I'm there, I'll consider it."

Danny felt his stomach knot, "Would you take it?"

The following Sunday, Joy and Danny went to the Old Mill for pancakes, then walked along several paths and looked for manatees in the lake. Danny couldn't get the job offer to Hawaii out of his mind. As they walked the path back to the car, he gave her a pair of emerald earrings for Valentine's Day.

"Oh, Danny, they're beautiful."

"Glad you like them. They are a lucky stone. With your gorgeous blue eyes, I can't think of anything better. What was that James Taylor song about choosing deep greens and blues? Tell me you'll wear them in Hawaii."

She kissed him. "I will. Remember, I'm going there to present a paper about the Asian economy. They want me to take the assistant director position. It's a great offer. I have to consider it."

"Joy, I would hate to lose you."

"While I'm gone, you can work on your book, don't worry about me. I want you to publish *Genuine Teaching*. It's a great idea. We need your ideas in education. Tell me that you'll do that and not worry about me?"

"I'll try," he said, and looked back to the huge wooden wheel where Angie got married.

"You said you'd send it to publishers."

"I will. I've got a few in mind."

"I'm rooting for you, Danny."

"Thanks, but it's hard to compete with Hawaii."

The day Joy left for Hawaii, Danny expected his brother Charlie to arrive from Michigan. Letting his answering machine screen the call, as usual, Danny heard Angie ask, "Danny, are you there?"

"Angie, yeah, just finished working out on my Nordic Track, so I'm a little out of breath. What's up?"

"The Devious Duo won," Angie said, starting to cry.

"What happened?"

"I got denied tenure. The letter came today."

"Doreen and Whitegloves sided with them?"

"I guess."

"And President Jackson?"

"His signature's on the letter."

"I can't believe it. You have to appeal," he said, pacing in the living room. He noticed the courageous turtle on top of the two larger turtles on the rocks near Buddha overlooking the pond and the fish swimming quietly in the clear water.

"It's not worth it, Danny. I'll just look for another job."

"You have to appeal. Get an attorney. If we have to go to the newspapers, let's do it."

"Oh, Danny, I'm devastated. I hate to think those two won," she said, and sobbed.

Danny listened, watching the water flow out from the pump creating ripples in the clear water as he looked from the fish to the Buddha surrounded by lilies. As Angie's sobbing slowed, his anger escalated.

"I've known you for twelve years. You're one of the hardest working nicest students I've ever had. And a great colleague. Tweedle Nasty, the hydra headed Scylla gets her jollies biting off heads. And Charybdis wants to suck you into the cesspool of his life. When I was chair, Tweedle Dumb pissed and moaned that he was afraid to come out as gay because he worried what would happen. So, he goes after others. Tweedle Nasty loves using him to get her way. She defies art and science. She went after you because you're good. She can't stand seeing you happy."

"Thanks, Danny. But I don't see how I can win. I'm through."

"Not as long as I'm at this university. We gotta go for it. Call Kajaw and Tony. See what they say. And look for an attorney. You've got to get tenure."

"Thanks, again Danny. I love you."

"I love you too, Sweetie. You'll win."

After she hung up, Danny went to the CD player and put on the album he brought to Ireland. He played James Galway's "Danny Boy" and stood looking at the pond while he listened. He turned the music up and walked outside, leaving the front door open so he could hear the flute. He grabbed the woven basket with cane handles from the porch and walked out through the screen door and dropped it on the tile walk.

He sat in the white wrought iron love seat at the pond's edge and shook the food container. The fish and turtles swam toward him slowly.

"Joy off to Hawaii with a job offer to paradise. Charlie on the road again. And Angie gets raped. Me alone to wonder what it all means."

Listening to the flute, he lowered his hand toward the large turtles scratching on the pond liner and waited for the small turtle to approach.

"OK, the courageous turtle! How goes it little fella? We got Buddha at the far end with Christ in the lilies and Mohammed or Allah is in the jar. And Yaweh in the mystery of it all. Who knows about the Greek and Roman gods. But what do you think about alleged Christians destroying a woman's career? What bullshit. Not what the courageous turtle would do, eh?"

He tossed the handful of pellets into the pond. The little turtle struggled amidst the large fish and turtle feeding frenzy to grab several pellets. "I wouldn't do what they did to reptiles and fish. Oh, Danny boy the pipes the pipes are calling. I gotta do something."

He watched the fish and turtles eat, admiring how the courageous turtle struggled among the larger animals. As Galway hit the final note on the flute, Danny started toward the grove. He inhaled the fragrant citrus blooms. The tangerine, orange and grapefruit trees still had ripe fruit. He walked around the lemon and lime trees in front of his bedroom window looking at the blossoms, enjoying their scent.

"How goes the grove, Dr. Danny?" his neighbor asked.

"Yo, Alexander the Great. My favorite next door neighbor. They're disappointed you haven't been picking their fruit. What kind of neighbor are you?"

"Is the fruit still good?"

"Of course, Dr. Danny's BB&G has the best citrus in town, and for you, free. You know that."

Danny picked several grapefruit and handed them to Alexander.

"Thanks. I love fresh grapefruit. But remember, I'm an orphan, adopted kids don't take things unless they're offered. This like the loaves and fishes?"

"Well, I'm no Christ, you know that. But there's so much of this stuff. My astrologer in Ithaca back in the Seventies predicted I would tend trees."

"What did he mean?"

"I thought it was figurative, thought it had to do with a dream I had in high school, but I guess it's literal. So, take some fruit."

"What was the dream?"

"Oh, I got a scholarship to play soccer at Brown and turned it down because I had a dream about a tree that morning. Very weird. The tree symbolized taking a different path. But the astrologer thought it was a call to my life's work. I had dropped out of Cornell. He said I should go back, my destiny was in teaching, the trees symbolized my students."

"You know what Schopenhauer said about destiny?"

"You still into him?"

"Of course. He even said more stuff about women."

"Didn't he hate women?"

"He didn't hate all women, just his mother because she got more attention than him. He said women would eat their young, but they are worse to women than men."

"Well, the female half of the Devious Duo just screwed Angie out of tenure."

"Angie?"

"Had you come to my birthday party last year, especially dressed in this NASCAR outfit and the pro-Bush bumper stickers on your truck, you would have met her. She was my grad student when we did the Mark Twain program for elementary kids, then I sent her to my friend Tony for her PhD."

"Oh, I met her at the opening of your pottery show. You gave her that brown vase I liked so much. She didn't get tenure?"

"No, Rheames and Slutski got to the committee."

"Is that it for her then?"

"She has to appeal. We might need you for a character witness."

"Well, I am a character," he said, tipping his NASCAR baseball cap.

"For sure. I mean you are HUGE at the gym. And anybody who knew Andy Warhol and Toots Shor has to be a character. But I'm so pissed the Devious Duo got away with it. Anyway, please, take some fruit."

"I will. Good luck with the appeal."

Danny picked several grapefruit and tossed them into the basket. He carried them back to the pond. He stood watching the turtles and fish and water streaming from the pump. He stared at the green metal roof and the blue sky above. He stood for a moment looking at where the blue and green met at the roof's peak over the dining room, wondering. Suddenly he heard someone pull into the driveway. Thinking is was his brother Charlie, he turned abruptly to see Dan's silver van.

"Danny, I brought back the drill bit I borrowed for the faculty show. What are you up to?"

"Thanks, Dan. I'm just wondering what Joy is doing in Hawaii and how my brother's doing on the highway. What's up with you?" he asked, holding the basket of grapefruit and reaching for the drill bit

"Just thought I should return the bit. Thanks."

"You OK? You look frazzled."

"Mallory just told me she's leaving me."

"Oh, no. Leaving you? C'mon in."

Danny opened the screen door to the porch and followed Dan through the front door into the living room. He tossed the grapefruit into the sink, and carried the basket back to the porch, then walked back to where Dan was sitting on the couch. He sat in the rocking chair.

"I don't know what I'm going to do. It's crazy. She told me on Valentine's Day that she doesn't love me anymore, and today she said she wants to split."

"That sucks. She's staying in the house?"

"We both are for now."

"You can move here, if you want."

"Thanks, Danny, I may need to. Is that *Danny Boy*?"

"Oh, that's Kate Smith singing. Yep. I just heard that Angie didn't get tenure, so I started playing Galway's *Danny Boy*. Now it's Kate Smith's turn. So she's leaving you, why?"

"Doesn't love me."

"Another guy?"

"I don't think so. She has a friend at the bank, but he's gay."

Danny looked at Dan, visibly distraught, near tears.

"Well, if you want to stay there's room. Brother Charlie will be here on and off this month. And his wife will be here. But there's always room for you, my friend."

A few days later, when Dan arrived, Tyrella, Raiz, Nicole, Danny and his brother Charlie were around Nicole's dining table passing spring rolls she was making. Dan blew in like a rip tide during a hurricane. He brought a bottle of red wine that he placed on the table where he stood as if he'd been mugged on the way.

"You look beat," Danny said, as he offered Dan his chair.

"It's over. I don't know how I'll survive, she's leaving me."

Charlie looked at Danny. Danny returned his brother's look with a lifted hand, sensing that Charlie thought Dan was too sensitive.

"Better that you end it, Dan," Tyrella said. "Lucky there are no children involved."

"Mallory says she's not getting enough attention."

"My word! Dan, you've done everything you could for her while she worked her way through graduate school and up the ladder at the bank. You haven't failed," she said.

"Thanks, Tyrella, but I'm lost."

"Let her go," Charlie said.

"Dan, this is my Brother Charlie," Danny added.

Dan and Charlie stood to shake hands.

"You ever been divorced, Charlie?" Dan asked.

"No, but if it's over, let her go. Just be fair."

Dan collapsed in the seat.

"What I get for loving a younger woman, a pretty face. I didn't get married when I was younger, so I figured I should marry a younger woman. What a disaster."

"Don't be so hard on yourself. You did your best," Tyrella said.

Nicole placed one wrap at a time into the pot of warm water on the table. She filled the soft circular rolls with shrimp, mint, rice noodles and the peanut butter sauce that Raiz made. After wrapping each one, she passed them around the table.

"What's with it with you guys and women?" Charlie asked. "Danny's worried that Joy will take a job in Hawaii. You have a young wife who wants to go out on her own. Let them go. You can't control women."

"I say, that's correct. I agree with you Charlie," Tyrella said.

Nicole and Raiz looked at each other then everyone looked at Charlie.

"Women, you can't live with them and you can't kill them. I've been married thirty-five years and have two daughters who are married. I've never been able to tell them anything. They're not like guys. You and Danny think you're gonna run their lives. You're not."

"I like your style, Charlie," Tyrella said, toasting her glass.

Charlie smiled, "Thanks Tyrella." Then turning to Dan he said "Dan, if she leaves you, you're better off. You'll survive, just get over it. It's life, Dan. If your wife doesn't love you, you don't want her around. And Danny boy, if Joy thinks Hawaii is better than you, fuck it. It's her life. You'll survive. What you should do is make sure your student Angie gets tenure. That you can do something about. You have to fix that. If Joy loves you, she'll come back. If she doesn't, so what? Geez, you artists are so sensitive. Get over it!"

Chapter 23: Penelope's Tapestry

Danny woke to the sound of the phone attached to the bed and reached for it after several rings.

"Danny? I'm on the deck at The Wharf on the North Shore of Oahu, the sun is setting. Oh, it's gorgeous Danny."

"Joy...you OK?"

"Very happy, Danny. I'm on my first Mai Tai. I'm with Margaret, my friend in Hawaii. We just finished our presentation about Vietnamese economics. Did I wake you? What time is it there?"

"It's around 1:30. Did your presentation go well?" he asked, trying to rally from sleep.

"We thought we were great and everybody applauded. I love it here, Danny."

He shuddered as he listened.

"But I've decided that I love you more. I'm not taking the job. I'll be home soon. I've decided I can't live without my philosopher artist."

"What a great wake-up call," he said, elated.

"I even bought that wheelbarrow sculpture I told you about. So get ready."

"You are a piece of work. I love you. Enjoy the sunset, think of me often, Sweetie."

"I do. I love you, Danny Boy! I'll be home Friday."

The key she gave Danny opened the lock, but Joy had the door chain connected. He put the bag with champagne, orange juice he squeezed, and soda bread he made that morning on the mat and worked his hand through the opening. Slowly, he managed to work the chain free. He walked to Joy's bedroom quietly. She was nestled in an array of pillows. He went to the kitchen, opened the White Star champagne, and poured it into the Waterford crystal glasses her daughter brought home from Ireland. Crouching next to her, he said quietly, "Welcome home."

As she came to consciousness dreamily, shaking her head gently back and forth, in a childlike voice, she said, "Oh, Danny."

"Welcome home, Sweetie," he said, holding both glasses and kissing her lips softly.

"Oh, Danny, champagne. I'm so happy to be home."

She sat up slowly, placing several pillows against the headboard.

He handed her the glass and clinked his against hers.

"And I'm so happy you are. To us, Sweetie. Quite the tan you got. Hmm, I thought you were at a conference solving the Asian economy?"

"The Asian economy is in great shape. If anything, America needs to worry. But that Hawaiian sun is irresistible. Like it?"

He kissed her then helped her remove her white lace nightgown and admired the tan lines around her breasts and hips. He caressed her breasts and traced the tan on her thighs.

"Gorgeous. You are gorgeous. And you came home. Wonderful. And, you had fun?"

"Yes, a lot but I missed you. Hawaii doesn't replace you."

"Well, sounds a bit exaggerated but thanks," he said. They toasted each other again and he refilled their glasses. "I squeezed orange juice for Mimosas if you want. It's in the kitchen."

"You are so good to me. I love it."

"I've never loved a woman as much as I love you."

"And I feel the same, that's why I came home. I kept thinking of those lines you came up with when we were talking about the 'Just Do Me' series. Remember? 'I love how we fit together. Your parts are where my parts want to go. I know you don't like me to think about you as a sex object, but you are the best object I've ever had sex with.' Danny, walking Waikiki Beach I realized we are meant for each other. I mean to go all the way to Hawaii to realize I want to be here with you, it was a great feeling."

"I am so happy to hear you say that. My stuff ain't the Sonnet from the Portuguese. I'm not sure I even have a soul. But I believe in heart. But what can you expect from a white boy born in Harlem? We have to celebrate with a Carvel banana barge. I love to lick the whipped cream and hot fudge off you and the way you lick it off me and we share the cherry. What do you say?"

"Great idea. You taste so good in warm fudge and the Carvel folks are still trying to figure out why we get it in separate containers. And let's go to Fresh Market, so you can tease me about the European cucumber that doesn't come with batteries. Let's celebrate all day."

"Anything you say, Sweetie. You know. Research is my life!"

"I forgot how much I missed you Danny."

They embraced and kissed and lay next to each other on top of the bed and made love.

Several weeks later, as they approached the rental boat at the dock, Danny's nephew Ron asked, "Have you seen this book Uncle Danny, Yogi Berra's *What Time Is It? You Mean Now?*"

"Berra has a book out?

"It's doing well," Rich said, as he pointed toward the boat.

Danny paged through it, reading several quotes after they boarded the boat. "Some great lines...the déjà vu one. Observing and looking... Just so cleverly understated and finessed. He's got enough stuff to make a writer's career," Danny said, as he sat on the bench to the left of Rich. "Ron, is your Dad qualified to drive this boat?"

"He thinks so," Ron said, placing his arm on the boat rail as he stood next to his dad.

"Since Ryan couldn't make it we cancelled the charter boat to go deep sea fishing. So, I'm captain on this one," Rich said, adjusting his cap and sunglasses.

"What happened to Ryan?" Danny asked.

"Was working on his boat and hurt his back. He really wanted to come to the First All Roarke Guys' Offsite, wanted to go for sailfish again. You saw the one he caught on his own?"

"Yeah, Rich. Off West Palm. The charter boat would have been fun. Last time everybody went, Charlie paid for the boat and his daughter Jeanne caught the only fish."

"Most expensive hors d'oeuvres I ever bought, Danny," Charlie said, handing cigars around as the guys found seats on the boat. "Today it's just around the Inland Waterway, Captain Rich?"

"Without Ryan, I don't want to take this on the ocean."

"Does the rental club have ocean going boats, Rich?"

"Not really, Danny. They asked me to look into the possibility, but doesn't look feasible. I don't think they could make money on it."

"But they came to you. They must respect your opinion?" Danny said.

"I told them I'd help, if I could," Rich replied, with his usual optimism.

"Well, we should run you for governor, you could replace Jeb Bush," Danny teased.

"I'm retiring next year. Maybe I'll consider it, Danny."

"Rich, the Pope just died, maybe they could use you there," Charlie said, flicking his cigar ash into the water

"I'll leave that to the College of Cardinals. But Danny, you should have been at that funeral."

"Me? How so?"

Rich revved the engine and the boat responded, taking them into the center of the river and toward the bridge. "I saw all the dignitaries at the Vatican. You're that caliber. You should be on the world stage, not teaching at that little university. What's happening with Angie's appeal?"

"Well, it's not the world stage, Rich. But we are still after the Devious Duo and hoping to overturn the university's decision."

With an edge on his voice, Charlie insisted, "It should cost them their jobs. Looks like they went for more than they can handle. The university administrators can't be happy. In Nam we said even eunuchs worry their balls will be cut off in public."

"We'll see, Charlie. But first, we need to get Angie tenure."

Rich said, "Danny, if you had more clout at the university, you could make it happen. I still think if you had gone to Brown you would be on the international stage. You could do so much more."

"Rich, I didn't take the offer. I went the route I went. I still got my PhD from Cornell. I'm not completely worthless."

"When we get your *Genuine Teaching* in print that will make a difference. Like Beth and I were saying at Christmas, and the last time you were here, I'll finance it. You've got to write it for a broader audience. Not just university people. The ideas are good. They'll sell."

"Thanks, I'm revising it. We'll see what happens," Danny said, drawing in on his cigar.

Rich took the boat under the bridge toward the mouth of the river. Charlie relaxed on the bow with his cigar and Ron stood behind his dad at the wheel. Danny shot video of each of them and then the shore, filled with expensive houses surrounded by tropical palms.

"You gotta get a condo on the ocean, Rich. Then you'd win at *Monopoly.* A house up north, one on the golf course, one on the inland waterway, and one on the beach. You'd have hotels on Park Place and condos on Boardwalk."

"Even after the hurricanes, the prices keep going up. Maybe I should," Rich said, with a laugh.

"Then I can retire here," Charlie said.

"After what the dean said about you when they invited you out of Penn State? I don't know if you could stay here untended," Danny teased.

"What did the dean say about Uncle Charlie?" Ron asked.

"Charlie didn't attend classes much, then one night he and friends allegedly borrowed food from the cafeteria and sold it in the dorm," Danny said, catching Charlie's glance.

"An aspiring entrepreneur, Danny, you have to appreciate that," Charlie said, and laughed.

"Rich, I loved the night the dean called the folks and said Charlie had organized a naked slip and slide in the dorm. They flooded the hallway and were sliding naked for distance. I just remember overhearing Dad say, 'Send Charlie home.'"

"Danny, I was a Phys. Ed. Major, not like I was studying rocket science. College just wasn't for me. You smart guys think it's cool. But I thought it was all bullshit. How you could do a pile it higher and deeper PhD amazes me. You shoulda stayed with soccer. You would have ended up playing with the Cosmos in New York and Pele. Didn't you play against the Cosmos' goalie in high school?"

"We did. Yeah, the guy was good. I knew his older brother because we were voted to All County that year. But the little brother had talent. They beat us for the county championship. You volunteered for Vietnam. But if I stayed with the Spartans, I would have gotten drafted. I had to teach."

"Couldn't you get a teaching job in Syracuse?" Charlie asked, flicking his ash into the water.

"I'd already signed a contract on Long Island. Dad insisted I honor it. And the Draft Board had already processed my deferment. I thought it was great after you came back from Vietnam that you went back to school."

"The only reason I went back was to finish college before my oldest daughter. Plus, Dad was right, without a college degree, life is tough."

"Amazing that you went back, got the degree and just retired to full time grandpa after selling your business. That's amazing. And your month on my porch drinking wine and smoking cigars was a great transition."

"I wanted to see how it felt to do nothing but drink and smoke cigars for a month. It was great. But now that I'm leaving, has Dan moved in?"

"Yep, he's there now. Filed for divorce. Also, finally accepted that Mallory was having an affair. Her gay banker colleague suddenly turned straight. When I told Dan he finally believed it."

"Guys believe bullshit until they can deal with reality. I'm glad you opened his eyes."

"Actually, he's been talking with another woman. He's keeping her identity a secret, but they're on the phone for hours. He bought her an orchid at the farmer's market."

"Guys alone are dangerous to themselves and others, Danny boy. You're lucky Joy didn't take the job in Hawaii. How she picked you over Hawaii I'll never understand. But, Rich, looks like Danny boy is in love."

"It's about time. He's the only unmarried family member in two generations. I hope your relationship works out. Maybe we can all go to Ireland together next year."

"It'd be a great place to get married, Danny boy."

"I loved it in '03, Charlie. Would be a great place, we'll see."

"Rich, Danny boy is really in love. Geez, artists! They get so romantic about things. But he is our little brother, so we have to look out for him."

Returning home after visiting with his brothers, Danny became increasingly passionate about getting Angie tenured. He confronted the Devious Duo at a department meeting about how they had treated Angie. But what truly startled him was when he got home after the meeting there were two phone messages on his answering machine from Dean White.

Pacing in the living room, he decided to ignore the messages. Instead, he went to check his e-mail, and found a message from the dean repeating the request to see him on Monday morning.

Upset, he powered on his cell phone.

"Tony, you won't believe it. I just got two phone calls and an e-mail from Dean Whitegloves that I'm a danger at PCU."

"Anybody knows that. But what are the particulars?"

"The dean wants to see me Monday. She implies my behavior is aberrant."

"Good observation on her part. But aberrant in what way, what did you do?"

"Typical administrator, no details just demands."

"Then you'll have to see her. Is it about Angie you think?"

"I don't know, but I guess I'll find out Monday. I'll let you know."

That Monday, Danny sat in the chair Dean White offered, listening to allegations against him, while he looked from her dark wooden desk cluttered with folders to the drab painting on the wall.

"Is this a yellow card or a red card, Clarissa?" Danny asked, impatient with her monotone.

"I do not understand," she said, tilting her head sideways.

"In soccer a yellow card is a warning. A red card gets you thrown out of the game. A red card gets me fired," he said, and flashed on his last game for the Spartans, back in Sixty-nine.

She continued in an emotionless monotone, "You poured gasoline on the fire when you confronted Dr. Rheames and Dr. Slutski at the faculty meeting. They felt threatened. If you do anything violent, you would lose your faculty position, yes."

"So this is a red card?"

"Dr. Roarke, you are big and strong. They felt intimated. They are afraid you are capable of violence."

"Be serious, Clarissa. I certainly didn't threaten them. What are their actual allegations? What did I do to them?"

"I believe they filed a grievance against you. I do not know the details. But perception is reality, Dr. Roarke. They feel threatened by you."

"Whose perception is reality?" Danny asked, frustrated. "What do they claim I did to them?" Danny asked, impatiently, angry that the dean sided with the Duo against Angie, but realizing the dean was probably concerned about her own future.

"Can you promise me that you will not become violent toward them?"

"Of course. Why isn't my perception that they're lying reality?"

"Dr. Roarke, you got angry. They felt afraid. That's the reality."

"Clarissa, you know this is nonsense. You think questioning them is a red card?"

"For now, just stay away from them. I guess this is a warning. A yellow card, as you would say. But do not give them any reason to think you will hurt them. That would be a red card."

"When will I hear about the grievance, about any allegations?"

"We should know in a few days," she said, crossing her hands in her lap as she finished.

Danny stood and offered his hand, looking up to focus on the tall frail woman's eyes; she strikes him suddenly as the image of the lanky school teacher Ichabod Crane fleeing from the Headless Horseman in "The Legend of Sleepy Hollow." Her handshake felt like a soft empty glove. Danny looked into the dean's dark glazed eyes, wondering where this labyrinth would lead.

The next day, when Danny got to his office, there was a phone message from the provost. He returned the call.

"Thanks for returning my call, Dr. Roarke. Are you in your office now?"

"Yes, what's this about?"

"I'll be right over."

A few minutes later, Provost Darren Sessions walked into his office.

"I put it in writing," he said, handing Danny the letter. "Dr. Rheames and Dr. Slutski filed a grievance against you. The letter outlines the restrictions on you."

Danny read through the letter vacillating between fear and anger.

"Darren, all I see are restrictions. What are the allegations?"

"Those are confidential until we go through the grievance procedure."

"You gotta be kidding? I thought we're innocent until proven guilty in America?"

"Now Danny, we are treating you fairly. We have to go through these procedures. You will have opportunity to defend yourself."

"So, I have to avoid any contact with them? What happens in the mail room or copy room? I even have to pass their offices to go to the men's room."

"Just ignore them."

As the provost got up to leave, Danny walked with him. As Provost Sessions walked briskly down the hall, Danny stood at the vending machine. As the Coke dropped and he had to twist his hand in to retrieve it, he watched Darren talk with Doreen outside her office. Danny unscrewed the plastic top and walked back into his office to prepare for class as he reread the letter.

In the classroom, his students showed the video of the play they made of the children's book *Bravery Soup,* about a timid raccoon named Carlin seeking courage on his movement toward authenticity.

When the video ended, Danny said, "Well, not exactly *The Odyssey* but a cute book. Nice work on the play. Looks like you folks had fun making it."

"Dr. Roarke, there's another piece. Some out-takes. Can we show it?" Jason asked.

"Hmmm. How come I'm worried, Jason? But, hey, you're a full time teacher, just taking this course for certification. Life is a team sport, so I gotta trust you."

"You'll like it," Jason said.

Jason started the video and watched Danny. They exchanged several laughs and looks as the story played out in a few minutes.

"I like that you got your son in it, with the mystery box."

"He enjoyed it. And he worked well with the others."

"Coincidence that it's about a soccer player on a quest to become a philosopher?"

"A philosopher of education. But that he finds his own book in the mystery box? Carlin found that there was no secret in the box, that courage is being who one is. Didn't you think that was clever?"

"As, I said, I'm glad you got your son in it. But, seriously, I appreciate it. Now am I supposed to think I'm as timid as Carlin the raccoon?"

"No. But sometimes you get down about education being all about test scores and not about kids' lives. My son Randy is four, and he gets the authenticity stuff now that we did the play. That's what the group of us realized. You're making sense of education. We appreciate that."

"Thanks Jason, I needed to hear that today. Now if only I could write another *Great Gatsby* to help people overcome their meretricious lives and appreciate the green light at the end of the dock as personal freedom with responsibility. Nice work. And thanks for the out-takes. Your group has a good feel for what I'm getting at. I worked with kids this summer and talked about authenticity as a common denominator in ethics. I told them that authenticity involves thinking about fairness and equality, feeling caring and intimacy, and acting through dialogue and reciprocity – all the philosophic stuff. Tanesha, an African-American girl, a good writer, and a bright fifth grader summed the principle of authenticity in five words 'be fair, care and share.' That did it for me. The kids all seemed to get that. Now Steffen, you and Nora came all the way from Germany for this semester. What do you think about *Bravery Soup* compared to the novel you two read, *The Old Man and the Sea*? Can we compare Carlin to Santiago?"

"Similar theme. The individual's quest. Hemingway's novel is great literature, however," he said, his German accent evident.

"You've talked about the affect your parents' divorce has on your life. And, Nora, you two are engaged, do you think that men are on quests?"

"For Hemingway, men are. But I think Steffen realized that his parents were not compatible, that's why they divorced."

"What did you learn in school about divorce?"

"Nothing. It was not talked about," she said quietly.

"Steffen, your reaction?"

"Nora is correct. In Germany, personal lives are not part of school. I was embarrassed because my parents divorced. They were not good together. But I keep that in mind. Santiago is the Hemingway hero, but his wife has died, so there is no relationship. He is lonely though."

"Is woman's quest for marriage then, Nora?"

"Dr. Roarke, I think women think about marriage and children, yes," she said, in warm, quiet tones.

"How many women believe their lives would be fulfilled if they were not married?"

Two hands rose tentatively.

"How many feel we should talk about interpersonal relationships and marriage in schools? By show of hands? Looks like everyone agrees. How about the play folks?"

Jason said, "Our group experience gave us a chance to talk about the characters and the play and their lives and our own. That's what amazed me about the experience."

"You are beginning to sound like a convert. I'm worried."

"No, seriously, Dr. Roarke, when I work with elementary kids, I think boys and girls need to talk about this stuff."

"Nora and Steffen, my German mother, serving Irish soda bread asked, 'How is it?' I answered 'A bit dry.' 'Well if you can get it better somewhere else, go,' she said. I went to my buddies' houses and watched their fathers beat their mothers or walk around the house and slap their kids. I returned and said 'Mom, not as dry as I thought.'" Several students laughed. "I think interpersonal relationships and marriage are like that, people test them and go out on their own and ruin their relationships. That's why when we talked about *The Giving Tree,* I said I thought it portrayed co-dependence, not authenticity. The tree teaches no lessons, but acquiesces to the boy's needs. I said Shel Silverstein promotes self-interest in boys and selflessness in girls. Absurd. But I see it everywhere. Justin, your little spoof gets my life right. Soccer is for boys. A man's life's work has to amount to more. As Camus said, life is a slow trek, and we have to embrace images that open our heart. I thank you for reminding me. I think all great writing is about that slow trek. And I think good teaching helps kids to understand that slow trek. And that life is a team sport. That's the point of genuine teaching. So, thanks again."

When Danny got home that evening after class, there was a message on his home phone from the Grievance Committee chairman, Dr. Caudell, that he scheduled a hearing. Danny called Tony.

"Danny, you've got to show. But get a lawyer."

"I did. He's looking over the paper work. He graduated from good old Politically Correct U. Says he's looking forward to dealing with the hypocrisy. He agrees that Southern charm is a public event. Venom flows in private, where the real deals get cut. And Angie's hearing is that afternoon. Looks like the rockets red glare is upon us."

"Danny, nothing you like better than a righteous cause. This is your chance. I have confidence in you."

"Well, if Angie goes down, I'll be on the road too. So, wish me luck."

Danny met the Grievance Committee in a small meeting room in the library. Two professors and several staff members who worked at the university comprised the committee. But he was surprised that the allegations implied his guilt.

Dr. Caudell started, "Dr. Roarke, Dr. Rheames and Dr. Slutski allege you have created a hostile environment for them. Please explain the offensive gesture that you made against Dr. Slutski."

"Can I see the allegations, Dr. Caudell?" Danny asked, and waited as the chairman handed him the printed grievance. He read through it for a couple minutes. "Where does he describe the gesture?"

"Now, Dr. Roarke. This is a hearing. We want your side," Dr. Caudell said.

"I'd like to know Dr. Slutski's side, it's not described here. Am I supposed to guess?"

Professor Trenton interrupted, "Danny, as a colleague, I understand your concern. But we are just giving you a chance to explain today. We will see if the case has merit."

Turning to the other professor, Danny said, "Thanks Don, I trust you, and I want to cooperate, but, I have no idea what Dr. Slutski is talking about."

"He says it was at the last meeting," Dr. Caudell said.

"Milt, all I can think is he interrupted me while I was talking to our chair, Dr. Hopp. If Don was Dr. Hopp and you were Dr. Slutski, I leaned toward Don and held my hand out in the opposite direction."

"That's it, Danny?" Don asked.

"That's it. No contact, no hostility. No harm, no foul. I think they're reacting to Angie's tenure appeal case."

"Dr. Roarke, there is no need to speculate about that," Dr. Caudell insisted.

The hearing went on for over an hour and finally Dr. Caudell dismissed the group, explaining that they would make their decision known within twenty days.

Dr. Caudell insisted, "Dr. Roarke the restrictions remain in place until we reach a decision. During that time, you should have no contact with either professor nor attend any meetings where they are present."

As Danny walked out of the building toward his office, he realized the benefit was that he did not have to deal with the Devious Duo, but like being ejected with a red card for the Spartans, he knew his career was at stake.

That afternoon, he met Angie and her attorney in the lobby before they were to present their case in the first stage of her tenure appeal.

"You ready for this?" Danny asked, as he put his arm around Angie, then shook hands with her attorney.

"Gotta let them know I'm not leaving without a fight."

"Glad to hear it, Angie. She'll do fine, especially with your help Tod."

"She's ready, Danny. And with faculty and student support, she'll win."

"Students?"

"Yes. We have several students that have had difficulties with Dr. Rheames and Dr. Slutski."

"Nice work. I wish you luck. I'm on for about 5:30. I'm gonna share my 'boy-toy' stories and the one about my future in her hands."

"What happened in the Grievance Committee this morning?" Angie asked.

"The Devious Duo alleged I created a hostile environment. And Lorrence said I committed an offensive gesture. At least in soccer everything was public. They're gonna tie me up with this as long as they can. But we have to get tenure for you. I wish you luck. I'll do my best when it's my turn."

"Thanks, Danny," Angie said, and hugged him.

At the evening meeting, Provost Sessions sat in. In their chat before the meeting, Sessions insisted Danny not mention the grievance against him. And so Danny read from a list of talking points he made in consultation with his attorney.

"I've been here fifteen years and witnessed Dr. Rheames intimidate faculty and staff. Within my first few weeks, she'd facetiously called me a 'boy-toy' and emphatically reminded me that my *future* was in her hands, referring specifically to clothed parts of my anatomy that were in her hands. As an old soccer player, I wondered if I should wear a cup," Danny said, and looked from the Appeals Committee Chair to Provost Sessions.

"Dr. Roarke, please," Professor Landsman, the Chair, interrupted.

"Just a style reference. I used to be an athlete. She intimidated untenured faculty. Angie was a student of mine and Rheames' animosity to me trapped Angie. Rheames intimidated her at meetings and so who knows what she did in private.'"

"Dr. Roarke, these allegations have little to do with Dr. Adams' case. Make your comments relevant to infringement of Dr. Adams' academic freedom."

"Sorry, Professor Landsman. But I want the committee to understand a broader picture. Rheames and Slutski tormented Angie. But the major thing, I believe is the dean knew about Rheames' attitude toward Angie and she allowed Rheames to be on the tenure committee, without having her present her position to our tenured faculty. This is blatantly unfair. These two plotted against Angie through the entire process."

"These allegations are not relevant to this case, Dr. Roarke."

"If you think not, Dr. Landsman, you don't understand these two. Angie is one of the most talented and compassionate professors at the university and that irritates the hell out of those two."

"We thank you for your input, Dr. Roarke. We will consider your suggestions. Thank you," Dr. Landsman said abruptly.

Danny looked at Angie and nodded. He made eye contact with Provost Sessions, then looked around the table to faculty members, many of whom he knew quite well and respected greatly.

"Thanks for letting me speak," he said, and stood. He patted Angie's shoulder as he passed her. "Good luck, Sweetie."

He saw Dr. Hopp in the lobby.

As he walked toward her, Danny said, "I can't understand why you let this fiasco happen."

"I di-di-didn't do a-a-anythi-i-ing."

He shook his head, looking at the ground, as she continued.

"I w-w-worry about how we can h-h-heal afterward. Like an election. B-b-both sides don't w-w-win."

"We're in the heat of it. I don't see compromise. I believe in honest invective. You'll change your underwear. Angie will change the world," Danny said, and walked off toward the studio.

He checked on several vases, amused by his primal people drawn in acrobatic sexual positions, that he called the "Just Do Me" series. Then he walked downtown. As he walked home, to his west the sun was a glowing orange orb sinking behind the green dome of the old court house. Passing a sabal palm, Danny said to the tree, "I just committed to social justice. Look, a red shirt, blue jeans and white Nikes, and so, as my astrologer said I'd have to become a patriotic guy. I was not destined to be a rebel. Let's see what happens."

When he got home, he started to dig in the back yard to prepare several plots for sunflowers. As twilight lingered, he finished planting a dozen packages of giant sunflowers. He walked out to the pond and tossed food to the fish and turtles who surfaced to eat. Then he walked into the grove.

Alexander Wilson pulled into his driveway in his pick-up truck as Danny picked fruit.

"Get aliens to do that, Danny Boy."

"Geez. Mr. Wilson, Danny Boy's BB&G can't hire illegal aliens. We can't afford them. I can only afford a philosopher for this work," he added, smiling, dropping several grapefruit into the clear plastic container then climbing down the ladder slowly.

"Oh, the family reputation, I should have realized," Alexander said, adjusting his hat.

"So, what's with the new straw cowboy hat and the 'Git er Done' button? What's that about?"

Alexander exaggerated a bow and laughed. "You don't know much about the South. I just came from my appointment with a good ole boy in his nineties, worth a fortune. He says it all the time."

"And so, even if you have the 'Support Our Troops' ribbons but wear your New York hat like yesterday, you'll get offed?" Danny teased.

"Gotta be careful, Danny Boy. New York liberals like you aren't welcome in the South. The red states are winning on American Idol."

"We know Americans are *idle*, but you, a Schopenhauerian watching it? Tell me how it's predicting America's political future?"

"Well, Carrie, a farm girl from one of the red states, Oklahoma or Tennessee won last night. That means the Walmart vote."

"Oklahoma is a hell of a lot different that Tennessee. What's it tell you about the future?" Danny asked, continuing to pick fruit and toss it into the clear plastic container.

"Schopenhauer said life is about will. And that women are subjective and men are objective. Carrie beat Bo, so she's got the women's vote. And the radio station 1310 AM comes out of Texas and they are political as hell."

"You mean they're preaching hell?"

"They want to change the laws to fit Jesus."

"Figuring they'll all get Raptured?"

"I guess. They're preaching from the book of Daniel."

"I thought Evangelicals only read the New Testament."

"Geez, where have you been? The Fundies think from Genesis to Revelations is the word of God. And they want to change the laws to fit."

"Well, you as a Muslim, I thought you were hawking the Koran?"

"Be careful, don't even joke about that, if any Fundies hear that, I will get offed."

"All because of American Idol?"

"They want to change the laws, like sodomy. They're making this a religious democracy."

Danny moved the ladder as he continued to ramble, enjoying the rapport between them. "Plato said democracy was bullshit. In the *Republic* he offers the Platonic oxymoron: philosopher kings. In his myth of the metals, he talked about the copper people – the regular people, artisans and craftsman and farmers, guys like you and me. We're ruled by our passions and so can't lead. The silver people are the military because they have allegiance to the state, are willing to invade Iraq. But the leaders were the gold people, the ones who could lead. What Tommie Jefferson and Ben Franklin said was, 'We hold these truths to be self evident that all men are created equal and endowed by their creator to life, liberty and the pursuit of happiness.' A republic requires educated people. But Bush and his Fundies don't fit the Plato image."

"Danny Boy, the Fundies believe that God is higher than the Constitution, that simple. When we put the Ayatollah back to replace the Shah, we thought it was a great idea. Now, Bush believes in the Rapture."

"And he's making America Sodom and Gomorra. Hopefully he'll turn into a pillar of salt. I've got Tweedle Dumb and Nasty after me. They're after my job *and* Angie's now. They accused me of threatening them. The New South needs to change."

"So, they're still after you, that's wild. Why do you think I wear this stuff? You gotta go along with it Danny Boy if you want to survive," he said, tipping his hat.

"Alexander, you may be great, but I've gotta change this foolishness. If Angie and I go down, I'm gone. But I don't want either of us to leave Palm City. But please, take some of these," he said, handing several grapefruit to his neighbor.

Danny walked back to the house with the fruit basket. The phone was ringing as he got to the porch. Waiting for the answering machine to respond, he emptied the grapefruit into the sink.

"Dr. Danny, you there?"

"Hey, Sweetie."

"What happened today?" Joy asked.

"Wild. The Devious Duo said I threatened them and the Appeals Committee is sorting through the Angie mess. Very interesting."

"You'll win. You have to. You're an honest caring guy. But, I've been thinking. We should get out of town for a few days. I made reservations as the Castaways on Captiva. I know it's one of your favorite places."

"What a great idea. For when?"

"This weekend, up for it?"

"Sure. Why don't we visit Ray and his wife on the way. I'd love to see their restaurant."

Joy took Friday off and they headed to his ex-student's restaurant for lunch and then drove over the Skyway Bridge to Captiva. The funky little cabin on the beach surrounded by coconut palms was across from the Lazy Pelican Restaurant and a grocery store. To Danny, it was the perfect town.

They dropped the groceries on the kitchen counter and changed into their bathing suits. They walked hand in hand on the beach collecting shells as the sun moved slowly into the west above puffy cumulous clouds in the blue sky above the calm green water. They dropped the shells on the blanket and walked into the water. Danny dove first and swam out in the cool water, loving the feel of salt water on his skin, reminding him of his days as a lifeguard on the beach. When he turned, Joy was standing at the waters edge.

"It's great. Dive in. Remember, you're a diver!"

She waded in slowly then dove. When she surfaced, she swam toward him with long fluid strokes.

"You *can* swim," he said, and they hugged.

"I'm so glad we're here. It is really beautiful. I see why you like it."

"Told you. It's my kind of town, a few wooden cabins on the beach, a restaurant and a grocery store. Everything we need. It reminds me of Lake Pleasant, where my brothers went on vacation with my folks. We should go there too."

They explored for shells buried in the sand under them and swam and hugged and kissed as the sun lowered in the sky. Danny took his bathing suit off and wrapped it around his wrist.

"Oh, much better. Try it Sweetie."

Joy took off her top and then her bottom and wrapped them around her wrist. She swam next to him and pressed her bare breasts against his chest and kissed him.

They continued to hug and kiss and explore for shells. Eventually, Danny went in to the quilt on the beach to get his video camera. He stood on the beach and watched as Joy stood in the water, her hair wet and curly in the sunlight. As she brushed her hair back with her long arms, Danny admired her gorgeous body, her broad shoulders and elegant features as he zoomed in on her. Slowly widening the shot, he brought in the water and sky and sun. Amazed, he said into the microphone, "She's like Bottecelli's Venus rising from the Gulf into my life to transform it and me. What a wonderful, elegant, classic woman."

Calling to her, he said, "Joy, I just want to get the fire started for dinner."

"I'll be here, Danny," she said and waved.

He walked the sandy path under the palms and started the charcoals in the small grill outside the cabin, next to the picnic table, under the coconut palm. As he tended the charcoal, Joy walked back leisurely from the beach. He watched her and smiled. As she approached the cabin, he went inside to get the shish-kabobs and champagne.

She carried the quilt and tossed it on the picnic table. He handed her a glass of champagne.

"The fire looks good. You tend it for a while. I've got an idea," she said, and shook out the quilt and took it inside. A few minutes later she called, "Oh, Danny Boy. I want your opinion."

He walked into the cabin through the kitchen to the bedroom. She had spread the quilt over the bed and placed the strawberries, Smucker's fudge, and the whipped cream.

"What do you think, Ulysses? The ice cream's in the fridge. We can have each other for dessert," she said, laughed and hugged him.

"I think that's what Penelope said to Odysseus when he returned to the bed he made for them."

Chapter 24: Danny's Day

"It's been weeks of this bullshit. The Appeals Committee hasn't decided yet, Angie?" Danny asked, as he stood at her office door next to the Mark Twain sculpture and the lunar eclipse photo he gave her.

"My attorney thinks it'll be over soon. He says in the meantime be as charming and professional as I can."

Danny walked to the antique student desk near her bookshelves that held the bowl with a purple orchid he gave her the day of the first hearing. He pulled a few dead flowers from it.

"This needs some water. I gotta tend it and you," he said, taking the plant to the water fountain outside his office. Returning with it, and looking at the clutter on Angie's desk, and the semester calendar behind her on the wall filled with red and black ink, he sat in the chair opposite her. "Have you heard anything?"

"Not yet."

"The Grievance Committee has been silent too. My feeling is the Devious Duo got out of hand and the university is trying to figure out what to do."

"I hope you're right Danny. I can't take more of this."

"You're doing great. I can't believe how professional you are. I think they figured you would have folded already. And when they went after me, I think they just spread too thin. But you never know how they'll blame us. Like my hand gesture Tweedle Dumb called offensive, wild. They are filled with bullshit. That's what my attorney is concerned about. And a family friend, a Jewish lawyer in New York I've known since we were kids, he's my brother Rich's friend, says I got to get out of the South. I'm not meant for it. He told me about a dry cleaner who lost his shirts when he was working in film in California. He took the cleaner to small claims court and the cleaner said he was hostile. The judge said, 'Of course he got angry, you lost his shirts!' Abe's saying that me getting angry at a meeting is the same thing. They're looking for any excuse. When the deals were behind closed doors, they won. In New York people are in your face. They go public about their anger and their allegations. I think the Devious Duo are worried now because it has all gone public."

"Everyone on campus knows what they've done. Several times during the hearing committee members were shocked by what people said. I hope they are piecing it together."

"My Dad's cliché, 'No news is good news' may fit. You know Provost Sessions is concerned. And if you're not hearing from President Jackson, you know he's assessing things. I've always respected him. He's got integrity. I remember my interview with him, when I applied to teach here. I was impressed by how forcefully he stood up from his desk and shook my hand. We're the same height, and so, when I looked into those confident green eyes and felt his firm handshake, I knew this was the university for me. He's aged gracefully over the years, and as his thick dark hair has started to gray, he reminds me of Antonio – both men of character with heart. It's a rare quality. He'll ensure fairness."

"I've always liked him. And yes, he does remind me of Antonio. Both great guys."

"But Dean Whitegloves has to be worried, because she supported Dumb and Nasty. Or they manipulated her somehow. I just wish it would be over. That orchid has a week or two before the blooms go. My hope was it would outlast the hearings. Remember Mark Twain's quote I put on the back of that eclipse photo, about the moon's dark side. Unfortunately, Tweedle Dumb paraded his tight gender confused butt and Tweedle Nasty paraded that rotund moon of hers. Hypocrisy like theirs can't win; there are good people throughout the university involved now. And all their allegations will unravel."

"Let's hope so."

"It'll have to be over by my birthday. I'm planning a birthday party. It will be one hundred and first anniversary of James Joyce's Bloom's Day. I was in Dublin for the ninety-ninth, my nephew's wedding for the hundredth, and so, I want friends for the hundred and first. It's gotta be a celebration."

"I hope you're right Danny boy. Is Tony gonna make it?"

"Would be nice if he could. But Mr. International is in New Zealand consulting."

Two weeks after graduation, which Danny was not allowed to attend because of the restrictions on him, he got a message on his home answering machine from Provost Sessions.

"Danny, the Grievance Committee has decided on mediation to resolve the allegations. We will be arranging for a mediator to come to campus to work with department faculty."

Danny called Sessions to clarify what the decision meant, then he called Angie. "I just heard from Sessions that they're gonna drop the grievance if I agree to mediation. Have you heard anything about tenure?"

"I got a call from President Jackson. He wants to meet with me and my attorney tomorrow."

"I think the Devious Duo will not be happy," he said, looking at the turtles sunning on the rocks and the fish swimming in the clear water. "Someone has to help the fish and turtles get along. Buddha is smiling in the pond. Christ is in the lilies. Jaweh and Allah are tending the butterflies. My neighbor Alexander Wilson just walked by with his dogs who I call Zeus and Apollo. So the gods are on notice. And the courageous turtle is on top of his reptile colleagues on the rocks. As your local philosopher, I say the signs look good."

"I hope I have something to smile about tomorrow. This has been hell."

The next day, President Jackson scheduled a special department faculty meeting for the following day. Jackson sat next to Angie in the meeting room.

"I want to thank you all for coming. I've reviewed the report of the Appeals Committee and met with their chair, and the dean, and the provost. I want to say that I thank you all for your hard work during this difficult process."

All department faculty were around the table. Rheames and Slutski were at the far end from Danny and Kajaw. Danny focused on Rheames face which was expressionless. Angie appeared near tears in black slacks and a blue blouse, which Danny felt spoke eloquently of what she'd been through.

"Awarding tenure is one of the most difficult decisions at any university. It is a life time commitment on the part of a university. I have reviewed Angie's portfolio and the comments by faculty and have thought long and hard about her place in the university. I've decided that she has earned tenure and welcome her to the university."

Everyone but Rheames and Slutski jumped to their feet and applauded. Danny rushed up to hug Angie and others gathered around congratulating her.

Danny extended his hand as President Jackson stood. "Paul, great decision. You really stood up for the university. John Palmer would be proud. She's one of the most talented faculty here," he said, appreciating the man's confident green eyes and strong jaw that exuded honesty connected through a firm handshake.

"I agree, Danny, and she was one of your students. Thanks for supporting her. That was courageous."

On the way out of the meeting room, Provost Sessions called Danny into a side hallway. Danny stood silently, wondering what Sessions wanted as the other faculty members were exiting in a happy group.

"Danny, here's a letter removing all restrictions."

"Thanks Darren. It's been a hell of a ride."

In the morning of his birthday, up early, Danny worked in the yard, first mowing the front lawn for croquet and bocce. He took the mower to the backyard and cut the grass he hadn't mowed for several weeks. The thick wet grass slowed and choked the mower. He had to restart it several times to carve around the sunflower garden in front of the greenhouse and the one along the south fence. He pushed it in front of the banana trees lining the fence and the cactus garden with the small Key lime tree in front of his south bedroom window. He sweated in the humidity and drizzle as he pushed it around the banana trees west of his bedroom window, then the thick growth around the stump of the water oak he had cut down before he went to Ireland two years ago, so that when he returned he could have the green metal roof over.

He continued to sweat as he pushed the mower along the path he called "Natural Florida" under the remaining oak, cypress, camphor and bayberry trees. He came to the oak that fell the previous summer in the series of hurricanes that blew across Florida. Looking at the fallen tree stretched the length of his property, he thought about the trees over his bedroom and garage that he had cut down before putting on the new roof. Shaking his head slowly side to side he thought about how lucky his timing was. Had he waited, any of the four hurricanes that blew through since could have blown those trees down to crush the house.

Inside, waiting for Joy, he made Irish soda bread, pie from the limes he picked that morning, and crab and shrimp for his birthday party. When Joy arrived with Bubba, she helped set the table. Danny cut sunflowers, black-eyed Susans and hibiscus, and they talked as they arranged the dining room table.

"It's a day of gathering the bounty of this small land, to share with friends to celebrate life and another birthday."

"Danny, you are a poet."

"No, I really mean it."

"I do to."

Walking past the pond, he tossed food to the fish and turtles as Tyrella pulled into the driveway.

"Tyrella Bishop bearing gifts."

"Happy Birthday, Danny. Yes, gifts. Humus and smoked salmon and wine from Australia. I so love the green metal roof, Danny. It makes your house look like a splendid sculpture."

"To build a roof over love and lust takes the luck of the Irish. Remember the leprechaun my folks gave me still sits on the bathroom window sill in the shell with coins from my travels," he said, as they walked onto the porch where Joy met them.

"Don't forget your German roots, Danny. That gives you the endurance."

"Our German roots, Sweetie," he said, emphatically.

"Believe it Joy. He will be considered a great writer some day," Tyrella said, patting Danny's shoulder.

"Then what? I'll get to play Danny Boy on the flute with Jimmie Galway?"

"Oh, you rotter. Joy, I wish you luck with this mad man."

"Thanks, I need all the help I can get. But he's mad in such a wonderfully lovable way," she said, and kissed him.

Danny looked at Joy and smiled. He put an arm around each of them as they walked through the living room. "I think the leprechaun my folks gave me was smiling because he knew all this would happen. When I put the Irish Euros in his shell and had the green metal roof put on, he seemed to know that I was ready for a woman in my life. And suddenly Joy appeared."

Joy looked at Tyrella and rolled her eyes, "See what I mean Tyrella? How can you not love this man?"

"Agreed, Joy. He is a charmer."

Danny escorted them to the dining room and moved the chairs so the three of them could sit and talk.

"How is your television show, Tyrella?" Joy asked.

"Going quite well. They want me back next year. So I won't be the restaurant critic for *The Chronicle.*"

"So, music on TV but no more free meals for a local philosopher? Ah, yes, celebrity. Tyrella, don't forget the little people."

"You are not little people. You are the real people," she said. "Those one loves and trusts, ones who make us better. Ones one would die for. And so friendship is like that."

"Well, geez. I was just teasing, but thanks. You are a magnanimous women. And your friendship is a wonderful birthday present. Even if I don't get any free restaurants meals ever again."

"Oh, Danny, you are such a scoundrel. Joy, how do you endure him?"

"When you realize his dark and gnarled heart is him doing his best, he becomes lovable," she said, and reached for his hand.

As they talked, Joy placed the watermelon she carved and added grapes and scoops of cantaloupe and honeydew. Danny brought out the Key lime pie and Irish soda bread he baked that morning. Then he put St. Pauli Girl, Guinness, and Harp on ice in a bowl he made.

They talked happily as Nicole and Raiz arrived and Kajaw showed soon after in a bright print shirt. The group settled around the dining room table and chatted.

"OK, we've been talking about the government and the future hopes for world peace and you're skeptical about it all. So let's get on with the party," Danny said. He handed Tyrella the book of poems by Yeats with the poem titles and page numbers written on the opening page.

She teased for a time and said, "Are you serious, I really have to do this?"

"I'm the birthday boy, Ms. Bishop. And you're a TV celebrity," Danny said, and raised the video camera.

She smiled graciously, then adjusting her glasses, taking command, moving her hand like a conductor, she said, "OK, I want complete quiet." Turning to the cover, showing it to the group, she continued, "This poem is by William Butler Yeats. It's called, 'When You Are Old'." Hesitating a moment, a smile developing on her face, she added "As you get old-er, you appreciate it more and more." After another moment, she started in her endearing English accent.

Comforted by Tyrella's voice and Yeats' words about the search for meaning through love, Danny focused the camera first on Tyrella, then around to Nicole and Raiz and toward Kajaw, sitting between Tyrella and Joy. As Tyrella read the lines so fluidly, Danny focused on Joy. She noticed and returned a smile and nod of appreciation.

This group of people had become close friends over the years, but Joy, in the eight months they'd known each other had become a great love. Hearing Yeats' words and remembering the trip two years ago to his grave in Ireland in sight of Benbulben, in County Sligo, Danny felt he had reached home. Finally, he built a roof over lust with love. This group of friends developed over the years was now complete with Joy.

As Tyrella finished everyone applauded. Joy, smiling as Danny videotaped her clapping, said "Wonderful, that was great, Tyrella. I see why your show is such a hit." Kajaw and Nicole and Raiz agreed, Nicole saying, "You should do books on tape. You would be great."

Acknowledging their compliment, Tyrella mumbled something about it being a wonderful idea, but moving on, she asked, "What do we have next?"

"'The Isle of Innisfree', it's a small island in Lake Gill, up in Sligo County, Yeats' Country. Near where he's buried."

Danny pictured the graveyard and tombstone and the hard edge of Benbulben's profile to the north of the little churchyard grave. He remembered when he landed at Shannon Airport feeling that he had to see Yeats' grave first before anything else in Ireland.

"Oh, I don't know that one," she said, adjusting her glasses after finding the page. Then suddenly thrusting her right hand in the air, she started. Stopping with a laugh, she shook her head. "I'm sorry, I guess I got carried away." But everyone cheered her on. She stopped, gathered herself then began again. "This is called 'The Isle of Innisfree.'"

As she finished in her melodious voice, Danny thought about Ireland.

"I was in Dublin for the ninety-ninth anniversary of the day James Joyce set *Ulysses*. June sixteenth was the day he met his lover and eventual wife. Joyce left Ireland soon after, to get beyond the strangle hold he felt it held on him. I loved the open country and the incredible shades of green on the hills and farms. And there are so few people along the Connemara coast and Dingle peninsula. The whole country is gorgeous. And that time of year the days are long. But Yeats was writing about missed love, during a time he felt stranded in Dublin. He was trying to live the life of an artist; as we folks know it is a tough gig. But he was without a great love. Sort of like Thoreau, to whom he paid homage with the reference to bean-rows that he would raise. Although I think Henry David really didn't want a woman. But anyway, I asked Tyrella to read it so we could reflect on life with and without love. And now, sitting next to Joy, her presence gives meaning to my life, like nothing I've ever known."

As Tyrella looked directly into the camera, she said "Danny, Ireland did great things for you. And, I must say, Joy has done wonders. It is so nice to hear you say that."

"Thanks Tyrella," Danny said, feeling great friendship toward her.

Joy reached over to hold his hand and smiled, and whispered, "I love you."

And as everyone applauded, Raiz said to Kajaw, "See, that's what people did before TV. They sat by the lake and listened to poetry, and fell in love."

Danny nodded his head, saying simply, "Well done, Tyrella. Thanks!"

Nicole, with a gently modulating hand said, "You have such great rhythm, Tyrella."

"For some unknown reason it works. I haven't the slightest idea what I'm reading, of course," she added, with a laugh.

"It's all about performance. After the next one you're done," Danny added.

"Do I have to do this one also?" she asked, finding the page. Starting quickly, "This is called 'The Song of Wandering Aengus' or Engus."

As Tyrella neared the end, Danny widened the camera and videoed the table that Joy and he set. It was filled with Key lime pie and Irish soda bread he made that morning while Joy napped on the couch under the palm tree. The Key West shrimp and Dungeonus crab came into view to remind him of Hemingway's home and his year in Oregon. He smiled as the watermelon that Joy scooped out after her nap and filled again with balls of watermelon, cantaloupe, honeydew and grapes filled the center of the lens. He remembered how she had him fill the small ceramic bowls he taught her to make with cashews and assorted nuts as she encouraged him to finish setting the table before Tyrella arrived. It reminded him how well they worked together under pressure as they arranged and rearranged the buffet on the glass topped dining room table. With a hushed voice, Tyrella finished and gestured with her free right hand.

Raiz said over the applause, "I like the plucking part," and everyone laughed.

Danny aimed the camera toward Joy. Light from the kitchen highlighted her blond hair, the tips of which lay gently on her shoulders, one covered by the sheer gray shawl, the other exposing a thin black strap that held her top underneath.

As Joy took the copy of *Ulysses* that Danny handed her, she flipped the pages and said, "Let me show you that this is all one paragraph that goes on for pages with no punctuation."

Danny talked as he continued to video her. "Ulysses is set on June 16, 1904. It is now one hundred and one years later. For those who saw that great American movie with Rodney Dangerfield, *Back to School* you will remember this scene where Sally Kellerman, who played Hot Lips Houlihan in *MASH*, starts her first class with this reading from *Ulysses* and Rodney Dangerfield as a student in her class has a fantasy about her. Joy is going to do a little longer reading, to include Algeciras and the Alameda gardens and the jasmine and geraniums that are so great there."

Tyrella said, "We read it that night we watched *Back to School*."

"Yes," Danny said, turning the camera back from Tyrella to Joy. "Have you seen it?" he asked to Nicole.

Raiz said, "She wants to. Kurt Vonnegut's in it."

"Yeah, Vonnegut wrote a paper for Dangerfield that Hot Lips failed, saying whoever wrote it didn't know anything about Kurt Vonnegut. So Dangerfield wouldn't pay him. It was hysterical."

"Ever see an interview with Vonnegut?" Nicole asked. "He's so bizarre."

"Yeah, well he's a Cornell grad."

"That's why," she responded, with a laugh.

"He's also one of the few writers who ever wrote back to tell me that he liked my writing and not to kill myself," Danny added, glibly.

Joy jumped in, as she paged through the ending. "I want to know why my English teacher told me I had run on sentences when this is a paragraph," holding the book up and flipping the pages. "All the way from here to here. One paragraph."

Danny kept saying, "Yeah, yeah. It's an impossible book."

Raiz said, "This is the only time you'll be able to read that book, because you'd never get to it otherwise."

"Tell me what a language arts teacher would do to someone who wrote like this?" Joy asked, looking at Danny.

"My junior high school English teacher wouldn't even let me try to write like Hemingway. She demanded structured linear sentences without slang or God forbid, swearing. So, whenever I was supposed to write from experience it became homogenized grammar exercises. In high school, my English teacher who was the school newspaper advisor told us that James Joyce developed the stream of consciousness style but that no one could understand what he wrote. So he never let me try it in my sports column. Then I go to Dublin in 2003 and they're reading from *Ulysses*."

"In the pubs?" Tyrella asked.

"Everywhere. But this was at the James Joyce Museum. And so, they're sitting around drinking Guinness, which by the way is in the bowl near the wine in the kitchen, and they're reading this book. And so, Joy you're on."

"Well, I'll try, but no brogue," she said, waving the book slowly, facing it toward Nicole.

"Joy, it's considered the greatest piece of literature of the Second Millennium. Now we're in the Third"

"Well not the way I'm going to read it Danny."

"You'll do fine. So, Hot Lips, you're on."

She held the book in front of her. Light from the kitchen behind her was bright yellow in the camera and on her hair. The old back cover black and the uncovered first page white with *Ulysses* in bold black and James Joyce printed below.

He kept the camera on her and enjoyed how she read and grimaced at moments when she confused a word, but finishing to applause as she repeated, "Yes!"

During the applause, Danny put his arm on Joy's bare shoulder and kissed her on her cheek. "Well done," he said, looking into her eyes. "Tough to read without punctuation. In the movie, Rodney Dangerfield goes into a fantasy where he is with her. Great job Joy," Danny added, and handed her the camera.

Danny showed Joy how to focus and record with the camera and he put the strap over her head and handed her the camera.

Tyrella spoke up, "Danny-boy, we are expecting this reading to be extraordinary. Can you see?"

He took glasses from his shirt pocket and ignored her with a wry smile. Clearing his throat for effect, he started "This is Homer's *Odyssey.* Where Ulysses – Odysseus in Greek – returns home after twenty years, ten years at war and ten years traveling." Looking at Joy leaning toward him with the camera he said, "Suddenly you're Steven Spielberg?" and they both laugh. "And so, he's back with his wife, his faithful wife Penelope. And so, I'm gonna read two paragraphs."

He opened the leather bound book containing Homer's *Iliad* and *Odyssey.* He had marked it with the gold ribbon and started to read the conversation between Odysseus and Penelope on his return home; Odysseus telling her that he was destined to travel again to teach.

Moving on to the next paragraph, he continued about their love making and conversations afterward.

"And that's actually the end of it?" Tyrella asked.

"No," Danny said, flipping from chapter twenty-three to the ending in chapter twenty-four. "I mean, they make love endlessly and talk intimately for hours after he strung the bow that none of the other guys could and she realized it was him, her man who built their bed from the tree that was in the center of the house. And then he shot arrows through a series of axe-heads that showed he was strong and accurate and a real man. And why we commemorate his victory with croquet wickets next."

"I figured you had a plan with the mallets. You are so cunning, Danny boy" Tyrella, quipped.

"Yeah, cunning. Anyway, Ulysses killed all the guys hitting on his wife. I'll read the last paragraph. This is how *The Odyssey* ends." Stopping, he tried to summarize. "After he killed all the suitors harassing his wife because he was the King of Ithaca and they were trying to take his kingdom, he traps them in his palace and he and his son kill them. In the last chapter, the families of the dead suitors attack him at his father Laertes' farm. Odysseus says they have to fight the angry relatives, but the goddess Athena intervenes during the fight."

"Where have all the goddesses gone?" Kajaw teased.

"What's everyone a critic? Anyway, Athena has been guiding him through the whole journey. And, the usual, Zeus sends a lightning bolt that scares everyone and Odysseus tries to rally everyone. But Athena tells them all to lighten up and stop fighting, and she suggests they achieve peace and get on with their lives. And so the *The Odyssey* ends. Applause to Homer."

"Danny, you are my Odysseus. I love that you made our bed. It's perfect for hours of love making and intimacy, and our research on the *Just Do Me* series."

"Thanks, Cutie. And, no doubt, you are my Penelope."

Tyrella, Kajaw, Raiz and Nicole applauded.

After dinner, they went out to play croquet. Danny explained the rules, with the camera around his neck and a mallet in one hand and his wine in the other, surprised none of them had ever played.

"Forget all the technical stuff. Let's get started," Nicole said, and Joy gave a rousing cheer.

Danny and Joy passed the camera between them to video as the other played. Kajaw and Raiz hit wildly and missed the early wickets. Tyrella played through quickly and got into the lead. Nicole moved passed Tyrella and was in the lead until Raiz caught up with her and hit her with his ball, which allowed him to send her in any direction he wanted by placing his foot on his ball and hitting the ball with his mallet sending her ball.

"I'm glad I'm not goin' home to your bed tonight, Raiz. Newlyweds, ah, competitive youth," Danny said, and gave Joy a quick hug and kiss.

Nicole recouped from the send and got back to the game, leading again quickly. Kajaw and Tyrella seemed amused but uncompetitive. Danny appreciated his friends and watching Joy and enjoying how well life had changed in the year since his last birthday. The game continued on as the light began to fade.

Kajaw was called away on his cell phone, saying, "I gotta go. Sorry."

Danny knew the pressure he was under and was glad he'd made it at all, since their garbled phone call a few days before when Kajaw was in New York with his friend still enduring chemotherapy. As Kajaw pulled out of the driveway, with his lights on, Danny watched, distracted, as Nicole caught up to Raiz and sent him and Tyrella played through.

"Gender collaboration, a sexist game," Danny said, as Nicole tapped Tyrella closer to the wicket, after sending Danny in the opposite direction.

Nicole and Tyrella chatted together as Danny took another shot back the distance Nicole sent him.

"But clearly the women have collaborated, Joy," Danny said, holding his hand up to catch Joy's attention. "I'd like to say it's a gender thing."

"Be happy you have someone of our gender who loves you Danny," she teased.

"Joy, you always say the right thing. But isn't evil collusion the undoing of the soul?"

"Looks like croquet. And the young newlyweds have something to prove, Professor Roarke."

Nicole moved ahead, got through two wickets then came back as Raiz tried to catch up. Danny and Joy were amused by the young couple and videotaping the game, leaning against each other and sharing wine as they watched. But Nicole kept advancing as Raiz chased her. Nicole was first through the middle wicket on the return. But Raiz caught her.

"Danny, should I send her?" Raiz asked, with a laugh.

"When I was at Cornell, I worked with Arab students. Their favorite phrase was, 'The enemy of my enemy is my friend.' Think about it, Raiz. You two have to sleep together tonight, wouldn't it be better to have a real friend?"

Raiz laughed, placed his ball next to hers, stepped on his and hit it with the mallet sending Nicole almost to the grove.

"Raiz, you bastard!" she yelled, then chased her ball.

Danny said, "Nicole, at least you get to bring it back into bounds. I don't know what we can do with Raiz."

Danny passed Tyrella, but Raiz still led. Joy preferred to videotape than to compete; and she and Danny enjoyed the show.

"It's a battle of the newlyweds," Danny said. "Raiz, remember you gotta go home together. Remember where you sleep," he added, but Raiz sent Nicole again.

"I have a mallet too, Raiz," she said, lifting and shaking it.

"Raiz, remember Athena in *The Odyssey*. Let's stop this war. Zeus will be angry."

"It's only a game. It's fun. And I'm winning."

"Wait 'til you get home," Tyrella said, shaking her mallet at him.

Danny tried to catch Raiz, but was amused by the dynamics between the young couple and wondered what would happen between them that night. The game continued on for a while and Raiz got to the final post first, ending the game. The group teased him for a while then brought their mallets with them and dropped them in the primal pot on the porch.

When they went to the living room, Joy wrapped Bubba in a white towel and put her in Danny's lap as she continued to videotape. Danny put in the *Bubba* DVD that he made of the blind dog. He handed the book *Guide to Sexual Fulfillment* to Raiz sitting next to Nicole on the couch. She looked at it as Raiz flipped through.

"Danny, have you and Joy tried all these?"

"Not yet, Raiz. This is a video of Bubba's guide to sexual fulfillment. She's my blind spirit guide."

Joy said, "Danny's on page three. But I have confidence in him and our research is great fun."

They all laughed. Danny started the DVD as they watched.

"That's Lammie-pie," Danny said, pointing to the stuffed toy in Bubba's mouth.

"You're twisted," Raiz said, laughing.

Danny laughed, "Check this chew technique. That's her chew and lick technique. Bubba's an artist."

Raiz shook his head, looking from the sex book to the video as he sat next to Nicole who kept laughing as she looked from Bubba seated on Danny's lap to her on video humping her toys.

"Its not just sex," Danny said, "The music is Mozart. She's good an hour."

Suddenly, the phone rang. Danny let it ring through. He heard Tony say "Happy Birthday, Danny boy!"

Danny grabbed the phone quickly when he heard Tony's voice. "Hard to believe, Antonio. We are almost twice the age of people we never trusted. Thanks for calling. Where are you?"

"New Zealand. It's not Bolivia, Sundance. But someday we'll get there."

"You'll be happy to know Angie got tenure and the Devious Duo surrendered on the grievance. I'm employed."

"Great news! I just wanted to wish you a great birthday and remind you how much our friendship means."

"Thanks, you are a great friend. And we're watching my spirit guide hump chew toys. You'd love it."

As Danny chatted, the others watched, amused as Bubba humped her toys. They chatted on for a while and Tony wished Danny luck with Joy and they ended the call.

Still watching the video, Raiz said, smiling, "Danny, you need to get out more."

They all laughed as they heard Danny chant, "Go, go, go," on the video.

"You should put this on the Internet. It could replace Paris Hilton," Nicole said.

"I'm telling you, Bubba is my spirit guide. She's a fifteen year old blind Yorkie who's lovable and enjoys a good hump. She knows lust and love. What more is there in life?"

As the video ended, Joy brought out the Key lime pie and started to put candles on it.

"Will there be enough candles, Joy?" Tyrella asked, winking at Danny.

"I've got plenty. Fifty-eight and one for next year," she said, patting Danny's knee.

When Danny started James Galway's "Danny Boy" there was a knock on the door.

Opening the door, Danny said, "Oh, my word, don't we look fancy. Folks, it's Dan and Iris."

"We're fancy. We just came from the Rotary Club," Iris said.

Danny hugged her. A few moments later as James Galway played his flute, Angie and Tim rang the bell.

"Well happy birthday to me. Thanks for coming. You missed croquet, but you get cake."

"Happy Birthday, Danny boy. Thanks for saving my career," Angie said, and hugged him.

"Hey thanks for being my friend. I got a call from Antonio in New Zealand. I told him you got tenure. He's really happy for you. And I'm sure Allison will get a hold of you to congratulate you."

"Danny, you are such good friends. I can't imagine my life without you guys. And now Tim. You've all changed my life."

Tim reached to shake Danny's hand. As Danny escorted them in and found chairs for everyone, Joy started everyone singing "Happy Birthday."

After everyone left, Joy and Danny hugged on the couch and talked about the party and what to do to celebrate.

"Sweetie, with you, the roof over has become a blend of love and lust, but mostly love and companionship. What I saw in my parents' love we have and more. I love you."

"And I love you. My parents never had this. What we have is so special, Danny. That I could feel completely loved, respected and cherished. Amazing, and you're a great friend."

After they embraced and kissed, Danny ran the bath and lit candles. He remembered the bottle of White Star champagne. He popped the cork and filled a glass to share and brought it to Joy submerged in the warm bubbles.

"Thanks for being here. I never thought it would happen last year at my party. Such incredible change. I cannot imagine another woman for me," he said, then kissed her softly and offered her the glass.

"And you've changed my life Danny. Just amazing. We really do connect. I never imagined I could feel so complete. Thanks."

He sat behind her in the tub filled with bubbles surrounded by candles as they drank champagne and talked. Afterwards, warm and amorous, they went to bed to make love. After kissing warmly for a long time, as he fondled her breasts and nipples and licked and sucked them hard, she eased on top of him. She rode him slowly, gently at first, but as they continued, she became animated, physical, athletic. He alternated between fondling her breasts and sitting up to suck her nipples, then rolled her nipples between his fingers with increasing pressure as suddenly she chanted, "Yes, Yes, Yes!" catching his eyes and smiling playfully as he acknowledged appreciating her Joycean allusion amidst the action as she climaxed.

Afterward, she lay quietly on his chest for a long time. He caressed her back and shoulders, as she seemed lost in a dream. They stayed that way, her on top, and him gently caressing her. Slowly, she returned, and smiling gently, looked at him. They kissed then rolled to their sides, embracing each other. She eased Danny on top of her. Kissing her softly, he entered her gently then deeper, enjoying her warm wetness as they adjusted their bodies to each other and kissed and he began to move more forcefully in and out. He caressed her thighs then moved them together so she could feel him slowly in and out over her clitoris. She moaned gently and adjusted herself so their movements aligned as he stroked her with the tip of his cock. As they kissed gently, moving slowly, they looked at each other smiling, and he stroked deep into her, then with his hands under her butt, he started slowly in and out of her, then more quickly and passionately, until they came together and lay exhausted and happy in each others arms.

Several hours later, Danny woke. He watched Joy sleeping quietly, feeling admiration for her and gratitude for how she transformed his life. He eased out of bed and took his journal from the night table. He grabbed a T-shirt and a pair of jeans from a closet hook and quietly put them on, then slid into his Nikes as he walked into the living room, turned on the lamp, sat in the rocking chair and started to write.

June 17, 2005 3:33 a.m.

My Block
Chapter 3: Beyond Scylla & Charybdis

I should call myself Danny O'Roarke — one needs to be "of" something or someone... They made Papa drop the "O" when he came to this country.

As Lincoln said in the "Gettysburg Address", we need to be "of... by... for... people..."

And so, what does a man care about if not his family, his work, or his country? Self interest is no interest of importance. As Hemingway said, alone man ain't worth shit... And so, to tell America's story in My Block I gotta swear... If the word "fuck" ended my soccer career, I gotta live with it, cause it was what I felt.

I swear by all that is heart felt that I care about this country and our people... I've been hired and fired and bought and sold like trash. And man, all I can say is that like George M. Cohan, my mother...father...sister...and I thank you.

And I know I was almost raped by some nameless guy they never caught. Who knows, he probably got offed by some other knife wielder or died of AIDS, like my gay buddy at Gulf Coast, who told me he was sick, then died a month later of a then mysterious disease.

But all I'm sayin is that we gotta be of, by or for something; or this country's gonna go down the tubes, and that would be a shame.

We need heroes. We want to believe in heroes, in myths and legends, and Ulysses and Helen and Penelope. But give me Penelope any time, cause beauty will get you a lot in this country, but we want love. And so, beauty may be something you are, a commodity you can buy or sell, but love can't be bought and sold... As Joy has so artfully declared, it just doesn't work that way... Beauty you see, but love you feel.

Take Elaine, she wanted to buy me. It didn't work for good reason.

And Maureen, she flattered me with all that Zeus and male and female being meant for each other. I believe it, like the Chinese ideas about yin and yang. A great relationship harmonizes male and female. But she lured me saying that my Shattered Images was a "minor masterpiece." Artists are vulnerable. She gave me money and bought me Hawaii and flew me to Spain to see the Rock of Gibraltar and the tip of Africa and the Pillars of Hercules that define the edge of the Mediterranean and maybe where Plato put Atlantis. But she lied about love...

Homer said Zeus had lots of women. Helen was one of the results. But can we trust poets and prophets? I mean, look at the book of Daniel... One night in the lion's den isn't The Odyssey.

With Angie's tenure, Tweedle Dumb and Tweedle Nasty capitulated because I put my career on the line for my student now colleague, and we stood up to them. It's time for justice. There's no justice unless people are honest. To be great, a university must transcend hypocrisy. As Don Quixote said, "Honesty and openness spell HOPE!"

And so, I gotta write My Block... If it goes to print there are some at PCU who will want me crucified. But that's the risk an artist takes. And so, like Holden Caulfield in Catcher in the Rye, who like David Copperfield was born *with a caul, I gotta tell my story. It's about what I've been through to get here. But I've learned you gotta dress + play the game today + the next day + until the season is over.*

I mean, I never got that hat trick for the Spartans against the Trojans. I just got red carded and ejected to end my career. Ulysses took twenty years to return to Ithaca and Penelope, but he killed everybody in the house. That's just not gonna play well these days with all the courts + lawyers + media. I mean, if guys are hittin on your woman because you killed Polyphemus – Poseidon's Cyclops kid + bragged about it – you got Hades to pay. And a trip to Hades just confirms that you gotta get on with life.

And so, yeah, other guys would love to hit on Joy, but if she loves me she will fight them off. Penelope did it for twenty years. She's the only woman in literature I ever respected. And Joy is my Penelope…

To Hades with Helen – the face that launched a thousand ships. Excuses that the gods made me do it or he seduced me are all nonsense. So I have to write about Elaine + Maureen + all the others along the way. But really, they were not the match I wanted. But be serious, Ulysses' seven year tryst with Calypso was consensual… Even the gods can't control a guy that much.

Just like the hypocrisy ambassadors at PCU, I mean, how do you listen to their crap? And so, I gotta put my ass on the line again. That guy that almost raped me didn't do anything worse. I mean, he stabbed the mattress and threatened my butt, took some clothes, the silver pocket watch Uncle Charlie gave me + he was gone. But being Black in this country is a tough way to go.

Tweedle Dumb and Tweedle Nasty have got to change. The word on the street is that Doreen resigned as chair and will retire this summer. Tweedle Nasty Scylla and Tweedle Dumb Charybdis are like mythological beasts that need to transform. But President Jackson elevated the university to Palmer's vision of "Heavenly Earth" and so, I applaud him and the university.

I just gotta get <u>My Block</u> out + if it gives someone courage, great. I'm not in it for the money. But, if I sell it, then I can talk about it. And say we all gotta try to be like the courageous turtle.

Yeah, it sucks getting assaulted + getting accused of threatening colleagues. Hemingway was pursued by cross-dressing J. Edgar Hoover because he went marlin fishing with Castro. But I'm not gonna swallow the barrel of a shotgun + blow my brains out over it. No one really knows how it's gonna end. But it's gonna end. As Jim Morrison said, "No one gets out alive." So, I gotta write. That simple.

As Tony said in his book <u>Elevate the Republic</u>, "It is up to each of us to make the world a better place." An artist feels it + a writer writes it. To get others to care is what it's all about. That simple.

Danny got up from the rocking chair and walked outside past the pond, listening to the soothing sound of bubbling water. As he walked toward the grove in predawn light and enjoyed seeing the young fruit, he noticed the full moon. He walked out to the road and looked at the house as the moon perched on the roof peak as if balancing his life. He stood immersed in the feeling then walked slowly back to the bedroom. He admired Joy sleeping peacefully. He undressed and returned to bed quietly and propped himself against the headboard to feel close to the woman he loved. He held the small battery light to his journal and wrote:

As Joy sleeps quietly and I think back on all the women I've known, it's good old Penelope that comes to mind. That never ending tapestry that she wove during the day and undid at night. That's a woman. Joy is that woman. She's the love of my life. And today is the first day of the best of our lives.

This journal has been a thirty-six year Odyssey, but now I have to write the novel <u>My Block</u> about everyone and everything I know...

Everyone's gotta fight the good fight. Everyone needs an "O'" in their name: Citizen <u>O</u>' the World. That's what we are. Oh, yeah, only a few have a great affect. But I've met some wonderful people along the way. And my mom + dad were good people. So, I gotta tell their story: "We named you because of the song Danny-boy and Daniel in the lions' den, but we figured you would be a writer. That's what Milani said because of the caul." And to be born Danny Boy on Bloom's Day... June 16 means I gotta write.

Aesop was right about the tortoise and hare: slow + steady wins the race. You gotta keep at it...and keep your eye on the sun and moon and sky. There just isn't a better way. Especially this morning with the moon balanced on the roof peak. A roof over lust must be built with love. And so, now with the love of my life in the bed I made, <u>My Block</u> has to immortalize the courageous turtle!